BESS AND

FRIMA

BESS AND

FRIMA

A Novel

Alice Rosenthal

SHE WRITES PRESS

Published 2018
Printed in the United States of America
ISBN: 978-1-63152-439-4 pbk
ISBN: 978-1-63152-440-0 ebk
Library of Congress Control Number: 2018935992

For information, address:
She Writes Press
1563 Solano Ave #546
Berkeley, CA 94707

She Writes Press is a division of SparkPoint Studio, LLC.

In memory of

My beloved sister Barbara Almond
and
My dear friend Robert Wernick

They both remembered so well.

PRELUDE

You might be out for a walk after a substantial meal this evening, or maybe you are crossing the street to kibitz with the card players sitting on the benches or camp chairs at the edges of the park's greenery. There is nothing remarkable about your dress or habits. You are very likely to be Jewish if you live in this cluster of streets, and you are an immigrant or the child of immigrants. But this is no teeming ghetto, and this is not 1848. It's 1940, and you are a US citizen, and you vote Democratic. Could be you have a framed photo of Franklin Roosevelt that you cut from a magazine on your wall, or one of his wife, Eleanor, in your kitchen. Two blue-blooded patricians as distant in background from you and yours as the tribal peoples who came to the Hudson River Valley ages before them, but with these two luminaries you feel a keen identification and affection. America has been good to you—this is a familiar bittersweet refrain in your heart—and when you look at what's happening in Europe, you realize this little corner of the Bronx is one of the safest places on earth for you. You are proud and grateful to be an American citizen, and to look and act and dress like a typical American is an honor. No long black gabardine for you!

So you see nothing extraordinary in the two young women, bare-legged and clad in light sleeveless dresses, idling on the stoop of an apartment house. You have seen them grow up, right here. Except you might notice yet again that the two are unusually good-looking and in contrasting ways. The slender blonde with the blue-gray eyes is Frima Eisner. That pretty, petite child grown into a lovely, graceful young woman. No wonder. Hannah Eisner, her mother, is still considered a fine-looking woman. The other, Bess Erlichman, is a repeated surprise. Who would think that gawky, dark child with the piercing eyes would become such a striking, statuesque young woman. She's not what you would call American-*shiksa* pretty like Frima, but she's as capable of turning heads as her friend. Both have very nice teeth, which still is unusual at this time and place.

They, like you, are denizens of this patch of earth in this section of the Bronx, the northwestern corner of New York City. It is a relatively new neighborhood compared to the Lower East Side, where you first experienced and studied America. It is spacious and leafy green, and it's easy to imagine the forests and farmlands of this hilly terrain that only recently were replaced by shopping streets and six-story apartment buildings. You can still sense the forests in the parkland that girds the neighborhood. You have read somewhere that this little corner of your universe is called Norwood, but that is the talk of realtors and city planners. No one who lives here would call it by any such name. After all, this is not the older, more settled Brooklyn, with its well-established suburban sounding districts: Brooklyn Heights, Flatbush, Sea Gate. Here you live on 228th Street or by the park or by Reservoir Oval. "Norwood? Very fancy-shmancy." All three of you would say this, smiling not with derision, but with a certain irony that is in your genes.

The two young women nod politely as you pass, but they waste no thoughts on you. For all the world, they seem absorbed in devouring hot dogs covered with mustard and sauerkraut, probably after seeing the two matinees at the Tuxedo Theater, just a couple of blocks away—that whole generation is crazy about movies. Bess finishes her hot dog and watches her friend with a little smile as Frima tilts her head back and tips the drippy sauerkraut and mustard into her mouth with the precision and elegance of a flame swallower. Frima gathers the greasy wrapping papers and neatly deposits them in a nearby trash can. She wipes her hands with the clean handkerchief tucked in her skirt pocket. Her lounging figure seems tranquil enough, but her expression is a bit preoccupied. She abandons the stoop to stand on the running board of a parked car, and looking skyward, she beckons Bess to join her. Your eyes follow hers, and you see the sunset over the slopes that will meet the Hudson. The darkening sky silhouettes the rows of apartment buildings that follow the curves and angles of the Bronx streets and lend the structures a mystery and beauty impossible in full daylight.

As the light passes, the teasing capricious breeze decides to fulfill its promise, and the night turns balmy. Those still lingering outside relax into a sense of hope and comfort. Anxiety about the far-off war is in the air, but also the scent of good things. The fearful Depression is waning, and people are shaking out and dusting off hopes and dreams. You'd guess that there is nothing dusty about the dreams of the two young women, though you can only imagine what they are.

It's time to go home now, for you and for them. You know that Frima will be leaving for the country tomorrow to spend the summer at her family's Catskill hotel, as she does every year. Bess, you've heard, will also be in the Catskills, working at a hotel in Monticello. An adventure for her, no doubt. Are they saying goodbye? They do an awkward, jerky little two-step in their effort to hug each other and not bang noses, but to you their shadowed figures are graceful—mysterious and lovely in the afterglow and as full of promise as the dawn to come.

CHAPTER 1

The journey from New York City to Monticello was less than a hundred miles, but Bess might as well have been moving by mule train through uncharted territory for all the dithering anxiety she felt about it. How to get there? Hannah Eisner, Frima's mother, had offered her a ride in their hotel station wagon, but they were leaving a full week before the "season," as they called it, and Bess's brother, Jack, was to meet them a day or two after they arrived in the country. Bess couldn't possibly be ready in time to travel with the Eisners or her brother, which was a good thing actually. She wasn't going to be overshadowed by anyone.

The train left from the wilds of New Jersey, which meant not only a long schlep on the subway but some means of crossing the Hudson— ferry or Hudson Tubes—and probably getting lost on the other shore. The Manhattan bus terminal she could find, even in a state of high anxiety, and though the trip took hours and hours with many stops, a bus stayed on solid ground, at least. Bess didn't count bridges as hazardous.

Once settled in a front window seat, she was joined by a slender (thank God) man at least three times her age. He spoke to her genially.

"So, miss, you don't mind I should sit next to you in this nice front seat? It's true, I'm not a handsome young man, nor rich, but I don't take up much room. Morris Ginsberg, at your service. Moe, to my friends, even the ones I am just meeting."

"Bess Erlichman, here. Bess, to you." She found herself smiling as she held out her hand. His familiar Yiddish-flavored English reassured her.

"And you're going where?"

"Monticello. And you?"

"Woodridge, where I live."

"Is that close to Monticello?"

"Close enough." Moe smiled. "You are going to work in the Catskills and this is your first time, am I right?"

"You can tell? Just like that?"

"One or two deductions only. If you were going up to the mountains as a guest, you wouldn't be leaving so early—not until next week or later. And if you weren't new at this, you would know that everything is near Monticello, in a way. Woodridge is not very far northeast of Monticello as the crow flies, but country roads make it seem a lot longer to reach. As the chicken flies, maybe I should say." He chuckled at his little joke, but seeing Bess's woebegone face, he continued gently. "Stop worrying. You'll have a fine time, a girl like you."

"A girl like what? I feel like a greenhorn. I'm afraid I'll make a fool of myself."

"Not possible. Only a fool can make a fool of herself. And you want to know from greenhorns? Look at me, who landed up in the mountains maybe a month after docking at Ellis Island, to join a band of immigrant Jewish farmers. Hah! What we knew about farming you could put on a postage stamp, and besides we were surrounded by gentiles who thought we were crazy or Christ-killers, or both. But that's such a long story. Even on a bus ride this long, I couldn't begin to tell." With a little yawn, Moe pulled a newspaper out of a small satchel and began to unfold it. "So now, I'm going to read the newspaper a little and take a nap. Take my advice and you do the same. And stop worrying. You'll have a fine time."

"Okay, I'll let you sleep." She felt dismissed, but she managed a smile.

"A good-looking young lady like you, I'm happy to talk to forever," Moe said. "However, my snoring is tolerated much better if you also are sleeping. Just ask my wife. Also, this is a long, tiring ride. If you can sleep now, you'll be more refreshed for the new scenery and adventure. Anyway, you'll wake up at the first rest stop."

"I wouldn't want to miss that." Aside from everything else, she had started her period last night—just what she needed!

"You shouldn't worry. No one could sleep through that stampede. Also, if I make too much noise, just nudge me with your elbow."

Too keyed up to actually sleep, Bess closed her eyes and for about the fifth time this day took inventory of her baggage and her life. The bus driver had tagged her valise and nonchalantly stowed it in some compartment outside the seating area of the bus. She had bit the inside of her lip as he did so. She hadn't brought many clothes beyond the bare necessities. It was her lifeline she worried about—the precious drawing pads, pencils, pastels, and small palette of good watercolors. Her art supplies, meager in themselves, were still too large and cumbersome to keep with her at her seat and took up most of the room in her suitcase. Her mother had been beside herself, watching Bess pack.

"Paints you wrap in a good dress! Are you crazy?"

"Yes, Mama, I'm crazy, but this is the way it has to be. All right? You want me to wrap them in sanitary napkins that I have to take on the bus? Besides, it's my suitcase and my life!"

The usual song and dance. No one in Bess's family, and very few in the world at large, could fathom how important her art was to her. They would smile in derision if she even said out loud, "my art." My art and my money. Such beautiful words, such joyous concepts. That's what she really longed for this summer. She might not have a lot of time to paint, but it almost didn't matter, as long as there was a little time alone and her paints were with her. If she was scared or sad or belittled somehow, they were there to give her courage, to make her whole. She smiled to herself a little grimly. Who in the ordinary world would suspect this about Bess? Frima or Hannah Eisner, or her teachers and fellow students at the High School of Music and Art. No one else, surely.

How she missed that school! It was the creation of Mayor La Guardia and was beloved of so many gifted teenagers, including Bess and Frima, who were members of its opening class. She remembered how ease began to seep into her pores each day that she and Frima descended into the depths of the subway, and by the time they had climbed to the school, she had shed her awkwardness and resentment and entered gladly into another world. Teachers and fellow students had complimented her work, even astonishing her by seeing things in her painting that she was herself unaware of. They had persuaded her that she was (or could be) a genuine artist. They encouraged her to think she was a young woman worth noticing, perhaps meant for something extraordinary.

She'd also grown into her looks, as Hannah Eisner had predicted she would. All those meals that never seemed adequate to her needs had finally abandoned their work of producing inches of gawky height and turned to creating a bust and curves. As she saw it, her figure had finally caught up with her nose and feet. She found she was attractive to boys—even those who were shorter than she was. She was invited to parties, asked to dance. Real dates were rarely in the offing, for most of the boys she'd known didn't have money to spend on taking a girl out. What was important was that they wanted to.

Unfortunately, high school ended each afternoon, and as soon as she entered her family's apartment in the evening, she was stifled by her own resentment and an aching sense of being undervalued. And then, alas, there was graduation. Listening to the commencement speeches was a torture. Commencement meant a beginning, didn't it? A hopeful beginning of a future. But was her future to be behind the counter of Papa's notions store on Bathgate Avenue? So dark and dank, with an aroma concocted of camphor, damp wool, oilcloth, and sweat. An aroma not so much of abject poverty as of an anxious, grim just-getting-by. And the air outside was just as bad. These were not the fresh leafy streets of the northwest Bronx. Walk outside the shop, and your nose was assailed by a rancid smell of overcooked carrots, tomatoes, onions, and congealed grease—the smell of poor people's cooking.

So the only answer was money, Bess concluded. Her own bank account. She would never again work in that shop to pay for her room and board in the soul-strangling atmosphere of what her family called home. She closed her eyes and gritted her teeth. How close she had come to another summer of indentured servitude. And this summer would have been the worst ever. If it weren't for a lucky break, there she'd be. No question, what made the Bathgate Avenue prison completely intolerable was that Jack was spending the summer in pretty, cool Ellenville, working at Eisner's Hotel. And of course, Frima would be there, too. The one last twist of the knife: Mrs. Eisner had also invited Bess to spend the summer up in the country.

"I wouldn't be able to pay you, dear, no more than I can pay Frima, but your room and board would be free, and you and Frima could work together, helping out in the office and with the kids. I think it would be fun for both of you. I could speak to your folks if you want me to."

"No, no, I can't. Not this summer." Bess was too quick to answer. And then remembering her manners, she added, "But thank you for the offer anyway. I really appreciate it."

Hannah Eisner, clearly surprised, had glanced at Bess curiously, but she didn't press the issue. "Of course, the offer is open, if you want to think about it and maybe change your mind."

That couldn't happen. What was there to think about except feelings that she could never express to Mrs. Eisner or Frima or Jack. A whole chopped liver of mixed emotions that made her stomach churn.

A summer at a hotel in the Catskills could be the gateway to adventure and experience she would kill for, but she'd be damned if she'd have her older brother watching her like a chaperone or deflating her efforts.

And if he ignored her? Just as bad. She'd noticed (who wouldn't?) how often Frima and Jack stole glances at each other; and the thought of them together, her brother and her best friend, with her out in the cold, left her with feelings of jealousy and abandonment she didn't even want to know about, let alone express. For the first time, she even found herself resenting Frima's mother, who had always comforted and encouraged Bess. Clever woman that she was, Mrs. Eisner had probably noticed Frima and Jack's interest in each other and was encouraging a match.

Bess, often referred to as "the mouth" at home, was unused to dissembling or fine-tuning her arguments for maximum persuasion. These were skills not highly developed in her family, where people mostly battled at top volume or sulked in glaringly obvious silence. Except for Jack. He had moved from the wailing and tears of childhood and the rages of adolescence to a persuasiveness she had to admire. It wasn't deceitful or anything, just a kind of presentation, a way with smiles and words. He was getting quite nimble at it—Jack be nimble. Her brother knew how to wait, to seize the best time to let his will be known. She had no talent for this. So ironic. She loved books, was an avid reader of fiction and an intelligent, sensitive critic. But, she came to realize, with books she was admiring someone else's words. For herself—for her own sense of meaning—words were not adequate. They were no way as powerful as light and line, color and texture.

Still, she and Frima had first become friends at the local branch of the public library, and had spent so many hours there together. Reading was one of the great pleasures they shared. Was reading one of the great pleasures Frima shared with Jack? She didn't think so. Jack read newspapers and magazines and scientific and technical books—college texts. Frima would never enjoy that stuff, and Bess was glad of that, even if she was being mean and envious in feeling this way. She had wanted to stick her head out the window and howl with chagrin that could not be expressed and would surely drive her nuts. Her only escape would be her own summer job in the country, away from them all. And goaded by her distress, she began hunting in earnest.

It turned out to be surprisingly easy. So easy that Bess was sure her luck had changed. Lillian Feinberg, a relative of a friend, had a job in the Catskills that she didn't need because she was getting married, and the boss was happy to get a good replacement at such short notice. The job meant a whole summer in the country, room and board free, at a fancier resort than the Eisner place. And she'd earn a hundred bucks—real money! Riches, practically. All she had to do was keep the guests happy by teaching their little darlings to paint a picture or make a clay ashtray when their parents wanted time to themselves. Really a piece of cake, according to Lillian. Why, Bess wouldn't even have to worry about clothes. The staff wore uniforms: cute little dark green shorts, slacks, or skirts with white shirts; or alternatively, cute little white shorts, slacks, or skirts with green shirts. Usually the staff had to pay for these outfits, but Lillian offered them for free. "After all," she said coyly, "I won't need them. I'm sure Nathan wouldn't want me running around Saratoga in a hotel uniform."

"I'm sure that will be lovely," Bess answered, casting limpid eyes at Lillian and thanking her enthusiastically with a straight face. Lillian had mentioned for about the fiftieth time that she was spending the summer with her intended's family in classy Saratoga. Bess was practicing holding her tongue.

Actually, she was thrilled when she tried on the hand-me-downs. They looked like new, and she looked terrific in shorts. The other things would be perfect, with maybe a little tuck here and there, and hems let down on the slacks and skirts. She was sorry she had resented Frima's mother even for a minute when that good women offered to do the alterations for her. Hannah Eisner was a professional dressmaker and could make adjustments in ways that would be invisible to any but the most practiced eye. Beyond these few items, she would need only a bathing suit. She could use the one she wore on the rare occasions she got to Orchard Beach, still in good shape since Bess almost never ventured into water over her knees. Also sandals, tennis shoes (not for tennis, of course), and a summer dress or two. With her height she never needed high heels.

Monticello, Bess learned, was the center of the vacation country and the town nearest to the hotel, the Alpine Song, and the area was hopping with Jewish vacation hotels sprouting up to replace struggling farms, boardinghouses, and small bungalows. Socially, these resorts could be goldmines, according to Lillian. "You'd never believe there had ever been a depression up there," she said. With luck, Bess could land herself a nice young Jewish doctor or lawyer, like Lillian had. Actually, Lillian's intended was a dental student, but still a catch. An "alrightnik," Mama would call him.

The Alpine Song, according to the brochure Bess had quickly committed to memory, was "nestled in the lovely Catskill Mountains on acres of sunny green lawn and unspoiled woodland, surrounded by Catskill lakes, walking and hiking trails, and a nearby golf course. Guests enjoy luxurious accommodations, a private pool, tennis courts, and superb cuisine. Dietary laws strictly observed." Which meant that the people who went there were prosperous (who else could afford all that?) and Jewish. A veritable happy hunting ground, Lillian assured her.

Bess had no wish to husband hunt. Her immediate experience of husbands—her mother's sorry specimen—wasn't exactly encouraging. But the rest of this Catskill adventure sounded just fine. She had quite deliberately lied to her parents about how much money she would make. She figured fifty dollars for the ten weeks would be believable to them, especially since her father didn't consider that she was worth much. Besides, that noisy adding machine he had for a mind would tell him instantly that he'd be better off pocketing her room and board, even if she earned nothing this summer. She hoped that she'd be in a position to not turn any of it over to him. But she wanted very much to give something to Mama. And then there were tips. Bess had never even thought about a tip before. But Lillian said if she smiled and looked cute, honest, and harmless, she could rake them in. She was curious as to how much Lillian herself had earned this way but was reluctant to ask. Still, she'd feel happy about any tips she got. Surely, this was money for her alone.

Surprisingly, it was her mother who was doubtful about the whole adventure. "So who is this Lillian? How come I don't know her? She never came to visit our house. She's from downtown? She's too good to meet us? And if this is such a great job, how come she doesn't want it for herself? Also, I don't like you should be all alone up there."

"So, for what do you worry about nothing? Money is money." This from the adding machine, of course.

Ignoring him completely, Bess explained gently and reasonably. "Mama, Lillian is a nice girl. She lives all the way over in Jersey, but she's Myra's cousin. You remember Myra—you liked her. And don't worry, I'll be surrounded by nice respectable Jewish people." Bess paused for the clincher. "And the reason Lillian is not taking this job is she's getting married this summer. A boy from a very good Jewish family, whom she just happened to meet at the Alpine Song."

So, hallelujah! Bess had crossed the ice. She was a free woman, ready for experience. When she took a break from the joyful labor of painting without someone looking over her shoulder, she would ride down country roads with carefree young men in convertibles. She would dance on moonlit patios in scented air. She would listen to the sweet rhythmic caress of the water as she reclined in a canoe, hidden in the shadows of purple mountains' majesty in the arms of one special young man: handsome, debonair, and sensitive—deeply sensitive—who understood her and adored her art.

"We'll be there in about ten minutes," Moe informed her, waking from his latest catnap.

"*Oy vey!*" she muttered to herself.

"Not another sigh. You'll have Monticello at your feet!" He picked up his satchel and blew her a kiss. "You need advice, you come to Woodridge and ask. Everybody knows me there. Remember, the only thing you need to know about Monticello is Thomas Jefferson never slept there."

She grinned and waved a kiss back, abandoning both panic and rhapsody. "Okay," she told herself, "keep your eyes and ears open and your mouth shut, except to smile sweetly and show those pretty white teeth."

CHAPTER 2

Six a.m., and Frima, clad in rolled-up dungarees and a faded plaid cotton shirt, slipped bare feet into old loafers, quickly braided her hair into a single plait, and pinned it to the top of her head, where the flaxen end of the braid bobbed around like a crest atop a bird's head. Very fitting, she thought with a sigh, for a chicken coop. Her hair was a trial to her, even though it was the envy of all the mamas in the city. They thought it made her look all-American, like a *shiksa*. What did they know? Did they ever try to curl corn silk or keep a hairpin in it? Well, never mind. She wasn't going to worry about it now. If she had to wear a braid or tie it back with a rubber band for the rest of her life, it wasn't the end of the world, was it? Jack probably wouldn't notice it anyway. Besides, he wasn't here yet.

She grabbed her basket and bounded down the back steps. Most times of the year, this ungodly hour would not find her so cheerful and energetic, but as she walked down the path to the chicken coops, she was aware of a gladness that made her want to skip like a child. She felt this way most mornings during the long summer days in Ellenville. At this first hour of daylight, she collected the eggs as she did every morning during the season. She enjoyed this task. Papa had taught her to gather them when Eisner's was still a modest little egg and dairy farm, and she'd acquired the same firm gentleness with livestock that he had.

Mama, now. She considered chickens to be witless, mean-spirited, and prone to hysterics. They evidently returned her hostility, for she could barely enter a henhouse without being pecked. Were it not for their obvious practical worth, she would have loved to see every laying hen and certainly any rooster slaughtered and turned into a roast or soup, preferably when she was not there to see it done. The Jersey cow and her yearly calf she tolerated, for although most of the hotel's milk came from a local dairy, there were still a few old timers who enjoyed the fresh unprocessed Jersey milk. Besides, what's a farm without a cow? The old horse of all work, Jessie, was pastured and would live out his life here because Grandpa and Frima loved him, and he had proved to be a major attraction to the kids. The aging hound, Rufus, also beloved by the two of them, Mama could put up with as long as Frima kept him clean, flea-free, and out of the main house. After all, she wouldn't deprive her father-in-law and daughter of the comfort of these old companions. The acquisition of more animals was another story. Mama was always against it, whereas Frima and Grandpa maintained a gentle conspiracy to increase their number. Frima grinned as she walked by the pasture and spied their newest freeloader, a shaggy donkey that had belonged before this summer to the kids of a neighboring farmer. The kids, growing up now, were no longer interested in their old pet, and the man's wife was delighted not to hear any more braying. Grandpa and Frima, mustering their arguments, had said nothing about the braying.

"Donkeys are strong, hardy animals," Grandpa said. "And this fellow is very gentle. He comes with a clean bill of health, also a cart and harness. He'll be pastured with the horse and will use the same shed in the summer and winter. Believe me, Hannah, it will cost us nothing. A little goodwill exchanged with another Jewish farmer. Who can it hurt?"

"Jessie will love the company, Mama. Horses are herd animals, you know," added Frima. "We'll call him Toby, like in Louisa May Alcott—you remember, *Little Men*? And just think how much fun the small kids will have going for a ride in the cart, which Grandpa is going to paint a bright red. It will be the most popular attraction for them."

"Until some three-year-old gets kicked in the head!"

"I've already talked with Moe, and we won't be liable. Everything is hunky dory, Hannah." Grandpa lit his pipe, signaling that for his part there was nothing else to say.

"You mean we'll have a notice: Approach at Your own Risk. How wonderful! Some heartbroken guests—probably dear friends of mine—with a child maimed for life or even worse can't sue us. That makes everything alright?"

"Now you know nothing is going to happen, Mama. I will personally supervise their time with the farm animals, as I always do. Here. I already have a new sign: Our animals are gentle but also large. Children under the age of 10 must be accompanied by an adult when visiting the barn or pasture.

Mama had sighed and eyed them sternly. "No goats!"

"Come to Eisner's and enjoy the matchless experience of a family farm vacation!" Frima quoted her mother's very own promotional slogan, softening her irony with an intimate smile. She and Mama, living alone together for most of the year, had developed an unusually fine judgment of each other's moods and limits. She had squeezed Mama's shoulder as she moved past her, noting as she often did lately that she had grown markedly taller than her mother. But this time the realization pierced her with a bittersweet tenderness. Was this because she knew, somehow, that she would be leaving this phase of her life soon enough?

As if reading her thoughts, Mama peered at her sharply. "It's all very well for you to think that you can take care of all this," she said, pointing to the pasture and outbuildings that were situated a distance from the guest accommodations. "But you are a young lady now, and I need my beautiful daughter at the desk and in the office to refresh the guests and the staff with her charming ways. A barnyard is not the aroma they should associate with you. And besides, you need to take care of your hands. There's no piano here at the moment, which is a pity, but there is the rest of the year to think of. And I think next year I will try to acquire one, provided you two can refrain from adopting any more four-legged refugees that do little more than eat, produce manure, and attract flies. Now Grandpa will have to hire another local boy to take care of those we have. I certainly can't spare Jack for such chores; nor would I expect him to do them."

Winning arguments was one of Mama's favorite pastimes, and she had certainly covered all the ground. Her parting shot about Jack was masterful. Frima wondered how often his name would come up this summer whenever Mama decided to rest her case. It was also true that a readily available piano was a joy to her, the intimate companion—and sometimes the solace—of her hours alone. Still, she could do without it quite easily for the summer. She was gifted musically. Her pitch was virtually perfect, and she had years of training under her belt. She was quite capable of studying a piano score and hearing the lines of music in her head, something she could do in a hammock in her off-hours or, if need be, in her own room with the aid of a silent keyboard. Besides, this was her summer life, as physically and spiritually uplifting to her as Mozart or Beethoven.

Domestic animals, of course, as well as the vegetable and flower gardens—everything really—needed year-round maintenance, but Grandpa lived here the whole year and hired local boys and maintenance people as necessary. He still had a dwindling but cooperative and friendly community of small dairy and egg farmers around him, and they had always looked after each other. It was essential to their survival. Most of these were Jewish, but Grandpa was a lively, genial man and seemed to dwell in harmony with neighbors of all persuasions. Unlike most of the small farmers who had turned to boardinghouse and hotel keeping, Grandpa would not leave the place during the harsh winter months, even after Grandma died. He was still a farmer, he insisted, and he intended to live and die here. Mama and Frima also suspected that more than one widow or single lady of a certain age contributed to his care and feeding.

As far back as she could remember, Frima had always wanted to be involved in the care of the animals. As a child, she had tried to adopt any stray tomcat or mutt that passed by, to say nothing of the wounded wildlife she was forbidden to touch. Perhaps it was because she was an only child. But she was never really lonely up here, and she would also have them increase the orchard, garden, and vegetable plots. She had the gift, if you could call it that, of understanding and enjoying this rural life. She was sure she had got this from Papa, who had spent his youth on the farm.

There was so much of Papa here. Even though he had been taken from them nearly eight years ago, she always felt his nearness in the country. In truth, almost any time she thought of Papa, she saw him here in Ellenville. Workdays in the city, which actually constituted most of his time on this earth, he was a more shadowy figure to her, gone from early morning to suppertime to his other life, where he labored at a civil service job in downtown Manhattan at the Customs Office. Often he came home tired. Probably, she realized now, because of the heart weakness that had cut his life short. Most weekends in the city he devoted to visiting friends and family with Frima and Mama, or taking them on outings to the zoo, the botanical gardens, the Museum of Natural History, as well as to concerts that he often slept through but which Frima and Mama adored. Nevertheless, the gentle refrains, "Shh, Papa's resting" or "Papa's studying," were repeated too often for Frima's satisfaction. It was only in the last few years that she realized what a feat it had been for him, through dogged work and long hours of study, to climb the civil service ladder and so bring his family through the Depression free from fear and want.

But here during his precious time in the country, mostly summer weekends and his too-short vacations, Papa had been a new man. He was invigorated by the outdoor life and work, and he seemed to exist only for Frima's care and amusement. He taught her to swim, to groom the horse, gather eggs, to know when an ear of corn was ripe or a berry sweet for picking, to identify poison ivy and sumac, which mushrooms and berries were poisonous and which good for eating. He had sown these acres with love and security for her, sufficient to last the year round. And Mama, that champion of urban culture, knew this. She might be finicky about manure and flies, but she had made these acres a charming, almost pastoral respite from the ordinary workaday city life. It was her tribute and memorial to her husband, and a way of telling her daughter that she was still loved by both of them and that she was safe. Frima's eyes suddenly brimmed with tears. She stifled an impulse to run back to the house and bury her face in her mother's lap. It was over in a minute, but she needed time to compose herself. She laid the egg basket aside carefully and sat down on the grassy knoll hugging her knees. What was wrong with her? Why was she acting like a twelve-year-old? It didn't take long to realize that it wasn't adolescence but womanhood that faced her. And it was because of Jack.

He was arriving tomorrow. What would he think of this place? She had been in such a tizzy since her mother had hired Bess's older brother for the summer. Bess was her best friend, but Frima had been so secretly relieved—and guilty that she was relieved—when Bess had refused Mama's offer to work up here also. She had said not a word to Bess about her crush on Jack. It was something she couldn't share with anyone, let alone his sister. She was even vicariously embarrassed when the neighborhood girls kidded Bess about her dreamboat brother. Fear, embarrassment, delicacy—any and all of these kept Frima quiet. And now that she suspected he was returning her interest, she was quieter still. As if her hopes would dissolve if she voiced them. But would Jack even like it here? Oh, please, God, make him like it here!

So, what's not to like? That's what Mama would think. Mama was so proud of the place, and she had every right to be. It was her vision, her driving energy that had made it into the charming vacation spot it was now. The Catskills were changing rapidly, vacation hotels growing and expanding from small farms; but Eisner's was in Frima's eyes unique. Through Mama's management, it maintained a carefully balanced position someplace between a boardinghouse and a resort. Frima looked around critically, trying to see it with a stranger's eyes, but she couldn't be objective. She loved every acre, and she approved of how Mama had preserved so much of the farm's rusticity, while making it comfortable and inviting.

The old barn had been rebuilt and painted a bright red, and the new whitewashed chicken coops were situated beyond a slope in back of the house, far enough from the guest accommodations to be out of sight and to keep the endless flies, droppings, cackling, and crowing from being a nuisance. Frima, still a child when the building and renovation began, had wanted storybook white structures with red trim. But with a mature eye, she saw that her mother's choices had been very smart indeed. The natural shingle Mama chose for all the hotel buildings, old and new, weathered beautifully and blended harmoniously with the selected old trees and lilac bushes that she retained for their beauty and shade. She and Grandpa had gutted the old farm house, adding a wing for the professional kitchen and dining room and a ground-floor modernized room and bath for Grandpa, whose knees were not what they used to be. The upstairs bedrooms were chopped up and renovated, and new bathrooms added. A large bungalow behind the main building housed the summer live-in help, with the cook ruling the roost. Jack would share space there this summer.

Frima giggled suddenly. Jack would live in relative comfort, at least. If he could see the farm as it was in the old days, when there had been an outhouse with a pile of rotting turnips behind it, he'd probably turn around and run back to the city. Now, with all the new plumbing and modern conveniences, she couldn't see anything in the physical setting he could possibly complain about. But, oh, there was so much more than the prettiness of the place, and she hoped he would appreciate this—the heart that went into creating it. She immediately rebuked herself for expecting too much. It took time and sweat and tears for someone to feel that way.

They sat around the kitchen table, Mama, Grandpa, and Frima, planning the remodeling and transformation of their property.

"Physical and spiritual renewal we can offer here, just like it was for Lou," Mama said. "A big fancy hotel we can't afford, nor do we want one. How Papa would have hated that!"

"Me too," Frima and Grandpa said in one voice.

"What we want is a place where reasonable, intelligent people of moderate means can enjoy a few weeks' relief from the city heat and daily worries in a charming country setting," Mama continued. "Where they can give their kids some nice new experiences they can't get in the city. And strictly family," Mama had said severely, though Frima wondered at that time how it could be anything else.

No luxury or pretension, but solid comfort was a must. With Frima's firm second, they argued down Grandpa, who was a bit too casual about the amount of indoor plumbing needed. Comfortably sized, airy rooms with good screens, good mattresses, adequate lighting, safe outlets. "If someone wants to read in bed, they should be able to without electrocuting themselves," Mama said. Good plumbing was another essential; little sinks in the rooms, with mirrors above them and lots of bathrooms—at least one for every two or three rooms.

Some of what Grandpa considered unnecessary costs or sanitary frills could be balanced in the kitchen. Not that Mama would ever stint on food. Meals were ample, varied, and skillfully prepared, using high-quality, fresh local ingredients whenever possible. But although there were separate tables, meals were served boardinghouse style. There was one mealtime for everyone, including children, who were not served separately, and with a few necessary exceptions, everyone would eat the same food at any one meal. "No kosher-style foie gras," she said, rolling her eyes—she had seen this on the printed menu of a larger hotel. "Chopped liver is chopped liver."

Making a virtue of necessity, Mama also scorned tennis and golf, dismissing these as sports of the rich. Instead she provided badminton nets, croquet sets, a couple of ping-pong tables, lawn chairs, and several hammocks, and their guests seemed quite content. "This is not a country club," she commented privately with lofty disdain. "If you come to the country to enjoy nature, then enjoy nature." Frima was in full agreement. After all, they lived right next to a golf course in the Bronx, so what was the big deal about that? So, except for a lawn, Eisner's did not go in for much formal landscaping. True to her vision of rustic charm, Mama had retained the old fruit orchard, grown half wild, the climbing roses, lilacs, and shade trees, some acres of pasture, and several of brambles and bushes full of berries for the guests to pick. Frima and Mama thoughtfully provided pails, printed warnings about poison ivy and sumac, and kept the most popular paths cleared. For the rest, they relied on the county to maintain the woody lanes, gentle hills, and quiet country roads for walking. A few minutes' walk brought you to a cool refreshing pond fed by a dammed-up creek, maintained by the county and civic-minded residents like Grandpa and Mama.

Indoor amusements were also casual and free. Mama considered her guests intelligent, resourceful people, with the taste and creativity to find their own amusements. She wouldn't dream of having a *tumler*—part hired comedian, part social director. Instead, they had fashioned a large common room in the main house, with well-used sofas and armchairs, a good-sized library of novels and magazines, usually left there by guests, as well as portable tables and board games. A radio and phonograph and a large collection of mostly classical records dominated one wall. Among the records, however, were some good dance albums, and on some Saturday nights, the floor was cleared. Mama didn't consider a little ballroom dancing or even a square dance or two beneath her or her guests.

Yes, Mama had very decided and distinct ideas about the kind of guests she wanted, so much so that Frima had good-humoredly asked her what kind of entrance exam she would give to screen them.

"Friends tell friends," said Mama. "And, of course, there is the secret handshake."

As Frima matured and became more aware of the business they were trying to maintain, she realized that Mama's achievement was truly impressive. She had so far managed to keep the place fully booked by a finely honed balancing act involving scale, resources, flexibility, and dawn-to-midnight work. And she was having the time of her life doing it. Mama, she came to realize, had a great talent for management that could not be fulfilled by sewing a fine seam and raising a daughter. She needed greater scope, and the hotel provided it. It had all worked out quite well, it seemed. Frima and Grandpa could have their little farm, and Mama could have her rustic inn. Who could ask for more?

But once again Frima fretted. In some other place, such a good-looking, bright, energetic young fellow like Jack might be a waiter, with specific hours and duties, free to court tips and call the rest of his time his own. Maybe Jack would be disappointed that Eisner's wasn't a grander place with more opportunities, more amusements, and more tips. Or, worst of all, more girls.

So, just who does he think he is? This place isn't good enough for him? He's never been in a place this nice in his whole life! By the time Frima reached her own bedroom, she had worked herself into a real snit. Okay, she thought, staring at herself sternly in the mirror. This way lies madness. Forget about Jack for a minute, and sit down and read a book or start studying the Beethoven you brought with you.

CHAPTER 3

So what if Bess's first exposure to Monticello was disappointing. It was flatter than she expected and quite hot. She instantly chastised herself: Well, what did she expect? Snow-covered peaks? Was the Alpine Song a yodel? She had little time for fretting as two young guys in an ordinary Ford station wagon hailed her.

"Woo-hoo! Going to the Alpine? What's your name, sweetheart?"

"Uh, Bess."

"Woo-hoo! Fresh fish for Max!"

"Looks like jailbait to me. How old are you, sister?"

"Nineteen."

"Hey, she ain't jailbait!"

She had no idea what they were talking about, these two lugs who looked like Abbot and Costello in their teens, but she had no time for questions. They drove off with the speed of a getaway car, and she clung to the roof strap in the back seat, heart in mouth. Before she could worry about anything except her life, they came screeching to a halt in front of a large house, where they dumped her suitcase on the wide front porch.

"In there, sweetheart," they said pointing to a screen door.

Numbly, Bess entered. A plump, friendly looking young woman with curly red hair looked up from a desk and smiled.

"You must be Bess. I'm Muriel. Welcome to the Alpine Song. Why don't you put your bags behind the desk for the time being? Give me about twenty minutes, and I'll be able to show you the place, get you settled. Max left me with a pile of bookkeeping while he went off to do something important. So, why don't you look around? Oh, and there's a restroom right down the hall to your left. I'm sure you could use one after that long ride. Would you like a drink—a Coke or something?"

"No, thanks. I'm fine. To the left you said?"

On first impression, the place looked nothing like the brochure, and Bess wondered for the second time why it was called the Alpine Song. To her Bronx-bred eyes, her own neighborhood was easily as hilly, maybe more so. There were a few pines, to be sure, but nothing could she see of the forest primeval and certainly no murmuring pines and hemlocks. So it wasn't exactly Longfellow, but perhaps the place had been named by a romantic who could hear music in the wind, music that she couldn't hear. Of course, you'd need wind to hear any such thing, and it was hot and still today. Okay, Bess, enough already. Shut up your imagination and open up your real eyes and ears. Besides, you should know that no place looks like a brochure.

There was a large swimming pool just across the road from the main house, empty now and undergoing a facelift, which no doubt would make it inviting by the time guests arrived. The lake she had imagined was nowhere to be seen. It did exist, she would soon learn, but it was a couple of miles away, and the hotel provided transport to shuttle guests to and fro. She suspected this was driven by the nitwits who had brought her here and promptly decided she would forgo seeing the lake until she could be escorted properly, preferably by that brilliant, sensitive young man, the one with the canoe.

Nevertheless, the Alpine Song was a pretty place, she found, if not the paradise of her overheated imagination. The main house, guest bungalows, and outbuildings were painted a fresh lemony color with attractive green shutters. There was a lush lawn with shade trees, and flower beds filled with petunias, snapdragons, and other blooms she couldn't name. Even better, there were some inviting and mellow-looking woods surrounding the main area. She might even find a spot to create a watercolor or two.

When she came back to the desk, Muriel was ready for her. "Let's get you settled in," she said. "Actually, you'll be rooming with me. I hope you don't mind."

"Of course not. Not if you don't, that is."

"I'm sure it will work out very well. There'll only be the two of us, which is kind of a luxury," Muriel commented. With a little sigh she looked at the scene around her, full of the noise of hammers and drills, workman popping up around corners. "You know the pre-season week around here is like a madhouse—it is at every hotel—and you probably won't meet Max for a few days. Don't worry about it. If he were to notice you too soon, it might give you the impression that you were someone special. He wants us all to remember that we are worker bees. But don't worry about it. He's really quite harmless, and at heart he's a worker bee himself."

"But I'm not really sure what I'm supposed to do. When and where do I work?"

"Don't worry about it. Just follow my lead. It will all begin to make sense in a couple of days, and there'll be plenty for you to do when the guests start pouring in."

Bess was beginning to warm to Muriel. She was quite friendly and helpful, welcoming, really, and Bess was grateful. Muriel would ease her discomfort at being the new girl in town.

The one-room cabin they were sharing turned out to be a decent size and rather private, maybe a little in disrepair, but close to the woods and away from the guest accommodations. It had a bare-bones but entirely functional bathroom, just for the two of them, which was in itself a luxury to Bess. There was even a little front porch. How lovely to sit out here and sketch or read. She turned to Muriel with a smile of genuine pleasure, which quite suddenly turned into an enormous yawn. Muriel gave a little laugh.

"Anxiety about the unknown is exhausting, isn't it? I remember the first time I came to this place. I didn't sleep a wink for two days before I got here. I bet you sleep well tonight!" Muriel gave her a friendly wink. The future was looking rosy.

It took Bess a whole three days before she allowed herself to wonder what she had ever done to make that skunk, Lillian, hate her so much. For only someone who bore her malice would have sent the city-bred Bess, blameless and defenseless, to this Garden of Eden without so much as a can of DDT. Years later, Bess had only to scratch a mosquito bite to conjure up her first week at the Alpine Song. She had arrived just at the onset of a heat wave that would blanket the state and most of the East Coast with oppressive humid air. It was little use to tell herself it would be worse in the city because there, at least, she wouldn't be eaten alive. Those welts all over her arms and legs, even her face! The quaint woodsy cabin she shared with Muriel had screens, but they were poorly fitted or the window frames had warped or something, and every bug that lusted for blood told all his friends that come nightfall it was party time.

Muriel, though less susceptible, was sympathetic, and she promised to use her influence with Max to get him to fix the screens. She wouldn't even approach him this pre-season week, however, so together they devised their own defense. They wheedled heavy plumbing tape from the workmen and plugged up the holes and spaces around the screens. They collected every flashlight they could lay their hands on and piled them in a box on the porch. The first one home at dark would immediately light the flashlights in a row across the porch and turn on the porch light, open the door quickly and duck as the horde of winged furies attracted by the lights whooshed out the door, and then rush inside and hurriedly slam the door. They slept with their heads under the sheets to avoid any stray bloodsuckers. They used up a lot of batteries and braved the wrath of Max, who was a stickler for saving electricity, but they were beyond caring. Then Bess discovered poison ivy. What good was it to look great in shorts if your legs were continually covered with blisters and calamine lotion?

Toward the end of her first week, a lean man with thinning white hair wearing outdoor work pants and shoes hailed her. Although she'd seen him around, she had thought he was a laborer, but it turned out this was her boss. Her first encounter with Max taught her two things: first, resort owners are not likely to be patrons of the arts; second, if an opportunity is too good to be true, it probably is.

"I don't know what kind of cockamamie story that Lillian told you, but our guests, they're not very interested in arts and crafts. The kiddies, they want to be in the pool or outside playing games. The mamas and papas, they want to get a little sun, rest, eat, maybe drink a little more than is good for them. For most of them, this is a once-a-year vacation, and they want to be waited on, entertained. Not very high-class entertainment, you understand. That's the way they like it, so that's the way I like it."

"But why did Lillian say . . . ?"

"Lillian, she's a friend of yours?"

"Not really."

"Good! But I have no time for gossip. Your contract says help out as needed. Maybe on a rainy day a kid wants to make a clay ashtray, but I don't think so. Mostly you'll help Muriel in the office. Also run errands, take over the reception desk when the girl's on a break, bring the livestock to the kitchen when the busboys are really busy, but no waiting on tables—that's for the waiters. They don't like nobody should interfere with their tips. So you'll hang around the canteen and the card rooms in the evenings and make yourself useful. No dancing with the help or the guests, unless the paying ladies already got partners. And no hanky-panky. You seem like a nice Jewish girl, so I'm doing you a favor. Not just the hundred bucks, which in these times is hard to come by, let me tell you, but also you got practically private accommodations; you get to live in a cabin with Muriel. She's also a nice Jewish girl, a little older than you. You won't get into no trouble with her. You understand?"

Bess nodded.

"Good! Meeting's over." Max turned to leave and then suddenly faced her. "And—what's your name—Bess? I'll get around to fixing those screens maybe after next week, but meanwhile eighty-six those shorts until those bites, or whatever, are gone. It's not nice the guests should think you got them here—hnyeh, hnyeh—and remember, turn out the lights!"Astonished, Bess nodded again. Did she imagine it or did Max actually wink at her?

She reported to Muriel. "I just got my orders from Max—hnyeh, hnyeh—where did he get that laugh?"

Muriel snorted. "Don't get me started."

"So what's eighty-six?"

"Kitchen slang for 'dump it.'"

"And I'm almost afraid to ask, but what is livestock doing in the kitchen?"

"It's slang for perishables, like butter and milk, anything that can spoil. It's vital to the survival of this kind of hotel not to waste food, to conserve leftovers. The kitchen is the heart of the place."

"Does that mean that now that the guests are coming, we dine on their leftovers?"

"You'll hardly recognize them." Muriel smiled. "Don't worry. The food will remain the same."

Which was quite good, Bess thought to herself. But what did she know? Her own mother was a lousy cook.

"It's just a first impression, I know, but I didn't think Max was a bad guy at all. I mean the way people grouse about him, you'd think he was an ogre. And he said he'd try to get to these screens after next week some time."

Muriel grinned. "If he said after next week, you can figure on August at the earliest. But it's because he's so busy and works all the time. And you're right, he's not a bad guy at all—one of the best I know to work for. My fiancé's boss, now, is really a slave driver. Most of the grousing about Max is because it's expected; you know, you don't want people to think you're buttering up the boss. As for Max, he doesn't want anyone to think he's a soft touch."

"Well, I didn't think he was that. He didn't think much of Lillian, I gather, though he didn't go into any detail." She said this rather carefully, not quite sure of her ground.

"Why would he think well of her? She pulled a fast one on him."

Bess was dying to know what she meant, but afraid of seeming overly curious. "She certainly wasn't very honest and open with me," she ventured. "I mean, if she had at least told me about the mosquitoes around this cabin, I could have come more prepared."

"She probably didn't know anything about them."

"But didn't she share with you last year?"

"Why would she? She was a guest."

"A what? She told me she worked here!"

Muriel was evidently as surprised as Bess. She was silent for a few moments, then sighed. "I guess you are entitled to an explanation, though, I beg you, don't say a word to Max or to anyone else. He'd die of shame if anyone thought he'd been hoodwinked. I only know because I'm his secretary and bookkeeper, and, even so, I don't know all the details."

"I won't let a soul know about it. But I'm sure there are some lessons for me in this story, so, please, let's have it."

"Well, Max is a friend of Lillian's parents. They've been guests here for a number of years. Evidently, Lillian felt ready for a little husband hunting, so she joined her parents last summer. As far as I could tell, she worked pretty hard at it, and at the end of the summer she seemed to have a good prospect. Anyway, at that time she begged Max for a job here this summer—probably because the prospect wasn't yet a sure thing. A few months later she borrowed on her future earnings here. A month or so before she's due to start work, she lands the guy and doesn't have to work here, but she owes Max money, so she can't just quit. She has to find a substitute—you—who will accept wages for the summer low enough to pay Max back for what she owes. I thought you would have known. She's a friend of yours, isn't she?"

"No, I'm happy to say. She was a cousin of a friend, or something like that. Jeez, what an operator!"

"That's a polite word for her," Muriel said. "But I hope she doesn't really affect your feelings about this place. I'm certain you'll have a good time here and you'll be glad you came."

Muriel certainly knew what was what, and the smartest advice she gave Bess that summer was to keep her mouth shut about things she was ignorant of (which was practically everything), then ask Muriel, who was beginning her third year at the Alpine. She was happy to be indispensable to Max so she could be near her fiancé, Jerry, who worked as a waiter at one of the grander Catskill resorts. That's where the really big money in tips was, Muriel said. He worked like a dog, but the money he earned allowed him to continue at City College during the next two semesters, at which time he'd graduate. They had planned very carefully. Jerry was earning a degree in mathematics; he had chosen math because there were no lab hours, which would free him to work part-time. Muriel had ambitions too. She wanted to become a librarian. After they married she would work for Max or someone like him until Jerry had a secure job, and then she would study for her librarian exams.

Bess couldn't help but be impressed by the detailed, determined planning involved, but it seemed such a respectable, plodding, pre-dictable path, so lacking in the romance and excitement she herself craved. Nevertheless, she found herself liking her roommate quite a lot. Muriel was from the first very good-natured about sharing the cabin. It would all work out very well, she assured Bess. They would be company for each other during the week, but there would also be time for privacy. As soon as her work was finished on Friday evening, Muriel was off to spend the weekend nights with Jerry, leaving the cabin to Bess. She wouldn't return until early Sunday morning, in time for the guests' check-out and check-in crush.

Now here was a revelation. Clearly Muriel was sleeping with her fiancé. Here was this girl—neither a femme fatale, a fallen woman, nor a tramp, but good-hearted, intelligent, and, to be honest, rather plain—this girl spent Friday and Saturday nights in her boyfriend's bed. Evidently, the famous mama's warning that "nice girls don't let" wasn't the last word. Muriel was a nice girl and she was letting, and she seemed neither guilty nor frightened of the consequences. Quite happy and enthusiastic, actually. It was food for thought, and Bess did think about it a lot. Just where would she, Bess, find herself in this would-be, could-be wonderland of summer romances, courtships, and less respectable, less permanent connections?

There was for sure a lot of what Max called hanky-panky going on. Bess had only to keep her ears and eyes open to realize this. The whispers of girls in the restrooms and the disappearance of couples after hours told her a lot. It was disconcerting that she, the city mouse, was less experienced about this then the country mice. She had in the last few years engaged in a very discreet amount of necking. Lack of privacy, and her own sense that school boys' fumbling advances were not worth the gossip or the risk, kept her from further experimenting. She had, after all, an older brother who was very popular with the girls. Stretching her ears to catch words of wisdom from his conversations with his friends, she was clear about the fine boundaries between nice girls and those they called pigs or bums. But here a lot of girls seemed to be "doing it," and the gulf between those doing it and those who hadn't yet done it yawned as wide as an abyss. It was humiliating that girls younger and far less sophisticated than she were in the know, while she wasn't.

"They don't know more," Muriel corrected her. "They just do more."

"Yeah?"

"Opportunity and boredom," said the sage Muriel. "Bored female guests and lots of young energetic busboys and waiters. Also, Max likes to hire local kids as maids and custodians—good community relations. And these kids, they don't have a lot of movies, museums, performances at the 92nd Street Y, concerts at Lewisohn Stadium, you know. But their boyfriends can get their hands on cars with back seats. And since most of them aren't planning on going to college or taking a grand tour of Europe, they figure they'll be getting married anyway. Result: too many pregnancies too soon."

Bess, sniffing a lecture in the air, backed up slightly. "You know, I've never been to Lewisohn Stadium. My brother goes to City College, but he's never even mentioned it."

"No? Well, that tells me you haven't been hanging out with the right crowd. Maybe in the fall you can come to a concert with Jerry and me. Who knows? We might be able to fix you up with some nice guy. Not like the ones who come here—you really need to watch your step with them—they've got more money than brains, believe me." Muriel gave a little laugh. "And that doesn't mean they're all that rich."

Bess just smiled. For herself, she couldn't be as dismissive of money as Muriel was. She hated not having any when it was so clearly a ticket to the freedom and experience she craved. She felt, also, though she would never be so unkind as to utter this, that she didn't really need Muriel's help finding men. She was very aware of the admiring glances they gave her. Muriel and Jerry were very nice and kind, but from the papers and magazines they read and the activities Muriel told her about, they appeared so earnest and socialistic. It didn't seem that the men they knew would be much fun or very exciting. Bess felt she only needed opportunity to do very well by herself when it came to guys. And weren't there opportunities here? There must be. All she would have to do is eighty-six the calamine lotion and wait.

CHAPTER 4

Frima turned in early the night before Jack arrived so she'd be sure she got her beauty sleep. "Idiot," she muttered to herself out loud as she slipped under the light cover and closed her eyes. "No schoolgirl fantasies or what ifs about tomorrow, please." She gave a mighty yawn, turning to her right side as she always did, but instead of slipping into sleep, she found herself caught up in a vivid memory. It was of a summer afternoon that she hadn't given a thought to in years. There was this boy, a very nice boy of her own age. She couldn't remember his name. Perhaps she had never known it—it didn't matter. She sat up, arms wrapped around her knees, eager to set the memory in its concrete time and place, recall specific details, lest it seem a dream, with time and images and sensations distorted and fleeting. But it wasn't a dream. It had really happened, and she was glad of it.

It was the summer before she turned twelve. Papa was still alive, and he and Mama and Frima were having an afternoon visit with some older couple her parents knew. These people were staying at a bungalow colony in the country, but it wasn't Frima's country. It was pretty far from Ellenville. Not in the Catskills at all, actually, but rather on the eastern side of the Hudson, in an area unfamiliar to her. It was very warm and sunny, but there were few people outside, so it must have been in the week after Labor Day when summer visitors had already departed. Otherwise she and Mama and Papa would have been in Ellenville at the farm. Perhaps they had stopped on their way back to the city. They were in the town of Rhinebeck. She recalled that without hesitation. Funny how that was the only name she remembered from that afternoon. But then, almost all of her memories of those few hours were sensory.

The bungalow was warm and muggy, and Frima was bored. Every few minutes a little breeze would come through the screened windows, but it was tainted with the smell of rotting meat. The area had been plagued with flies, she was told, and some residents had hung a piece of meat high on a pole to draw the flies away from the houses. Maybe the meat was poisoned. Frima didn't really want to know. She thought it was a disgusting device, even though it seemed to work. Mindful of her manners, she made no comment, but she was relieved to know that they would be there for only a few hours. Luckily she had her bathing suit with her, and Mama, after some consultation about the safety and depth of the pond that was in full view of the screened porch, said she could go down and swim. She put on her light-blue suit with the red piping that Mama had bought for her new that summer. She was proud of it, for it made her look grown up, even though she was fully aware that she hardly needed the top at all yet. Still, she looked nice in it, and she had hopes of next summer bringing some longed-for changes.

Frima tentatively put a foot into the water. It was cool, very clear, and its bottom seemed free of any mucky stuff. It was lovely, actually, with shimmering rainbow colors when you looked at the water up close, and tiny minnows swimming among the water lily pads. The lake was shallow, just deep enough to swim, and silent, except for hushed and secret little water sounds. The air was fresh and sweet, without a hint of that tainted breeze. Were there other people there? The lake was so inviting, there must have been, but the only person she remembered there was this one boy. She couldn't recall his name.

Did he tell her? Did they even bother with names, exchange any history? All she remembered clearly was that he was slender and tan and a good swimmer. Did she think he was beautiful then? Who knows? But she thought of him so now. He looked like he'd be popular in a schoolyard and good at outdoor games. He was friendly and unselfconscious in seeing her there, which put her very much at ease. They swam out to a small white raft together, and Frima couldn't hoist herself up on it, but he helped her, and there was no awkwardness or embarrassment. She was exhilarated at having been able to swim so far without tiring. They spent the entire afternoon in the water. He showed her plant and rock formations on the almost transparent pond bottom, the minnows and even a few sunnies—he was sorry he didn't have a fishing rod with him, she recalled—but mostly they would surface dive and swim between each other's legs. They didn't say much, but they were entirely absorbed with the water and with each other until their respective mothers called them home.

"I hope you aren't burned to a crisp," said Mama, who worried about Frima's fair skin. "I called you to come out of the water and put a T-shirt on, but obviously you didn't hear me," she said pointedly.

"I'm fine," Frima replied. She felt profoundly happy that afternoon and deliberately said nothing about her encounter. She had really liked this boy, and he'd liked her. They'd had a lot of fun. If only they had lived close to each other, they could have been boyfriend and girlfriend. It was a delicious secret she wanted to think about at will. She felt clean and refreshed and so natural. Yes, that was the word, natural.

Sitting there in bed, Frima smiled. She had been in the sixth grade before that summer, a year in which she had discovered boys, and they had become the preoccupation of every unscheduled moment, it seemed to her now. She was not alone in this, of course. Virtually all her girlfriends had more or less the same reaction to these creatures, who only a short while ago had been ordinary brothers, cousins, playground and sandbox buddies, or rivals. They must now be approached with shrieks, giggles, and posturing, or conversely with pretenses of ignoring their very existence. But with this boy, there was nothing like that at all. They had touched each other a lot; they had held hands, and he had lifted her onto the raft. They held each other's legs and arms without shame or pretense. She felt that had they more time together, he might have kissed her. She would have liked that. He would have been nice to kiss.

Just like Eden before the apple, Frima thought. And tomorrow in this place that was so natural and refreshing to her would come this other boy, and this one she knew was beautiful. Could it be like that little bit of Eden again? She sighed, feeling a telltale wetness between her thighs. How could it be? They both had already tasted the apple.

The next afternoon, as soon as Grandpa drove off to pick up Jack at the bus station, a decidedly unnatural Frima dashed upstairs to primp. Gleaming newly washed hair behaved itself when parted on the side and held off her forehead with new barrettes. With clean smooth fingernails and hands giving off a subtle floral scent, she changed into a thin, light blue, cotton dress, nothing fancy or out of the ordinary, but still highlighting her fair coloring and slender figure. She had calculated the time it would take for Grandpa to drive back from the station so she could be doing something fetching but casual when they arrived. Nothing involving chicken droppings, hayseed, or dirt under her fingernails. Arranging flowers for the reception area—that would be perfect. She didn't want to be seen awaiting him too eagerly. The only problem was that Grandpa was late returning to the hotel. Flower arrangements could take only so long, and even with stalling, she was finished before the station wagon appeared. So she stood with Mama, ready to greet him on the front porch.

Funny how when Jack stepped out of the station wagon, he seemed diminished in stature compared to the man of her dreams. He was wilted from the heat, and he mopped his brow with a clean white handkerchief and dried his hands before he shook hands rather stiffly with Mama and Frima. His eyes darted around nervously, and he barely looked at Frima while he greeted them and made small talk about his journey from the city. It was questionable if he even noticed Frima's efforts to be enchanting. Her disappointment was momentary, however, for she quickly realized that he was only rather nervous and shy, as well he should be. He'd never been to the Catskills before nor worked at a hotel. This was entirely new to him. She couldn't expect him to be the smart, cocky, wise-cracking Jack who charmed the girls on the Bronx street corners. Those city streets were his natural milieu, it dawned on her. For so many of the young men of her time and place—girls too—real life was on those Bronx streets. That's where you went for connection, pleasure, recognition, and, paradoxically, peace and solitude. Small space for any of these comforts in apartments crowded with overworked and overwrought families. Her own experience was different and rather privileged, she knew, for she could find so much that enhanced her life at home. Frima felt suddenly a keen sympathy for Jack that went beyond her attraction to him. She smiled her understanding and encouragement. In a couple of hours they had both loosened up, and Jack's stature miraculously returned to normal.

Back in her bed and ready for sleep, Frima suddenly thought of that unnamed boy again. His natural milieu was the country lake. Jack's was the city streets. What was her place? Was it both? Profound as the idea seemed to her, she was too drop-dead tired to think about it now. Besides, she had all the time in the world, didn't she?

—

Jack's first hurdle was to transform himself into a driver and a mechanic. He knew how to operate a vehicle and had habitually discussed the features of the new-model cars with his friends, even though none of them could yet dream of affording a car. He had decided to take his driver's test up in the country where it was less of a hassle. For his first two days, he spent most of his time in the hotel station wagon with Grandpa, driving the country roads with his permit, practicing changing tires, and probing the mysteries of the internal combustion engine. The ease and enthusiasm with which he learned won him Grandpa's admiration and trust—which was no mean feat—and on the fourth day he drove into the yard, elated. Jack waved the license at Frima as he got out of the car. Then he grasped her around the waist.

"This means, Frima-Dreamer, I can take you out for a night on the town if we can find one!"

"Oh, I'm sure we'll find one. We're not a complete bunch of hicks here." She was very happy, though careful not to gush. She was relieved that Mama was not there to witness her enthusiasm. As for Grandpa, he just beamed. Jack had won a friend for life.

Frima ran the encounter over and over again in her mind for the pure pleasure of it. Frima-Dreamer, he had called her. Now just what did that mean? Was it just a silly rhyme you might use to amuse a child, like Josie-Posie, or higgledy-piggledy? Or was she a beautiful dreamer à la Stephen Foster? A lovely girl with the gift of imagination and dreams? Could he mean, by chance, that Frima was dreamy— gorgeous and sexy? That would, of course, be best. No matter how she interpreted his words, they were personal and intimate and compli- mentary—altogether fine.

There were in the few days before the guests arrived still enough spare hours for Frima to give Jack a crash course in the Catskills, as she knew it. It didn't take him more than ten minutes to absorb all the warnings about poison ivy, sumac, mushrooms, and skunks, but the vacation world of bungalows, guest houses, hotels, and bigger resorts was a whole other planet. How could she explain that the peaceful, pastoral facades in no way mirrored the complex and fractious yet cooperative world hidden behind them? Frima herself was only really familiar with Jewish life in the Catskills, and there was much that she was ignorant of, but there was a new fascination in revealing to Jack what she did know.

"The number of Jewish vacation places is increasing pretty fast, but there's still a lot of prejudice around here, with its own not-so-secret language, and each brochure and advertisement makes it perfectly clear who is welcome. Menu descriptions tell you a lot, you know. Glatt kosher means a lot of beards and black clothing. Strictly kosher, kosher style, kosher, and non-kosher available. These are signals down the line from the orthodox to the totally nonobservant."

"And the 'restricted' places?"

"They won't be so crass as to say no Jews allowed, but they'll usually advertise 'Convenient to all Churches,' if they're serious about no Jews. Maybe some say 'All-American Cuisine,' or something, if they just don't want you to act Jewish—that I don't know."

"And colored? Do you see any here?"

"Porters and red caps at the railway stations, some kitchen help, or laborers I imagine, but I haven't seen Negroes who seem to be guests in these parts. Perhaps we're not that advanced, or they simply can't afford it."

"Well, they probably wouldn't be comfortable where they're not wanted, anyway."

Frima was not entirely happy with this response—the all too familiar refrain of the genteel biased—and just what they would be likely to say about any Jew. Didn't he realize that? She refrained from saying anything, lest he think she was preaching at him. After all, she couldn't expect Jack to be as liberal and enlightened as her family. Yet Bess was. How odd. She quickly moved on.

A couple of miles down the road they came to a guest house catering to ultra-orthodox Jews, where the bearded men, bewigged wives, and kids dressed like tiny grownups seemed more alien to both of them than the Italian Catholics on Villa Avenue in the Bronx. In a nearby village there was a summer colony of socialists where it was rumored that free love was practiced openly. Jack seemed particularly interested in this.

"You're not going to see anyone making love on the lawn, you know."

"Well, is there a nudist colony close by, at least?"

"I wouldn't be the least surprised if there was one somewhere. Of course, not every place has a special bent, but for the smaller places, it's an asset if they can attract guests who will be comfortable with each other. I guess when you want to develop a big resort, you have to accommodate a whole lot of different people to stay full and in business. For any hotel, if you can't fill every room you have, you are in big trouble."

"And Eisner's? What kind of people come here?"

"Why, those who want the matchless experience of a family farm vacation, of course."

"Very funny. Now, tell me, really. Don't you think I need to know?"

"Okay, okay. The farm remains a farm because Grandpa is still a farmer and owns the land, and it's also a memorial to my father who loved the old place. Also my mother knows that I love the farm, so it is still here. Beyond that, the hotel is my mother's vision and energy, and she is urban to the core—sophisticated, intelligent, confident of her taste, but not snobbish or exclusive. She will be the first to tell you that you have to have more money than brains to be exclusive."

"I've always thought she was a looker and a charmer—like her daughter," he said winningly, "but you make her sound downright intimidating."

"Strong-minded is what I'd call her. And, like all of us, sometimes opinionated."

"So her opinions determine your guest list? All your guests are sophisticated and liberal, with taste and intellectual curiosity? How does she find them? And how will I be able to talk to these people? I'm feeling a little out of my class." His smile softened his words.

"Well, that's just silly. Our guests are really nice people and not in the least snobbish or demanding. I mean, if they are sunning themselves on the porch, and they want some extra ice for their drinks, they are generally happy to get it themselves from an ice box that Mama keeps in the side yard rather than have you serve them. I'd say that compared to the larger hotels, our guests are a breeze. You're not so much at their beck and call."

"Terrific. Means I have more time to be at *your* beck and call."

Frima was not all that comfortable with this open flirtation and continued as if she hadn't heard him. "And they are appreciative of our efforts."

"Meaning they are good tippers?"

"They are. But Eisner's is a comparatively small place, after all, so you can't expect as much in tips as at the bigger resorts."

"So, tell me. How does your mother find these select guests?"

"Oh, family, friends, word of mouth, ads in the right small journals and weeklies, you know."

"Actually I don't, but tell me more."

"Well, Eisner's is not strictly kosher, so you won't see people who are really observant. Most guests are Jewish, but more secular, and there are some who have married non-Jews. It's not a big deal here. Many of the folks who come up here are in what Mama likes to call the 'lower-paying professions,' men and women who work all week and have pretty steady, if moderate, incomes. You know, teachers, nurses, and other civil servants, a few low-fee lawyers and family doctors, accountants, librarians. Mostly they want to spend time on vacation with their kids, because they don't have that much time with them during the work week. That's why we call Eisner's a family farm. We don't regularly have a separate mealtime for the kids, and we don't have a real day camp like some of the other hotels, though we help plan activities for them. I'm a part-time counselor when I'm not doing ten other jobs. You'll probably get recruited too. Now what else can I tell you? Our guests are mostly first- or second-generation Jewish immigrants, well-educated, even if some are self-educated. They like to read, listen to music, keep up with the arts, science, and politics. They are liberal and Americanized, but for some, I think, cultural life in the United States is a bit of a come down from their past. Of course, this is just my personal impression."

"Isn't it usually the other way around? America is the land of opportunity and all that?"

"During the Depression?" She smiled a little ironically as she said this, then immediately backed off, not wanting to appear a smart aleck. "Still, I think you're right, really, if you think of this country as an opportunity to escape from oppression and change yourself or your vision of life."

"And do you have a vision of life?" His smile was intimate, as if he really cared to know things about her that others couldn't.

"Not yet," she said, suddenly shy again.

In truth she was afraid of saying too much, doing too much, for she enjoyed these pre-season hours no end. Jack would take her hand while they walked or put an arm lightly over her shoulder or around her waist. She loved the nearness, the body contact. How different he was from some of the boys of her teen years who initiated physical contact with so much anxious over-planning and discomfort that she would spring away from their touch as if it came from a hot stove. She was elated when she had the opportunity to accidentally lean against Jack, take his arm when he helped her out of the car or over some brush or stones. The first time he kissed her, it seemed the most natural thing in the world. Except, she thought silently, was it natural to be so stirred by it? Oh, she was ready to fall in love. Slow down, Frima, she cautioned herself, totally without conviction. There's a whole summer ahead of you.

CHAPTER 5

It was turning out that everyday life at the fancy-schmancy Alpine Song was really quite nice. Good food, fresh air, pretty country, her new friend, Muriel. Bess found that guests liked her because she was young and friendly and funny, and she was starting to collect tips. Not a fortune, but very gratifying, even more so because she didn't feel overworked. She was just pleasantly ready for sleep at bedtime. So unlike the weariness she felt working at Papa's store. Since, as Max had predicted, no one seemed interested in making ashtrays or pictures, she had a few free hours to paint and pursue her own path as she was doing now.

She had abandoned the pretty woodland that had first attracted her—too many biting creatures—for this sunlit meadow full of wildflowers and Queen Anne's lace. The sun was kind to her dark complexion, and it was so beautifully quiet here, except for the sound of one of Max's dogs licking his paw. The pooch had felt it necessary to accompany her here. She didn't mind his company. She liked dogs, even though the heat made this one's doggy scent very evident. At least he didn't look over her shoulder and make comments. She put her sketch pad down to stretch her shoulders. She would be due back at the hotel office in about half an hour. Just a few more minutes with her face toward the sun and she would go. She leaned back to fondle the petal-soft flap of the dog's ear and looked at him attentively. She didn't know what breed he was. Probably a mutt, but he looked to her like the essence of dog, rather like the one she had first created on paper when she was in grade school—her first artistic triumph and her first heartache.

Her teacher had announced that there was to be an art contest—not just for her own fourth grade, but for the whole school and many other schools in the Bronx. The contest was sponsored by the Dime Savings Bank. The best picture for each school was to be exhibited on the walls of the bank with the artist's name and school printed under it. Furthermore, each winner would receive a prize: a personal savings account with a bank book in the child's own name showing five dollars already deposited in the account. A veritable fortune in the Depression! There was tremendous excitement in the classroom. Virtually everyone was a contestant. Of course, Bess would try out—any excuse to create a picture. The rule was this had to be a picture of something you wanted more than anything else. Now here was a difficulty for the innately honest Bessie. The things she wanted most she couldn't articulate, let alone put on paper. After some ethical struggle with herself, she decided to create a dog—because after all she really would love to have a dog—even if it weren't the most important thing in the world. So much for originality. At least half the children in the class had chosen a dog. But here the resemblance ended. It turned out that some of these dogs were so elegant and beribboned, so sophisticated that Bess had the ungenerous notion that they were not painted by her schoolmates. The same was true for the next most popular category, a baby sister or brother. Some of the pictures were painted in oil colors! Bess's work was only in what she liked to think of as pastels (colored chalk, actually), for that was all she had. Her dog took up the entire paper with nothing more than a leash and a girl's leg in a white sock and a black Mary Jane shoe to suggest herself as the owner. She had considered this composition seriously. Certainly it was easier to just create a dog and not have to worry about the colors or drawing skill she would need for an entire girl. Besides the dog was the wish— she was just the wisher.

When she came to submit her picture, she almost backed out, so formidable did the other more elaborate creations seem. But she didn't back out and—guess what?—she won. Looking back at that wonderful moment, Bess smiled ironically. There was a lesson there somewhere. At first she had been dazed by the adulation of the other kids in her class, the beams of her teacher, and the wintry smile of the school principal, a formidable woman whom Bess usually feared and avoided. But still the sense of victory had been so sweet that she was afraid the triumph would show on her face. Then everyone would hate her for sure.

She needn't have worried. The triumph disappeared, and the heartache came soon enough. "Home is where the heartache is," she quipped to her doggy companion, whose only response was to try to lick her face. But at nine years old, there was nothing funny about the deflation and anger that overwhelmed her by the time she went to bed that night. At first, it had been okay. Jack had tousled her hair and departed with a casual "Good for you, kid" before escaping to the street to join his friends, who were far more important. Papa had been Papa. "For that picture she was scribbling they pay her five dollars? Go figure!"

Mama, the first one she told before the others had come home, was different. She had hugged Bess. "My Bessie, I'm so proud of you." There were tears in her eyes when she said this, and that had made Bess cry too. She didn't mind that kind of crying. It was later when she was alone in her bed that the tears were bitter. For she had learned that Mama couldn't really fight for her.

The little artists were to be feted a couple of Fridays hence at the local Dime branch, where the winning pictures would be on display for a month. The honored winners invited to the party were to be accompanied by a parent or legal guardian in order to be able to open their individual savings accounts. Simple enough, Bess thought, but in her family it was out of the question. Papa would never consider leaving the store on such an errand and absolutely refused to allow Mama to accompany Bess. On a Friday before Shabbos, the busiest time on Bathgate Avenue? She should leave the store? Never! Bess could go by herself. She and Mama could open the savings account another time. Mama stopped arguing and retreated into one of her frozen aggrieved silences. Still, she did enlist Jack to write a letter in his fine penmanship to the branch manager, explaining the situation, and Bess did eventually receive her bankbook. As if she cared about that at the time. The real issue was her shame at not having a proud beaming adult to accompany her to the celebration. But the bankbook did matter, it turned out. It was the beginning of some vague, fuzzy hope and ambition. And she thought with tenderness now of the times through the years that her mother had passed her a crumpled dollar with a whispered, "Here, Bessie, buy for yourself an ice cream cone or a Hershey Bar, and the change you put into that bank account—just for you!"

As she started to walk back to the hotel, she stopped suddenly with a thought that had honest-to-God never occurred to her before. Why didn't they get Jack—he'd already had his bar mitzvah at that time and was thus a man—why didn't they get him to help Papa at the store for one stinking Friday afternoon after school and let Mama go to the bank with her? "Oh, give it a rest," she said out loud. "He is their bright-eyed boy and always will be. But I'm the one with the savings account." Her faithful companion, tongue lolling, trotted at her heels. "And I even have the dog!"

Back at the cabin, she hopped into the shower for a quick cool rinse, and shivering with pleasure, looked down at her long legs and elegant smooth tan. No more poison ivy blisters—it was time to show off these gams. The white shorts she put on fit snuggly but respectably over her rear end and flared just slightly where they ended at mid-thigh, as if they had been tailored just for her. Thank you, Hannah Eisner! With a fresh green shirt tucked into the waistband and a couple of buttons opened at the neck, she knew she would draw admiring glances because, let's face it, she looked fetching. Not easy, just fetching, and she suddenly loved who she was—Bethesda. This was the secret name of her heart and soul. As of now, the only one who knew it was Frima, and she was sworn to secrecy until Bess was ready to reveal it to the world and make it legal. Would the time come this summer?

Bess loved the movies and had longed for the screen-image fun and romance—the happy ending. But in her one attempt to experience this here in the country, she had barely escaped with her clothes. There he was, a guest at the hotel: your average bouncy, boyishly handsome, suntanned, athletic college boy, born Bruce Stein, but secretly referred to as Alphie Pie by Bess and Muriel because of his habit of boasting to anyone who would listen about his fraternity at NYU: "The oldest Jewish frat house in the world." That was all there was to say about him, except that he had the brains of a potted plant. A cactus, she and Muriel concluded, since he turned very prickly if his vanity was hurt. As clearly it had been when Bess whacked him with her flashlight to prevent him crawling all over her and ripping her one good dress. Naturally she had talked over this adventure with Muriel.

"My first and probably only experience with an alrightnik, and it practically ends in disaster."

"He certainly is that," Muriel yawned. "Probably more dimwitted than most."

An alrightnik. Would Bruce even understand the term? Bess doubted it. And he'd never get its particular mixture of envy and grudging admiration, often salted with contempt. A struggling immigrant Jew, like Bess's mother or Muriel's, who mixed English and Yiddish in their everyday speech, might label a richer Jew as an alrightnik. The rich one would never think of himself as that. No more than he would see himself as a social climber or a gatecrasher. Why did it make any difference? "Why is old money always superior to new money, anyway?" She didn't realize she had asked this out loud.

"It isn't," Muriel answered. "Old and new money—it's all gained from the sweat of the working class."

Bess judged this exactly the right time to fall asleep.

And then along came the big catch. His advent was anticipated with much excitement by the staff, for he had stayed at the Alpine several times before. He was known as a good tipper, an avid and highly skilled card player, and a lady's man. Still in his mid-twenties, he had graduated from an Ivy League law school and currently was a clerk for a federal judge in New York City. A law clerk, Bess was made to understand, was no mere office worker. It was a very prestigious position, and this man was destined to go far. And Bess, as soon as she had laid eyes on him, knew what the fuss was about. This was truly a splendid specimen of young manhood, inches taller than Bess, in itself an excellent attribute, with blue eyes and ashy blond hair that looked gray in certain lights. Very sophisticated. He had a vague resemblance to some regular in Hollywood detective movies who played a sophisticated nogoodnik. Bess could never remember his name. The good catch's name she was unlikely ever to forget.

"Arthur Midland. The name sounds like the president of a big bank or insurance company. Very goyish. What's he doing at the Alpine?" Bess asked Muriel.

"Supposedly he's half-Jewish," Muriel replied. "But I think he comes here to be a big fish in a little pond. He makes money playing cards with the ordinary husbands and likes being ogled by their wives, who think he's the most romantic and dashing thing they've ever seen outside of the flicks. He's famous for having affairs with one or another woman whose husband only comes up on weekends. Very safe for him and no commitment."

"You don't seem to think much of him."

"I don't."

Bess didn't stay around to hear more and shrugged off Muriel's comments. Muriel had taken on the role of big sister, for which Bess was usually very grateful. But this time, no. She didn't want anyone ruining her excitement. It's like having Jack around, she thought resentfully. Then suddenly she felt oddly forlorn that he wasn't around, and that if he were, he wouldn't have time for Bess anyway.

Arthur Midland spent most of his first two weeks not noticing Bess at all, and it didn't take her long to understand why. The staff grapevine let her know exactly which devoted young wife and mother he was comforting, whose husband slaved away Monday through Friday in the city. She was a petite blonde (in itself enough to irritate Bess) and had a pretty-ish face with pencil line eyebrows and a mouth that was made to look sexy-mean with the careful application of lipstick above her thin natural lip line. She was clearly looking for it, Bess thought resentfully. Oh, yeah? Well, what about you? What are you looking for? She was torn between humiliation that she herself was invisible to this desirable man and relief that she was not in his line of sight. It did dawn on her that if you are nineteen and really just beginning to fish, perhaps you'd best not hook a shark. Still, the sense of danger was fascinating.

She found that Arthur Midland was becoming something of a constant companion in her head. She imagined him eyeing her appreciatively from a card table and fancied his flirtatious complaint that her presence was so distracting that she put him off his game. Or, alternatively, that he asked her to stand close to him and bring him luck. She envisioned him watching her while she worked in the office and imagined him gracefully slouched in a corner of her cabin, legs crossed, arms folded, a cigarette in the corner of his mouth, watching her take off her clothes. She told herself she was a fool, letting him continually insinuate himself into her consciousness, but this did not stop her from going out of her way to be in his line of vision and standing taller, moving more gracefully and sensuously even when he was nowhere around. All her movements and poses were more consciously come-hither.

If Arthur Midland was smitten with her in her fantasies, she was still taken aback when he actually asked her to dance one night. Bess cautioned herself that he was probably using her as a cover, since it was the weekend and the devoted wife was dancing with her husband. She was immensely pleased, however. After all, he had asked her, Bess, and not some other woman to provide this service for him.

"I understand you're an aspiring artist—a painter? I'm surprised you aren't installed in a quaint bohemian studio in Greenwich Village, instead of idling away your time up here in Max's cultural desert. Husband hunting?" His tone was light.

"I'm not idling away my time. I work here, if you haven't noticed. And I'm not looking for a husband. Besides, studios cost a lot."

"With your figure you could be an artist's model. All those artsy type guys would be lining up to paint you. I certainly would, if I had any talent."

"And how many artist's models do you know who can afford charming studios in Greenwich Village?" She was surprised at her own sharp retort. Perhaps it was because she was nervous. "Besides, that's not what modeling is about," she began more gently, but broke off at his teasing smile, flattered in spite of herself.

His attentions increased over the next week. More dances, a squeeze of the hand, gentle, casual caresses of her shoulder, her arm, a touch at the small of her back. Nothing obvious that would jeopardize his affair. But the devoted wife was leaving on Sunday; and he would still be here. What would happen then? Bess wished she could talk to Muriel about this, but Muriel didn't like Arthur and remained discreetly silent. Just as well, probably, since Muriel would have nothing to say that Bess really wanted to hear. She wanted only to be encouraged in this adventure. Pushed off the diving board, so to speak.

The next couple of weeks were like the continuation of her fantasy, except that Artie, as he asked her to call him, wasn't as ubiquitous as he was in her daydreams. In fact, he didn't spend all that much time at the hotel after the devoted wife departed, and he frequently drove off to town in the afternoons and absented himself in the evenings. But when he was there, he was very attentive, indeed. He took her for strolls on her hours off, danced with her, bought her drinks from the bar, even drove her to the fabled lake (alas, no canoe). He had all the attributes she dreamed of in an accomplished lover, and she was aroused and greatly pleased by his kisses and knowing gentle caresses. He wanted her, that was obvious, but he seemed to be in no hurry, as if he were at leisure to contemplate and enjoy his seduction of her. If only he would just shut up and sweep her off her feet.

Unbidden as this thought was, that was the problem. In fantasy your dream man says exactly what you want him to. In reality, the more Artie said, the less she approved of him. The first time he told a bartender, "The lady will have one of your very dry martinis" without asking her first, he seemed elegant and masterful. The next time, she raised her eyebrows a little. Not being stupid, he was quick to notice.

"You don't mind my ordering for you, do you? It's just that I know this place, and I want you to have the best experience here." He treated her to his charming smile.

"Fair enough," she replied, treating him to hers.

She'd noticed that Artie didn't eat many meals at the Alpine, even though the well-prepared and abundant cuisine was a main attraction to most of the guests, many of whom seemed to live for the next meal. He soon enlightened her.

"Have you ever eaten pork? Wait, wait—don't tell me—you eat pork and shrimp, but only in Chinese restaurants, and you wouldn't dream of eating bacon, ham, and shellfish anywhere else."

Bess's experience of any restaurant was pretty meager, but he didn't have to know that. "If you're so sure of my answer why did you ask me?"

"Now, now, don't get huffy. I'm simply thinking of rescuing you from Max's kosher swill by taking you out for pork ribs, Kansas City style, of which there is nothing finer."

"You know, I don't really understand why you stay here. You say it's a cultural desert and that the food is swill. Yet you come back here. It's not your first season or your second, is it?"

"Truth is, I'd rather be in the Adirondacks or at some elegant hotel in Palm Beach, but I'm not a millionaire yet, and with all its faults, Max's place is comfortable and convenient for me. Besides, I'd never have met you in one of those fine resorts. They don't take kindly to Jews."

"And you would consider staying at one of those anti-Semitic palaces? You're part Jewish, yourself, I understand. If that's your idea of a joke it isn't very funny!"

"Sweetheart, calm down! I'm only trying in my not very clever way to get you to come out and have ribs with me."

She agreed to go out with him for a late dinner on her Saturday night off, but as soon as he was out of sight, she began to regret it. No part of their last conversation had pleased her. It took her some effort to cast aside the negatives about him. She was determined that he would be her first lover. He was good-looking, intelligent, and clearly sexually experienced. She didn't have to marry him, did she? And he'd be leaving the hotel soon enough. Surely, everything would be easier after her first time. Her life, her art, would gain a passionate, a sensual depth. And after all, she couldn't wait around forever for her romantic ideal. What if she were hit by a car? Who wanted to die a virgin?

He made it quite clear that he wasn't going to wait around forever either, when he suggested that they stay at a guesthouse adjoining the restaurant. That way, they could relax, have a few drinks, privacy. He promised to get her back early in plenty of time for the check-out, check-in rush. Bess had to respect him for that; no surprises, unlike Alphie Pie. But still, she had to be frank.

"You know, Artie, I've never. . . ."

"Not to worry, sweetie, I know you're a babe in the woods—it's part of your charm. I'll take care of everything. No slip-ups. I promise."

He was sparing her embarrassment and worry, which was nice. It was a relief to feel good about him again.

The restaurant looked like a roadhouse, a little run down, but there were plenty of people there, some of them quite well-dressed. They had a long wait for a table, so they sat at the bar, where a quite interesting looking bartender managed to mix drinks and serve them very efficiently while pleasantly fielding customers' jokes and bantering. He had these terrific hazel eyes with slightly drooping lids—very sexy! A couple of women were busier flirting with him than drinking, and Bess had to stop herself from paying too much attention to this. Not a great start for this big evening. Artie suggested she have a beer, since that was what they would want with their meal. He didn't think she was up to a boilermaker yet. She had no idea what that was, but she noticed that he ordered a scotch on the rocks for himself.

"Double?" the bartender asked, impassive.

"Right. You know your man."

When he ordered a refill, she noticed that the bartender diluted his drink. It had crossed her mind that Artie drank a lot, but what did she know? She came from a family that drank alcohol only as ritual wine, with maybe a glass of schnapps for the men at celebrations. What seemed excessive to her was probably just more than she was accustomed to. Besides, he never seemed adversely affected by it. Still, it was clear by the time they got a table and started on a pitcher of draft that he was having too much. He was losing his gloss, becoming touchy and impatient about the long wait for service. And suddenly, things began to fall into place for Bess. He did his drinking here. The bartender knew him, didn't he? He drank here and at other places like this. That was why he was away from the hotel so often—to drink and probably to gamble. She began to be very sorry she was here with him, sorry and scared.

Lost in thought, she hadn't paid attention to what Artie was ordering and only noticed the dozen oysters on the half shell when they were placed on the table. Artie was determined that she try them as an appetizer. "Like this," he instructed her. He squeezed lemon on an oyster and expertly slid the whole creature into his mouth. She found it impossible to follow suit. She found them revolting.

"Oh, God. I'm sorry! I simply can't eat this," she managed to apologize. "I know you think that's silly, but I can't!"

"Oh, now, don't be such a drag, sweetie. They get these babies from Cape Cod, the best damn oysters on the Eastern Seaboard." He was keeping his disapproval in check, she could see, sure that his persuasive charm would carry all before it. He leaned toward her intimately. "They are sex on the half shell."

Yeah, for you, maybe, she thought. All she could manage was, "No, I can't."

"Then why did you let me order them? They're not cheap, you know!" His irritation was showing, but then, catching himself, he switched tactics. "Come on. sweetheart, try one—just for me!"

Again, that smile. She was really sore at him now, and it was a relief. Angry at him and disgusted with herself. She really didn't like this guy at all. Why was she here with him? "Why is it so all-fire important to you that I try one? If I do, I'll gag, or even worse. Is that what you want?"

"No, I just want you to stop being such a provincial little kike!"

She didn't plan to throw the beer in his face, she just did it. And probably he didn't plan to slug her, but he did; and the bartender came over and elbowed him out of the way and asked if she was okay and sent a waitress for some ice for her cheek and a towel for her jerk of an escort.

Artie didn't wait. "Find your own way back, you stupid bitch!" he hissed at her, slamming the door as he left. It was all over in a minute, it seemed.

The waitress took her to a little room off the kitchen where she could sit down with her ice pack and collect herself. She thought she might throw up, but her nausea passed, and then she thought she might simply drop dead of shame, but that didn't happen either. After some minutes, she found her way out to the front again to see if there was such a thing as a taxi. There was a lull in the activity of the place, and she saw that it was after eleven. The dinner crowd had thinned out. The bartender greeted her with an iced Coke with a slice of lemon in it.

"Take this, you'll feel better. And you ought to have something in your stomach. Do you want those ribs your date ordered for you?"

"God, no. I mean, no thank you. Do you think I can find a cab?"

"Not around here. I'm off duty in about a half hour. I'll drive you back to the Alpine."

"Really, I can't let you do that."

"Yes you can. You can't walk there can you? And don't worry. I don't bite or use my fists, for that matter. Do you know Muriel? She'll vouch for me."

"She's my roommate. How do you know her?"

"Oh, politics, same crowd in the city, and I've worked with her boyfriend. How about if I order some eggs for you? You need to eat something."

"Okay, thanks." He was being so nice, but what did she know? He could be a Jack the Ripper. Well, she'd have to risk it.

They were both quiet on the way to the hotel. The guy was tired, Bess could see that. As for herself, she felt like bawling, but she resolutely refused to do any such thing. She had disgraced herself enough, thank you. A few minutes from the Alpine, the bartender spoke, stifling a yawn.

"Feeling any better?"

"Yes, except for behaving like an idiot. First a whack with a flashlight and then a beer in the face. Oh, God!"

"You hit him with a flashlight?" He was alert now.

"No, that was another one. Oh, please don't laugh!" She felt her voice trembling on the edge of tears.

"Sorry."

He turned the car into a narrow dirt lane used only by the staff that led directly to her cabin (so he really did know Muriel!). He stopped only a few feet from the porch and went around the car to open her door and help her out. He slapped at a mosquito. "Watch out, these buggers are out in force tonight."

"Tell me about them," she said with her first genuine smile of the night.

"I'll leave my headlights on until you're safely inside so they don't gang up on you in the cabin."

At the door he turned her face toward him, and for one sweet second she thought he was going to kiss her. Instead he ran his fingers over her bruised cheek.

"I don't think you'll have a shiner. It looks like he just grazed your cheekbone. Your boyfriend will never make a prize fighter."

"He's not my boyfriend, just an awful mistake. And one that will probably cost me my job."

"Why?"

"Staff are not supposed to throw mugs of beer at guests—especially free-spending regulars."

"You didn't throw any mugs at him, just the beer."

"Very funny."

"Seriously, you don't think for one moment he's going to tell Max about this, do you? He hit you because you humiliated him with that beer. A guy like that, he can't face it. Also, he figured the night he planned was down the drain, and he was sore about it. It would be even more humiliating to tell anyone about how he didn't score. Besides, even if he were dumb enough to complain, Max wouldn't pay any attention. Under all that bluster, your boss is really an okay guy who came up the hard way—he used to be a cook—and he knows a grade A bastard when he sees one, if you'll pardon my French."

She smiled a little, even though her cheek throbbed. "I noticed that you put water in his drinks but you didn't do that to anyone else."

"You are very observant," he said smiling. "I didn't know you were paying any attention to what I was doing."

"Why did you do that?"

"Well, you looked like a nice girl, and I know that guy can be an ugly drunk, though I've never seen him slug someone. On the other hand, I've never seen anyone throw a beer in his face. You must be a woman of strong convictions. I admit, I enjoyed seeing that, and I have to say I'm curious about why you did it. Maybe you'll tell me about it sometime. But not tonight. Tonight you need to rest, and keep using a cold compress on your face, on and off, twenty minutes at a time. Here, I brought you some ice."

Bess smiled and held out her hand. "Well, thanks so much for the ride. I really appreciate it, uh . . . I don't even know your name."

He didn't shake her hand, but held it gently. "Vinny. Vincent Carmine Migliori on my driver's license. And you?"

She hesitated for a fraction of a second. "Bethesda Erlichman. Beth for short."

"Well, Beth, I'll call you tomorrow to see how you're doing. Would that be okay?"

"Okay, sure, thanks," she babbled. "Oh, and, by the way, some people at the hotel call me Bess," she added a little lamely.

"Beth, Bess, whatever. Use that ice and then try to get some sleep."

Bess shed her clothes and covered herself with a long T-shirt. She was suddenly so tired that she was tempted to forget about the ice.

But that was what he told her to do, so she wrapped some cubes in a washcloth.

She sat down with a hysterical giggle. Start the evening dressed up for Arthur Midland, super-duper alrightnik, and end up with Vinny, the Italian bartender. And guess what? If Vincent Carmine Migliori wanted her to spend the night with him at a guesthouse or anywhere else, she'd be only too eager to do just as he wished.

CHAPTER 6

Whatever hope Frima and Jack might have harbored about nights on the town, the first week of the season left them too exhausted for more than a few words on the porch, stolen from valuable sleep time. Jack felt aches in muscles he had not known he possessed, and he began to look on five minutes on the porch swing to smoke a cigarette as a luxury. Frima, besides working in the office, babysitting, to-ing and fro-ing, fetching and returning, had undertaken a small flower garden so there would be fresh blooms on the table. She could barely keep her eyes open by the time she reached her room at night. Still, in a week or so, both of them had settled into routines, and feeling able-bodied again, they found the ways and means to spend more time together.

Grandpa was their chief ally in this. Despite his original protests that he was as fit as ever and needed no steady help during the summer, he had taken to Jack right away. "He's a Jack of all trades," he said and repeated this to anyone who would listen. Mama rolled her eyes the way she used to at Papa's silly jokes.

"Frima, why don't you take the kiddies down to the barn to visit Jessie and Toby. You could give kids a bareback ride or hitch up the little cart. It wouldn't hurt either of those animals to get a little exercise. After all we don't want freeloaders," he said, with a significant wink at his daughter-in-law. "And you'd better take Jack with you. Those kids are too heavy for you to lift."

Another time he'd announce, "I won't need the car tonight. Why don't you kids take the night off, drive to Monticello or Liberty. Have a hamburger, a couple of beers. You need a little relaxation."

"Not too much beer," was Mama's only comment. Frima was relieved that Mama made no objection. She should have known she would hear from her mother soon enough.

She and Mama were taking a break from office work, watching Jack from the porch.

"So handsome," commented Mama. "And so much like Bess, in his looks, at least. Isn't it amazing that their parents, those small-minded sour pusses, could have produced such bright, charming children?"

"I think he's beautiful—they're both beautiful, he and Bessie."

"And you, my darling. Aren't you just as beautiful, to say nothing of being talented and bright?"

Frima peered suspiciously at her mother. "Just what are you getting at?"

Mama sighed, and when she spoke it was with an unusual hesitancy. "I think you admire both of them, and that's fine. But you also seem to envy them a little. You've always looked up to Bess—a bit too much maybe. Exotic, you called her, original, courageous. Yes, yes, I know. I'm very fond of her myself. It's just that now I see you have a crush on her brother, and you look at him as if he has so much that you don't. As if he's better than you somehow."

"I thought you liked him!" Frima found herself close to tears.

"I must be expressing myself badly. Of course, I like him—I hired him, didn't I? He is very likable—a fine young man. . .but Frima, you are impressionable and inexperienced. I am just saying, go slow. Be careful."

"If this is going to be one of those lectures about how he won't buy the cow if the milk is free, I refuse to listen to it. Do you really think Jack would take advantage of me with you and Grandpa here?"

"I think you are deliberately misunderstanding me," Mama said firmly. "And I will tell you this. I see how much he is on your mind, how you study him, attend to him, fret about whether he is happy, wants to be with you. Do you think he does the same? Does he devote half as much care and energy to what you think and feel? What's important to you? Oh, he likes you a lot, that's obvious. He finds you very attractive and sweet and bright—who wouldn't? Maybe he is even falling in love with you. But believe me, my daughter, you are not the center of his life, as he seems to be for you. It's not possible. He's a twenty-three-year-old man, and they aren't made like that."

Frima kept her voice light. "Papa wasn't much older when you married him. Was he the same as Jack?"

"Could be he was," said Mama, smiling. "But your Papa, he was very trainable."

"I think you underestimate Jack." She felt quieter now.

"Perhaps. But I don't want you to underestimate you. Listen to me, darling. Go dancing with him, have a good time, even fall in love a little. But remember that you are a beautiful and talented young woman with such potential and so much to offer. He's lucky to spend time with you."

"Well, I'm not thinking about anything beyond the summer. I just want to enjoy this time." She really believed she was speaking the truth.

"Which is just what I want for you. Enjoy it in good health." Mama kissed Frima on the cheek and they parted friends.

She did not enjoy quarreling with Mama, and she was relieved to end it at that. But Mama was wrong about some things. She, Frima, was not so dewy-eyed and worshipful that she couldn't see imperfections in Jack. And she was far from devaluating herself. For one thing, she knew very well that she was a lot more at home with the finer things in life than Jack was. She had noticed, for instance, that he was uneasy about his table manners when he first sat down to dinner with the family at the staff table. He had watched Frima surreptitiously and followed her lead about which cutlery to use, where to put his napkin. His eagerness to learn these fine points touched her. She recalled that Bessie had done the same the first time she had a meal at Frima's house. Both of them, brother and sister, had this same desire to absorb the niceties, to better themselves. Well, she was their model, wasn't she?

And then there was music. She had shown this talent from a very early age. She barely remembered this herself, but she had been told so often how her mother and father had discovered her picking out familiar melodies on a piano (some relative's, no doubt) before she could read words, before she was even in school. Frima knew she wasn't the wunderkind her parents thought she might be, but she had studied the piano and musical theory seriously for the love of it; not to perform professionally, but perhaps to teach. Jack knew nothing about classical music, but he wanted to learn, he said, if she would teach him. Didn't that mean he looked up to her and admired her?

Yet, reluctant as Frima was to admit it, Mama was on to something. Frima did admire, even envy, both of them, Bessie and Jack. It was so hard to explain, but in some unarticulated way, she felt they were her more confident superiors. Now, why was that? She knew she was good-looking, bright, that she enjoyed more material comforts, more opportunities than either of them. But Mama's perception plagued her, and she found herself coming back to it as the hours passed. She looked back over the years at her connection with both brother and sister. She and Bess had become fast friends in grade school, and since then they'd been in and out of each others' homes virtually on a daily basis. The Erlichmans' cramped apartment was as familiar to Frima as her own, and it was impossible not to make comparisons. Though it was obvious that Frima and Mama's home was way more comfortable and inviting, she found it oddly stimulating and pleasant to spend time with the Erlichmans, loud, angry, and excitable though they were. Now for the first time, unbidden, Frima divined what the attraction was. They were a family—an intact family—secure even in what seemed to be their pervading dissatisfaction. No matter how much they hollered at each other, everyone who was supposed to be there was there—right where they ought to be. They didn't have a papa who had died suddenly without a word of warning.

She stood very still. Was this what Mama was hinting at? Did Mama understand this something, this feeling that Frima had hidden from herself? If she did, Frima was devoutly relieved that her mother had done no more than hint at it. It was a something that would not bear airing and close examination. She had firmly closed the door on it. From the porch where she stood, she could see that Jack had finished mowing and was driving off to town with Grandpa to do errands. It was almost three. She was free until about five. She would work on some music. The Beethoven. She could lose herself in it—just what she needed.

Frima had opted very willingly for having a really good piano in the city rather than a mediocre one in both town and country, but Mama still talked about providing her with a good instrument up here in Ellenville as well. It was always next year that this miracle would occur, and Frima knew that in reality it was too much of a financial stretch—a sacrifice was more like it—for Mama. She, Frima, would not allow it. Never would she be such a selfish daughter. She could study with a silent keyboard to practice fingering and phrasing. She was adept at reading and breaking down a score, even the characteristically dense pages of Beethoven. This required discipline and concentration, and she looked forward to a couple of hours of happy absorption on her own.

When not seated at an actual piano, or a dinner table, Frima habitually avoided chairs. Despite the comfortable desk and chair and quiet study space her conscientious parents had provided for her, she preferred to sprawl on a sofa or hammock to do her reading, and for quiet study she preferred the floor or her bed. In very short order, she was happily ensconced on her bed with the window wide open to the breeze (after all, nobody could hear her) and her keyboard propped up against the footboard in easy reach if she wanted it. She hummed as she flipped through the pages of the "Moonlight Sonata" to the movement she planned to work on. It was many minutes before she realized that though she turned pages, her thoughts had wandered far from Beethoven and moonlight. It was on just such an occasion as this, about a week ago, that Jack, finding himself with a couple of free hours, had come up to her room in search of her.

"Now what in the world are you doing?"

"I'm trying to work on this sonata."

"In bed?"

"Well, it's a large flat surface. The floor is too hard."

"I can think of better things to do right here," he said, half reclining on the bed and stroking her bare ankle. He raised his eyebrows like Groucho Marx.

"Get off!" She giggled as she said this and pushed him away gently. Probably too gently, as she thought back on it. She would not let him lie down here, but the thought of him there in bed with her had been distracting enough to push serious practice quite out of her mind.

"Well, if you won't let me stay here with you, come out for a walk with me."

"I'm studying," she said, sounding lame, even to herself.

"Studying? Oh, come on!"

"Now don't you laugh. It is study—serious study," but she had smiled in spite of herself.

"Okay, I believe you. Some day you'll have to teach me about classical music. But are you going to waste this beautiful afternoon when you could spend it with me? Come on, honey, how often do we get the chance to be alone together?"

She had needed no more coaxing. She grabbed a bathing suit and a towel in case they decided to end their walk with a swim.

Mama had seen the two of them running down the back porch steps and seemed a little surprised, but she had said nothing.

"Too beautiful today to practice—we're going for a walk," Frima called out to her, responding to her mother's question before she could ask it.

The entire incident discomforted her now in light of her talk with Mama. Surely it was that occasion that had spurred Mama's cautions to Frima this afternoon.

"Some day you'll have to teach me about classical music." Jack's words, reassuring when she first heard them, suddenly were dismissive: some day, but not now. Could he simply brush past Frima's love of music and her talent—this most special and defining part of her—like some bracken in his path to an afternoon's pleasure? No! She refused to believe any such thing. Mama was making far too much of this. She was being a mother hen with one chick, and that was sweet of her, but she didn't understand. Jack wasn't riding roughshod over her talent, her special qualities. It was only that he wanted to be with her during his precious hours off.

Armed with this comforting interpretation, she turned to the score again, but it was no use. She couldn't practice or study anything today. Maybe never this summer. She lacked the concentration and discipline—that was the problem. She never really wanted to practice diligently during these months. It was only to please Mama that she made the effort. Summer was her time off, like it had been when Papa was alive. Papa was not that caught up with Frima's talent; he was proud of her and supported her, but that was all. It was Mama who was always pushing. A sudden keen anger toward her mother overwhelmed her. She felt her gut wrenching, and she began to perspire. She splashed her face with cold water and rushed outside. This visceral response was over in a few minutes, leaving her troubled and confused. Suddenly she longed to talk to, to be with Bess.

This was an unexpected feeling. Normally they were separated during the summer months and didn't expect much contact, except maybe a postcard, if something exceptional happened. But this was no ordinary summer. Jack was in the picture, and it was clear if unspoken between the two girls (and very likely true for Jack also) that this made all the difference. Probably the very reason that none of the three spoke openly about it. She had been content to not speak of Jack at all, but now she longed to know whether Bess, too, was experiencing this whirlwind of confusion, conflict, joy and enchantment this summer. And this rebelliousness? Well, Bess was always rebellious. She was an expert at that.

Frima had on her bureau at this very minute a letter Bess had sent her several days ago. It was brief enough for a postcard, but it had come in a sealed envelope so Frima knew it was for her eyes only.

Hey, Frima,

Guess what? I've met this guy. He's a guest here. Very intelligent, glamorous looking—may be the next Clarence Darrow. I don't know, but he may be the one! Love to talk to you. Anyway, let's try to connect by phone. What's a good time?

Love,
Bess

Frima was, of course, dying to find out more. She could have called the Alpine Song and left a message if she didn't reach Bess directly, but she couldn't seem to get around to it. Now she made herself sit write down and write a card:

Great news! Can't wait to hear more. Best time to call is late afternoon.

Love,
Frima

Now she could relax a little and wait for Bess to call. It would be so much easier to talk if Bess had a boyfriend of her own.

CHAPTER 7

"**R**emind me, Muriel, to have my head examined if I do so much as smile at another alrightnik. From now on, Bethesda Erlichman will keep a safe distance from anyone remotely resembling one." She said this over her shoulder, as she sorted through her clothes laid out on her bed Sunday morning.

"I take it your date was not all it was cracked up to be?"

"I can't even talk about it yet—it was so awful."

Muriel looked at her, baffled. "Well, okay, but who is Bethesda?"

"That's the name I'm going by from now on. I'm going to change it legally as soon as I get back to the city. So please, Muriel, call me Bethesda or Beth, or even Bethie, and nothing else, except maybe 'idiot,' when I act like one."

"Whatever you like, but, tell me, are you planning to pack your bags and go, just because of that Midland creep?"

Beth, blushing, turned to face Muriel. "Well, no. It's just that I met this other guy, and I really liked him and he said he'd call, so I think he may ask me out, and I'm just checking to see if I have anything I can wear—though he probably won't call. But he said he knew you and Jerry."

"Whoa, slow down. And how did you get that bruise on your face? Did you bang into something or did somebody hit you?"

"Artie." Beth was hardly audible.

"What!" Muriel steadied her voice. "I think you need to sit down and tell me the whole story."

"Okay, the short version. Artie took me to a place for pork ribs and he drank too much, and he ordered oysters and I refused to eat one, so he called me a kike and I threw a beer in his face, and then he slugged me."

"That bastard!"

"Yes. Well, anyway, the bartender, this Vinny Migliori, sort of rescued me and drove me back here."

"Vinny Migliori? A lot of women would call him quite a fine end to a lousy evening."

"He probably won't call."

"Oh, I think he will."

He did. That very afternoon.

"So, Beth—that's right isn't it?—how are you feeling? Recovered from your night out?"

"Oh, great, great! You were right about the ice—no black eye, just a little swelling, and that's almost gone." She felt she was gushing but couldn't seem to control it.

"And the welterweight? Is he out of the way?"

It took a moment to understand. "Oh, he'll be leaving in a few days, I hear. Anyway, he's staying out of my way, which is all right with me."

"Then he's smarter than I thought. So, Beth, I hope you won't hang up on me if I ask you a question?"

"I won't, I promise." His voice, a little hoarse and gravelly, was somehow endearing to her, caressing, really.

"Well, this impulse of yours to use whatever is at hand as a weapon—a flashlight, a beer, maybe a rolling pin? Does it come over you often?"

Beth laughed. "Never a rolling pin, and the other two, well, only once each."

"So, I guess it's safe to ask you out for dinner. I promise I won't take you to the same place, and you can eat anything you want, I assure you."

(Yes, yes!) "I won't even bring a ping-pong paddle. I promise."

"Good. Now let me see what I can do about changing my schedule around. I wouldn't want you to wait until eleven p.m. to be picked up. When are you off?"

"Any time after eight, if that's not too late."

"Sounds good." After an almost imperceptible pause, Vinny continued. "I thought I'd take you to a steak place I think you'd like, but if you'd rather eat kosher food, that's no problem."

"Who says I'm kosher? It was just the oysters I couldn't manage. Steak would be just fine! Er, should I dress . . . I mean dress up?" (Idiot! Stop asking questions.)

"Whatever you wear, you'll look great. Me, I'm kind of informal and out of uniform on my night off, but I'll try not to disgrace you. But take a jacket or a sweater. It might get cold."

Beth gave a little laugh.

"Uh oh! Do I sound like your mother? Or even worse, my mother?"

"Believe me," she said. "You could never sound like my mother."

"Good. I'll call you Tuesday."

———

For the first time in her life, Beth found she was actually enjoying a beer. Here in this steak house with Vinny, she felt she would enjoy anything he had to offer. They hadn't done much more than make small talk, which was okay with Beth, since their first introduction to each other had been so intense, to put it mildly. She was relieved that she wasn't being interviewed, for she would have so little to say.

"So, life in Monticello—are you getting to be an old hand?"

"You're kidding me, right? The only thing I know is that Thomas Jefferson never slept there."

"So, you've already met Moe Ginsberg! I think he meets every train."

"On the bus, actually, on the way up here." She grinned.

"The old boy certainly gets around."

"He was a great comfort to me. He seemed such an authority, though not in a high-handed way."

"He knows a lot, and he's very sharp, though he can lay it on a little thick with pretty women he meets on buses. Actually, it's thanks to him that I've got this summer job—his connections."

"So you don't live up here?"

"No, I live in Manhattan—Minetta Street, downtown. I'm just bartending this summer, before I start a new job in another theater of action." He smiled a little as he said this. "Pretty heady language for what I'm doing."

"Which is?"

"I'll be working for the American Labor Party, as an organizer, so my business is really labor. My West Coast buddies seem to think I should be right out there with Fiorello LaGuardia and Vito Marcantonio drumming up other Italian-American working stiffs, like me. As if I could match them! Have you heard either of those firebrands? That's real theater for you."

He pronounced it *thee-ay-ter*, which surprised her. She'd never heard a real person say that, who wasn't a hick in the movies, that is. Her surprise must have shown in her face, for Vinny laughed.

"*Theahtah*, I should say. I'm showing my San Francisco roots."

"Well, my accent screams Bronx," she said. "Anyway, I've seen and heard Mayor La Guardia. He's always in the news. He opened the high school I went to—I was in the first graduating class—and I've heard him read the comics on the radio, of course. But that's not what you meant, is it?"

"It's certainly part of what I meant. And why do you sound apologetic? You're not even old enough to vote yet, are you?"

"Two more years. It's just that I feel so ignorant since I left the city.

Muriel says that's because I need to get a social conscience. Maybe I should. What are you smiling at?"

"You sound like you're thinking about buying a new dress or choosing fish rather than chicken from the menu."

"I'm not as superficial as all that! I really want to learn more, see more. You know, Muriel talks about civil rights, human rights, class conflict, working-class values. Well, I never heard a word of that in my family, and my mother and father have worked their lives away, and they're poor to boot, and I have worked every summer in their miserable little shop for the last six years. So maybe some people haven't had the time or background or education to have a social conscience."

"I don't think you're the least bit superficial, and you're right." His voice was gentle. "People aren't born with social consciences—or consciousness. They learn from their families, as I'm sure Muriel did, maybe a few from their religion, or because something happened to them and they need—and learn—to make connections."

"And you?"

"Me? Something happened. My father was a dock worker on the San Francisco waterfront. He was badly injured during the big strikes of the early thirties, but he lived long enough to join the dockworkers' union headed by Harry Bridges, the man who still heads the ILWU today. My dad loved that man. Harry became a personal friend of the family. He made sure we had all the benefits coming to union members, and he was a mentor to me. I learned practically everything I know about the wide world from him without ever really thinking I was being taught. He's that kind of bloke."

"Bloke?"

"Excuse me—sometimes I do that. Harry is an Aussie by birth." Vinny was silent for a moment. "Well, enough of that. Stick around me and you'll get more social conscience than you want. But now let's eat. How do you like your steak?"

Beth had never had an evening like this. Vinny was so exciting and yet so comfortable to be with. They had talked together easily, and yet they hadn't really spent much time telling each other things. Vinny certainly knew a lot of people, a surprising number in Beth's opinion, and seemed to be very well liked. He didn't go out of his way to be hail-fellow-well-met with them—he mostly paid attention to her—but she felt proud that he was so popular. To top it all off, a dance band came out, really just a combo, but the waiters pushed back some tables, and people were able to dance. Beth thanked her lucky stars she had practiced dance steps privately with Frima so often, and even on rare occasions with her own brother. She could have danced with Vinny till the lights were turned off, and even after, but when the musicians took a break, he kept her hand in his and led her outside.

"Sorry, but I've been on my feet all week, and I'm bushed from the ankles down. Could we just look at the stars for a few minutes? Then I guess I'll have to get you home. Sunday's a busy day at the hotel for you, I know." A convenient porch swing appeared around the corner, and they sunk into it.

Of course he kissed her, first gently and then more deeply, and Beth felt she could be happy to just stay tangled up with him forever. Except she wasn't all that passive; he had to push her away.

"Beth, honey, slow down. I'm only flesh and blood!"

Instant humiliation. For a moment worse than being slugged in a restaurant. She managed to extricate herself from him and the swing and moved to the edge of the porch. After what seemed an excruciating long silence of about fifteen seconds, she turned to Vinny. "Do you think you can take me home now?"

"Yes, but. . . ."

"Thank you." She cut him off and walked quickly toward the car. Vinny followed her silently, opened the door for her, and watched as she curled herself up in the far corner of the front seat. Still silent, he slipped into to the driver's seat, but instead of starting the car, he just turned around, folded his arms, and looked at her.

She couldn't stand it. "The Alpine is that way, I believe," she said quietly, her face full of woe.

Vinny kept his voice even. "I know where it is," he said. "But we're not going there until I know just what the terrible thing is I did to you. Not if we sit here all night. You can start explaining now."

She certainly didn't want to, but it all came out in a rush. "Oh, you must think I'm the biggest kind of fool—and a tramp, which is worse still! No, don't deny it. I have a big brother, you know, and I hear what he and his friends call girls who are easy—even though these guys are tickled to death when they are. They are dumb broads, tramps, sluts, and even whores!"

"What the hell? Wait a minute—my turn—so shut up and listen. I am not your brother, I'm happy to say. And I'm not one of those horny fraternity boys you've met up with here. You know I couldn't possibly think you are a fool—though you may be a bit of a screwball sometimes—and I'd never think of you as any of the things your brother and his swaggering buddies call women. I don't think of any woman like that." He paused to expel a sigh. "But you are a dish, and don't think it's been so easy keeping my hands or anything else off you. It's just that I thought you were kind of young and would need to go slow, and so I didn't bring anything with me, you know, to protect us. My fault, I should've known better."

"I'm not sure I know what you mean."

"Yes, you do. So, what do you say, Beth? Want to try again?"

"Well, I don't know."

"You have about a half hour to think about it before we get back to the hotel."

Vinny started the car and neither of them spoke again, but about half way there, he reached over and took her hand in his and held it there, and she let him.

Don't get your hopes up, Beth thought, hardly daring to take comfort from this gesture. By the time they parked at the cabin at the Alpine, Vinny was whistling under his breath.

"How do you feel about square dancing?"

"Why, I don't know. I've never done it."

"I haven't done much myself, since I grew up on the wharfs, but I've tried it once or twice and it's kind of fun. Anyway, there's this shindig I've been invited to next Saturday out near Woodridge, lots of guitars, banjos, singers, and dancing. I sort of have to be there, but it would be a lot more fun if you'd go with me."

"Uh-huh. What about your tired feet?"

'What about them? I intend to spend all afternoon Saturday in a hammock with my feet propped up, now that I know what an energetic young thing you are."

"Well, okay," she said, controlling her need to bob up in the air. "Woodridge is where Moe Ginsberg lives, isn't it? Do you think he'll be there? It would be nice to see him again."

"I wouldn't be surprised. He's all over the place. So, I'll call you midweek." He lifted her chin, kissed her gently on the lips, and left.

The cabin was empty, per usual on Saturday night, for Muriel was at this very moment in bed with her boyfriend, and just where she, the newly fledged Bethesda Erlichman, wanted to be. "But not with Jerry, of course," she cried out with a whoop. "Slow down, girl, he's not your boyfriend and may never be," she cautioned herself. "But, oh! He thinks I'm a dish, he told me I'm a dish. And I think I'm falling in love."

When Muriel came in early the next morning, Beth was already dressed, lounging on her bed, a sketch pad on her knees. "Ah, Muriel," she said. "You look so relaxed and refreshed. Just as you should in this vacation paradise."

"And you look remarkably calm and happy. You had a good time, I assume?"

"I did." Beth gave her a brief, highly edited version of the evening. "And he's taking me to a square dance next Saturday."

"At Woodridge? How nice! Jerry and I will be there too. I'll fix it with Max to let us both get off early."

Any doubts about how nice it would be with Muriel as chaperone vanished as her roommate emerged from the bathroom with another piece of advice.

"Bess . . . uh . . . Beth, we're good friends, right?"

"Absolutely. Why?"

"Well, then let me say this. Vinny is an adult, unlike the overgrown juveniles you've spent time with. Oh, he's charming and persuasive—he has to be in his line of work—but if I know him at all, he's not a guy with a lot of leisure for candy and flowers and prolonged courtship rituals. So I want you to take a half-day off and see a very nice medically trained woman who lives and works not far from here. Judith Ginsberg is her name. She's devoted her life to protecting women up in this backwater. She takes care of me. I'll go with you, if you want me to."

"Yes. I'd be very grateful if you would. Is she related to Moe Ginsberg?"

"She's his wife."

Beth grinned. "Thomas Jefferson never slept here, but Moe Ginsberg sure did. Well, I'm starving. Let's go get breakfast."

For Beth, the next couple of weeks were a cram course in safe sex, contraception, women's rights and responsibilities, and the intricate connections of same to the class struggle. Muriel and Judith (who immediately insisted on first names), were kind, enthusiastic, and thorough. So much so, that Beth occasionally wondered whether it might not be better to die a virgin. But that wouldn't happen. She and Vinny made certain of this about a week after the square dance. Vinny was careful, reassuring, and gentle with her, and her first time was painless and happy, and continued to improve from there. She was quite oblivious, really, to struggle of any kind. Their only concern was getting up early enough to get Beth back to her hotel and to find sufficient time and place to continue their lovemaking, expanding and refining their pleasure in each other. They were both smitten.

A few days later, Max had an especially busy day planned for Muriel and Beth. All kinds of bookkeeping and clerical work that had piled up, he said. As soon as they had finished one pile of papers, he was ready with another. They came back to the cabin late after dinner, grousing.

"There was absolutely nothing left that couldn't have waited until tomorrow. God forbid a staff member might need a little slack. I could just shake him—" Muriel broke off suddenly and turned to Beth. "Oh, my God, look at the windows!" They rushed to inspect. There were new sills, new panes, brand new tightly fitted screens. Unpainted or varnished yet, but still perfectly functional.

"Now that's Vinny for you!" Muriel exclaimed.

"What are you talking about? Vinny couldn't have done this."

"Oh, I don't think he did it himself. He wouldn't have time for that. Probably he twisted Max's arm in a friendly fashion, or maybe he supplied the workmen, somehow. But it's his doing, believe me." Muriel giggled suddenly. "Now I know why he was so casually quizzing me about the cabin when we were at that square dance. Congratulations, you vamp, you! You must have something really special, Bethie!"

Beth was in seventh heaven. A better summer even than in her dreams. Of course, she asked Vinny about the windows right off when they next spoke.

"Well, I didn't do the work," Vinny answered. "Max always meant to fix the screens. I just kicked his butt a little—nothing serious. And speaking of butts, I intend to spend more time at your cabin if that's okay with you. With Muriel and Jerry gone on Saturday nights, it's actually easier for me to stay at the cabin than schlep you back while it's still dark. I don't work on Sundays, and you do. So if I spend the night there, I don't want any saber-toothed bugs gorging on my naked butt or yours."

What with hotel work and love, it was more than a week before Beth even thought of her sketchbook. But on this rather cool overcast day, she had an hour or so free, and since the cabin was comfortable this afternoon, she decided to work there. She liked the indoor light just now. She looked at the portrait she had begun of Vinny's face. Primitive still, and not really a likeness. It would never be what people called realistic—her true work never was. But it might be good, she thought. A good start. The strong, bony nose was easy to delineate, but not really that important; the mouth firm but with curved sensitive lips was not yet what she was after, but she'd get there. The eyes, bright hazel, a little turned down at the outer corners and slightly hooded, were his most distinctive feature and the most difficult to capture. Thug's eyes, people might say, at least those who saw all Italians as gangsters, but they were anything but—so direct, and caressing that the hooded lids seemed a way to control, even soften, their power. Still, it was so frustratingly easy to slip into caricature. She had to get the features, the light—everything right.

Well, she had to be patient, she had plenty of time. Would she ever show it to him? She lay down pencil and pad with a sudden realization. Vinny didn't even know she was serious about art, let alone that she had a deep, compelling attachment to this work. With something like panic she raked through their conversations of the last few weeks. Had she even told him she liked to paint or draw? If she had, it was some passing casual reference that she had quickly put on the back burner, as if it had no importance between them. She had done that, not Vinny. She was shocked and frightened by her own behavior. As if this wonderful, vital part of herself were an embarrassment to be hidden like a scar or a birth defect. Well, hell! No more of that. She would enlighten Vinny and soon.

Now calm down and think—strategize. Vinny did that all the time, didn't he? It was almost second nature for him, and she'd do well to learn from him. She decided to show him a couple of watercolors that she'd done up here. Nice, actually, well done they were, but pretty conventional. He'd probably like them. But not the portrait. Not yet, if ever. And certainly not the other stuff that was more abstract and intense—closer to the bone. Was she selling him short? She didn't think so. Vinny was intelligent, sharp, well-informed. But the handsome, intellectual, sensitive young man with the canoe who adored and understood her art? No way. What started as a sigh turned into a grin. What a half-baked insipid fantasy that had been. She vastly preferred the bright-eyed, red-blooded, somewhat hairy Vincent Carmine Migliori, any day.

CHAPTER 8

Frima returned from sorting and delivering the hotel's daily mail puzzled and chagrined. It had been two weeks since she had replied by postcard to Bess's letter. So why hadn't Bess called her? Was she so caught up in this new romance—this next Clarence Darrow—that she had no time for her best friend? Oh, yeah? And you've been so open and communicative all summer about your new romance? Maybe Bess won't intrude because she knows it's her one and only brother you've been slipping off into the shadows with? Why don't you call her? Because you're a coward, that's why. This irritating internal argument was becoming a real drag on her spirits, but who else could she talk to about this? Certainly not Jack about his sister's romance and not her mother about her own. Besides, it was Bess who was her habitual confidant. Okay, no more. I call her tonight. Period. She called the next night, which was good enough.

Beth was breathless as she picked up the phone. "Frima! Oh, Frima, I'm so sorry I didn't get back to you. Don't hate me, and don't think I'm crazy. It's just complicated!"

"I thought it might be because you were occupied with Clarence Darrow."

"Clarence Darrow? Oh, him! No! Now, Frima, please don't think

I'm completely off the rails, but it's another guy. That first one turned out to be a horror story, which I'll tell you about when we have more time. But Vinny rescued me from him."

"Vinny?"

"That's his name. He's an Italian—Italian American, I mean—and he's a bartender this summer but he's really a political organizer. Kind of a left-wing labor leader, and brilliant in his way, I think. Totally great with people. Anyway I'm in love, and I very much want you to meet him. I'd love to have you come over here—you and Jack both. He could drive you here couldn't he, hmm!

"Bess, please think about this. I'd love to meet this Vinny. But do you want Jack to meet a left-wing Italian bartender whom you happen to be in love with?"

"Now it will be just fine. You don't have to say a word about any of this to him. Just that I want the two of you to meet my boyfriend."

"Well, okay, but I don't know his name, right? His name is boyfriend until you reveal the details. Now I can just see the look on your face—so innocent—like what can she mean? I mean, to be perfectly clear, do you know any Jews named Vinny?"

"Nope, can't say that I do. Just leave it to me and Vinny. And speaking of names, I'm Beth now. You remember, short for Bethesda."

Frima stifled a guffaw. "After all, what's in a name? Well, you tell Jack. I'll be busy looking for cover."

"Don't you worry your pretty little head about a thing. Vinny and I can take care of Jack."

"Uh, Bess . . . Beth . . . my dearest friend. Maybe you should leave it to Vinny, if he's as great with people as you say."

"Good idea. So what do you say? Would a week from this Saturday be okay?"

"Sounds good. Why don't you count on us getting to Monticello around seven, unless you hear otherwise."

"I simply can't wait. Love ya," Bess trilled.

Well, I can, Frima thought, as she hung up the phone and allowed herself a loud groan.

That name! She wished she and Bess had never gone on that trip to Washington their senior year in high school. That way they would never have seen a train schedule with the fateful words Bethesda, Maryland, and Bess wouldn't have lost her head over the name. On the other hand, she might have come up with something like Hepzibah. It was all part of the need to make herself over. Jack would hate the name change, but that wasn't really Frima's problem. Brother and sister could take potshots at each other, but she was staying out of this one. She just had to remember to be surprised when the four of them were introduced.

Jack was completely amenable to the double date Frima and Bess were arranging, after he heard the highly expurgated version of their phone call. "Let's hope he's a nice normal guy with a little gelt," was his only comment.

Mama was enthusiastic too, and she promised to make Frima a new dress for the occasion. The very next afternoon they set off for town to choose fabric and a pattern. They agreed on a fine, light cotton, a subtle small white print on a sea-colored grayish green background, "A color that only true blondes can wear," Mama said. When it was done, Frima slipped it carefully over her head, ran to the mirror, and then hugged her mother. Cut and sewn so skillfully it fit like a glove, and the skirt would swing when she danced. And when she removed the little matching jacket, the bodice made the most of her usually modest cleavage, her smooth skin and lithe arms. Also, Mama promised to do Frima's hair in a chignon, which was always fashionable, and certain to last the evening.

Jack whistled when he saw her dressed for their night out. He was looking pretty spiffy too, in his only good sports jacket and slacks, and they looked at each other and grinned, pleased with themselves, each other, and the drive ahead of them. The weather was warm and sunny, but with a gentle late-afternoon breeze, and neither of them was in a great hurry to reach their destination. Jack parked the car at a shaded little vista point, took her hand, and led her out of the car. They stood quietly, gazing out across the rise to a blue lake in the distance. Jack put his arms around her and kissed the back of her neck. In a moment she turned to him.

"I wish this summer would never end," she said.

"I don't want us to end. We don't have to, do we?" He looked sober, a little afraid.

So sweet, Frima thought. "No we don't."

What more was there to say? Frima moved toward the car, lest they ruin her makeup entirely. The passionate necking, the "Oh, please" and "No, we can't" could wait until the end of the evening. She was sick of those dishonest "nos;" she didn't want to hold back. And sometimes she felt that she was actually more open-minded than Jack about this. He might have more of the good girl–bad girl mentality than she did, if his sister's comments were any guide. For herself, marriage might not be necessary, but lovemaking—sleeping-together sex, as she defined it—was something inseparable from deep commitment and love.

Back on the road, Jack broke the silence. "Well, at least I know now that your mother approves of me," he said smiling. "After all she made that pretty dress for you to go out on the town with me."

"Well, I like that!" Frima retorted, half indignant and half amused. "Maybe it's just that she approves of me, you know."

"Oh, of course—"

"Never mind," she interrupted him lightly. "The real reason is that Mama is ever the competitive hotelkeeper. She wouldn't want me showing up at the fancy Alpine Song looking like a *schlump*." They both smiled, content now with silence.

As they neared Monticello, however, the atmosphere became edgy. She could see a tightness around Jack's jaw. Her own uneasiness was all about her sins of omission. That she had not been entirely candid with Jack was no more than prudent, but his sister, her best friend, was quite another thing. Bess had guessed at the growing intimacy between Frima and Jack, and if she hadn't alluded to it, Frima would probably have said nothing. It was of no use now to tell herself she was naturally reticent, whereas Bess wore her heart and everything else on her sleeve. That wasn't even fair. It would be quite natural if Bess felt some resentment and jealousy about this new state of affairs. At the very least, Bess would think Frima had been cowardly about not mentioning it, and she would be justified. She glanced at Jack. Was he feeling something similar? She almost dreaded the reunion upcoming in about five minutes.

Happily, Bess made it easy for them. As soon as she spied them from the main house desk, she let out a whoop and embraced them at the same time, almost knocking their heads together. Good old Bessie! The silent sigh of relief from all of them was almost palpable.

Bess looked really smashing. In a white scoop-necked peasant blouse and skirt that showed off both her tan and her bust line, she looked healthy, relaxed, happy. Frima silently and swiftly sized up her best friend. There was that same Mediterranean skin as her brother's, the kind that effortlessly bloomed in the sun, while Frima's own fair skin had to be coaxed ever so cautiously into a hard-won layer of tan, lest she spend the summer sporting a gorgeous peel. And that thick wavy hair; cooperative hair that did what Bess wanted it to do. Was she always going to envy her looks? Maybe. But it was an easy, sort of genial envy that they shared, for both of them knew by now that they were good-looking young women, and the contrast in their looks put neither of them in the shade. They had heard this often enough.

Bess was eager to show them around the Alpine, talking it up like a real estate agent, and Frima took a professional interest in comparing their two summer homes. Without question she preferred Eisner's casual rusticity, even though she knew it was as carefully planned as the Alpine Song's more formal grounds and buildings. But this was a pretty place, nevertheless, and surprisingly unpretentious looking. The owner was not trying to imitate Newport.

As they walked toward the cabin, Muriel came out to meet them.

"Jack and Frima, at last we meet. Beth has told me so much about both of you!" They all exchanged cordialities easily, but when Bess and Muriel moved away for a moment, Jack didn't hesitate to comment.

"Who's this Beth?" Jack asked Frima out of the side of his mouth. "This Muriel, does she have a lisp?"

Frima just shrugged, smiled, and looked a little surprised. "We'll know soon enough. No wisecracks, now," she murmured.

"Muriel is a peach," Bess said, as she rejoined them. "Usually I'm not off for another hour, but she's covering for me, even though it's her night off, because this is the only day Vinny is free this week, and we want to take you to this special place. It's a bit of a drive, but it's worth it."

"Vinny? And just who is Vinny?" Jack's tone was ominous.

"Surely you know I'm seeing someone." Bess answered offhandedly.

"Oh, yeah, and I notice this is the first time I've heard his name."

"Perhaps I neglected to mention it."

"A nice Jewish name—Vinny!"

"His name is Vincent Carmine Migliori," Bess enunciated slowly and carefully, "though he answers to Vinny. And I, by the way, am now Bethesda, but you can call me Beth or Bethie if you like. Those are the names I answer to." She said this lightly and evenly, but her eyes challenged him. You will behave yourself, her look said. You will be nice to him and to me. We'll settle this at another time.

This was not her friend's usual style, and Frima was impressed. Had she been coached? By this Vinny who was so good with people? She looked at Jack, who obviously was taken aback.

"Suit yourself," he said shortly, to Frima's great relief.

At that moment his sister waved to someone a little distance away.

Obviously Vinny. His appearance was unexceptional, a little shorter than Jack and more compactly built. He looked like he's done a lot of physical labor, might be formidable in a fist fight, if challenged. As he came nearer, Frima saw he had a really attractive face, interesting, intelligent, good-humored. He was only a few years older than Jack, but there was nothing boyish about him. What surprised her were his hazel eyes, light brown hair, and skin fairer than either brother or sister. She'd thought all Italians were swarthy.

Vinny greeted Beth with a squeeze and a kiss on the cheek and had a firm handshake for both Frima and Jack. "My pleasure," he said easily. "Did you have a good drive? Did Beth tell you what we thought of doing? I understand you like to dance, and there's a place we think you'd really enjoy. A very good pick-up band and good food too, though nothing fancy." He paused for a moment, and they nodded. "So how about we take my car, Jack? This place is kind of off the main road and not too easy to find. And I imagine you'd like to sit back and relax with this pretty lady." He spoke deferentially, making his words a question.

Admirable, Frima thought. There was something about this man that took in the situation at a glance and took charge of it. Something masterly and at the same time diplomatic and very courteous that defused the electric atmosphere. In a few minutes, they were settled in Vinny's large sedan and on their way, making pleasant small talk. They chatted about the dry, cool weather, a rarity in the dog days of August. They joked about guests, big tippers, small tippers, the usual nut cases. They compared sore feet and aching backs. Jack seemed determined to be on good behavior, and Frima was proud of him, rooting for him. She figured Vinny would look after Bess . . . uh . . . Beth. (Get used to using that name!)

When they got to The Shack, as it was called, Frima knew immediately that they had crossed some invisible boundary and were no longer in the Jewish Catskills. It was a jagged boundary at best, but there was no question that for the time being they were in a different culture. The place had a rustic look, like some of those fake cowboy bars and grills on the main rural routes upstate. There was no western influence in the dimly lit interior, however, which offered very ordinary wood tables and booths with candles in wine bottles throwing off a warm but shadowy light. The place reminded her of the Greenwich Village hangouts that she had seen and heard about but had never entered. Sort of working class, but not quite. With the exception of a few quiet men at the bar who were obviously stag and looked tough and wary, the people seemed kind of arty—bohemian, she'd describe them. Also there were several colored customers there. This surprised her. She'd never been to a public place up here in the country where the races mingled, as equals. This one must be a rarity.

Frima looked at Jack. He seemed a little puzzled, but he remained quiet. He just pursed his lips at her and opened his eyes wide, mugging surprise. As their eyes become accustomed to the dusky light, they saw that The Shack was a substantial structure with an upright piano and a set-up for about six musicians who would come in a little later. Vinny ushered them into a comfortable booth near a screened window, and after a couple of beers, they all relaxed. Frima had perused the menu carefully, which was distinctly American bar food, including pork, shellfish, cheeseburgers, and so on. Frima had been afraid that Bess would provocatively order pork, but they all followed Vinny's recommendation for steak, which turned out to be excellent.

A whole lot of people knew Vinny, and several knew Beth, too, probably because she was his girl. They came over to greet them, and he was cordial to everyone, no matter how often his meal was interrupted. He rose a little as he greeted each newcomer and was careful always to introduce the people at his table. Frima started counting off some of these names in her head. Bob, John, Pete, Pancho (could that be right?), Claire, Ida, a colored woman named Adella—Frima made a special effort to remember her name—and several other women, all named Felicity or Olivia. Now that wasn't possible, was it? Or maybe, Frima decided, she'd better lay off the beer.

Beth seemed in her element, getting up to hug this one or throw a kiss to that one. She appeared to be entirely at home, ostentatiously so, and this was beginning to irritate her brother, though he said nothing.

"The band's starting," said Frima, grabbing Jack's hand. "Let's dance!"

"Let's all dance," said Vinny.

The band was terrific, and they all began to have a very good time, not stopping until the musicians took a break. When they returned to their table, Jack turned to Vinny. "Who are those bruisers sitting at the bar? Are they bouncers?"

"Sort of. They are just working stiffs, like the rest of us. But they are ready and willing to scare off any troublemakers."

"There are Klansmen in these hills, or White Brotherhood, or whatever they like to call themselves," said Beth scornfully, and they don't like to see Negroes and whites mingling. And those guys over there make sure they don't come in and bother anybody."

"The Ku Klux Klan is here in the Catskills? I thought they were only in the South," said Frima.

Jack's glare went from Beth to Vinny. "And you let me bring Frima here where there might be violence?"

"Nothing is going to happen here," Vinny said calmly. And then added more pointedly, "And do you think I'd bring Beth here if there were any danger? These men are just a precaution because a few years ago, some drunken teenage punks came in and tried to pick a fight with a few people. They've never come back. Oh, there are some white supremacists up here, like anywhere, but they're not too eager to bother people who have the power and the means to fight back. And you, Beth," he said cheerfully. "Stop scaring away the customers with that kind of talk." He gently smoothed a lock of her hair off her forehead.

Frima smiled at Vinny. "You seem to know everyone here. Are you running for Congress, or something?"

Vinny laughed. "No, I'm just a bartender in another place not very different from this one. You get to know a lot of people that way. That's where I met Beth."

"In a bar?" Jack looked at his sister.

"That's right. Vinny rescued me from the jerk I was with. Remind me to tell you about that some day."

Frima took Jack's hand under the table, and he visibly relaxed.

"Is that your job all year round? Up here?" Jack asked. They all knew it was a way of finding out whether Beth would continue seeing this guy in the city.

"Just for the summer," Vinny responded easily. "In New York, I'll be working for the American Labor Party: the ALP."

"You mean with Vito Marcantonio and those other guys? Wasn't he kicked out of the Republican Party for being a red?" Jack asked.

"He's the guy who won the Congressional seat anyway," Beth retorted.

Jack ignored her. "Is he a red?"

"He's an American. An Italian American like me."

Frima refrained from telling Jack that her own mother looked very kindly on the ALP. She felt it impolitic to say so at this moment. Instead she turned again to Vinny. "So you are in politics, in a way, after all."

Vinny winked at her. "I confess that I love the political fray, but I'm not running for anything. But enough about me. What do you do?"

"Me? I do clerical work and bookkeeping for the hotel during the winter and I study the piano. I hope to teach music, some day." She was a little shy talking about this. "And Jack's studying chemistry at City College."

"Only part time, unfortunately," Jack added. "The rest of the time, like my sister, I have to help my folks with the store. Hard times, you know."

"Talk about exploited labor," Beth put in. "We could use Marcantonio in that hole." She faced down her brother's look.

"My sister, as you may have seen for yourself, exaggerates. She imagines she is slowly pining away in a sweatshop. Poor thing, she looks tubercular, doesn't she?"

Vinny reached over the table and took Frima's hand. "We haven't had a dance yet, Frima. Let's leave these two to their family squabble and hope it will be over it by the time we get back." He turned to Beth and caressed her cheek lightly with the back of his hand. "Don't throw anything," he said, and led Frima to the dance floor.

She approved of this guy, Frima did, and she had an idea he could be very good for her friend. Beth's volatile energy, her quick enthusiasms, and equally quick disappointments—Vinny could handle them, Frima guessed. He could help Beth, teach her a lot. That social ease he possessed, that diplomacy. You might be born with the temperament for it, but it was a talent and a skill, and it took experience and lots of practice. It wasn't Jack's strong point, and Beth had none of it. As for herself, she was a peacemaker, which wasn't saying all that much. She was a poor fighter, anyway. Yet with all the tensions, these undercurrents going on with the four of them, it was still turning out to be a fun evening. This was Vinny's doing. Yes, he would be good for her friend. And she, Frima, would be good for Jack. In some ways she could teach him, guide him. He was, as Mama put it, trainable. She was pretty sure of that.

The band began a slow romantic foxtrot, and Jack cut in. Beth came to join Vinny, and they all relaxed into the music.

"More coffee, Jack?" Vinny asked, when they at last sat down again. "You've got a ways to drive back."

"Good idea," Jack said, taking out his wallet, "and a check, I guess."

"Forget it," Vinny said with a self-deprecating smile. "It's on the house. Owner owes me a favor."

—

"Morning, sunshine. Sleep well?" Frima moved to the porch swing, bringing a cup of strong black coffee to Jack and sat down next to him. "You need this, I'm sure."

"She's sleeping with him, you know."

Now that was getting down to basics. "No, I don't know. And how do you know?"

"Didn't you notice? We were both parked near the cabin. He drops us at our car, then he walks Bess to the cabin, which is dark, by the way. He puts on the porch light, takes the key out of his pocket, opens the door, and goes in with her. Didn't you see all that? It's obvious. They're making it obvious."

"I didn't see any of that, I was already dozing off. Besides, that doesn't prove anything."

"Don't be naive, Frima. This guy is older than she is, knows his way around. And besides, he's a red. Yes, Marcantonio is a red, and so is he. They believe in free love. It's part of their politics—marriage isn't. Not that I want her to marry him, God knows! But it would be just like Bess to get pregnant."

It was just like Beth to avoid it, Frima thought, but kept this to herself. "All this detective work. I can't believe how you are letting your imagination run away with you. I'm sure all this will come to nothing."

"It's not my imagination. I know how these Italian Catholic guys talk about Jewish girls—I remember from high school. That guy's up to no good, believe me. I'm a guy and I should know!"

Frima almost laughed at his shamed-face look when he realized what he'd said. "Oh, so you're a guy like him? How would you feel if people around here said, 'That Jack is up to no good with Frima. He's only out for what he can get.'" She hesitated for a moment. "And what would be so very terrible if they were making love? Isn't that what you—what we—want to do?" She held her breath.

For a moment Jack didn't look at her. Was he ashamed that he'd shown such rancor in front of her? Or maybe he was startled by her frankness. Then suddenly he flashed a smile, the charmer's smile that made her feel like lying down with welcoming arms. He took both her hands in his. "You and me, we're different." He said this softly. "I love you, and I'll always take care of you."

Which was, after all, what she wanted to hear, and she wasn't about to spoil it by worrying about his sister's affairs.

CHAPTER 9

Beth woke before Vinny that same Sunday morning. She was a lighter sleeper than he, or maybe just not as tired. Also she was squeezed against the wall, for her bed in the cabin was small for a couple, and Vinny had chivalrously insisted on the outside spot, lest a single toss land her unceremoniously on the floor. In about ten minutes the alarm would go off, and he would jump up comically and zoom into the bathroom to make himself presentable before Muriel came back from her nights away. Beth actually didn't mind the tight squeeze. She loved to lie there feeling him breathe, occasionally still getting a whiff of shaving cream or aftershave. Vinny had a strong beard, and to save her skin, he said, he showered and shaved before bed on the nights he was with her. No one he worked with cared a hoot if he had a five o'clock shadow during working hours, he assured her. "Owners and bosses shave and shower in the morning, but the worker does this at night—kind of a badge of honor," he informed her.

"So it's terribly bourgeois of me to shower in the morning?"

"You know, I don't know if the rules apply to women—never thought about it," he replied, grinning. "I'll have to check it out with Marx and Engels."

"Somehow I'd be happier with you sticking to Marcantonio and LaGuardia," she retorted. "At least they're not Germans."

"You like Italians better, don't you?" he said into her ear.

"Well, I'm not so sure. There are Mussolini and his thugs, you know."

"Now that's my girl! I say we stick to Italian Americans of a certain stripe. No fascist animals, especially not that one—part strutting rooster, part hyena. You know, I'd like to see that son of a bitch in a room, stripped of his uniform, his guns, his henchmen—put him in a locked room alone with those two little New York politicians—no weapons except their voices and minds. Marc and the Little Flower would reduce him to mincemeat without breaking a sweat."

Beth was finding herself quite interested in politics and the world situation at large. She, who before this summer, had been reluctant to spend more than ten minutes on such matters. Of course a lot of it was banter with Vinny, with its pleasing innuendoes, but she actually felt that focus on larger events sharpened her mind and expanded her vision. If the United States entered the war, well, that would be another story. But for now, lying here in the early sunlight after a night of lovemaking followed by safe, restful sleep, war seemed very far away, and she could just be pleased with herself. She was beginning to feel sophisticated—that was the word.

Add to this the satisfaction of reviewing last night's double date with Frima and Jack. It had gone remarkably well, she thought. Frima and Vinny had obviously liked each other, and this was no small thing. And Jack? Well, things had gone as well as could be expected. Only a glance at the calendar on her dresser cast a shadow on her mood. The days were going so quickly. Little more than three weeks left to the season. What then? She absolutely could not go back to her family apartment in the Bronx. She would die there in about a month. But to live in Manhattan, she needed a job. And it had to be in Manhattan. How else could she see Vinny? Muriel, understanding her urgency, unearthed a touch-typing instruction book, and left the office unlocked after regular hours so she could practice. Vinny was delighted when he heard about this. He wanted her to be near him.

If she wasn't, their time together would be limited. His hours were irregular, and sometime he worked well into the night.

Irony of ironies, she was finally learning to type. Her father's most cherished wish for her. She had fought like a cornered animal when he wanted her to take a commercial course at the neighborhood high school rather than attend the "fancy schmancy downtown high school," the one that had practically saved her life. And here was this other man in her life encouraging her to learn office skills. But what a difference! One, contemptuous of her talent—totally dismissive of it—wanted her to throw herself away. The other wanted only to make her life easier. Oh, she knew that Vinny might not have much understanding of her creative work. That was pretty clear to her when she showed him a few of her paintings.

"I admit that I don't understand a lot of this, not being artistic myself. And for me, I guess I prefer more realism—a clear message. But don't get me wrong, I am impressed, ignorant as I am, and, you know, I really like the two paintings you did up here. I think they're beautiful."

"If you really like them, they're yours. My gift to you." She held her breath.

"I do, and that's very generous, sweetheart, but—"

"I'd want to frame them first." She deliberately interrupted him, before he could reject her offering.

"Great, I'll be proud to hang them on my walls, though you'll have to decide where to hang them." He smiled a little ruefully. "Unfortunately, they illustrate the fate of the artist in our society—the young and unknown, at any rate. Most people, me included, can't afford to pay what your paintings are worth in terms of your labor and love and creativity. So if you want to paint, I'm afraid you'll still need a day job."

"No kidding!"

Beth wasn't sure whether she had created or discovered it—this little cabinet in her mind to which she alone had the key. Either way, she was finding it very useful to file away thoughts, parenthetical comments and questions that would do no good to ask out loud, such as, Why is it that people who don't get it, don't understand a work of art, always judge it by whether they would want it on their own walls? Or, Why does everything have to be interpreted in social and economic terms? Was it worth hiding these spontaneous and rebellious thoughts? Even from Vinny, who had first been attracted to her because of her spontaneity? Yes, even from Vinny. He could not follow her to that deep unknown place from which her art sprang, and she wasn't sure she would want him—or anyone else for that matter—to go there with her. If she asked Vinny either of those provoking questions, she would wound him, and they both were still being very careful not to hurt the other. "Lesson one in couple-ship," she announced to the empty room. "First, cause no pain."

Lesson two was find your girlfriend a job! This she discovered only a few days later, when Vinny approached her with an offer. The National Maritime Union, where he had connections (naturally), needed some office help. He didn't know how much the job would pay yet, certainly not very much, but if she shared rent and lived frugally (as if she had ever done anything else!) she'd be in pretty good shape. She knew that Vinny was vague only because he had not yet negotiated the wages for her. Or, for that matter, rent. She was quite sure he would. Vinny seemed to have a natural talent and pleasure in taking care of things, including Beth.

So it wasn't much of a surprise when after a week of quietly setting the stage with his landlord, Vinny asked her to move in with him. He had arranged to move into a larger apartment in the same building, which would be vacant after September. She said yes without a moment's hesitation. It was as close to perfect as she would get. Perfect would be Vinny and a studio space of her own to paint in—all day if she wanted to. Still, the life she was about to embark on was wonderful enough. A good nine-to-five with interesting people, the man she loved mornings and evenings, and the Art Student's League only a couple of local subway stops away for studio space and connection with other artists. She was young and strong and energetic. She could do it all. And, most glorious, she felt loved and cared for, a totally new and entirely delicious feeling.

Beth approached the office typewriter with determination, if not enthusiasm. She'd made rapid progress and could actually type correspondence now, not just clusters of individual alphabet letters and symbols, which was a relief. Except, *oy vey*, the first letters she needed to write would announce her new life and complete departure from the old. She'd start with Frima, sister in spirit, before venturing into the enemy territory of her biological family. Her letter took hours to produce.

August 18, 1940

Frima, my dearest girlfriend!

Get ready to visit me in the Village, and I don't mean Monticello or Liberty. It's Greenwich Village, New York City, USA, I'm talking about. That's right—I'm not going back to the Bronx. I'm going to live with Vinny. Actually, I'll be sharing an apartment with Muriel for a month or two while Vinny gets a bigger place painted and furnished for us. There's a nice apartment that will be available in the same building he lives in on Minetta Street. Isn't that lucky? I think it's fate!

And I'll have a real job! It's with the NMU (the National Maritime Union). Vinny has connections there. Just office work (notice that this letter is typed by me—it took me hours but I'm learning), but also the chance to do some posters and graphics. I can't tell you how exciting all this is to me, meeting interesting, forward-thinking people, and I'll be able to take studio classes at the Art Students League. But most of all I'll be living with the man I love. Oh, Frima, he's really special, and I'm learning so much from him. He has answers to things, and he can open doors I thought would always be shut against me—and they would be if I were stuck back with my folks in that prison of a store where I was almost buried alive with boredom and hopelessness. From the moment I met Vinny, he seemed to me so strong and calm and sure of himself, and yet there's this sense of possibility and excitement and action about him. I know that Vinny's not your typical dreamboat—not like my brother, right? Oh, yeah, I can tell how you feel about him! But, believe me, this man of mine is so romantic and sexy, and going to bed with him at night and waking in the morning with him makes me feel so wonderful. I know I'm gushing like a schoolgirl, but I've really never felt so adult before, and I really, really seriously hope you'll be happy for me.

No, we're not getting married. Neither of us wants that yet. Also I think it's better to try out living together before we even think of such a thing. Besides, I don't think I believe in marriage. Lots of progressive, forward-thinking people don't, you know.

I feel like I'm jumping into a new life, and the only one I'll really miss in the old one is you, kiddo (and your mother also. I hope she won't think I'm too shocking) and, yes, Jack. So please be part of my new life, and if you have influence over Jack—and I know you do—make him be part of it too.

Whew! I see I've run off at the mouth again, and I haven't really asked about you. You seemed very happy when I saw you. Happy with Jack. I was a little surprised and yet not surprised you fell for him. I thought maybe you'd go for someone less conventional and more artistic or musical. Still, in his own way, he can be quite a guy, and he's obviously stuck on you, which shows good taste. If you should ever get permanently stuck on him, I think it would be great to have you as a sister-in-law, and if anyone can, I think you'd be just the one to keep him from being a disapproving stick-in-the-mud about things—like about me flying the coop!

Anyway, Vinny sends his best to you. He really likes you, and, of course, I send lots of love from me.

Beth

P.S. Don't say anything to Jack about this letter. He'll only have a conniption, and it'll be easier for everyone if he finds out after it's a fait accompli.

P.P.S. I really love signing my name like this, but you can call me Bethie if you like, or if you're really mad at me, Bethesda. But I hope you're not. Please be happy for me and with me.

Beth

She read through it quickly once more, then hurried out of the office to drop it in the mail before she changed her mind.

CHAPTER 10

Was the girl crazy? Running off with this guy? Why, she'd only known him for what, maybe six weeks? Ridiculous! Frima almost laughed—from shock, mostly—as she read the opening lines of Beth's missive. There was nothing remotely amusing in the lines that followed, and she sat down abruptly to try to digest the rest of it.

Please be happy for me and with me. Now just what was she supposed to make of that? She felt frustrated and trapped. Beth was leaving her no room to feel anything but complete happiness and approval of what she was doing. Which was impossible and completely unfair to boot. And just what did she mean by *Don't tell Jack*? She had some nerve! Did Beth think so little of Frima's feelings for her brother that she could ask that? Couldn't she understand what a personal betrayal that would be? And didn't she realize that his life would be radically changed if his sister ran away from home? Well, she was going to tell Jack, and she would tell Beth so. He had a need and a right to know. What she wouldn't repeat to him were Beth's not too subtle hints about them as a couple. How many times in this letter had she used the word *stuck*? Stuck on you, stuck on Jack, stuck in the Bronx, stick in the mud. Beth's love for Vinny was freedom, but Frima's for Jack was paralysis. Yet the only one boxing her in was Beth, herself. Her face grew hot and she felt almost choked with rage. It was not a feeling she'd had much to do with in her life. She flung down the letter and ran out of the room as if she could leave fury behind.

What she couldn't escape so easily was the sudden sense of loss that overwhelmed her. Oh, God! She would miss Beth so much, this sister she'd never had. Beth living down town could never again be the Bessie living just down the block. And for sure Beth was never coming home again. Home was a prison for her.

Well, she had to talk to Beth and she had to talk to Jack. But before she did anything, she needed to talk to Mama. She had a sudden nasty vision of Beth sneering. There goes Frima running to Mama like a little girl. Now where did that come from? Beth was so fond of Mama and had longed to have a mother she could talk to—she would never sneer about that. But maybe she was jealous of Frima's closeness to Mama. Even worse, would Beth think it was a betrayal to tell Mama? After all, the letter was confidential. Well, too bad!

She felt anger filling her lungs, again. How dare Beth bring these troubles upon her and ruin her, Frima's, personal happiness! She wanted to scream out loud, but that wasn't her way. She forced herself to breathe deeply, splashed cold water on her face, and deliberately slowing her pace, she walked over to her mother's office.

"So, do you want to tell me about this letter? Do you want me to read it?" Mama spoke gently, noting her daughter's woebegone face.

Frima hesitated only a moment. There was nothing to hide, really. Mama's eyes were wide open. She knew what was brewing with Frima and Jack, and the whole world would know about Beth soon enough. She handed over the envelope.

"Why are you smiling?" Frima asked.

"That Bess!" Mama said. "Always so intense, so dramatic. 'Personal and confidential,' as if the wrong person might get hold of her letter." She unfolded the pages. Her smile faded as she quickly scanned the lines. "Put the latch on the door, Frimaleh," she said. "You don't mind if I read this again a little more carefully?"

"Go ahead."

"So she is Bethesda now—or Beth? Well, Beth writes a very young and very thoughtless letter."

"It's . . . ruthless," said Frima, slowly, finding the word she sought. "I never thought I could say that about Bess . . . Beth. But that's what it is."

"So it seems. But it is also a desperate letter, and desperate people sometimes are ruthless. You know, don't you, that she really can't go home to her family. Her life there was bad enough, but after a taste of freedom, and some experience of what good is, it could be intolerable. You know what her daily existence has been, who she is. And she needs and wants you to be her friend. That, at least, is perfectly clear."

"I know, Mama, but she puts me in such a position!"

"Very true. And what are you going to do?"

"I'm going to call her. Tomorrow, I guess. I'm too upset with her today. I can't tell her not to do this, to think about it a little longer, but I will tell her I won't lie to Jack. I really wish she'd tell him herself, though, and right away."

"Yes."

"I mean, doesn't she know that this will really change his life? That if she's not there, he'll have to spend more time at the store and less at his classes?"

"And less time with you?" Mama spoke very evenly.

"That's not the point!" Frima felt herself flushing hotly.

"Well, maybe not. But perhaps Beth knows, as I do, that she doesn't really have to worry about Jack, that he's quite capable of taking care of himself."

"There you go, again. Don't you like him at all?"

"Now, you know better than that! Of course, I like him, and what I said is not a criticism. It's a compliment, actually. Why would you think otherwise?"

"I know, I know," Frima answered in a small voice, "but I'm so mad at her, Mama. I've never felt like this. What on earth can I do?"

"First, you can calm down. This is not the end of the world. For you or for her. She must get away from that house where she feels so miserable. Then, who knows? Maybe the great romance comes to nothing. Once she's away from her family, which is the main thing, she may not be so anxious to move in with him."

"I believe she loves him, Mama."

"Ah, well, you girls fall in love so quickly." Mama smiled, but she gave Frima a significant look. "He's a nice young man, you say?"

"Very. I've only met him once, spent that one evening with him, but I really liked him. He's smart, too, and steady—mature. I believe he's been good for her."

"Well, then, maybe their living together is not such a bad thing. People have to live their lives." Mama gave a big sigh. "Still, I feel sorry for her poor mother."

"Her mother?" Frima was taken aback. She was caught between laughter and tears.

"Yes, her mother. You're so surprised?"

"The woman you once referred to as equal parts nudnik and harpy?"

"Well, I was wrong about the harpy." Mama gave Frima a wicked little wink. "Harpies shriek. That one suffers in sighs and murmurs. But, seriously, you must persuade Beth to keep in touch with her mother. The father, he's a nasty piece of goods—a *poskudniak*, as Papa would say—but the mother, she may be a nudnik, but nudniks have feelings too, and no mother can bear to lose her daughter."

Frima promptly burst into tears and rose to leave. Mama came round her desk and hugged her. "It's been quite a summer, hasn't it? Now, see if you can relax, get a little rest. Don't do anything more about this today, but tomorrow you'll call Bess, yes?"

Frima nodded, unable to say more, and left the office. She stopped in the the kitchen to get some ice and a dish cloth. Happily, none of the staff were there to ask uncomfortable questions about why she was crying. The puffiness of her eyelids that always accompanied tears was a blasted nuisance and a dead giveaway of her distress. She meant to put the icy compress over her eyes to erase the puffiness before Jack returned with his deliveries from town. Twenty minutes with her feet up wouldn't hurt either, but in half that time she was up knocking on the office door again.

"Mama, do you think it would be okay if we reached a compromise, kind of? If I was able to persuade Beth to tell Jack just this much; that she is moving in with Muriel—which is true enough. Then if she does move in with Vinny, she can tell him when it really happens. Sort of let Jack and the family down easy. And if she doesn't move in with Vinny, well, nobody is the wiser and nobody is upset or unhappy."

"Very diplomatic, darling."

"Not dishonest?"

"Who says diplomacy is honest? Just necessary. You know you could tell Beth that if she doesn't agree to do this, you'll tell Jack everything—right away."

"I was thinking of doing that. It's sort of blackmail, though, isn't it?"

"Another kind of diplomacy." Mama smiled for the first time since she'd read Beth's letter. She was silent for a moment or two. "Forget about diplomacy and blackmail. Think of yourself as a peacemaker. There are only those two—sister and brother in that bitter house—and they need each other. The mother and the father are no support, no solace. And, you know, Beth loves you, and so does Jack. Yes, yes, I think he does. So? Why do you look so surprised? Just because I cautioned you about falling head over heels for him doesn't mean I don't recognize real feelings when I see them. You know, it seems to me, my Frima, you have matured so much in the last few months. Sometimes I forget to tell you that. So go, go be a good influence on both of them."

"I'll try. I think I'll write to her, instead of calling. Maybe I'm a coward about confronting her, but, after all, she wrote to me, and it gave me time to read and react. God knows what I might have said if I received this news by phone. Besides, writing helps me think;

deliberate, I suppose. I'll write to her tonight and mail it tomorrow, first thing. And, Mama—don't be insulted—but I won't show it to you before I mail it. I need to be a big girl now." She forced a smile. "Only thing I'll tell you is that she will know she has to agree to talk to Jack immediately, or I will."

"So, good!"

Crying always gave Frima a headache. A walk in the fresh air was what she needed. She started down the path to the chicken coops and the barn, meaning to follow the path out through the pasture to a dirt lane seldom used by the summer people. It was a walk she'd taken often with Papa. As she entered the shaded lane, she stopped abruptly, struck by a realization, a feeling—she didn't know what—a something, as if layers of controlled, rational thought were suddenly cracked and pushed aside. She was never going to see Papa again. Never, ever. Well, of course she knew that, had known it for years, but this was a realization from the depth of her being. Not painful or frightening, so much as vivid, intense. Papa was gone. He didn't go on purpose; he didn't want to leave Frima or Mama, but he had gone.

The intensity was short-lived, and she walked on, puzzled by the experience. *Ah-ah* and *pa-hoi-hoi*. Suddenly, oddly, these syllables came to mind, words dredged from her science classes in high school. They were terms for the lava that erupted from the earth's volcanic depths. Hawaiian they must be. This intense experience she'd just had—not the first one this summer—it was like something from her own depths breaking through a divide and into her awareness. Very strange.

A slightly hysterical cackling broke into her thoughts, alerting her that one of the hens had strayed from the coops. Looking about her, she spied the bird on a low-lying branch, too far for her to reach and just enough above the ground to destroy any eggs the nitwit would lay or injure the hen as it tried to fly down. With sudden irritation she picked up a stone to hurl at the bird. Her arm froze. Was she crazy? She could kill the hen with a stone that large. What in the world was the matter with her? The hen's behavior was not uncommon. The younger hens, in particular, would often ignore the comfortable, safe roosts built for them and lay their eggs according to their own internal logic. Not for nothing were they called birdbrains. How could she react so strongly to a chicken that had simply flown the coop? She stopped in her tracks. Well that was it, wasn't it? The bird flew the coop. Papa had flown the coop, Beth was flying the coop. Mama would have to some day. No one else was going to fly the coop and leave her if she had anything to do with it.

As she came out of the lane and into the pasture she saw Jack walking toward her. Clearly he had come looking for her, for there'd be no other reason for his coming this far from the hotel. She ran to meet him and almost knocked him over with the enthusiasm of her embrace.

"Whoa, wait a minute," he laughed. "Who would have thought a delicate thing like you could have such strength?" He was obviously delighted. "Why all this enthusiasm?"

"Just high spirits," she replied and took his hand.

With Jack there, she gave no more thought to the incidents of the last hour. But by the time she returned to her room to write to Beth, she knew she wanted to marry him and that she'd do everything in her power to make that happen.

CHAPTER 11

For the next few days, Beth approached the ringing phone at the hotel desk as if it sizzled, and since it rang almost continuously, her daily two hours of desk duty were hours on the hot seat. It was ridiculous. Did she expect all the members of her tribe, from the Bronx back to wandering desert ancestors, to rise up and send their wrath crackling through the Bell Telephone wires? Because she was deserting them? Oh, if only Vinny were sitting at the desk with her, silently coaching her, holding her hand.

But, no, none of that, she told herself firmly. Vinny was a grown man doing what grown men do during the day: working at his job. And she was a grown woman, working at hers. Besides, it was only Frima, her dearest friend, who would call, and Frima was not wrathful. Okay, then, why didn't she call already?

So it was with considerable relief that she received Frima's letter a week after she posted her own. She could stop worrying about the phone ringing. Why shouldn't everything be all right? Wouldn't her best friend be happy for her? She remained unconvinced. Well, you are not a child. You will read it now and, if necessary, report an edited version to Vinny. Relationships required using your discretion, such as it was.

Rhubarb, Max's hound-like creature who seemed to have adopted her, looked up at her with pleading brown eyes, and she allowed him to follow her to her cabin. Soft-coated, and completely uncritical, he would be a warm-blooded teddy bear, a comfort to her if Frima's letter proved to be anything other than happy and supportive. Now what kind of name for a dog was Rhubarb? Why didn't Max name him Scout or Pete or Jack? Well, lots of people did name their dogs Jack. Even pets they really loved. Enough! She hastily tore open the envelope and began reading.

My dearest Beth,

It's taken me a good hour to try to begin this letter, I was so taken aback by yours. Not that I'm surprised you're in love with Vinny—he seems like a great guy, and I liked him immediately. And, believe me, I was so happy that the four of us had that time together. I'd like nothing better than for those kinds of times to continue. But I have to say, isn't this decision hasty? You've only known him a month or so, and this is such a big, life-changing move in which you'll be burning bridges, to say the least. Of course, I know how important it is for you to be able to live your own life, how desperate you are to get away from the way things were before the summer, but I wouldn't be much of a friend if I was totally enthusiastic about all this. You know that I love you like a sister and will support you in any way I can, however much I'll miss having you just around the corner. But, I beg you, be a little cautious about burning those bridges. Of course I understand your wanting to leave your father far behind you and not look back. But your mother and brother? Don't do that. You know your mother loves you, even if she hasn't been able to be much help to you, and she will miss you terribly. And Jack, well, I realize that he hasn't always been the brother you'd wish for, but, remember, he's been struggling too. I know he'd be very upset at any real rift between the two of you, to say nothing of the added burdens your leaving will make in his own life.

I guess I sound kind of preachy and formal, and really I don't mean to be. It's just that it's not easy for me to write about all this. But here goes—the part that is most difficult for me. You know without my telling you that Jack has become very important to me this summer. You're used to girls getting crushes on your big brother, but this is different, and I expect you know that. We really care for each other. So, it's impossible for me to keep all the news about you from him. Don't worry, I haven't said a word to him yet, and I won't until I get a chance to talk to you—hopefully in a few days. Meanwhile, I have a strategy in mind, a compromise. Tell Jack that you have a job downtown and that you're moving to Manhattan and will be sharing an apartment with Muriel. Don't say a word about living with Vinny until you actually move in with him. Let Jack and your mom down easy, and give them a little time to get used to things. You and Jack are so much the same—bright, charming, colorful—but you are the impulsive one who may jump from the frying pan into the fire. So take a tip from him and go a little slower. Talk it over with Vinny. I bet he'll agree with me.

I'm going to get to Monticello next week to see you—maybe for lunch? I'm sure Mama can find something for Jack to do that will keep him here. I can catch a ride in with one of the guests or Grandpa. We need to talk. So please, Bethie, call me when you've read this.

Love,
Frima

P.S. Mama sends her love also.

Beth sat on the steps of the cabin waiting for Frima. Rhubarb, napping rather heavily against her, let out a big sigh and Beth echoed him. "We need to talk," Frima had written. And I need to paint! Talk—she wasn't much good at that. No matter that in the Bronx apartments where she grew up in that so close and so unloving family, she was Bessie the Mouth. Blustering, hollering, whining, babbling—that wasn't talk. Her deepest, clearest expression was in color and line, light, shadow, texture. And most people didn't speak this private language. Frima didn't. Vinny didn't. But they respected it. "You don't respect it," she said to the dog, as she nudged him gently away, "but you don't talk either. Maybe that's why I like having you around."

The dog stood up, ears alert, and woofed before Beth even heard the wheels of a car. He began to bark loudly, making a show of protecting her. It was all for show, of course. If someone even looked at him funny, he would back away. Just like me, she thought, all bravado.

A surprise. The car was not the Eisner station wagon, but a more spiffy four-door sedan. Oh, my God, was that Jack at the wheel? No, an older man. There were three people in the car. A delegation? She walked over a little tentatively to greet them, just as the stranger, sportily dressed and nice looking in a middle-aged way, moved out of the driver's seat to open the passenger door for Hannah Eisner, who emerged a carefully created vision in blue polka dots. Frima, barelegged in loafers and a familiar casual skirt and blouse, bobbed out of the back seat, a taller, younger version of her mother.

"Mama left Jack to man the front desk, and Grandpa was too busy to drive, so Leon—he's a friend, one of Mama's suppliers, actually—drove us over here. He and Mama are going on to Woodridge to talk some insurance business and have lunch with Moe Ginsberg—but, how silly of me—you don't know who he is." Frima was obviously babbling to cover awkwardness, which was fine with Beth.

"But I do," she said. "He's the first person I ever met from the mountains. He sat next to me on the bus traveling to Monticello. Also, he's a friend of Vinny's."

"In which case I'll get a report on your young man from him. How are you, Bess—Beth, darling?" Hannah effortlessly joined their conversation, and kissed Beth on the cheek. "You look blooming!"

"So do you!"

"Well, you know, one doesn't want to get frumpy, even in this backwater. Let me introduce you—Leon?"

"A pleasure," said Leon. "Sorry I can't shake your hand." He was carrying a picnic hamper, evidently heavy.

"I thought you might like a little change from Max's food, so I packed a little picnic for you and Frima," Hannah said. "Leon and I will go on to Woodridge and pick Frima up around three at the main house. That way we can say hello to Max, if he's around, and that nice Muriel—I've met her once or twice."

"Well, sure, if you like. Muriel's covering for me right now. Tell me, does everyone know everyone in this neck of the woods?"

"I don't know a certain young man yet," Hannah answered coyly, "but I look forward to it. Now have a nice lunch and a nice chat, girls. We have to dash."

"Your mother should be secretary of state. What diplomacy!"

"Amazing isn't it? And wait until you see the Italian-Jewish picnic she packed for us. Cold blintzes, and Genoa salami, sour pickles, challah, olives, Danish—don't ask me how she got some of these goodies, but she is always one to make a statement."

How much easier to talk and plan now that the ice was broken. They both were suddenly ravenous, and attacked the food like starving things. Thus fortified, Beth had a brain storm.

"Listen, Frima, don't say anything to Jack about my plans. It's better if it comes from me. I'll write to him, this afternoon. And, don't worry, I am taking your advice. Not a word about moving in with Vinny."

Frima nodded her head. They were both silent for a few moments.

"I haven't even said anything to Vinny about this compromise." She heard herself saying this somewhat shyly, but proudly. "Uh, Frima, do you think you could . . . you should . . . help me?" Beth asked in a small voice.

"Could–would–schmould, I will!" Frima gave a small ironic laugh. "With these two guys we've fallen for, I think we'll need to help each other and frequently. So let's put our heads together."

"Okay, I'll start. Dear Jack. Now it's your turn."

"Very funny. Now just continue. You've got this job, and so on. Not too much detail, because that's a dead giveaway that you're unsure and nervous, that you're omitting some things. Only you need to know the details yourself, know what I mean?"

"How did you get so smart?"

"Detective stories," Frima retorted.

Relief that they were thinking as one again made them feel hilarious, but they managed to put together a brief, well-intentioned, diplomatic—you could say friendly—letter and had dropped it in the outgoing mail bin to make sure it went out that very afternoon. Frima had insisted on this. She wanted no opportunity for either of them to revise any more and delay getting this to Jack.

They returned to the main house to see Hannah, Leon, and Max seated in the shade with glasses of iced lemonade in their hands. They were relaxed, chatting pleasantly like old friends.

"Here they come, the belles of the Catskills," Max greeted them. "You girls get yourselves a cold drink from the kitchen, and join us." Could this be the same Max?

"We're only staying a few minutes," Hannah said. "Just enough time to kiss this girl goodbye."

"That's all the time Bess has—hnyeh, hnyeh. Of course, if she came up here and caught herself a nice Jewish dentist or doctor—even an accountant—she wouldn't have to work. But no, she falls for an Italian radical—a labor organizer, yet. *Oy vey!* Just what I needed. Hnyeh."

"He's a fine young man, according to Moe Ginsberg, and he should know. Furthermore, Judith Ginsberg told me he looks something like the actor, John Garfield," Hannah replied. Frima and Beth looked at each other with raised eyebrows and grinned. Of course, he did! They'd both noticed his resemblance to someone in the movies.

Hannah rose with a little sigh. "Well come, Leon, Frima, dear. We can't keep Jack at the desk forever. Beth, you look wonderful—you stay that way. And bring your young man to the farm one day soon, as soon as everything is settled, of course," she said airily, but with a significant smile. She kissed Beth on the forehead.

A benediction, Vinny would call it.

CHAPTER 12

O n the way home to Ellenville, Mama informed them that she would sit in the back since she and Frima had some talking to do.

"Frima, my love, you know I depend on Leon for his good practical business sense. He is also the soul of discretion, and I've talked some of my plans over with him. He has kindly consented to drive and leave us time to talk."

Frima looked at her quizzically. She barely had time to do this before Mama had them both seated and was charging ahead, full steam.

"I don't know whether you and Jack have an understanding, or if he is your intended," she paused meaningfully, "but that is not necessarily of the greatest importance at the moment."

"Then why mention it?"

"Now bear with me, darling. What I mean is, your relationship doesn't have to be affected by this, particularly. I am thinking of hiring Jack for the winter months to help me manage the hotel from the city. I find him so bright and capable, and it would free you to concentrate on your music more. Also, he could continue his studies, and I'd give him a wage that would ease his situation, even allow him—and Beth, if she contributed—to hire someone to take their places at the store. My offer would only be part-time, but not as taxing as working at the store."

"Whoa, wait a minute! You've got this all figured out?"

"Only the business part—the money issues—which I've discussed with Leon and Moe. I would do nothing about this without your agreement. What I'm trying to say is, I don't think it has to affect your personal situation with him. If you didn't care for him, I could have come to the same conclusion, based on his abilities. Also now there's this situation with Beth. It might ease her way in leaving her family, if Jack knew he would not be their sole support and labor. It would certainly soften the blow. Think about it."

"Yes, I will." She felt incapable of saying more. If Mama expected her to be ecstatic in her gratitude, well, she'd have to be disappointed. She sat back in her seat, trying to get a handle on the puzzling resentment she felt at an offer that would undoubtedly make everything easier for everyone, herself included.

After a few moments, Mama pulled a cigarette case from her bag. She offered one to Leon, and lit one for herself. She didn't smoke often, but, Frima knew, it was a prop that could ease uncomfortable silences. "You look troubled, Frima," she said.

Frima managed a reassuring smile. "No, Mama, It's just a lot to think about."

"Yes, it is, my love." And like the skilled salesperson and manager she was, Mama didn't belabor the point but stubbed out her cigarette and closed her eyes for a short nap.

Well, that was it, of course. It was the feeling that she was being managed that Frima resented. It was all happening too fast, out of her control. Was this plan to her benefit? Well, yes, but she had no room to maneuver. Maneuver what? With two fingers she massaged the space between her eyes, as if this gesture could shed some light on her puzzlement. It didn't. This was just nuts. What was she bellyaching about? She deliberately leaned forward to talk to Leon to distance herself from these thoughts.

"How is my old friend Moe? Any more corny jokes from him? You know, I met him when I was about eight, and I thought he was the funniest man I ever saw."

Evidently, her voice roused Mama from her catnap. "Are we there already? You must be speeding, Leon."

So she managed him, too. Leon doesn't seem to mind, why should I? "Almost there," Frima informed her. "And Mama, remember, not a word to Jack about your offer until he's heard from Beth. We mailed the letter before we left Monticello, so it should only be a couple of days."

"As if I would do such a thing!" Mama let her know she was a bit offended, but Frima felt a lot better. More on top of things.

Jack was busy at the desk, jotting down a message with the phone cradled between ear and shoulder. He looked relaxed, efficient, exceedingly handsome. He smiled when he saw them, politely ended his conversation, and jumped up to relieve Mama of packages. When his arms were unburdened again, he turned to Frima to give her a quick kiss.

"Careful, I reek! Genoa salami—Beth and I saved some for you."

"Genoa? Is it from that guy, Vinny?"

Frima giggled. "No, from my mother—would you believe it? There it was, packed in that humongous picnic basket."

"Is it from Italy?" he asked suspiciously.

"I'm sure it's just Italian style."

"Then it has pork in it, right?"

"Well, yes, I guess so. But you eat pork outside of the house, don't you? Because Mama and I will eat it, if you don't."

"Not so fast," he said, smiling and taking her hand. "I may be suspicious about Italian men, but I'll eat their food any day—as long as it doesn't support Mussolini."

It was all going to be okay. Fine, actually. The sight of Jack, the nearness of him was completely reassuring. She could hardly wait to be alone with him. And so it continued for the next two days. Until he came storming over to her where she had settled after lunch for a few blissful minutes of quiet in a hammock tucked behind the house.

"Just what is this?" he demanded.

"What is what?" For a moment she was completely startled. He sat down on the edge of the hammock, nearly dumping her out.

"This sweet little letter from my sister—this little hand grenade. Do you know anything about this?"

"Jack, just what is the matter with you?" She ignored his question. She was genuinely indignant. She didn't expect this anger directed at her.

"Okay, just in case you didn't know." He proceeded to read the letter, punctuated with his own angry asides:

My Dear Jack, [Dear, my foot!]

I wanted you to know before I announced this to the family. I have made a major change in my plans. I've got a job starting in September, working as a secretary downtown, and I'll be rooming with my friend Muriel, who is renting an apartment near my office. Vinny helped me find the job. [Big surprise, there—she can't even type.] *It's at the National Maritime Union, and it will pay me enough for my rent, living expenses, and some over, which I plan to contribute to Mama and Papa so they can pay for some help in the store. I hope this will ease any extra burden on you caused by my moving.*

This is a necessary and, I believe, right move for me. [Deserting her family, her religion, her values!] *I want to remain in touch and I hope that we can remain friends* [Ha! That's what people say before they never talk to each other again] *and help and support each other as brother and sister. I will be in touch with more details later.*

Love, [This is love?]

Beth

"Quite a letter isn't it?" he continued, studying her reactions.

"Yes, it is."

"Carefully written, wouldn't you say? Reasonable, agreeable, diplomatic—not the way my sister usually talks to me or my parents. She had help—You, Vinny, that Muriel—maybe all of you. Very nice! Very loyal!"

"Good God, what is it with you? Is it the letter or who wrote it that enrages you?"

"Both, I guess," he said, visibly moderating his anger, and speaking more evenly. "I don't like her plans, obviously, since I can't approve of her boyfriend or what he represents, but if you aided and abetted her, I would be really upset, disappointed. You taking her side."

"Side?" She suddenly abandoned strategy for the plain truth. "I'm trying not to take sides," she retorted, her voice shaking with anger. "What has this to do with sides? Yes, Beth told me about her move, just a few days before she wrote to you, swearing me to secrecy, and I told her that if she didn't tell you and very soon, I would. And, yes, I helped her word the letter. What's wrong with that? I care for you both, and I don't want to have to choose one of you over the other. There is no need—there shouldn't be. Beth understands this and accepts it. But, believe me, if you insist that I choose, then we are through—you and me. Think about it!"

She didn't wait for a reply. And no, she wasn't going to weep over this. She was too indignant. How self-centered could he be? She went back to the main house to take over the desk. Tears could wait until she was alone tonight, because alone she would be, for sure. She returned to her room early. No tears. She felt so numbed and desolate that the only relief was sleep, and she felt incredibly sleepy. She set her alarm clock for five-thirty, so she would awaken to gather the breakfast eggs. Without it, she was afraid she would sleep all day.

She and Jack were polite but avoided each other as much as possible during their working hours. She noticed throughout the day that his ordinary, spontaneous, charming smile was rather forced. For herself, she went through the motions of her job with a gray numbness that she hoped was not evident. How long would it last? What would life be like if Mama actually offered Jack a city job and he accepted? If she offered it, Frima was sure he would take it. What would she feel like then? It wasn't a thought that lifted her spirits, but she was deeply reluctant to say anything to her mother. She wasn't sure why.

The next morning at six, she found Jack standing quietly on the back steps of the house, waiting for her. He must have been waiting for her, as ordinarily he wouldn't be dressed, shaved, and ready to face the world quite so early. She hesitated for a moment, and he took her arm.

"Please, Frima, please wait a moment or let me walk with you. I need to say something, to talk to you." Taking her silence as consent, he began. "I am so sorry. I've been a complete idiot, about Bess, about Vinny, but mostly about you. I don't know what got into me, talking to you like that. I was very upset with my sister, but I had some nerve taking it out on you. I can't excuse myself by saying I've been brought up badly—even though it's true. Being with you, I should have learned better by now, and I promise you I will try." He continued, his voice almost breaking, "I love you, I need you, Frima. I want to marry you and be able to take care of you, make you happy." He paused for a moment. "Can you forgive me? Will you try? You don't have to answer me this minute, but will you try?"

Frima melted, immediately and completely. She answered by bursting into tears and throwing her arms around his neck. They stood silently rocking together.

"You'd better help me gather the eggs," she said, recovering herself.

"Sure. Uh, Frima, would you do something for me? Will you help me answer Bess? At least I'd feel better if you would sort of run your eye over my response to her."

"You mean Beth?"

Jack sighed. "For all of her nineteen years she's been Bess. I'll never remember to call her anything else. Besides this change—it's really dumb. *Bethesda*, I ask you. Isn't that a little ridiculous? Pretentious?"

"Not really. But maybe it's because I understand a little better why she changed it. So, for now, at least, call her what she wants to be called—if you want my advice, that is."

"You know I do."

She stopped herself from rhapsodizing—that would never do—but, God, how happy and relieved she was. She still had Jack, he was hers, and she was ready to show him that she was his. After all, Beth had "given herself" to Vinny, and look at her—absolutely bloomingly happy. And, God knows, she, Frima was equally eager to do the same. She had been, in truth, all summer. Still, it would not do to sing this out to anyone who might be listening. It took all morning before a little worry found its way through her pink cloud. Had Mama already offered Jack that job, and had that influenced him? Well, what if she had? It didn't mean he doesn't love me. Nevertheless, she found herself at her mother's door a short while later.

"I wonder, Mama, did you talk to Jack yet about working for you in the city? He hasn't said anything to me about it."

"Of course not. You told me to wait until he heard from Beth, and far be it from me to cross my daughter, in such matters," she said pointedly. Frima ignored her huffiness, judging it was mostly for show.

"Well, he did hear from her, so you'll probably want to talk to him now, right?"

"Was he upset about Beth?"

"At first, but I think he's coming around."

"That accounts for the two gloomy faces I noticed yesterday. Well, I'll talk to him today. Would you ask him to come to the office directly after lunch?"

"I sure will," she said cheerfully, trying to control her elation until she was by herself again. She slipped out the back door, and did a little dance in the shadow of the house. Oh, joy, joy! What could be better?

He loved her—entirely for herself. Nothing self-serving about that. It was staff lunchtime and she saw Jack walking up to the main house. A few kids ran up to him, and he swooped down and lifted the youngest one to his shoulder. How sweet he was, how altogether fine he looked. Oh, it was going to be a wonderful year in a wonderful world!

CHAPTER 13

Beth was out early this Saturday morning. Minetta Street, tucked away between the longer Bleeker and MacDougal streets, was still very quiet, except for shift workers coming home and dog walkers. Her eyes followed one man in pajama bottoms and a raincoat. He was half asleep and crabby as he stood by the curb while his pooch took his time checking out the territory. "Crap already, will you please? It's cold out here," she heard him mutter. Nevertheless she envied him. The dog reminded her of Rhubarb, whom she missed keenly every time she saw a mutt who resembled him. She had longed to take him back to the city, but this yearning was more of an *if only we could* than a *we simply have to* because she knew Vinny was absolutely right in refusing to consider this.

"Baby, this is not a lap dog. He probably hasn't ever had a leash on him. His house training is questionable, especially since he isn't allowed anywhere closer than the back door of the kitchen—except for you spoiling him in this cabin."

"Spoil? I do not spoil anyone."

"Okay, okay, wrong word. But he's not an anyone, he's a dog—a country dog."

"A second class citizen to you!"

Vinny just looked at her until she smiled reluctantly at her own idiocy.

"I'm thinking it was a mistake trying to raise your social consciousness. But really, Bethie, leave him to do what he needs and loves to do—eat, sniff other dogs, and hump any females in heat or objects he wishes were in heat."

Beth had rushed into the car and sunk down in her seat to hide when they were all packed and ready to leave for the city. She couldn't bear the thought of looking into those tragic, abandoned brown eyes for the last time. The dog dashed up to the car, ready to jump in or chase it, when, surprisingly, Vinny got out, took something from his pocket and called to him. "Here, Rhubarb, you go get it, boy!" The dog bounded off, joyfully grabbed his prey mid-air and trotted off with it.

"Now, what was that?" Beth asked.

"A lukewarm frank I scrounged from the kitchen."

"And kept in your pocket?"

"Old pants," he answered, starting the car.

"You old softie!"

"Well, I didn't want a scene. A howling hound laying it on thick."

"Me, neither. Still, you know, I'll really miss him—sweet dog—I'll never be able to eat rhubarb again without thinking of him."

"How often do you eat rhubarb?"

"Almost never," she admitted.

"When you do, just think how nice it is to still be in bed at six a.m. on a cold rainy day, instead of outside walking your dog, because for sure I won't—"

"Okay, I get the picture."

It was part of the bargain, the give and take of the relationship. So was her shivering in a patch of sunlight so early this Saturday morning, while Vinny, feet up on the coffee table, was consuming hot black coffee surrounded by newspapers, which were, in order of importance, the *Daily Worker*, *The New York Times*, *The Compass*, and the *New York Post*, this last mostly because Beth liked it. These represented in his eyes about the entire spectrum of respectable reporting. The other popular New York dailies were of use only when you ran out of toilet paper. This comfortable warming of feet and mind were quite all right with Beth, since he would be doing the cooking tonight. Beth had warned him before they moved in together that she didn't cook and couldn't cook; that her mother was the worst cook she knew so she had no model, blah, blah, blah.

"You can open a box of cornflakes, right? Make a sandwich? Coffee? I'll teach you to make coffee. I'll do the rest," he said without rancor. And to his credit, he didn't complain, probably in the service of self-preservation. They also tended to share a lot of meals with other people potluck, a term Beth had never heard before. Tonight was not a potluck, however. Vinny was going to prepare a special meal, celebrated traditional dishes learned from his mother, and Beth would do the shopping from his very specific list. Two long, skinny crusty loaves from Vito's, then over to Pete's for other specialties: a wedge of aged Parmesan, fresh flat-leaf parsley, extra virgin olive oil. What made it virgin, let alone extra, she wondered, but she said nothing. She knew Vinny treasured these rare moments of quiet in his noisy, hectic life. He looked up from his paper, as if reading her mind. "Ask for Savvy, not that new young clerk. He'll know just what I need and answer your questions."

As she entered the small Italian grocery, she sniffed the pungent air appreciatively. It was amazing how the smells of Bathgate Avenue that used to so offend her were transformed into quaint old world aromas on Minetta Street. Okay, so it wasn't Paris or Florence, and it might be true, as Vinny said, that most of Greenwich Village was a slum, to say nothing of the adjacent Little Italy and Chinatown, but it was a picturesque, exciting slum, full of vitality. Besides, some of the houses surrounding Washington Square and lower Fifth Avenue still retained their nineteenth-century elegance, and it was fun to imagine being lucky enough to live in one. She felt that she was absorbing knowledge and sophistication like a sponge and was once again exhilarated by that sense of possibility she'd experienced in high school. Walking hand in hand with Vinny on a Sunday morning to spend a few hours in Washington Square Park, she watched men her father's age playing chess on park benches, while squirrels, dogs, and children ran around them. She eavesdropped on political and philosophical arguments. Without envy she enjoyed looking at young women and grandmas chatting, keeping an eye on offspring or carefully doling out coins for Popsicles and Dixie Cups, while NYU students tried in vain to study. Minetta Street was in the heart of the Village, within walking distance of all its sights and offerings. She explored a crazy quilt of crooked streets and alleys, storefront galleries, bakeries, small foreign restaurants and groceries. She saw people in little coffee shops immersed in newspapers and magazines, or sipping thick black coffee in little glasses with a strip of lemon peel on the rims. Evidently they could sit there for hours.

All this panorama of Village life she enjoyed as if watching a Movietone travelogue, but it was the indoor life she really savored. To her it was privileged. For this life you needed a house key or a boyfriend such as hers. The true creative, exciting life was indoors, within the walls of studios, basements, and flats where people wrote, discussed, sang, painted, and shared inexpensive rice dishes or spaghetti and red table wine. "Dago red," Vinny called it, which was okay because he himself was Italian.

Last week she'd had a surprise. Vinny had taken her to a Sunday afternoon party at a really fine place—a remodeled Federalist house, people said, with a garden and huge windows and more space than even a large family could possibly need. It was owned and occupied by just one middle-aged couple who that day were having a fundraiser for some local candidates; councilmen, she recalled. She hadn't paid much attention to which candidates, for she was preoccupied with her limited wardrobe.

"We won't have to stay long," Vinny informed her. "Just long enough for us to grab a drink and for me to introduce the honorable candidates and shake some hands. And stop worrying," he added. "People don't look like swells at these things. Besides, you'll be a knockout whatever you wear."

"Spoken like a man," she muttered, interpreting his compliment as a dismissal. Beth had some time ago decided that she would never look dowdy, taking Frima and, even more so, Hannah Eisner as her model.

"A clever woman makes the most of herself, and the world appreciates this, even when they don't know quite what they're appreciating. And you don't have to be rich to do this. Taste is everything in dress," Hannah had proclaimed loftily. In this case, however, Beth shouldn't have worried. Everyone seemed quite determined to look ordinary. Still, she was shy and a little overwhelmed by her surroundings, and spent most of her time examining the paintings on the walls and drinking enough wine to make her a little unsure if all the art was original. Hopper, Bellows—Ash Can School—and a few of those Mexican lefties she'd heard so much about and that she kind of liked. Maybe all a little too obvious in the message department for her private taste, but all the same, she had to be impressed.

It was only a short while before she saw Vinny edging his way out of the crowd, mopping his brow. "Let's get out of this crush," he whispered.

"So, it seems you don't have to be poor to be a lefty," she commented on the way home. "Not a proletarian among that crowd, I'd say." She was feeling a little miffed that she had been pretty much ignored by the other guests.

"Except me," he answered good-humoredly. "Somebody has to support us working stiffs."

A working stiff, that's what Harry Bridges called himself, she remembered. "Now what would old Harry say to that?"

"Nothing much. He didn't need much to live on. Neither do I, but anyone willing to support labor—no strings attached—would be fine with him. However, at these digs, they tend to be a little too heavy on the fundraising and light on the refreshments. Not bad wine, but those canapés—do people really eat those things? I'm starving. Let's head over to Thompson Street for a real meal."

The thought of food recalled her to the present. She'd better get back so Vinny could start his preparations, with her as kitchen maid. Vinny was cooking veal tonight, accompanied by pasta, a new word, indeed a new concept to Beth, who had before now had only eaten spaghetti or macaroni and cheese at the Automat or her mother's gummy noodles. She didn't remember what kind of pasta it was— there were so many shapes, sizes, names. The veal was a recipe from his mother, who still lived in San Francisco with her daughter's family. They were all practicing Catholics and disapproved of the life Vinny led. Beth pictured some black-frocked, white-haired old crone who considered Beth a disgrace, who would cross herself and hurl curses at her for living out of wedlock with her son. She allowed herself a guilty smile. Pure stereotype this image was. Something to keep in that private cabinet in her mind. It was not really such an unpleasant image to her, and far easier to contemplate than the real reaction of her own mother when Beth moved out of the house.Mama had wept. She'd wept often and silently, though she knew nothing of Beth's plans, didn't even know there was a boyfriend in the picture. She kept touching Beth, gently putting her hands on her; "My Bessie," she would murmur, and Beth didn't dream of correcting her. Only her Mama could use her old birth name. Beth was so stricken by Mama's sorrow she could hardly bear it. Who would have thought Mama would care that much? She vowed to herself that she would send her a few dollars from her salary every pay day and would call her frequently. She figured she could hang up if Papa answered. The Adding Machine, of course, didn't give a damn.

"We're not good enough for you? You're too high class from working in the mountains to go to the store? Fine! One less mouth to feed," was Papa's comment.

She was almost grateful for his niggardliness. It made it easier for her to leave. Happily her move didn't take long. She had so little to take with her, and Frima and Jack had helped. She never expected this aid from her brother, who remained inscrutable about her move and just busied himself with hauling her stuff in the Eisner's station wagon, which Hannah had lent them. Beth knew that Jack had huge respect for Hannah Eisner, who was essentially offering him a path to his own success and who had tremendous influence over him. And, of course, he was in love with Hannah's daughter. Wisely, Beth did not comment to him about either of these happy circumstances, but to Frima, in private, she spoke almost daily. There was so much diplomacy in that elegant little blonde head, and she was at heart a peacemaker. Still, Frima could be tough, too, when she felt she was right. Whenever Beth wavered about keeping her life with Vinny to herself, Frima was right there to keep her firmly on the path of discretion.

"No matter how much you'd like to throw this in your father's face, not a word to any of your family about Vinny. Time enough to tell them when it really happens."

"You know that sounds as if you're thinking maybe we won't go through with this. That Vinny and I are not serious about being together."

"Nonsense. Now, you know I'm right. No blurting of anything. You're living with Muriel, a very nice Jewish girl you met during the summer—an advantageous move, and simple economy."

"Yeah, but it's duplicitous."

"Duplicitous? Will you listen to her?" Frima rolled her eyes, exasperated. "This from the girl who wasn't even going to tell her brother she was moving away from home—who wanted me not to tell him!"

"Well, they'll all have to know some time."

"And so they will, when the time is right."

Beth, comforted once again by the wisdom of Frima's approach, immediately switched gears. "My advisor, my confidante—I'm going to miss you so much! I wish you and Jack were doing what I'm doing. We could be neighbors again."

"She needs to have her head examined," Frima commented to an invisible audience. "Now, Bethie, you know that won't happen. But we'll still see each other, talk to each other all the time. Then there is the D train. The Village is just a subway ride away."

Beth was convinced the right time for her big announcement was now. Tonight, to be exact, at dinner. They had invited Beth and Jack and Muriel and her fiancé, Jerry, to a little summer reunion dinner at Vinny's place. She would make her big announcement then, though of course it would really be news only to Jack. This was fine with Vinny, whose only caution was to wait until after they'd had coffee. In truth he didn't much care whether her family or his approved of their actions. He would behave well, friendly and hospitable as usual, but it wasn't a real concern to him. What he refused to do was ruin the pleasure of good food and drink through useless combat. Her silent response was a little dry: he knows what's important, that boy does! Nevertheless, Beth knew he would protect her if things got rough, and that was the essential thing. She was safe with Vinny.

The table, moved from the foyer and opened to its full extent in Vinny's living room, provided just enough room to fit six people seated around it. It forced intimacy when it was open and surrounded by chairs, for there was really no other place to sit. Beth set the table with candles and thick white crockery. They didn't have stemmed wine glasses, which was too bad, but Vinny assured her that Italians often used these plain short glasses for less formal occasions. Happily, it was a cold night for October, and they could light a fire in the small corner fireplace. The flames reflected in the old-fashioned, half-shuttered windows gave the room just the right warm atmosphere. None of the guests were used to drinking dry red wine, but after the first tentative glass they seemed to enjoy it, and things were going well. Everyone was friendly and animated, telling war stories about their summer jobs by the time Vinny brought in the antipasto.

"Vhat's dis?" Beth peered at the platter. "Wrinkled holives. How many times I got to say this. I already told duh other vaiter—no wrinkled holives at this table!"

"Sorry, ma'am, the kitchen was extra busy this evening. No time to iron them. It won't happen again."

"Just see that it doesn't and dhat's all. For this kind of service we're paying? For wrinkled holives?"

Jerry chimed in as if on cue, "And next time you should please remember, the tea bag is on the side of the cup, not in it. How many times I have to tell you?"

"But see?" Vinny replied deadpan. "There's no water in the cup, sir. We always bring a pot of hot water separately."

"So who's the customer here, you or me? You never heard the customer is always right?"

Lots of yucks after this. Frima almost choked on her wine. "I guess we're lucky, Jack. The only complaint that we ever had was that an egg wasn't cooked right."

"Seems so," he said, laughing along with the rest.

When the stories, the routines continued, however, Beth could see that her brother was growing solemn.

"Something wrong, Jack?" she asked, knowing as she said it she probably should have kept her mouth shut.

"Not really. Only thing is I wonder why it's necessary to use that exaggerated Yiddish accent."

"It's not exaggerated," Beth retorted. "It's perfectly accurate. That's the way they talked—the older ones, anyway." She was proud of her gift of mimicry. "Besides you've used that accent yourself many times, when you tell Jewish jokes."

"But those were jokes, and these are real people you're making fun of. And I would tell those jokes only to members of our tribe. We're not all Jews here, you know."

There was an uncomfortable silence for a moment. Frima looked embarrassed, and Beth noticed her take Jack's hand to remind him not to get into an argument.

"You've got a point, Jack," Vinny said quietly. "I meant no offense, but my apologies anyway."

He shot a look at Beth, which told her quite plainly to drop it. Then he went into the kitchen to bring in the main course.

The food was delicious. The spaghetti in a light sauce of olive oil, garlic, and parsley, the simple romaine salad, the veal scallops sautéed with Marsala wine—all were a novelty, and provided sufficient chatter to again lighten the atmosphere. Vinny's generous pouring of wine also helped. "Kind of fun being a bartender again," he said affably. "Nobody's driving, right?"

It wasn't until they were having coffee that Jerry, with a heartiness and lack of judgment brought on by wine, opened Pandora's box.

"Italian, Jew, what's the difference? They both love good food, right? And you know that gag, don't you? Stiff, buttoned-up Protestants go to Jewish psychiatrists to learn to live like Italians."

No one did more than smile at this, and Muriel gave him a quick squelching look.

"There are differences," said Jack quietly. "According to Hitler they are very different, and Mussolini is one of Hitler's best friends."

"Whoa, just hang on a minute," Vinny said. "I hope you're not implying what I think you are. There are plenty of people in Italy and Italian Americans right here who hate that bastard. He's killed and tortured plenty of his fellow Italians. Also, it may be news to you, but it's nevertheless true, that there were some Jewish fascists in Italy who helped him come to power. Not as helpful as the Holy Roman Catholic Church, perhaps, but still useful to him."

"I never heard that," said Jack.

"Well, you're hearing it now. Fascists are fascists, no matter what religion, and they come in all shapes and sizes. You're right that Mussolini does whatever Hitler says, including hunting down Jews, but before you get all hot under the collar again, remember that if anything, I have more reason to hate that pig than you do. Unless you have relatives in Italy that have become his victims."

"I don't, thank God, but I do have or had relatives in Poland."

"Do you know any of them personally?" Frima asked. "I mean we hear these terrible stories, but how do you know who is gone?"

"Honey, the letters stopped coming. My folks used to hear from their cousins, uncles, and aunts in Poland every couple of months at least. Nothing now; no explanation."

"I'm afraid Jack's right. That's certainly what I would assume." Vinny sighed.

"I'm so thankful all our relatives are here," Frima said, "but the others!"

"My God," Beth looked chastened. "I never really thought about it, I'm ashamed to say, or . . . you know, felt what's happening—not in any personal way. You see movie newsreels about Storm Troopers, all those monstrous crowds giving Nazi salutes, but the human tragedy is hidden from you; you don't really have to look."

"Perhaps you wouldn't have had to look if your great red hero, Stalin, hadn't made that miserable anti-aggression pact with Hitler, carving up Poland and the rest of Eastern Europe." Jack's tone, though quiet, was ominous. He was supposedly responding to Beth, but he looked directly at Vinny and Jerry.

"You think the Poles are incapable of persecuting Jews on their own, pact or no pact? Besides, Stalin was probably buying time," Jerry retorted.

"So they say." Jack responded smoothly. "And the same could be said for Hitler." He barely looked at Jerry now, keeping his attention on Vinny.

Vinny looked evenly at Jack and took Beth's hand under the table before he responded, which she correctly interpreted as, "Let me handle this."

"Could be you are both right," he said. "But don't look at me. I hate the damned pact, whatever the strategy."

Jack shrugged his shoulders, clearly realizing he couldn't win an argument with a man who refused to fight. He grew quieter. He politely refused more fruit or coffee, responding almost exclusively to Frima. At one point he excused himself and went into the bathroom. When he came back, he looked even graver and avoided his sister's eye. Beth chickened out. She would make no happy announcement of her living arrangement tonight. If Jack hadn't guessed already, a short note would be enough.

The sobering war talk continued but was becoming desultory. Catching Vinny stifling a yawn, Frima spoke up.

"Well, I can't speak for the rest of you, but I'm almost besotted with wonderful food, drink, memories. Jack, you'd better take me home before you have to carry me."

Offers to clear the table and do the dishes were graciously shooed away, and the goodbyes began, the men shaking hands, the women hugging and kissing. Frima thanked Vinny directly as they were leaving.

"That was a truly great meal. We don't get lettuces like those uptown where we are. And that veal! I'm sure my mother would love to have the recipe. Do you think you could send it to me?"

He put his hands on her shoulders and kissed her on both cheeks, European style.

"For you, any time," he said, "though I have a feeling veal will be pretty scarce soon. Still, I'll give it to Beth or send it directly to you."

Beth stood by smiling. It was obvious that she, Beth, was not leaving with the others. No need to say anything to anybody about her living arrangements.

A delicious quiet descended, and Vinny and Beth collapsed onto the couch, loathe to start cleaning up after the feast.

"I think it all went very well, don't you? Except for Jack's MOT comment."

"What?"

"Member of our tribe. He simply had to point out that you were the only one here who wasn't Jewish. He doesn't approve of you, of course. He thinks you are a corrupting influence, that you carried me off, seduced me, and are turning me into a godless red."

"I guess he doesn't realize you're pretty capable of doing most of that by yourself," Vinny replied easily. "Now, think how I would feel if he ran off with my sister? No, wait—bad comparison—I'd probably pity the poor SOB. She'd be after him to join the Knights of Columbus, maybe try a little flagellation."

"You're a real comedian."

"But, seriously, Beth, Jack's no fool, and he does have a point. There is a difference between what you can say among your own and outsiders. It's like my objections to *Amos and Andy*. A harmless radio show, right? Maybe not in great taste, but funny, people laughing at themselves—except that both Amos and Andy are played by white men, so the show promotes denigrating stereotypes."

"Oh, God, Vinny," she said standing up. "No lectures now, it's way too late!"

He rose, looking slightly shamefaced. "Well, I guess the only answer is to go to bed," he said, patting her rear end.

"What about the dishes? Won't it be roach heaven?"

"We'll do them first thing in the morning."

Beth grinned. "You are corrupting me, no question!"

CHAPTER 14

They were eating again, which was hard for Frima to believe after the meal consumed the previous night, but both she and Jack were devouring bagels and lox with enthusiasm. Perhaps love made you hungry. These Sunday morning leisurely breakfasts at Mama's ample table were becoming an institution since Jack had accepted her offer of year-round work for the hotel. Frima was relieved to see that he was finishing his second cup of coffee now, quite at ease. Far more so than he had been on the subway ride home last night. There he had been silent and morose, and she'd worried that he counted her as one who was encouraging Beth in her "outrageous and irresponsible behavior," as he liked to phrase it. He had made no such accusation, but she felt guilty anyway. Those sins of omission again. Well, what was she supposed to do if she was caught between these two intense, temperamental creatures? Peacemaking meant you omitted things and compromised and tried to see both sides of an issue—activities that Jack and Bethie couldn't be bothered with. To hide her own tension, she chatted more than usual when they sat down at the table.

"That Vinny is some marvelous cook, Mama. He promised to send the recipes for the veal and the spaghetti. Also the salad dressing. You'd love his food. It's delicious, but all quite simple, I understand."

"The simpler, the better," Mama commented.

"An ordinary man who can cook like that," Frima mused. "Chefs, of course, but in a home it's different."

"It has been my experience," said Mama, "that men who are home cooks usually have one or two specialties they are very proud of, but when it comes to preparing meals day after day and cleaning up after themselves, give me a woman, anytime."

"In that case, Vinny had better get used to veal Marsala every day," Jack said. "My sister can't boil an egg."

"Many people can't," said Mama.

"You know what I mean. Now really, Hannah, what do you think of this business of Bess sneaking off to live with this guy? This girl here seems to think it's perfectly fine. She finds old Vincent Carmine Migliori positively charming." He tugged gently on a lock of Frima's hair to soften his words.

"I do, and I'm not in the least ashamed of it." Frima retorted.

"It isn't an orthodox arrangement, certainly," Mama said mildly. "But you know Beth will never be conventional. Frima tells me that he is a very nice young man." Mama appeared all candor and innocence as she spoke. "Tell me, what bothers you about them as a couple? That they're not married?"

"For sure. But more that he's not Jewish, and he's a red, to boot. Now tell me, when has Russia ever been anything but trouble for the Jews?"

"I never heard Vinny say anything about Russia." Frima said.

"Maybe not. He won't talk frankly to just anyone. But didn't you notice the *Daily Worker* folded up in their bedroom? Also he's a great big fan of Vito Marcantonio and that West Coast agitator, Harry Bridges. That tells me a whole lot."

"I rather like Marcantonio. I'd vote for him if he were in my district," Mama commented.

"Uh-oh, you, too?"

"Come now, Jack," she said soothingly. "Don't fret about this. Beth will be okay, and so will you all. This is the twentieth century. People do these things, and sometimes it works out for the best."

"I know, I know that. But Jews need to stick together, especially these days. Somehow, I can't help feeling that under this guy's influence, my sister will become an anti-Semite."

"Now that's unfair, Jack," Frima said. "Vinny has never shown the slightest prejudice! And, remember, he was the one who apologized for the kidding around. He doesn't want to offend anyone."

"That's part of his political line, honey, but what about those jokes last night? Listen to this, Hannah. You be the judge."

Hannah smiled about the wrinkled holives. "Ah, Beth! She can be quite a wag. But seriously, Jack, was there any harm done among friends in a private home? You all laughed, didn't you? Beth wasn't being mean-spirited or unkind, was she?"

"Well, no, but she was getting there. You know as well as I that she can run off with a notion and go right over a cliff with it. Besides, this wasn't joking around among ourselves. Vinny was there, and he isn't one of us. There are times when it's us or them, and right now with the war, with what's happening, it has to be us—only us."

Mama looked troubled. "I know that your sister can overdo things—we all know that—but her heart is in the right place. And, Jack, don't you see? If it's only about us, we're all lost."

Jack had no ready response for this.

They were startled by Mama's sudden spurt of laughter. "Forgive me, children, but I just had this thought. If Vinny is an anti-Semite, hoo boy, is he in the wrong job! A labor advocate in New York City, a negotiator, a leftwing activist? What would he do with the garment workers, to name just one contentious crowd. A whole lot of Jews, right? Quite a few Italians, of course, also. All these impassioned union workers with very strong opinions, and he has to try to herd them all in the right—I should say left—direction. He'd be an imbecile to undertake such work if he were anti-Semitic. Besides, according to

Moe Ginsberg, a man whose brains and convictions I greatly respect, Vincent Migliori is anything but an imbecile and exceedingly good at what he does." Mama got up decisively. "Enough gloom now. How about a Danish? I just bought them fresh this morning. More coffee, Jack? Now, how is school going?"

"Pretty well," Jack replied, reaching for a pastry. "It's a lot easier to organize my time, working for you."

"Uh-huh. Also a little more money and space? Less quarreling? Maybe you could think of Beth's moving out as less of a desertion and more of an advantage. And as for Vinny, who knows? It might all turn out for the best. So now, for a little business," said Mama, decisively closing one door and opening another. "I may need you to come up to Ellenville, with me next Saturday. Could you do that and stay over until Sunday?"

"Can I bring this girl with me?"

"So where else should she be?"

"It's a deal."

"I notice that nobody at this table consulted me about how I want to spend the weekend," Frima said.

"You're absolutely right, and I apologize," said Mama. "Do you want to go?"

"Well, yes, but that's not the point."

"Sorry, honey," said Jack. "It's just that I always assume you'd prefer our sweet haven in the country to anyplace else."

Somewhat mollified, Frima smiled but remained silent. Jack spoke fondly about the hotel. Calling it their haven or sometimes their heaven in the Catskills. She was pleased by his romantic descriptions, knowing he felt that way because she was there with him, but she didn't imagine that his feeling for the place could be deep. She was surprised at her own quick resentment that his attitude was too easy. How contrary and ridiculous she was! How could she expect him to put heart and soul into a place where he had spent only a summer?

Even if he knew some of the story from her own telling, how could he experience the powerful meaning of it all? He knew, of course, that after Papa had died, Mama had almost singlehandedly saved the family farm. Like the heroine in a melodrama—a comparison Frima made completely without irony—Mama was the driving force behind every hard-won success that created Eisner's. But those long sessions around the farm kitchen table, where Mama, Papa, and the adolescent Frima dreamed and planned, the false starts and worries, the endless work—how could Jack possibly fathom what it meant? It was a closing of family ranks, a defiantly optimistic response to loss. Also an act of love.

And here they were, sitting around a kitchen table again planning, but with Jack substituting for Grandpa, who remained firmly rooted in his little haven in the country. Now they were talking of improvements. With large parts of Europe and East Asia at war, there was a demand for both raw and manufactured materials. People were beginning to earn again, and they might be looking for a few more amenities.

Once again they spoke of putting in a swimming pool, a project Mama, Frima, and Grandpa had roundly rejected before in favor of the pond for swimming.

"Personally, I have always hated the idea of a pool, and I still do," said Frima. "No matter what you do to it, it's still ugly concrete and smells of chlorine. Furthermore, the fake color of the water is a blight on the landscape. What happened to enjoying nature?"

Mama sighed. "Well, yes, dear, but it might make us more competitive, and it looks awfully good in a brochure." She said this without enthusiasm, evidently waiting for a better argument than Frima's to talk her out of it.

"Well, if you don't mind my butting in, I agree with Frima," Jack said. "Not that I'm bothered by chlorine or anything. I've been in enough public pools to be immune to it. But aside from the building expense, you'd have a whole different atmosphere. People lying on beach chairs and lounges, jumping in and out of the water; they'll demand more services—drinks, towels, snacks. You're at their beck and call, as if you don't have enough of that already. Besides there's the maintenance and cleaning. People always worry about polio where there's a pool, even if it's not in the city. You'd probably need a pool guy. I don't know what the laws are about lifeguards, but certainly there would be risks, insurance headaches. At the pond there's a county lifeguard, and the whole issue is out of your hands. Also, while so many guests are away at the pond, the staff gets a respite, or at least a chance to catch up."

"Smart boy, this one. I'm convinced," said Mama. "No pool, and we're all happy. Any other business to bring up?"

"Yes, there is," said Frima emphatically. She was determined not to be taken lightly in this planning. "Just where did you think of putting that pool?"

"Oh, I don't know. Maybe a thousand feet behind the cabins? What does it matter now?"

"I'd like to put a kitchen garden there. Way easier to dig than excavating a huge hole for a pool. I know we get fresh vegetables from the truck farms, and this plot wouldn't substitute for those; but I bet guests would get a kick out of corn, tomatoes, cucumbers, fresh peas growing right out in back. The kids could plant radishes—supervised of course."

"A nice idea, but who will make this garden grow?"

"Who do you think? With maybe a little help from my friends," she said, nudging Jack's knee under the table.

"I can see it all now," said Jack, grinning. "*Potage de petite pois à la Frima* on the menu, or perhaps *le choux farci à la Frima* to give the menu a little more class."

"So you speak French now, college boy?" Mama gave him a sidewise glance.

"I'm a poor boy, but I've been to a fancy Jewish wedding, you know. I've been around."

"When I want a *tumler* I'll hire one," said Mama rising from her seat and giving him an affectionate rap on the head. "You watch out, my boy. My daughter is an enthusiast and a romantic about farming," she said as she left the room.

"And I'm an enthusiast and a romantic about you," he said softly to Frima.

"I was beginning to think you were in love with my mother."

"So whose mother should I be in love with? Mine? Listen, honey, let's get out of here and find some of that greenery you love so much. The park or the botanical gardens, maybe?"

She smiled wholeheartedly now, and nodded.

"And don't worry, I'll make your garden grow. That's a promise."

The rose gardens had none of the fragrance of midsummer, being pretty bare in October, but no matter. It was the perfect place for Jack to pop the question. They talked of an April wedding up in Ellenville. He was sorry he couldn't give her a ring now, but some day he hoped to. As if she cared a whit about that! All resentment and contrariness melted away. She wanted him to be about love, about closing ranks? Well, she'd got what she wanted.

—

"So, *mazel tov*, Frima. My own daughters should have such luck," one of the ladies said. "Enjoy your engagement, dear, it's the best time of your life," said another of the gaggle of women who had greeted her outside the neighborhood bakery. There was a communal sigh from them. It was cold out, and Frima was eager to get into the warm, quiet apartment, but she was well brought up, so she smiled politely. "Thank you, I will."

So the vital thing was to catch a man—a matter of luck, not

merit—and once you were married, it was downhill from there? Enjoy your engagement? Were they crazy, those women? They had only been engaged a month and their wedding wasn't until late April, but both Jack and Frima had begun to wonder why they just didn't elope. All the hoops they had to jump through just to get married. The only one who actually enjoyed their engagement was Mama, to the extent that she could exercise all her tact, charm, and management talents, while her daughter and future son-in-law, full of opinions and convictions, essentially wandered around helpless.

At first it surprised Frima that Mama hadn't urged them to take their time and not rush into anything, for those maternal cautions of last summer were still vivid to her. But there'd been a lot of water under the bridge since last summer, and Mama had provided a lot of that flood by hiring Jack and weaving him into their lives. Also, since her mother was no fool, she certainly realized that their passion wouldn't be kept at bay by anything so mundane as a career or a marriage license. Well, why wait for anything? Life was moving at a compelling pace with the war in Europe, jobs in the war industries at home. Would America be in the fray any time now? Grab your happiness while you can! Only thing was their happiness was in being together, not in an obstacle course ending in a wedding ceremony.

The first stumbling block was housing. Frima would have loved to live up in the country, as they couldn't afford their own apartment yet. But she knew that was out of the question. Jack couldn't commute to his classes from Ellenville. Naturally, Mama had a solution, and it was gratefully accepted. For the time being, until Jack was earning full time, they would live in her apartment. Mama's large bedroom would be theirs. She would use the smaller bedroom because she planned to spend more and more time at the hotel. Grandpa was getting frail and there was so much to do. At the hotel, of course, Frima and Jack would have their own private room. They weren't bound for a rose-covered cottage, but it was a good solution for now. Many couples lived in far more uncomfortable circumstances.

Mama had not commented on the pleasures and convenience of living so near to Jack's folks, an omission not lost on Frima. If Jack noticed, he said nothing. Very wise of him. Mama did invite Sam and Sarah to dinner, bowing to convention.

"This is not an engagement party, I hope." said Frima. "I won't have anything to do with such a thing if Beth and Vinny aren't here."

"Do you take me for an imbecile? This is a duty, not a pleasure. Later, you can have any kind of celebration you want with your friends. As for me, you know I'm always happy to see Beth, and I find this Vinny intriguing. For now, with Sam and Sarah, just think of them as difficult guests at the hotel. You know how to behave."

The dinner was pretty much as anticipated. Sam Erlichman, somewhat pacified by Mama's brisket and potato pancakes, managed to toast the coming union with a glass of schnapps: "*Mazel tov, mazel tov.* But watch your step. Marriage is no picnic." He managed a smile.

Sarah glared at him. "From me, I say every *mazel* to the young couple. You're marrying a fine, beautiful girl, Jack." And then without missing a beat, a big sigh. "This should only happen to my Bessie— and with a nice Jewish man!"

"Don't worry, Mama, you'll see," Jack said heartily. "Bess will come to her senses."

Or you will, Frima thought unbidden, stifling a snicker. Jack's folks made her nervous, and when she was nervous, she had a tendency to laugh, the more so if it were forbidden.

There was nothing amusing, though, about the little interchange she and Jack overheard as her future in-laws departed. Sarah and Sam were waiting for the elevator in the hallway, a space that exaggerated every sound. In a voice that could be heard above a subway train, Sam gave free rein to his feelings.

"He needs a wife now like he needs the cholera. What good is this for him?"

"Shah! Keep your voice down! She's a nice girl from a good family. I like her."

"There'll be a baby before you know it. And then what?"

"From your mouth to God's ear."

"*Tsuris.* That's what it will be. He has to marry so soon? You heard maybe the expression a shotgun wedding? Don't you know *tsuris* when it's right in front of your face?"

"Me, you're asking? When it's standing right in front of me? I married you, didn't I?"

The happy couple inside the apartment looked at each other and groaned.

"At least your mother is pleased," Frima offered. "And your sister is, I know."

Jack nodded his head. "More so than I am about her." He sighed.

All of which was true.

CHAPTER 15

"**I** knew it!" Beth exclaimed. "I felt it in my bones. My brother, the heartthrob, following you around like a puppy. And you know something? I'm really truly pleased about it. Sisters at last! So when does it happen?"

"The wedding?"

"What else?"

"Late April in Ellenville. We haven't set the date yet."

"So soon? And you told me to slow down! Ahem, no hurry is there? Okay, okay, don't bite my head off, I'm only kidding."

"One of these days, you will allow me to bite your head off after you say something provoking without heading me off at the pass," Frima replied testily. "And if you don't stop, I won't let you be maid of honor."

"Oh my God, you want me to be maid of honor? Really? Now, that's what I call exciting! But what about Vinny?"

"Won't work. He's a man."

"Hilarious. You know what I mean."

"Well, I doubt that Jack would choose him as his best man. But, believe me, if you and Vinny aren't there together and openly, there ain't gonna be no wedding."

"Atta girl! Well, I am tickled pink to be your maid of honor. I don't have to wear pink, do I? I mean I will if I have to, but—"

"Pink? Wear anything you want, even if it's as bright red as the worker's flag. Just don't overshadow me."

"Strong words."

"I need them these days. Ever been engaged? Well, don't be. Not that I wouldn't be quite happy to see you married. Any chance that you and Vinny are thinking along those lines?"

"I wouldn't count on it. I don't think I'm the marrying kind."

"But you love Vinny, don't you?"

"Yes, and he loves me, but remember I grew up the daughter of a terrible marriage."

"So did Jack. But I guess one marriage among the four of us is enough for now," Frima said lightly, backing off. It was evident that Beth didn't want to talk about this.

Beth sat by the phone after they hung up, relieved that she was home alone. Her feelings were too roiled up to talk to another human being, and for a wild moment she wished that Rhubarb were there with her. She could talk to the dog, say anything whatsoever, and he would look at her with complete acceptance in his soulful eyes, hoping for no more from her than a dog biscuit. "One marriage is enough for now," Frima had said. That was a mouthful. She wondered if Frima was aware of how loaded those few words were.

She was pleased that Frima was marrying Jack. She had learned to be optimistic about this union. She tittered to herself. Now that was a Jane Austen attitude, if there ever was one—you learn to be happy, you endeavor to be satisfied—and you are amiable, always amiable. Funny how much she loved Austen. Probably because she was so unlike her. Those witty, elegantly written fantasies, always a well-deserved happy ending—in marriage. Well, Beth couldn't take refuge in a novel now. And for her there would be no happy ending in wedded bliss. Could Frima find it with Jack? Maybe she could. He loved Frima, that was obvious, and though he was the son of that same bitter marriage, he had always had the best of it in their family. The older one, the handsome son. Smart, ambitious, so engaging. And he looked up to Frima and her family. Not a bad formula for success.

She glanced down, pencil in hand, at the word she'd unknowingly jotted down on the message pad: *pleased*. How odd. She was pleased about the coming marriage. Pleased wasn't quite the same as happy for the couple. But it was accurate, and it made her uneasy. Pleased, as in gratified. Yes, it was gratifying that Jack was marrying into the Eisner family, for it suited her own need to remake herself. She'd always secretly longed to be a part of that family—who wouldn't want Hannah Eisner as a mother, Frima for a sister? But it still made her sad, guilty. It was disloyal to her own poor mother. Nevertheless, Jack's marrying into that family would make both sister and brother more Eisner and less Erlichman. A big step up for both of them. Okay, so it was ambitious. Nothing wrong with that. It wasn't the whole story, was it? It would be a loving connection. Besides, couldn't she some-day achieve a new family by marrying Vinny and creating her own? No way! The thought of marrying Vinny and having his children was almost as terrifying to her as the thought of losing him.

The pencil broke in her hand, startling her. Time—time is on my side. I've only known Vinny for a few months. Nobody would expect her to marry so soon, let alone have a baby, especially not Vinny. He's a responsible guy. Let Jack and Frima be the impetuous ones, for once.

Except it wouldn't wash. True, neither she nor Vinny felt ready for marriage and children, but Vinny didn't panic at the thought, and she did. Timing was everything to him. She'd come to realize how different she was—how unnatural—on one occasion when they were being a little spontaneous in someone else's bedroom and she hadn't been wearing her diaphragm. Vinny had been taken aback at her fear.

"It's only once—what time of the month is it?"

"Rhythm method? You know that doesn't work! Judith Ginsberg says—"

Vinny put his hand over her mouth. "A hell of a time to quote

Judith Ginsberg." He paused. "Okay, no coitus," he annunciated carefully. "Just shut up and pretend you're underage in the back of my car."

"Just like a man," she muttered wrathfully. "Thinks all he has to do is unzip, wave it around."

"Are you trying to imitate my mother or yours?" Vinny spoke evenly, even smiled a little, but she knew he was not happy.

"I'm sorry, love, maybe I'm being a nervous ninny, but I worry. I can't get pregnant!"

"But why all the terror about it? Would it be the worst thing in the world? We could have a child. Or not have it, if necessary. I mean, I'd be sorry to have it happen, but there are ways, safe ways."

"No! I don't want either—at least not now."

"You really are terrified," he said slowly, and rolled over.

She waited anxiously—would he get up and walk out on her? But she had underestimated him. In a few minutes he rolled over and nuzzled her again.

"This is a very big bed," he whispered intimately. "It could accommodate all kinds of acrobatics, unlike ours at home."

"Yes?" She giggled.

"And pleasures that don't require any perfumed spermicide."

"You mind that?"

"No, not really, but face it, Bethie, you do sometimes lay it on a little thick, and I prefer the fragrance of you."

Well, she'd mend her ways, which was easy enough. She knew what the instructions called for, yet she'd used about twice as much diaphragm jelly as necessary just to be safe. It just showed how important not getting pregnant was to her. The mildly perfumed jelly was virtually an aphrodisiac to her, it so freed her from anxiety. Vinny could tease her about Judith Ginsberg, but that good woman had opened her eyes to a world that young men like Vinny or her brother could only see dimly, if at all. An unwanted pregnancy was serious trouble; but an unwanted child was a tragedy. Diaphragms were the safest, best means of avoiding this, as well as the best prevention of that other tragedy, an unsafe abortion. Before this last summer, abortion was barely in Beth's vocabulary; she had never encountered anyone who had experienced one.

"You think you haven't, my dear girl, but the practice is rampant," Judith had informed her. "Terminations are readily available in safe clinical conditions for women with money. For poor women, they are also readily available, but rarely under safe conditions, except with the aid of some generous and courageous doctors and midwives. The worst is when a woman is desperate enough to try to end the pregnancy herself. You are shocked? Well, it's true and has always been true, here and in the rest of the world, civilized and uncivilized. Your own mother, she is alive and healthy? And she has only two children? It's probable she has had one or more."

"My mother? I thought she just didn't have sex with my father, which I can really understand, as he's pretty grim. This is amazing!"

"What's amazing," Judith smiled a little dryly, "is that you think of abstinence as a likely explanation. She might not enjoy sex much, but she is his wife, and your parents aren't old, except perhaps as seen through your young eyes. Remember, life begins at forty! But let's concentrate on you. What we want for you is to enjoy lovemaking, knowing that you will become pregnant only when and if you wish to."

In those rare dark hours when Beth visited the issue in that private cabinet in her mind, she could not envision herself married and pregnant without evoking an image of a caged wild bird, squawking over an alien egg. At those hours, as now, she clung to two comforts: Judith's words and time. Naturally she became a true believer in birth control and wanted to proselytize. But to whom? Certainly not to any women of Vinny's acquaintance; they had long been far more informed than Beth, herself. Instead, she had tried to convince Frima to follow her example and visit Judith. This was a blunder, to say the least. Frima had no interest in doing so. Her intimacies with Jack were just that—intimacies, and therefore private. She was entirely kind about this but also quite firm. What was good for Beth didn't mean it was good for Frima. Beth had only succeeded in feeling less fastidious than she should be. So what else was new?

The shrill ring of the phone again. Resisting the impulse to hurl it across the room, Beth answered it. Another mistake. It was her mother, in tears.

"What's wrong? Everything is wrong. Wherever your Papa is, is wrong. You know that Jack and Frima are engaged?"

"Well, yes, but you're happy about that. You like Frima."

"Of course—a darling girl! But your father! He says if you're at the wedding, he won't be there."

Beth, stabbed by pain and rage, was silent, but her mother continued without noticing. "He says—you don't have to know what he says—I shouldn't repeat it. But who is Vinny? You're living, God forbid, with an Italian? I know nothing about my own daughter?"

"Mama, shh, calm down!" Holy shit, who told him? Jack? She couldn't believe he would do that.

"Anyway, Frima says if you're not there, and with this Vinny—she likes this Vinny—she says if you're not there, there won't be a wedding. So you don't go or Papa doesn't go and I go alone, which makes me so ashamed. What to do? Hannah Eisner says not to worry, that everyone will be there, but what can she do? She says she's going to call you. But still, what to do?"

"What you can do is not worry about any of this. Papa isn't home, right? So go put your feet up, make yourself a cup of tea, take a nap. Everything will be fine. Believe me. It will be a very lovely, happy occasion. You know Hannah and Jack and Frima will make everything just fine." Beth was pleased with herself. This last had been a heroic effort—Vinny would be proud of her. He'd also suggest that some of his Dago red was what her mother needed most.

What she, Beth, needed now was some time with a paint brush.

Did she have time to go up to the studio at the League before Vinny came home? Probably not, but she could get to her sketch book. When the phone rang not five minutes later, she picked it up, thinking she might go nuts. She greeted Hannah Eisner's voice with a little bark of laughter.

"I say hello, and that's funny?"

"Oh, Hannah! Forgive me, but first Frima calls, then my mother, now you—one after the other. I half-expect Jack to call me, and I'm sure Vinny will have something to add before I've even had time to digest the big news. It seemed to me suddenly like a speeded up scene in a one-reel comedy. But first, *mazel tov!* I'm quite sincere about that."

"Thank you, my dear. I won't keep you long—we're both busy woman these days. I just wanted to assure you, Beth, that we are all delighted that you will be maid of honor. Who else so fitting? Also, everyone will be there as they should be, and if one of them isn't happy, he will still behave himself. Don't you worry your pretty head about any of it. You know, I've never become acquainted with your Vinny, except by reputation, and he sounds quite fascinating. I'm eager to know him."

"Oh, I knew you'd feel that way, Hannah, and I'm so happy that you do, but my father, oh my God, a royal pain in the you know what."

"To say the least." Hannah gave a comfortable little laugh. "But I've not been a successful hotel manager for nothing. Also, remember I'm a dressmaker, and your Papa sells notions—buttons, ribbons, zippers? He and I will have a little talk. Just you remain deaf and dumb to all of this idiocy. I'll take care of Sam."

"No blunt instruments?"

"What a thought, my dear girl. I am a diplomat."

Just how Sam Erlichman had divined that his no-good daughter had been up to even more no good was a mystery. Neither Jack nor Frima had a clue. But secrets were hard to keep, and gossips talked. Sam, it was clear, was happy to have anyone see his rage.

"That's it! I won't have a whore for a daughter, a *nafkeh*. I never set eyes on her again. She can't get married like a normal person? Not her! She has to shame us by living with an Italian? A Dago? A gangster? If she goes to the wedding, I don't. And that's all!"

"You can sit here and soak your feet, or your head, though it won't give you any more brains. I'm going to my son's wedding if I need to walk there," Sarah retorted. The battle was joined.

Jack's first reaction was to mutter that whenever his sister was involved there was trouble. Why did she have to entangle herself with this guy anyway? But greeted with stony silence and Frima and Hannah's eyes boring into him, he promptly thought better of complaining. He knew quite well which side his bread was buttered on; Frima and Hannah were his sister's champions and thereafter he wisely left the combat with Sam to them.

Sarah, arriving at Hannah's door, marched into the kitchen and planted herself on a chair.

"I'm going, he isn't, and that's that. In the ground he should be!" Then, more quietly, "I hope you'll have room for me in the car."

"Of course, Sarah," Frima assured her. "Why, you're part of the wedding party, you know."

"Ah, well, thank you, dear." Sarah managed a little smile. "I hope I have a dress fancy enough for the occasion. From that *schnorer*, I'll get nothing."

"Have a cup of tea, Sarah," Mama said calmly. She set a steaming cup and a slice of apple cake in front of her.

"Thank you, but I have no appetite—I'm too upset."

"This is just what you need. Now, Sarah, don't you worry. I promise you right now, you and Sam will both be there. He doesn't have to say a word to Beth or anybody for that matter. The wedding is a small country celebration, nothing fancy, but Sam will be in a suit and you'll have a nice dress. I'm making it myself, just like I'm doing for Frima. After you finish your tea, I want to take your measurements. Then we'll talk."

Masterful, Frima thought. Still, Sarah was a piece of cake compared to Sam. Mama would need a bludgeon to get anywhere with him.

She did, nevertheless. Neither Frima nor Jack knew exactly how. She sent them on an errand, announcing that she was going to call Sam. No, she didn't need them for moral support—they'd just be in the way. They dawdled around, full of curiosity, but she closed the door on them. Ears to the door they could hear that she spoke in rapid Yiddish, her voice rising in intensity and determination. They couldn't make out much more.

When they returned Mama was at her sewing machine. She greeted them with a smug look of victory.

"And?"

"And what? Frima, my dear. He's coming and that's all. Though maybe we could put a piece of plumber's tape over his mouth. That would be nice."

"Hannah, how in the world did you convince him?"

"Jack, Jack, when will you learn? A little blackmail, a little bribery, a little flattery. You know, diplomacy."

CHAPTER 16

And so it happened, and on a lovely spring day, as planned. The bride was beautiful, the groom handsome. Beth was bridesmaid, and Jack's cousin was best man. The four stood under the canopy, while Sam, Sarah, Mama, and Grandpa sat in the first row: Sam stony-faced, Sarah smiling through tears, Mama and Grandpa beaming proudly. Vinny, discreet as usual, sat further back, next to Leon, who had offered to listen for the phone and to generally take care of business and free Mama to bask in her glory. The rabbi intoned, the groom stepped on the glass and broke it decisively, everyone shouted *mazel tov*, the bride was kissed, and the formalities were over. Now the real celebration could begin.

Mama's hospitable table and bar were everything they should be, as was the wedding cake. The happy couple, dazed by the hugs, kisses, and congratulations, had barely begun to enjoy the celebration when the dancing began a little later, and they didn't stay for long. Mama had declared that the newlyweds should have at least a couple of nights of honeymoon and had booked them into a very nice guest house for the weekend, far enough from family and friends for privacy. She must have called in a few favors for this luxury, Frima thought. Also, she admired the dexterity with which her mother had kept antagonists apart. Moe Ginsberg, who had a home in Woodridge, offered his guest room for Beth and Vinny. The older Erlichmans would stay at Eisner's, none the wiser. The festivities continued, and, as Beth later related to Frima, everyone behaved after their fashion.

Beth, delighted with Moe's hospitality, took his arm. "Well, we're grateful, of course, but, I don't know, would Jefferson sleep there?"

"In Woodridge? I don't think so, but he might condescend to stay here. What a delightful party. Hannah has certainly outdone herself."

"But I don't see Judith anywhere. Couldn't she come?"

"Unfortunately, she had to be in New York, but she was so sorry to miss it. Everyone is having such a good time," he continued, gazing around, "except that couple over there, especially the man. I don't know them, but joyful, they're not."

Beth groaned. "My parents—father and mother of the groom. They don't approve of what they see here. At least my father doesn't. My mother simply disapproves of my father. Nothing new there. It shows she's human and redeemable."

"But what is the objection? Not to the wedding or the bride, surely!"

"Now don't play dumb with me, Moe. You know perfectly well the problem is Vinny and me."

Moe gave a little smile. "So Vinny hasn't won them over yet?"

"He hasn't met them. They won't acknowledge his existence, or mine, if I am with him. But I think I'd better go over and talk to them."

"Gently, my dear girl—if you don't mind my offering a little fatherly advice?"

"From you, Moe, anytime."

When Beth approached, Sam ostentatiously moved to the far side of the room and spoke to no one. Beth took courage and boyfriend in hand and introduced Vinny to her mother.

"So nice to meet you, Mrs. Erlichman, and on such a happy occasion. *Mazel tov!*"

"Likewise, I'm sure. Head full of sawdust, a heart of stone—stubborn, don't ask! A *schnorer*, a *vantz!*"

For once, Vinny was at a loss. Beth, unable to contain herself, dragged him out of earshot, and over to the bar. "She's talking about my father, not you. Oh, my God, the look on your face—don't make me laugh. I swear I'll have an accident."

"I know what a *schnorer* is, but what's a *vantz*?"

"A bedbug," she said, giving way again.

"You know, she wouldn't be a bad looking woman, if she could stop looking so woeful."

"My mother?"

"Uh-huh. I can see your resemblance to her. Well, don't look so horrified—I'm not insulting you," he said, carefully edging her away from the glassware.

"Oh, don't worry, I won't throw anything. I am just amazed you could say that." She hesitated a moment. "Still, you know, I remember when I was little, I used to think she was pretty."

"I'm sure she was. Oh, maybe she wasn't the dish you are, but you got your looks from someone."

Beth smiled. Clever, of him, she thought. He knows I melt when he calls me a dish.

"She might even be something of the knockout Frima's mom is, if she were happier." He smiled winningly as Hannah came waltzing up to them.

"Vincent, my dear!" Hannah exclaimed in a lah-di-dah voice. "I'd dance with you again, if I weren't so pooped. People are beginning to say their goodbyes, and I can't say I'm sorry. It's been a long day. I believe I could use a drink."

"I'll mix it for you myself," said Vinny. "You look like a lady who'd enjoy an old fashioned?"

"Wonderful."

"This guy is at his most charming when he's bartending," Beth confided. "Also, he packs a wallop when he makes a drink, let me tell you. By the way, you want me to stop the music? That's usually a signal that it's time to depart."

"Perfect."

Vinny came back, drinks in hand. "I made one for you also, Bethie. Why don't you two ladies take a load off? The place is beginning to empty. No, I won't join you just yet. I see Leon beckoning." He left them, and they sat not speaking, enjoying the almost unnatural quiet that marks the end of a successful celebration.

"You should be so proud of yourself," Beth murmured.

"And you, too, my dear. This whole shebang can't have been easy for you."

They sipped their drinks in satisfied silence for the next few minutes, waving a hand languidly at departing guests until they saw the two men coming toward them. Leon was white-faced, as if he'd had a shock. Vinny was grim and tight-jawed.

Hannah sat up alarmed. "What is it? Why do you look like that? An accident? Frima and Jack!"

Leon spoke gently. "No, nothing to do with the kids. But something very sad, very disturbing has happened. Judith Ginsberg is in the hospital." He hesitated for a moment. "They don't think she'll live."

"Is she so sick?" Beth asked. "Moe said she had to be in the city. He didn't seem worried, though." Her voice trailed off as she looked at Vinny's face.

He took her hands in both of his. "Judith was shot," he said carefully into the silence. "In the back of the head. Just as she left the station on the way home. We don't know anything more, except it was someone with a rifle in a car."

Hannah, shocked into silence, looked like she might faint, and Leon edged her gently back into her seat. "I'm going to stay with Hannah tonight," Leon said. "Vinny, here are my keys. You can stay at my place. Moe will want to be at the hospital, I know. You kids make yourselves at home there. We'll see you back here in the morning." Leon paused for a moment. "I'm so glad you're here. Moe will be also."

He sighed. "I need to tell him now. No need to tell anyone else tonight. They might as well get a good night's sleep."

"I'll drive Moe to the hospital and come back for Beth later," Vinny said. "If you stay here with Hannah while other folks are still here, it will seem more normal."

"I'm going with you," Beth announced. "Don't argue with me, Vinny. I'm going! I'll sit with him in the backseat. He'll need me there. You just drive!"

Vinny didn't argue; one look at Moe was enough. Moe's face seemed drained of blood. He suddenly looked like an old man, carved in stone, except that he leaned on Leon's arm. In the car he sat silent and bolt upright in the back seat, but he allowed Beth to hold his hand and returned the gentle pressure on hers until they reached the hospital.

Beth had no sense of where they were, what medical facility they had come to, only that she felt a fierce protectiveness toward Moe. As if she were his strong healthy daughter who loved him. She must not lose him. And Judith? Ah, God! Would she lose her? She was sweating suddenly, and she stepped out of the waiting room into the outdoor chill. Her head was crowded with thoughts. Here she was with three people of such importance to her, and yet she hadn't known of their existence before last summer. Three people who loved, protected, and guided her, who freed her in ways she'd never experienced from her own blood. They were the Catskill people, as she thought of them. As were Hannah and Frima. Her own folks and Jack were not. It didn't matter that some of them lived in the city. It was a frame of mind or maybe soul. A year ago, she'd had silly fantasies of what might happen to her at a mountain resort. She couldn't have imagined how vital were the attachments she would make. If she ever ran into that lying Lillian, she would thank her for conning her into taking that job at the Alpine. She was suddenly very tired, and she dozed in the waiting room until Vinny came in to drive her back to Leon's.

"It's after midnight, and it doesn't look good. Moe refuses to leave Judith. He wants to be alone with her for a while—until his sons get here. They're flying in from California. He insisted on me taking you home, which is probably an excellent idea. I need to stay awake on the road. Talk to me, Bethie, but not about this."

No, not about this—nothing about loss for now. But it was easy to talk with Vinny. He liked to teach her things, and at the moment this was a useful and very comforting trait.

"You know, Vinny, I came up here last June knowing pretty much nothing about this whole area. My folks would never even think of coming up here ordinarily. It's even strange seeing them here now for the wedding. A vacation to them is maybe a few days with cousins in Rockaway or Sheepshead Bay—all they can afford. When I was growing up I'd hear people talk about spending two weeks in the mountains, and I had a cockamamie vision of—I don't know—snow-capped peaks, craggy wilderness."

"Your boss, Max, named his spread The Alpine Song, after all." Vinny smiled. "Maybe he had the same kind of vision."

"Uh-huh. I always suspected that Max had some romance tucked away under his obsession about saving on his gas and electric bills. But it's not just Max. It's Moe and Judith; it's Frima's grandfather, Jake Eisner. How did they get here and why? I remember Moe told me that what he knew about farming would fit on a postage stamp. Yet they are here with Max and the others, poor immigrant Jews from Eastern Europe spread over a rural area already inhabited by unwelcoming gentiles. I mean they didn't originally come here to be hotelkeepers— why would they? How could they afford it?"

"Probably a number of things come into play. From what Moe tells me, some prosperous Jews—businessmen and bankers here and in Europe—acquired these tracts of not very valuable land, to be distributed among their less fortunate brothers from Poland and Russia who were being murdered in the pogroms at the turn of the century.

As I understand it, the people who came before them were mostly poor Irish immigrants who labored for the tanneries that were a main industry and cut down the hemlocks that fueled the works. To eke out a subsistence living, they had farm plots on this same stony land, where they could keep a pig, a milk cow, maybe a few chickens. Have you ever been near a tannery, by the way? The stench can be terrific. No place for a resort community. Evidently, when the tanneries closed, their workers left, and here were these small plots of land available for the next crop of hopeful immigrants who wanted to farm. They became egg farmers mostly—you don't need huge rich acreage for chickens—a dairy cow or two, a farm horse, a vegetable plot—you might be able to make it, especially if you could rent out rooms boardinghouse style during the summers. Without heavy industry here, this whole area could be a breath of fresh air for paying summer guests, especially your—what do you say—*landtsmen* who are laboring in sweat shops and factories in the city. And, of course, there were no Cossacks. Some hostile gentiles, but that's not quite the same thing. There's a similar egg farming community north of San Francisco, though I never thought much about it when I was living on the coast. Maybe these settlements are in other areas of the country also. At any rate, what started as summer boardinghouses to keep the farms alive expanded to hotel keeping. These folks worked their heads off and still do to keep going. They are a very cooperative community, you may have noticed."

"What I notice is that everyone seems to know everyone else, though I imagine it's more than so-called small-town friendliness—if there is such a thing. I don't know anything about small towns. Here, it seems there's a lot behind the scenes that I'll never see, but that I sense. Nothing bad, you understand, just a lot of quiet activity."

"Sometimes, not so quiet. Full of arguments, though generally peaceful. And Moe has a whole lot to do with it. Do you know what these farmer-hotelkeepers fear more than anything?"

"No one coming here."

"Even more than that is fire. That's the big one, whether from nature or arson, so insurance is of terrific importance. You can imagine how much the big insurers want to take on the risks of these precarious little dreams people have. Moe Ginsburg, the guy who is everywhere, was one of the primary movers in organizing the insurance cooperative that kept these places going. And one thing leads to another. It's work together, help each other, or go under. What I admire is that no one is excluded. It's Jews, the latecomers, who did this, but anyone of goodwill is welcome. That's the way to build community, a real social order. The center of all this has been Woodridge, but it's bound to spread."

"Just up your alley." Bess stroked his face gently with her fist.

"Well, I think that attitude springs from the same source, but I'm not giving you a lecture—I know how you love that. And, of course, I'm more of a waterfront and seaman-type guy."

"Whatever you are, you're my type," she answered.

Leon called before they were out of bed in the morning. He and Hannah and her father-in-law, Jake Eisner, were at the hospital, along with many other well-wishers. Judith was gone. Moe was with her, though she never awakened.

"How is he?" Vinny asked.

"Dazed. Numb, I think. Jake wants to stay with him until his sons get here in the early afternoon. Moe and Jake are long-time friends, you know; they sojourned up here at the same time." Leon sighed. "Anyway, why don't you and Beth come over to the hotel for breakfast and we'll figure things out. We need to get Jack's folks home. If it weren't for the father of the groom, they could go with you two. And since Hannah simply refuses to interrupt the honeymoon weekend by enlisting Jack, I guess I'll drive them in."

Beth and Vinny did not stay for the immediate funeral required by Jewish tradition, but they returned for a private memorial service some weeks later. Everyone Beth had met in the Catskills was there except, happily, most of the paying guests. Even her old boss, Max, showed up, though Beth was no longer surprised by this after the mini-history lesson Vinny had provided. The tributes were moving and sincere, but the question on every mind was, who had murdered Judith? Who would want to? A man with a rifle in a nondescript black car; that was all anyone knew and all they could get from the police. No license plate, no suspects, seemingly no motive. Vinny thought this murder—this assassination—would be buried in a back file in no time flat.

Beth was aghast. "No investigation, no motive? No justice? Why, it's like a lynching!"

He expelled a big breath. "If the police don't have a motive in mind, no one who knew and respected Judith is about to suggest one. We all assume the murderer must have been the father, maybe a husband or brother, of a woman, or girl, who came to Judith in trouble. For all we know, Judith may have escorted her into the city to consult with a doctor willing to help out. There are such courageous souls who will do procedures safely and cheaply out of conscience, and Judith knew them. The only decent response possible is for someone to carry on the work she was devoted to." Vinny was silent for a moment. "Now that some bastard has made very clear how dangerous this is, I don't know who that will be. But someone will, in time."

CHAPTER 17

Barely two weeks after the wedding, Frima was kneeling in front of the toilet bowl for the second morning in a row. Yesterday, it could have been an upset stomach, but today again? She'd missed a period, but that wasn't all that unusual, and she'd dismissed it as wedding nerves. How about you put two and two together, genius? A baby! She was so flabbergasted she wasn't sure how she felt. Of course, she wanted children, and she knew Jack did. From what she had seen last summer, he was great with kids. But so soon? Should she tell anyone? No, it was too early. Not until you're sure. They say you couldn't be sure for the first month or so. She'd better wait a few days to see if things went back to normal.

Normal? Now just what was that? Not this emotional seesaw. On one side was panic: oh, God, we can't afford this, and I can't even take care of myself, let alone a baby, and Jack is working his head off for Mama and studying for his degree, and I don't do anything but a little typing for him or Mama and tinkle on the piano and cook and clean, and my husband barely has a moment for me until his exams are over in June. On the other side was this secret and protective elation about what might be happening inside her. Was she growing something beautiful? Of course, she or he will be beautiful with Jack and Frima as parents. She saw the three of them—such a good-looking proud couple with their beautiful bundle of joy. All the oohs and ahs, as they paraded on the Bronx avenues or on the lawns of Ellenville Isn't it amazing what I've . . . we've . . . done? There was no such thing as normal anymore.

Nevertheless, well before her test results came back, Frima had shed her initial dismay and had so settled the issue with herself that she knew she'd be disappointed if she weren't pregnant. After all, what could be more special, more affirming of the love between husband and wife? Starting a family—this was what marriage was all about, wasn't it? And the timing? Was it so bad? Not at all.

"Healthy as a horse," the doctor informed her, "the picture of a young expectant mother, though you could afford to gain a few pounds. You can start eating for two—I'll tell you when to stop." It was standard patter but very reassuring to Frima. Everyone will be proud of me, and I'll be everyone's pampered darling, she thought, secretly delighted.

"And when will the baby be born?"

"First week in November, though it may be a little later. First babies sometimes are."

Frima nodded and smiled. I don't suppose you could make that January, she thought, but said nothing. That's between me and the baby. And now for Jack. She'd wait until they were in bed, she decided. She already knew it was there that she would have the most influence.

"You can forget those for a while," she said, when she saw Jack fumbling in the bedside drawer. "We won't need them." She smiled at his quizzical look, and said gently, "I'm already pregnant, you see."

A brief but excruciating silence followed while Jack erased dismay from his face and substituted a tentative smile.

"How? When?"

"You know how. When, I couldn't say exactly. You're not unhappy are you?" (Oh, come on, Frima, how did you feel when you first suspected this?)

"Just give me a minute, honey. This is quite a surprise. I thought we'd wait a while."

"So did I, but—"

"But it looks like our kid can't wait to be born," he said grinning at her. "I admire his determination."

"It may be a *her*, you know."

"Determined, like her mother, which is okay with me."

She was keenly relieved and felt a burst of love for him. He was taking it like a man. Why did she ever think he wouldn't?

They told only Mama; the rest of them could wait.

"It's maybe a little early, but I don't argue with this kind of joy, whenever it comes."

"We were kind of surprised ourselves," Frima admitted.

"Oh, I wasn't," said Mama. "And it all works out very well, in fact. The baby can have my room. When I baby-sit, I can sleep on the couch."

"What are you talking about? This is your place. We are not going to turn you out of your own home."

"You're not. It's not only work that brings me back to the hotel so often. I have an intended, you know, and we're planning to make it official pretty soon now."

"Leon?" Frima asked carefully.

"Who else?"

"Well, I knew you were friends, but—I must be an idiot—I mean, I really didn't pay too much attention. Too wrapped up in my own life, I guess."

"We were not particularly interested in your noticing. The second time around for both of us should be a quiet event. Besides, I didn't want to steal your thunder."

Oh, really? Frima was skeptical of her mother's modesty, but good humouredly so. She felt an accord with her mother that had too often been missing in this crazy year.

She waited another two weeks before saying anything to Beth. It was all very well to tell herself that it was wise not to tell people too soon. But Beth wasn't exactly people; she was her best friend and now, of course, sister-in-law. The thing was, she felt uncomfortable giving her this news. All that talk they used to have about doing creative, original things with their brains, talents. Marriage and children could wait, blah, blah, blah. What of all that? How much time had she spent at the piano since the advent of Jack? Why, she'd barely listened to any serious music. And with a baby? Was she kidding? Beth was braver and more true to her art than she, Frima, would ever be.

Then there was her own hoity-toity response to Beth's urgings about birth control. She had actually felt a little superior because Jack was taking care of things, taking care of her, and she was happy to let him do so. That way their sexual life could be romantic, spontaneous. She could tell herself she was swept off her feet. She didn't have to worry about any of the un-fastidious, unromantic details of lovemaking, like Beth did. And so she was pregnant, and Beth was not. Beth was out there chasing her dreams.

Oh, Frima was happy she was pregnant. She really couldn't help it. She was eager for her still-flat belly to grow and announce her achievement to the world. But when she thought of Beth, there was this nagging guilt that she, Frima, would be a disappointment to her, someone who had capitulated too soon. She saw with a momentary clarity that, being pregnant, she didn't have to put her talents, her ambitions, to a test. She could relax into the sheltering arms of her immediate family, let nature take its course, and put her other dreams on the back burner.

Okay, enough stalling. She picked up the phone and called Beth.

"Are you sitting down? Congratulations, you're going to be an aunt."

"What are you talking about? Who? Jack?"

"Who else, you pinhead?"

"Of course, sorry, but I'm barely used to your being a married lady, yet. And you're happy about this, right? I can hear it in your voice."

"I am. I'm very excited."

"Well, then, I'm happy too. Wow, Aunt Bethie, I like the sound of that. And Jack?"

"Ready to hand out cigars, like a proud papa!"

"Now, that I'd like to see. He is one appealing guy when he's feeling good, isn't he?"

An odd thing to say, Frima thought, but nothing she could argue about.

"Uh-huh. And you can tell Vinny."

"Will do—he'll be very happy for you, I know. He's not exactly an uncle, but he'll act like one, if he's allowed to."

"Absolutely, and any time," Frima said heartily. She'd handle Jack if there were problems.

"The grandmothers, I take it, are thrilled, which is all to the good. My mother, she'll be so wrapped up in her grandchild it'll take the pressure off me to reproduce. The grandfather? Well, too bad he doesn't know what joy means."

"I suspect that's true, but the great-grandfather is delighted; never thought he'd live to see the day—you get the picture."

"So, when's the happy arrival?"

"Oh, around December." Frima knew her tone was vague, a little too casual.

"Not quite sure, are you?" Beth said good-naturedly.

Frima, feeling relaxed again, didn't bother to respond. "So how's with you?"

—

They were in the country again, back at Eisner's and preparing for the season. Mama and Jack were frantic with responsibilities, while Frima felt far less so. Mama stopped rushing in and out of her office to watch Frima as she walked up the steps to the porch.

"Now look at you! You have that proud, yet careful, walk of a woman expecting, like you're carrying something oh so precious and fragile—which you are. I love to see it. Why, you're positively blooming. Not the least pale and tired. And didn't I say it would get better?" Mama smiled. She seemed to be smiling all the time these days.

Frima smiled back. Gone were those first months when it was an effort to get herself out of a bathrobe she was so tired; and the nausea, the morning sickness made her think the cool rims of the sink or toilet were the only places she could lay her head. Now it had all passed, and in the middle months of her pregnancy, she was filled with a sense of well-being and self-importance, more like a shared self-importance really: she and the baby. She savored the attention and smiles she received up here at the hotel where she was the only pregnant woman. Not only Jack but the hotel guests and staff were tender and solicitous. Full of advice, comfort, and happy-ever-after stories. Now she lay back on the long cushioned porch swing, listening to the music on the radio in Mama's office. It came through the window, just loud enough for her to hear every note if she concentrated. The baby kicked energetically. "Do you hear that, baby? That's Beethoven, one of his early string quartets. Isn't he wonderful? Listen carefully to this last movement." She talked a lot to her baby these days, and took any opportunity she could to expose her unborn child to this special world she, herself, loved. There might be something, after all, to prenatal influences.

Mama came out to the porch and joined Frima on the swing, lifting her daughter's feet into her own lap to make room. She gently massaged Frima's feet as she spoke. "Frima, darling, you know we talked about you and Jack taking over the apartment in the Bronx when the baby comes. Well, maybe you can move in a little earlier. I've decided to stay up here after the season. I'm sending you and Jack home with the car, so you can easily get back and forth from here to the Bronx. A young couple needs some privacy. So now that you're feeling good, I'll stay up here with Grandpa, and with Leon, of course."

"Are you going to get married here?"

"Well, yes, eventually. We thought early spring. We're in no hurry—after all I'm not pregnant."

"And you're hinting not so subtly that I had to get married in a hurry?"

"Darling, you started throwing up only a few days after you were married, and it's a little soon to be feeling all that kicking. But don't worry. Nobody's counting. By the beginning of November I'll be ready to come down and help you when the baby comes."

"December, you mean."

"November. I'll wager you an ice cream soda."

"At Krum's, on the Grand Concourse?"

"It's a bet," said Mama.

CHAPTER 18

"A Broadway for me," Mama said, wasting no time. "That's coffee ice cream and chocolate soda, isn't it?"

"Yes, ma'am," the waiter replied. "And for the young lady?"

"The same—no, make it vanilla ice cream for me."

"Double scoops and extra whipped cream, please," Mama added. "And oh—I almost forgot—the check goes to the little mother. I mean, the young lady."

Frima grinned. "Go on and rub it in a little more."

"Ah, well, it isn't often a mother is proved right these days. Well, we might as well enjoy these goodies while we can. If we get into this war, who knows? Rich cream will probably be hard to come by."

They were silent for a moment, the almost obligatory silence that followed mention of the looming war.

"Of course, I'm surprised that a daughter of mine would choose vanilla when there is coffee or chocolate available. So bland!"

"Vanilla is the choice of the discerning palate," Frima answered, burlesquing an upper class accent. "Don't you know, Mother, that professional ice cream tasters always choose vanilla to determine quality. Now, you want to talk about bland? I'll tell you what's bland—that music someone is listening to on the radio."

Krum's was quiet this early on a Sunday afternoon, its seemingly endless soda fountains and seductive display counters relatively empty, and they could hear a sentimental foxtrot wafting from the tinny radio in the back rooms, hidden from the customers. The waiter, bringing their sodas had overheard them.

" Does the music bother you? I can ask them to turn it off."

"No, it's fine, thank you," mother and daughter answered almost as one. They were old hands. They knew how important a little entertainment was to kitchen workers.

"'Sammy Kaye's Sunday Serenade,'" said Frima with a little smile. "My mother-in-law likes to listen to it. She's probably listening right now, while the baby is sleeping. What's that crooner singing? 'The Shrine of Saint Cecelia?' *Oy vey*, she'll love that!"

"Better Sarah should listen to Danny Kaye."

"I thought you didn't like Borscht Belt comedians."

"Not true, I like anyone with talent. I just don't want to hire any of them. But on second thought, he's such a fast talker, I don't know if Sarah would understand his patter. Perhaps it's better if she listens to 'Soothing music for a Sunday afternoon.' That's what Sammy himself says, so let's just blend him into this soda shop atmosphere."

They sipped their sodas slowly, stirring the ice cream around to make it last, and slipping into a comfortable silence. Frima sat back savoring the quiet of the place. It must be around two, she thought. All the crowds at the Loew's Paradise for the matinee will come rushing through those doors in a couple of hours and the place will be jammed far into the evening. She smiled, thinking of the Loew's Paradise, the Grand Concourse's answer to the downtown movie palaces. Its most celebrated feature was a high-domed ceiling displaying a firmament with blinking stars and gently moving gauzy clouds. Very romantic. The ultimate Saturday night date for the Bronx teenager was a double feature at the Paradise and an ice cream soda at Krum's. But Frima hadn't known any boys rich enough to treat a girl to such luxuries. Still, it was the ultimate treat for kids, too, a reward for good report cards or to celebrate birthdays. How much fun it would be if she and Mama could just go across the street and catch a double feature at the Paradise, as if she were a little girl again. But she had her own little girl now—Lena, beautiful and demanding—and she couldn't possibly leave Sarah with the baby that long.

Lena. A lovely name. It had just popped into her head, and she knew instantly it was right. The baby was named for Papa. Jack and Frima had agreed that if it were a girl it would be Frima's choice, Jack's choice if it were a boy. Papa's name, Lou, brought to mind Louisa. Frima was partial to feminine names ending in *a*, but it also conjured up Louisa May Alcott, which was unfortunate. Not that Frima hadn't loved her books, but she envisioned the writer as lean, dark, somewhat homely, and constricted by her life in the last century. Frima's baby had been beautiful from the start. Everyone said so, of course, but Frima could see how true this was. Yes, it was a musical name, Lena, lilting, whimsical. So fitting for this peaches-and-cream beauty. Her skin was neither rashy nor irritated, her head a pretty shape, and she was long and filled out (not like some of those wrinkled monkeys). Supposedly this was because Frima had an unusually fast and easy labor for a first-time mother. Or so they told her; she hadn't been aware of much at the time. The baby had practically popped out as if she couldn't wait to get out of there, yelling her head off to let everybody know about it. Frima was in total agreement with her. Big, beautiful, and brash, this child would prove to anyone who bothered to think about it that she was full term.

Then came the days in the hospital, with nurses bringing the baby to her at exact intervals, instructing her about bottles and formula, lecturing about "regular schedules for baby," and sterilizing practically everything. All those rules and regulations, the timing of everything, it all seemed positively nuts. Frima had seen calves born and raised at the farm. They nursed when they were hungry and mama cow ate placidly or gently butted the calf away when it was annoying her, and the calf didn't expire because the barn wasn't as sanitary as an operating room. Yeah, yeah, no one had to remind her that human infants weren't as developed as calves at birth and were much more fragile and precious. But still, it was food for thought. Secret thought. She had thought about nursing, but she found no encouragement for this at the hospital—quite the opposite—so she was quick to give it up and accept without protest the advice of the medical profession and government pamphlets.

Both she and Jack were baby-obsessed, naturally, and were weary from interrupted sleep. Every too-early morning was greeted by schedules tacked up on the kitchen walls, bottle sterilizers on the stove. The apartment always seemed steamy and too warm, even though Mama had given them a diaper service, thank God. Jack, who had not had the privilege of almost endless prenatal advice from the ladies in the neighborhood and postnatal lectures from hospital personnel, was more nervous and over-cautious than Frima, and very likely just as tired. It wasn't easy trying to study and work with an infant in the house. For once, both new parents were truly glad to have Sarah so close by.

"These hotsy-totsy rules and schedules—*meshugge!*" said Sarah. Mama, more subtle, simply nodded and raised her eyebrows.

Grateful as she was for the help, these exchanges made Frima cross. It was irritating to have her own rebellious thoughts so openly expressed. She, who needed to do everything science and the medical profession advised in these critical first weeks. Besides, Jack, the science lover, would have been far too uncomfortable with anything else.

And then there was this secret Frima had: she knew in her heart that she would never qualify as mother of the year. Oh, she would cherish and defend her child to the death, all right, but that seemed to have more to do with biology than conscious thought or feeling. Some of the time she was positively entranced with her baby; when Lena slept, or even more so when she was full and content, busy flailing her arms and legs around and producing sweet little noises for her own purposes and amusement, or looking ridiculously critical and deep in thought when she focused on Frima's face. But there were other times when the infant was a demanding little tyrant that sucked in formula with the sole purpose of producing pee and poop from the other end. And she was barely five weeks old. How long would Frima have to be imprisoned by the four Ps as she thought of them: pee, poop, park, and playground? The fifth P was, of course, the piano, and had nothing to do with imprisonment. It was her release, but it was reduced now to a half hour, if she were lucky, between the demands of her baby and her overworked student husband.

"Now what is all this hubbub?" Mama broke into Frima's thoughts. They both looked around, startled by a roar from the back of the place and seeing waiters, soda jerks, and customers rushing toward the sound of the radio. The waiter hurried to their table.

"Did you hear? The Japs have bombed Pearl Harbor!"

"Pearl—what? Where?"

"I don't know—somewhere in the Pacific. We have a fleet there, or something."

CHAPTER 19

Frima sat at the window, eagerly awaiting Beth's appearance. Just how eager she was for her company made her feel a little pathetic. If Beth were with her, taking Lena to the park for her daily outing would not be the lonely and boring experience it had become. Not quite the vision she'd conjured up during pregnancy: Jack and she and the baby makes three, parading around and modestly smiling at the coos of admiration for their picture-perfect little family. She hadn't anticipated the feelings of isolation and boredom. There were other young mothers in the park, of course, but Frima didn't want to talk about babies and children. She could do that at home, thank you very much. So here she was not two months after Pearl Harbor, and her life in this corner of the world had not changed.

Well, yes, there was relief, of course. Relief from the first panic that Jack would be called up. He had registered with the draft this past summer, as had all men over twenty-one, and God knows he was able in mind and body—even high-minded and patriotic—but evidently the draft board wasn't calling up fathers of young children. Not yet, anyway, and besides there was serious talk of his being stationed as a technician at the Bronx VA when he graduated in June. So she had reason to hope he would be in the army without the threat of bullets and bombs (just the havoc of their aftermath). Evidently he had impressed one of his chemistry professors who had influence. So, what else is new? She thought of her husband's talents with pride and a little fortifying irony mixed in. If he weren't Jewish and could shed the Bronx accent, Jack could be elected president. Certainly mayor—look at Fiorello La Guardia. She thought with affection of the rotund, clever "Little Flower," who had some Jewish roots as well as Italian, and could charm his way out of a prison, speaking Yiddish, if necessary. And Jack had the added advantage of good looks. Luckily, her husband's ambitions ran toward science. Well, if he was awarded with this safe VA position, Mama would have to do without him. She'd have to rely on Leon and on her daughter. This was actually a pleasing prospect, spending the summer in the country with the baby. Frima was never bored there, and Jack would surely get some days off. But there were these months to get through. Ah! And here was her colorful sister-in-law to help her.

Beth stood at the door, her cheeks becomingly rosy from the cold, oozing vitality. Hugging Frima, she swiveled her head around. "Jack here?"

"Off to the library."

"My mother?"

"Playing cards with the ladies—you're safe." Frima grinned.

"And the papoose?"

"Fat and happy and waiting for you to admire her."

Beth leaned over the crib to gaze at her little niece who was cooing to herself. "Do you know, Lena, that I'm you're Aunt Beth, you beautiful creature? Isn't that remarkable?"

The baby peered at her calmly, a little speculatively.

"You're wondering, who is this one and what's in it for me?" Beth said softly. The two women laughed and the infant responded with a toothless grin.

"Can I pick her up?"

"Sure."

Lena, fixated on Beth's dangling earrings, which were just out of her reach, seemed content in Beth's arms, so she held her until they arrived at the front door of the building. Beth laid the baby in the carriage to be bundled against the cold, while Lena wailed at being put down.

"You know, in the Soviet Union they swaddle infants. It makes them feel secure, or something," Beth commented.

"Tell me you're not recommending this. What do they do when they have a diaper full? Unroll them?" Frima giggled at the image. "And how did you get to be such an expert on Russian baby-rearing?"

"Not me. Vinny. He's interested in all things Soviet these days. Besides he really loves children." A big sigh followed.

"And you don't. Is that what you're saying?"

"I like them. This one I could love, but she's not mine. That's the crucial thing. I don't want—I can't imagine—having any of my own. I know Vinny wants marriage, children, the whole shooting match, but I'm too selfish. Or infantile, I guess."

"Sometimes, Bethie, it's hard for me to believe that you learned what you know about sex and babies sitting at the knee of Judith Ginsberg, God bless her. I wonder what she'd say to you."

"I don't know," Beth responded in a barely audible voice.

Frima, seeing her close to tears, changed her tone. "Come on, let's walk a little further, where we can talk, or have a good cry, maybe. That's always helpful." She put her arm around Beth and guided her to a park bench somewhat isolated from the others. After a silence of some moments, Frima began to talk slowly, tentatively.

"You know—of course you do—that Lena was an accident? It seems ridiculous to say that now, for how could this miraculous creation be any such thing? But, of course, we should have been more careful. It would have been wiser to wait a few years. The thing is, though, Lena wasn't a mistake. And that's crucial. I always assumed I'd have children. I never really thought about not having children, and from what I could see, Jack was good with them. I loved to see him interact with the kids at the hotel. It seemed such a happy sign for the future. The sadness, the tragedy, is having a child when you don't want one or can't care for it—that's what Judith would tell you, I'm certain of that. She would fix her eyes on you. You, the essential one. You shouldn't have children because your husband or boyfriend or king or church wants you to, or because you can't help it. I'm sure half the children in the world are born into those circumstances, unfortunately. But mothering is too important to be left to chance."

"Wow! I'm really impressed. You could write a treatise."

"I've had a lot of time in the last year to think about all of this."

"Well, anyway, I feel better talking to you. I think Lena is pretty lucky to have such a good mother."

"Hah! That's what you think! What's true is I was lucky to have such a good mother."

Beth stood up, restless. "This bench is cold. Can we walk a little?"

They pushed the carriage up one of the cobblestoned paths.

"Vinny signed up with the Merchant Marines," Beth said quietly.

"Really? But why? He does such important work here, doesn't he?"

"He feels that he has to get into this war, and he doesn't want to wait until he's drafted. He grew up on the docks of San Francisco, and he has so many buddies in the Maritime Union. It makes sense for him to be on a ship. Besides the Merchant Marines are integrated racially— the regular military forces aren't, you know—and that's a very important issue to Vinny." Beth interrupted herself with a big sigh. "Vinny is a very principled guy."

"A little trouble in paradise?" Frima asked gently.

"More like we're not in it anymore, but we're still together. We still love each other, but I guess I just don't think of him so much as my teacher these days. I don't really mind Vinny's positions or the theoretical basis for them—I've even gotten to like old Harry Bridges, his hero, though I've never met the guy. And I really want most of the things Vinny wants. It's just that I'm more naturally irreverent than he is, though he's the big-time radical. You know, he was brought up as a Catholic, of course, and though he has rejected his religion, there's a certain kind of . . . I don't know . . . need for rules. Thing is, he's so good-natured you wouldn't really notice it."

"Maybe it's that opposites attract? You're the spontaneous, impulsive one. That's the first thing that attracted him, wasn't it?"

"My God, you're all perceptions today, aren't you? You're right." Beth hesitated a few moments. "There's one thing that really bothers me, though. And I'm only telling you because you're the one person I know who would understand."

"Bethie, there's no one here. You don't have to whisper."

"He doesn't approve of my work—my personal painting—the creative stuff. He doesn't understand it, and he thinks that everyone should be able to see the message in art."

"What has he said about it?"

"Nothing, really. Just an expression, a click of the tongue. Maybe a question like, 'Will anyone understand what you're saying?'"

"You know, Beth, I don't always understand your work either," Frima said carefully. "But I like it."

"Okay, so you can't always articulate what it's about, but you don't disapprove. That's a big difference. Vinny tries to hide his disapproval, but it is there."

"If it's any comfort to you, Jack doesn't particularly like classical music. He doesn't understand what it means to me."

"But he approves of it, doesn't he?"

"I guess so, I don't really know. Funny, both of us loving and attached to men who don't understand a big part of us."

"Not so funny, I'm afraid." Beth's voice quavered. "You know, I switched my work hours so I could be away from Vinny more. So I could be alone, to paint for myself, while he was out working. And now he's joined the Merchant Marines. I feel terrible. I don't want him to go. He'll be away from me so much. And those ships are so danger-ous—they can be torpedoed just like the Navy ones. I'm afraid maybe he enlisted to get away from me, or because he knew I wanted to be away from him sometimes. Because time alone, free time, is like a breath of fresh air. I feel so ungrateful. Like a selfish child who takes and takes and doesn't care enough, and really wants him only for bed and breakfast. I swear, sometimes I think I'm a disloyal worm."

Frima put the brake on the carriage and put her arm around her friend. "Bethie, please. You're no such thing! Will you please be a little easier on yourself? It seems to me perfectly natural to feel the way you do. I'm afraid conflict, mixed feelings are part of the whole relation-ship deal."

"Have you ever felt anything like this about Jack?"

"Well, I've been pretty angry with him sometimes, but nothing last-ing. Maybe because the baby makes him super important to me. Not to say that I won't feel like putting a pillow over his face sometime or other. I mean, what you're describing doesn't shock me in the least. It seems inevitable when you're living together."

After a few minutes of quiet, Beth was calmer. She could turn to Frima and ask with genuine interest, "So tell me, how are things with the new father? He was so eager to go out and fight. What now?"

"Well, he's crazy about Lena, which is great to see. He caught her very first smile. He thinks it was meant entirely for him, silly man. And as for the rest of the world, he knows the war can wait for him. He's likely to enter the army as a medic or lab technician right here at the Bronx VA, did I tell you? With any luck that's where he'll be sta-tioned, and Jack seems to be a lucky guy. To tell you the truth, I don't think it's so important to him to personally fight the Japs. Nazis, that's another story. But we're not there yet, and when we are, well, we'll see. And don't ask me how I feel about that. I haven't the faintest idea."

"Men! Can't live with them, can't live without them," Beth said airily, her spirits beginning to lift.

Frima suddenly gave a cackle of laughter. "You remember those fairy tales where the prince charming turns into a swan at midnight and flies away until the next night of love? Wouldn't it be great to have a prince charming who stays beautiful and energetic until about one a.m. and then turns into a nice hot, crisp potato kugel?"

"Or a pizza!" Beth sputtered, and they simply fell over each other in stitches at their own wit.

CHAPTER 20

January 1943

A year later, the country was at war on all fronts, yet Beth felt more at peace with herself than at any time in recent memory. It was only a little heartburn from the celebration of the New Year that had kept her awake in the wee hours to usher in 1943 with a fizzy Alka-Seltzer. She gazed down at Vinny, who was snoring gently beside her. He was about halfway through a two-week leave, and he would be shipping out as soon as it was over. His body, lean and battle-ready from shipboard rations and active duty, at this moment radiated only comfort and satiation with good Italian food, wine, and love. She smiled at his peaceful expression. Here it was way after midnight, and she had no wish for him to turn into a pizza.

So what had changed? Were the personal conflicts and differences gone? Not really, she knew that. They were just pushed aside. But if their problems were eased by their forced separations, so be it. It made their time together precious. And if they were living in the moment, the moment felt good. Besides, wasn't everybody? Everyone talked about fighting for the future, but the now was also precious—at least right here in New York. What had changed? The war had changed. There wasn't any happy news coming from Europe or the Pacific, but the conflict, itself, was truly popular. It was patriotic to support the war, fight the good fight, even root for the Russians, for God's sake. Here she was, Beth Erlichman, riding lightly atop the mainstream, the majority, in her external life at least, and that was a big part of her existence. For once she didn't see herself as bucking a crowd that was all going the other way. She wasn't fighting for breath or a voice. For the bastards were now silenced or at least forced out of the limelight. Okay, maybe it was still us against them, but there were so many of us. She and Vinny could go to a double feature and see Hollywood working-class heroes with working-class accents, brave and free Jews, beautiful peasant girls singing in the fields, even a few Negroes in dignified roles. It was the rich, high-falutin' ladies and gentlemen with that hoity-toity accent of mysterious origin that you laughed at now; not the low comic gangsters or knuckleheads with the coached Brooklyn (sort of) voices.

Then there was this music, completely unknown to Beth just a few years ago. All this singing. Was there ever a movement so shaped and directed by song as the leftwing labor movement right here in New York? Maybe in churches, she guessed, though she knew practically nothing about those mysteries. But the radical movement she had jumped into while tagging after Vinny was steeped in song—special song that the more conventional population knew nothing about. If you knew all the lyrics of "This Land is Your Land" or "There Once Was a Union Maid," that was a sure sign, a secret handshake signaling your views. It was all called folk singing, and the instruments of choice were guitars, banjos, mandolins, harmonicas. The more you sounded like you were born in Appalachia or the Mississippi Delta, the better. Musicians borrowed freely from church hymns, mountain music, work songs, blues, and cowboy songs. Anything tuneful and easy for ordinary people to sing was fine. Almost all the lyrics were in plain folksy English, except the songs that came out of the struggle for the Spanish Republic; these were always treated respectfully, almost reverently. It wasn't only the Depression, but the Spanish Republican cause, Vinny had informed her, that had pushed so many students and intellectuals to the left. All of this song was called people's music. She had been surprised when Frima had examined a couple of sheet music pages Beth had shown her and identified themes from Bach and Beethoven, that had been simplified and made easier to sing. The only music that was never heard, except maybe to spoof it, was American pop—the for-profit stuff. Beth was a little sorry about that. She liked Frank Sinatra singing anything.

She and Vinny had just hours ago returned from a fundraising concert for Russian war relief, so her head was full of songs, or lyrics, anyway. The Almanac Singers were featured—no surprise there—and as usual, the audience was encouraged to join in the choruses. Vinny loved this group, and he had a pleasing baritone voice, himself. Beth had the lung volume but a very tin ear. He always urged her to sing on these occasions, because it broke him up to hear her veer way off pitch in another direction. It was funny, kind of, she had to admit.

For the concerts this year, at least, she could be comfortable with every word sung. Last night, the most popular song by far was Woody Guthrie's "Sinking of the Reuben James," about the first American convoy ship sunk by Nazi U-boats.

And now our mighty battleships will steam the bounding main
And remember the name of that good Reuben James.
Tell me, what were their names, tell me what were their names?
Did you have a friend on the good Reuben James?

Beth had heard this so often, she knew the words by heart. Some difference from the song none of the Almanacs sang anymore—not since the Nazis invaded the Soviet Union. What an about face!

Oh, Franklin Roosevelt told the people how he felt.
We damn near believed what he said.

He said "I hate war and so does Eleanor.
But we won't be safe 'till everybody's dead."

Beth would never sing this. She wouldn't dream of not admiring the Roosevelts. Where she came from, that was like saying a Hershey Bar would poison you. She knew that Vinny had been uncomfortable with isolationism, but even more so about any leftwing split, and he'd padded around the apartment in his socks muttering about unity, which wasn't much of a big fat help to Beth. The thing she realized more and more was that Vinny had no real irony in his views of a social order. Oh, he had a sense of humor, no question about that. He could be witty and penetrating about people, but about his politics he was earnest. Beth, ironic to the bone, had learned to quietly store her dry contradicting comments in that private cabinet in her mind, including the biggest irony of all: that happy unity on the left—the United Front, as Vinny spoke of it—came only at the cost of this devastating Nazi invasion of Russia, with its staggering death toll.

Well, seize the day, she said to herself. The sigh that accompanied this soon became a grin, as she thought of tomorrow morning. She sang softly to herself,

Old Paint, Old Paint, a prouder horse there ain't,
Cause my Old Paint is a horse with a union label!

She couldn't recall who was responsible for this ditty, but it was Vinny's favorite union song, not least because it wasn't all that easy to sing, and Beth invariably blew it. It had become their intimate joke on those occasions when they made love with Beth in the saddle, so to speak, like tonight. And it was particularly fitting for the next few days, for Beth would drive a horse and wagon in the streets of East Harlem for a scrap metal drive. Old Paint! She gave a snort of laughter. The first time she had driven a horse and wagon for one of these events, the horse was called Jack.

Frima hadn't even known the horse's name, but she had burst out laughing at the thought of Beth, a comically physical coward if there ever was one, driving a horse.

"Nice, Frima, very nice! I come to you petrified—you, supposedly my dear friend—and you think it's funny. And you are the only person of my acquaintance who knows anything about horses."

"Farm horses, not city horses, I'm afraid. Isn't there a fruit and vegetable wagon that comes around your neighborhood? You could consult with the driver."

"Are you finished?"

"Bethie, I'm only trying to jolly you along, a little. There won't be much traffic, will there?"

"I don't think so. They close off the streets for a while, like a block party."

"Will there be other people on the wagon with you?"

"I think they don't want too much weight on it. They need room for the stuff they're collecting, but Vinny will be there, walking next to it. And someone will lead the horse," she added, in a small voice.

"And your job?"

"Well, I'll hold the reins and wave and call out, 'Support the war effort!' You know, stuff like that."

"And look fetching and attract all the men on the street, you poor thing!"

"I wish you could be there with me, but I guess you couldn't bring the baby."

"Right. Your mother, to say nothing of your brother, would have apoplexy. And I need them around, you see, because I too am supporting the war effort. I'm taking a course with the Red Cross—first aid, and so on. I pray I never have need for any of these skills, but I want to do this. Jack and your mama are both very proud of me, to say nothing of my own mama, and that's nice. Lena doesn't seem to care, one way or the other. So far, so good, my dear. Now wear something that shows off your charms, knock 'em dead, and ask Vinny to send me a snapshot."

The new cart horse was named Sea Biscuit, God help us. But this second time in the driver's seat, Beth felt like a pro. She sat in her bright red beret and scarf (wonderful how red showed off her vivid coloring), looking "dishy," as Vinny said, while he hopped around snapping pictures. Too bad they couldn't show color. Later she sat with him at a table with a few of their friends at his favorite Italian place on Thompson Street, toasting the successful drive and waiting for their spaghetti with white clam sauce. Beth had loved this from the first time she tasted it. With Vinny beside her, she could probably even learn to like oysters.

This restaurant reminded her of the one in the country where she'd had her first date with him. No live music and no steaks, certainly, in wartime, but the warm, easy atmosphere was the same. She felt as gleeful and proud as in those carefree summer days before the war. Beth tried to scold herself about her ease, her happiness, when half the world was dying. She was conscientious about blackouts and rationing, and she saved scrap metal, rubber bands, meat fat. She obeyed all the restrictions of the home front without complaint. But she remained buoyant, confident of her safety, optimistic. She was not born to this attitude, she told herself. A lack of angst was alien in her family. But in truth she had not experienced any personal loss. Her brother, now serving as an army medic at the Bronx VA, would very likely do his part for the war effort bomb-free and close to his family. Her guy had so far spent months training on Staten Island and had shipped out to the Caribbean and to the West Coast. Warm waters, close to home. He was back on duty in a few days. Maybe he would ship out to the North Atlantic, but she could not worry about this as she had in the past. They were a lucky couple, they'd constructed a good life for themselves: this was his, this was hers, this they shared. Beth clinked her glass against Vinny's. "Oh, we are a lucky girl and boy—here's to us!"

—

Beth had walked home from work this Saturday afternoon, a long but leisurely stroll in the fresh chill air. She had the stretch of weekend before her, with no obligations except to herself. Vinny was now back on duty, this time indeed somewhere in the North Atlantic. Sometimes fear about this plucked at her sleeve, but not today. All this time to herself! She kicked off her shoes and sank into an easy chair staring at the wall. If it were stripped clean of shelves, mirrors, and her own two soft watercolors hanging there, what a canvas that wall would make. She could paint something huge. Like "Guernica." Now that was a crazy thought. Whenever she got over to the Modern, she would stare at the painting, unable to move away from it. She and everyone else. Sometimes she resented Picasso for his power to make her confront the horror, the pity of that bombing. Well, she certainly was no Picasso, nor did she want to imitate him. What would she do with a canvas as big as a wall? She had no ambitions to be a muralist—she didn't want to do a big stolid monument that was determined to lecture or shout at you forever. Still, wouldn't it be nice if there were such a thing as a completely erasable wall. She could throw colors on it any way she saw them—clashing, smashing colors, textures, light and shadow—pow! Then she could erase it before anyone saw it. Coward! She scolded herself. Could you see Picasso or Rivera or that strange Frida Kahlo doing any such thing? No! They'd confront the world with their truths—or even their delusions.

So what had happened to her carefree afternoon of creating art for art's sake? That child-in-a-candy-shop sense of letting her pencil or paint brush roam free? She couldn't be free here, for some reason. She should have gone up to the Art Students League to be in the comfort of others in shared space. She couldn't work here with that sketch tucked away in the closet. Jesus! She was absolutely astounded by her own thought. That portrait of Vinny that she had started with such elation the summer she had met him. She had never finished it, hadn't thought of it for months. She couldn't finish it, she knew that now. She didn't know how to complete it—she didn't want to—but she couldn't just dump it. The phone rang, and she grabbed the receiver. It was her friend, Jeanette, who was married to one of Vinny's maritime buddies. Did Beth want to catch a flick tonight? They could grab a bite before the show.

"Good idea. (Oh, yes!) Nothing about the war, I hope."

"No closer to it than Judy Garland and Mickey Rooney."

"Wonderful." A dose of Hollywood's sugar-coated optimism, buoyant and resilient as rubber—just what she needed to sustain her. That and maybe a toasted cheese sandwich at Nedicks before the movie.

She came down to earth, flat on her butt, only a couple of days later, when the doorbell rang and she heard the low voices, the shuffle of footsteps outside. The real war had come home to her. She knew before they spoke what the two sober seamen had come to tell her. Vinny's Liberty Ship had been sunk by the Nazis. There were no survivors. He was gone. Beth looked at the men numbly, barely reacting to their words. Who were they? They looked familiar. Friends of Vinny? Had she met them before? She didn't know. She didn't know anything.

"Are you all right? Do you have someone to stay with you? Do you want us to call someone?"

"No, no. But please sit down." These guys were seamen, less formal than the army or navy would have been. Ordinary men with New York accents in work clothes.

"You know, we're here to help. You're not alone. Vinny wanted . . . we want . . . to take care of you, if we can. We don't have military benefits for you. Merchant Marines don't get them, but Vinny contributed to a fund, a less formal arrangement. But we can talk about that later, of course."

"Yes. Thank you."

Murmansk! A name, a place she hadn't known existed before the war in the North Atlantic. Now it was a name she would never forget. So cold! How awful that her sunny, warm-blooded man should die unclaimed in those freezing waters. He didn't deserve it. Oh, God, poor Vinny. Words she believed but couldn't feel. She couldn't cry. She slept fitfully, wandered around the apartment, finally got around to informing friends who weren't serving with him and wouldn't know of his death. Some of them cried, but she couldn't. She heard Frima choking back tears when Beth called her—she'd had a real soft spot for Vinny. Hannah Erlichman cried for both of them, Beth and Vinny. Even Jack was sympathetic: "I'm truly sorry for your loss. Can we do anything to help?" He sounded awkward but quite genuine. She would have to thank him some day, but not now. Now all she could feel was a depressed numbness, and words beating in her mind: this is what you deserve. She didn't know why she deserved this. She didn't know anything.

Life went on. She went to work, which was a relief; it seemed so normal. She had an occasional meal with a friend, went to the movies, leaving her seat during newsreels of the war at sea. She visited with Frima and her little niece, but she felt almost nothing. And she could neither cry nor paint. How long this went on, she couldn't say, but gradually her mind took up a new refrain:

Full fathom five thy father lies
Of his bones are coral made
Those are pearls that were his eyes

The Tempest—she remembered it from high school. Beautiful words, they were. But surely Shakespeare didn't mean for them to sound like an advertising jingle with an underlying tinge of mockery and reproach. And he couldn't have meant these lines to be repeated *ad nauseam.* They seemed to slip into her consciousness at every opportunity when her mind was not focused on something else. It was driving her mad. Was she going mad? Maybe she should see someone about this. Like a psychiatrist? A psychoanalyst? She almost laughed out loud. On her salary? Certainly she wouldn't dream of using the small stipend Vinny left her for any such purpose. He would have hated the very idea. So bourgeois—so antithetical to solidarity and common cause. Beth didn't agree, actually. She found the little she knew about Freud and his followers intriguing. It must be a streak of bourgeois individualism coming out in her. But if she was going to analyze her way out of this jingle madness, she would have to do it herself.

Vinny's fate was wrapped up in Shakespeare's words; nobody needed to tell her that. Coral and pearls, now. Didn't they come from warm tropical seas? From vacation paradises? Not the unrelenting cold of Murmansk. Well, Vinny was—had been—her vacation paradise, for a while at least. Coral bones? Now that was easy. He had been red to the bone. She was suddenly impatient, irritated with herself. What was she doing? Break the code and you win? As if the mysteries of pain were some kind of parlor game? Beth knew she was in great pain. If only she could cry or scream or throw things, she might feel some relief. But she couldn't. She remained numb and depressed with those damn words beating in her head.

How long this lasted, she couldn't say, but quite suddenly there was silence. It sort of sneaked up on her. She found she was free of this misery, as if chains had broken or a fog had lifted without her volition. She entered the Minetta Street apartment with a renewed eagerness and sense of purpose, quickly shed her work clothes for an old pair of paint-stained dungarees, and sat down at the table with charcoal and a sketch pad. She needed to paint. Shakespeare could paint with words. She couldn't—didn't want to. She had to have oils and water-colors, brushes. Unbelievably strange how the greatest word conjuror in the English language had been shouting at her: "Paint, paint! Here it is, I'm practically giving you the image. Paint, you fool—it's the way you mourn and celebrate!"

This would be her most important work so far. This painting of Vinny. She thought momentarily of the sketch hidden in the closet. Should she throw it out? No need. It didn't disturb her now. She hadn't been able to finish it because she didn't really know what man she was trying to portray. Perhaps she would finish it some day, but no urgency about that. Her real need now was to create the Vinny she would always think of when she thought of his end. It was the sea change she was after. This man, a warm-blooded Mediterranean—she would not let him disintegrate in those frigid waters. A beautiful sea change he would undergo; no bloated or frozen flesh, but there would most certainly be coral bones—a whole skeleton of coral, like finely wrought chain. She already knew the name of this creation: "Those are pearls that were his eyes." Sea-washed hazel pearls.

She had been sitting in the same position for hours. It was after two in the morning, and she was covered with charcoal. She hadn't eaten anything, but a shower was what she needed now. A shower and sleep. She ran the shower long and hot, soothing the stiffness in her shoulders. Suddenly she began to cry, huge hiccupping sobs that brought her a blessed release before she was conscious of thought.

Full fathom five, thy father lies . . . Shakespeare had to hit her over the head with this before she could see. Vinny was her emotional father. Her lover, yes, but she had cleaved to him, rushed into living with him because he could guide her, love her, keep her safe. So unlike her own father, who never could. That heavy weight of guilt she'd felt since his death; would Dr. Freud call this an Oedipal thing? That's what the parlor "Freudians" would call it. She didn't know, and she didn't care. The weight had lifted now, and she could feel her grief.

She dozed off, then woke fitfully to more tears. She was stabbed by a certainty: she hadn't loved Vinny enough or properly—that's what made her weep now. He needed a woman who would be his wife and a mother to his children, as well as a companion, and she couldn't do it. She wasn't a real partner, just a girl who needed him to prop her up. Oh, Vinny, I am so sorry I couldn't be more for you. I truly am. Forgive me! Without sense or reason, she began to believe he did. Bethie, will you forget about all this screwball remorse—we had a great time didn't we? That's what he would say. It was his farewell gift to her. After all, Vinny was not a guy to hold a grudge.

It was late in the morning when she woke again. She got up immediately, refreshed but starving. She bolted down toast, a piece of cheese, black coffee. Thank God it was the weekend and she could work on the portrait all day. This painting, now. It would not be easy. It might be a struggle to get it right. One thing she was certain of: the coral Vinny would be content and at ease. No agony there, no fear or loneliness. She would put him in a relaxed, lounging position, maybe glass in hand, shooting the breeze with his buddies. Discussing Marx? She didn't think so. Much more likely gassing about the women and food they missed. She didn't know how she would portray the other seamen yet. She'd have to experiment, see how things developed. She only knew the eyes were Vinny's alone—that he was at peace. As was she.

CHAPTER 21

The white greasy margarine, looking exactly like lard or Crisco, sat on the table in its squeezable transparent bag waiting for Frima's attention. Embedded in its surface was the familiar small orange capsule. For an instant and at just the right angle it was a vision of sunrise over Arctic snows before it reverted to mundane artificial food coloring. You squeezed out the orange goop and mixed it with the white fat to emulate the rich yellow of summer butter. The government, in its wisdom, did not want anyone to confuse margarine with real butter, which was rationed of course, so they left the task of transforming this white mass to the patriotic American housewife. The country girl in Frima knew and sympathized with the dairy farmers who benefited from this decision, but she also knew what fresh summer butter looked and tasted like, and she glared at this blob balefully. Three-year-old Lena, in contrast, was entranced. "I want to do it, Mommy. Let me!" To Lena it was magic to see the orange coloring oozing through the white as she squeezed the bag. Better than any sandbox. Of course, her small hands wouldn't be able to finish the job; they would quickly tire, and soon enough Lena's interest turned in another direction. Michael in the playground, she reported, had a whole closet full of bubble gum, and he would only let his best friend have some. All the big kids who were already in kindergarten or first grade wanted to be his best friend. "I'm too little," Lena informed her without rancor.

So bubble gum was a casualty of war. Frima doubted that her daughter knew what it was, actually. If it were available, she would keep Lena away from it as long as possible. She didn't look forward to cutting it out of her child's tresses or scraping it off furniture. Bubble gum gone; margarine a new plaything. So this was war to an American three-year-old. On impulse she picked up a week-old news magazine that Jack hadn't gotten around to finishing. It was opened to a picture of a string of advancing Japanese tanks.

"Do you know what this is, lovie?" She pointed to a tank.

"Yes, it's a Jap."

"A person?"

"Don't be silly, Mommy! That's not a person."

"Is it an animal—like an elephant?"

"No. . . ."

"Can you squeeze it—like this?" Frima picked up the package of margarine.

"No, it's too hard."

"Well, what does a Jap do?"

"Bad things. Let me make the yellow again, Mommy." Lena was clearly tired of silly questions.

And why shouldn't she be? A lucky child, thank God! A lucky Jewish child! No fear of any bad things; no one lost. Nor had she, Frima, had any close losses, except for Vinny. He was gone and she had wept for him, but he wasn't her personal sorrow. He was Beth's. Frima had been puzzled by Beth's response to his death. It was unlike anything Frima would have expected from her volatile sister-in-law. Beth had been quiet and numbed, and after a month or so she became immersed in her painting, her job, her political activities. "I still expect to hear his key in the door or to see him around the corner in another room. I miss him, but it isn't the hurt it was," she told Frima.

What a completely unnatural position Americans were in. Their country was at war on two fronts in a conflict that had killed or permanently maimed unimaginable numbers of people; an urgent and completely justifiable conflict against fascist enemies of humanity. Frima believed this wholeheartedly. The threat was real. Yet both war fronts were thousands of miles—oceans away—from American civilians. How could the war be real to civilians here in North America? There were no burnt ruins or bloody body parts or stench of war on your own streets or in your own fields. Frima was not uninformed. She read newspapers, listened to the radio, saw newsreels at the movies; but she also realized that she was getting no more than a tiny glimpse of the whole story. News and images were carefully censored. Jack knew something of the reality, perhaps. Working in a military hospital, he had to see some of the damage and breakage, but he wouldn't talk of it at home. Besides, those who made it to American hospitals couldn't be the worst casualties; obviously none of the overseas dead were there. The hospital wounded were a distressing sight, but more like the burn and trauma units in ordinary civilian hospitals that she'd seen in her Red Cross classes. Most of the mass horror was hidden. Even soldiers and sailors returning from overseas didn't seem to talk to their families about the real war.

Well, did she want to see the real war? Of course not, who would? Still, she was uncomfortably aware that innocence is only cute in a child. For the rest of us, it's seriously dangerous.

—

The Battle of the Bulge, with its enormous American and Allied losses came and went, and finally the Nazis seemed to really be losing ground. Now Frima found it hard not to feel that, fair or not, she and her charmed circle of family were going to escape unharmed. And for the most part, they did. Except that in the early spring of 1945,

Jack was suddenly, unaccountably, shipped overseas. To Germany! It seemed completely crazy to Frima. The Germans were losing, weren't they? Did the Americans need so many medics in Europe? Why not send him to the Pacific, God forbid? Jack didn't know; she didn't know. If you weren't overseas, most of the war was still a great unknown.

Again they were lucky. He was gone barely two months. Two very anxious, lonely months, to be sure, but they could be pushed aside once he returned sound in mind and body. If Frima thought he would enlighten her about his experiences or say anything of why he had been shipped back so soon, she was disappointed. "Nobody understands why the army does anything," he said. Frima didn't pressure him. So many returning men seemed to feel that the ugliness of war was not for mixed company. They wanted just to rush back to civilized life: good food, baseball, making babies. Jack was no different. Lena was a renewed miracle to him. He couldn't believe how beautiful and charming she was. Nor could he keep his eyes or hands off Frima, and she only wanted to wrap him in passionate, romantic love and anything else that would give him (and her) pleasure.

"A couple of kosher franks, dripping sauerkraut and mustard, real sour pickles, then bed with you. What could be better?"

"Pastrami," she answered straight-faced.

By the time the war in Europe ended, she was pregnant, and this time there was no doubt or conflict about it—a planned baby, completely wanted.

The last person she mourned personally was Franklin Roosevelt. Was he also a casualty of war? Who could say? There were plenty of people at home and abroad who would be happy to see him gone, but not in these parts, Frima thought. His death was a complete shock— to ordinary people, at least. None of them had the faintest idea of how sick he must have been, just as they had not known of his daily struggle with his paralyzed legs. For Frima's generation, he was really the only president: the courageous, proud standard-bearer of American values. She, herself, could barely remember Hoover. FDR had brought them through the Depression and the war and had rekindled hope. Of course, except for newsreels, ordinary Americans seldom saw the living, moving image of him, but his face was as familiar to people as a kindly father or uncle. And that voice! So powerful, persuasive, reassuring—whatever was needed—familiar to every American who listened to the radio. It seemed that everyone she knew was crying at his death. Frima did, as did her mother and Sarah; grown men and women on the street wiped tears from their eyes. Jack was still overseas, but she had seen news photos of GIs weeping. Even Arthur Godfrey, the undisputed king of morning radio, broke into sobs as he reported on the funeral procession.

Major radio networks repeatedly broadcast a folk cantata, "The Lonesome Train," commemorating the death of Lincoln and fostering the idealistic connection of the two leaders. Frima was usually only politely interested in this type of music, but it turned out that its creators, Millard Lampell and Earl Robinson, were men Beth knew from the old days with Vinny, and at her urging, Frima got to know the cantata quite well. She found she was impressed with it.

Some in the North and some in the West and some by President's side,
They cursed him every day that he lived and cheered on the day he died.

"Lonesome Train" was, after all, a pretty fitting and affecting tribute, Frima felt. Newsreels and newspapers showed people lining the tracks of the funeral train for Roosevelt. They evoked Lincoln's death. For surely Lincoln and Roosevelt were, each of them, the most revered and the most detested presidents in history.

And now? Now there was Truman. Would anyone have intense feelings about him? Just let him finally end this war altogether and not undo any of the good things Roosevelt had wrought.

—

Frima and Jack were up in the country for the Labor Day weekend, basking in the afternoon sun. Just last month, the US had dropped atomic bombs on Hiroshima and Nagasaki, devastating Japan. Like most Americans, their personal reaction to this was a deep relief—the war was over. Jack, dozing off in the chair next to her, dropped her hand, and the newspaper with coverage of the official VJ observance slipped off his lap. Frima smiled and gently picked up the paper. She wouldn't disturb him. His sleep had been restless at night. She didn't worry too much about that—she had heard from other women that their returning GI husbands also slept fitfully, and she believed time was the remedy. Still, she wanted Jack to get all the rest he could. By springtime it would be baby time again. "Sleep all you can now, Papa," she murmured. Also, Jack would be starting school again in a week, earning a degree with the help of the new GI Bill that would prepare him to teach chemistry. A good, happy career path for him. Babies and study robbed you of sleep, but for such good, hopeful reasons. She glanced at the news photos again, thinking that the war years were beginning to seem like a newsreel to her, one that quickly passed. Mamas still admonished children to "think of the poor, starving children in Europe," when they refused to finish their breakfast oatmeal. Kids on the Bronx sidewalks played games— "Step on a crack, you love Hitler"—but these were turning into leftovers, slogans and images that were losing their history.

Except for those liberation photos of the concentration camps. Good God! Human beings in the country of Bach, Beethoven, and Schiller had willfully planned and created this hell. Had any humans in known history ever acted as cruelly, sunk so low? Probably. But they didn't have the modern German efficiency and technology. And they didn't have Margaret Burke White's camera or Edward R. Murrow's broadcasts from Buchenwald forcing this reality on anyone who looked or listened. She stirred uncomfortably. Jack wouldn't look at those pictures or listen to the descriptions. He didn't need to, he said, and he would talk no further about them. Perhaps he was right. She had been horrified, for sure, but also resentful that she should have to see such nightmares. Well, the civilized world would punish the perpetrators. They would expose those monsters, and hang them. It would all be in the past soon. It couldn't affect their future. Now, Frima, happy thoughts. Just close your eyes to the Brahms lullaby. "Lay thee down, safely rest."

CHAPTER 22

On a sunny morning in late October, Frima entered her kitchen with an energy frequently missing so early in the day during these first months of pregnancy. She had taken her wet laundry up to the roof to dry on the clotheslines there before the other housewives were even up and about. This was a chore she actually enjoyed. She savored the smell of sun-dried sheets, and she loved the panorama of buildings and water towers from that height on a clear day like this. Up here in solitude, she always recalled the daydreams she and Beth used to have about converting those towers into studios, full of light and magical artistic energy. No time for daydreams today, though. She had bundled Lena off with Sarah, who would take her to the playground. Her mother-in-law was something of a pleasant surprise these days. Having a grandchild to care for and another on the way had given her a new lease on life. If Sarah could somehow dispose of her miserable husband, who knew what possibilities awaited her? Now why should she, Frima, be so surprised? Jack and Beth were Sarah's offspring, and they were exceptional: charming, bright, beautiful. She must have done something right. Their stubbornness came from Sam, that was for sure, but Sarah was at a loss when confronted with it, so Frima had to counteract it with her own strategies.

Beth was coming up to see her mother today, and she would have dinner with Jack and Frima and her young niece this evening. It was a Thursday. If they were a normal—that is, warm, generous—Jewish family, it would make far more sense for Beth to come on Friday, the end of the work week. That way she could share a Shabbos meal with the whole family, all three generations, especially now that Vinny was gone. But this wasn't a normal family. Sam refused to be in the same room with his daughter, and she in turn loathed him. Jack was still testy about Beth's living situation, convinced that the influence of Vinny lingered on in an alienating way. Since returning from overseas, Jack was more eager to keep to Jewish traditions, more sensitive about his Jewishness than he had been, and Beth unwittingly brought out the worst of his touchiness.

Frima recalled uneasily the great bacon fat controversy of a couple of weeks ago, when Jack, Frima, and Lena were downtown and had made a rare brief visit to Beth's apartment. Like a good patriotic American, Beth had some rendered meat fat chilling on the window sill. It was still collected as part of the war effort (used for munitions or something), and Lena had trotted over and tasted it. It was bacon fat, unfortunately, and Jack had a fit over it being there. The argument was sotto voce in deference to the child, who, happily, was more interested in exploring the apartment than listening to the adults.

"How can someone who calls herself Jewish keep that garbage in the house?"

"Why not? Plenty of Jews eat bacon. You eat it yourself—I've seen you."

"Never in my home! And never lately. It's Kraut food."

"So is cabbage. You're being ridiculous," Beth hissed back at him.

Frima entirely agreed with her, but not being a fool said only, "Stop this nonsense, right now, both of you!"

Despite all of this, Jack would have heartily approved of Beth joining them for a Friday night meal with the ritual lighting of the candles. He would think it a good influence on her. But knowing full well that this would be impossible at his parents' table, he left the Friday night decisions to Frima. Besides, she was pregnant, and allowances had to be made. In truth, what Frima would have liked was for her mother and stepfather to do the whole Friday night deal. They could flatten Sam if he made trouble, and of course Mama would do all the cooking and baking. This was impossible, she knew. Even if they had wanted to do this, Mama and Leon couldn't drive to the city every week. Rubber tires were precious and irreplaceable, their wear and tear a serious consideration, and gas was still rationed. So Frima had come up with this furtive, somewhat convoluted plan; good for this week, at least.

She surveyed the refrigerator. She was going to make her mother's famous stuffed cabbage, a great big pot of it, enough for tonight and Friday. She had hoarded her meat rations for this. She had some sweet butter also, so she'd make Mama's unadorned but delicious butter cake, maybe accompanied by stewed fruit. She had all the recipes. Butter and meat at the same meal? Absolutely. Jack knew she would never agree to a kosher home. Kosher style food sometimes, but that was all. It was a good plan. Jack adored Mama's stuffed cabbage, and Beth would also. There would also be plenty of food for tomorrow. She had ample time to prepare this ambitious meal. Beth would take her mother and Lena out to lunch and stay with them until about five, then bring Lena back here before Sam came home. Enemy ships that passed in the night. The whole day would be just fine with Lena, since she and Aunt Bethie were buddies.

Usually Beth bought her some delightful children's book as a present, and they would read it together, probably several times over. Lena loved books, and Frima was sure her child would be reading before she reached first grade. Beth was so good with Lena. Too bad she had no desire to have a child of her own. Or maybe not too bad. She would certainly be better off waiting for marriage to the right guy. She hummed to herself as she pulled off the outside leaves of the cabbage. She'd get the cabbage rolls in and out of the oven before she baked the cake. Then just a half hour before dinner she'd reheat them. They'd taste even better that way. With good planning she could even get to practice some Shubert for an hour before the others got here.

Jack was home earlier than expected. He came over to the piano and kissed the top of Frima's head.

"Don't get up, honey. Last class was canceled today. Something smells wonderful, by the way."

"Stuffed cabbage."

"On a Thursday?"

"Your sister is coming, remember? Besides I made enough for tomorrow night also, with your folks."

"Well I hope it will influence her in the right direction—remind her that her roots aren't in pizza. Do you need help? Want me to set the table or something?"

"Uh-uh. Everything's ready. Take a load off."

"Okay, I'll be on the couch reading the paper. Probably full of stuff about Nuremberg—the trials will be starting soon." A big sigh followed this. "Right there in the city where it all began."

You would be much better off closing your eyes and listening to a little Schubert, Frima thought, but she held her peace. It was inevitable that they would talk of the trials this evening, but why should she be uneasy about fireworks between brother and sister? On this issue at least they were all on the same side, weren't they? Still, she was glad that Lena would be sitting at the table to dampen any desire to argue.

"Aunt Bethie, tell Daddy about the boy with the pot on his head. It was so funny! Grandma Sarah laughed and laughed and her eyes got wet. But she said she wasn't sad."

"What is this kid talking about?" Jack asked.

"It was just something I saw on the way here." Beth answered. "The weather was so nice I walked from the subway, and I saw this woman and a kid get off the bus at Montifiore. Probably going to the emergency room. This poor kid had a pot—you know, a saucepan with a handle—on his head. And his mother, loud enough for the world to hear, is badgering him: 'You had to be General Eisenhower, yet! I don't have *tsuris* enough? No, you have to be General Eisenhower—" Beth broke off with a little snort of laughter.

They all had to laugh. "Poor kid," said Frima. "He must have been so mortified. How would they get it off?" she asked Jack.

"Soap or some lubricant, like you would if you had a ring stuck on your finger, I guess. The kid's mother probably could have done it herself, if she'd been thinking."

"But she had *tsuris* enough," Beth and Frima said in one voice, and that set the two women off again.

"Very funny," Jack said quietly. "But you know, don't you, that you're using that exaggerated Yiddish accent again? Considering the times, it's not in the best of taste."

"That's the way she talked, Jack. Like a Bronx Jewish immigrant. We all do, at times, so what's the big deal?" Beth answered evenly.

"Lena, lovie, say goodnight to Daddy and Aunt Bethie." Frima interrupted them smoothly. She could see that Lena was beginning to nod off. And just in time, she thought.

It took her about fifteen minutes to read Lena a story and get her settled. She could hear subdued but rapid conversation from the kitchen table, but had no idea how much the antagonism had escalated until she returned to the room.

"Six million of our people exterminated like rats. Extermination—the word makes me want to puke. The Nazis would have been kinder to rats—just a little arsenic—they wouldn't work them to death, humiliate and torture them, deliberately starve them! Those Kraut bastards aren't even human—hanging is too good for them."

"What they did is unbelievable, unspeakable. But the Nazis are human—that's what is so horrifying. And we have to remember they also killed political prisoners, gypsies, homosexuals."

Frima stood frozen for a moment. Oh, shut up! Beth was perfectly right, but didn't she realize that her preachy, proselytizing tone was infuriating to Jack? For a discerning woman, she could be such a blunderer.

"Oh, spare me that all-men-are-brothers crap! It's just a way to undercut the fact that Jews were the main target—the main victims. Who do you think a Nazi would kill first, a Jew or a Gypsy? If you weren't such an anti-Semitic Jew—which is unforgivable—you would realize that."

Beth's voice was low, but it shook as she spoke. "How dare you? Do you think I don't know that I would have been incinerated if I'd lived in Europe? I'm an anti-Semite because my view is broader than yours? I'm Jewish and proud of it—I'm just not your kind of Jew. And we most certainly are talking about crimes against humanity, brother of mine, whether you like it or not."

"Who are you calling brother, comrade!"

"Jack! Stop this at once! He doesn't know what he's saying, Beth— he's just upset by the horrors. We all are."

Beth was silent for a moment, stricken. She spoke slowly, trying to keep her voice from shaking. "No, Frima, no peacemaking. Not now. I know when I'm being personally attacked." She whirled on Jack. "You'd better explain just what you mean by that comment, brother."

"Oh, come on! I'm talking about Saint Vinny the Red. You know you took his word as God's."

"I did no such thing, though I'd much rather take his word than yours. 'Saint Vinny the Red?' You didn't just make that up, did you, you clever bastard? You've had time to refine your nastiness. And whatever you think, Vinny was a fine man, a brave man who died for his country—which is more than you did!"

"I doubt he died for *this* country!"

They glared at each other, murder in their eyes. Then just before Frima was forced to intervene to separate them, their glances fell, and they stood appalled at how far they had gone to injure each other.

Beth quietly picked up her bag and walked out of the apartment. Frima immediately followed her.

"Please, Bethie, he didn't really mean it. I'll call you tomorrow, okay?"

Beth stood silent for a moment. Then she nodded her head and gave Frima a quick hug before entering the elevator.

Returning to her living room, Frima opened fire immediately. "How could you say such things to her? She's done nothing to deserve that from you. She's had enough loss. Do you want to disown her, like your impossible father did? Well, I won't—I'm telling you right now, and you'd better believe it. You have got to call her and apologize. Maybe she'll be generous enough to forgive you. Are you listening to me, Jack? Look at me when I speak!" She was suddenly taken aback by his face. All the fight had gone out of him. He looked exhausted.

"Do you think it was right that she practically called me a coward?" He asked this quietly, without anger or rhetoric, as if he really didn't know the answer.

"Of course, Bethie was wrong, but she was very upset. You really attacked her. I know she can be irritating to you, but you must apologize." She paused for a moment, but he did not respond. "On second thought, I think you should write to her. I'll look it over before you mail it. I'll talk to her tomorrow—"

"Frima, can't this all wait until tomorrow? I'm suddenly unbelievably tired, somehow. I've got to take a nap or just call it a night."

He really did look exhausted, and she relented. "Okay, I'll be in later. I'll try not to wake you."

She cleaned up the kitchen, emptied ashtrays, feeling tired herself, but unwilling to face any of these chores in the morning. She wanted tomorrow to be a clean slate. Still perturbed, she wasn't ready to join Jack. She lay down on the sofa with her feet up, trying first to distract herself with a magazine, then a half-read mystery when a sudden sound of something crashing to the floor brought her to her feet—Lena? Jack? She ran toward the back of the apartment to find her husband lying in a dead faint in the hallway just outside their bedroom. He had been sweating profusely. She knelt over him. What to do? Fear made her momentarily an idiot—she could recall nothing about fainting from her Red Cross classes. Cool water? A cold compress? But before she could get to the bathroom Jack was rising to his feet. He pushed her roughly out of the way and slammed the bathroom door. She heard him lean over the toilet, vomiting.

"Jack, are you all right? I'm coming in."

"No, don't! I don't want you to see me like this. I'm okay. And you're pregnant," he added lamely.

"A pregnant woman doesn't know about throwing up?"

She heard him flush, then move to the sink. He opened the door.

"It's just food poisoning," he commented, by this time able to rinse his mouth and squeeze toothpaste on his brush quite competently.

"Funny, I don't have it."

"It affects people differently."

"But you fainted."

It's over now. I'm sorry I pushed you," he said, gently caressing her stomach. "But I think I'll sleep on the sofa so I don't disturb you if I have to run to the bathroom again."

He was looking better now, his color was coming back. "No, the bedroom is closer if you need to get up, and you'll sleep better in bed. I'll sleep on the sofa. Don't worry, I'm not made of glass."

Jack didn't protest, and she left him as he fell asleep again. She wasn't convinced that he was entirely recovered, but she was weary and she quickly dozed off on the sofa, only to awaken to the sound of her husband entering the bathroom again, more quietly than before. This time she didn't go after him. Some ginger ale over ice is what he needs, she thought. If it helps me, it ought to help him. He needs fluids sipped slowly.

She felt in charge now, as she approached the bathroom, glass in hand. But when she came to the door, it was not retching she heard, but sobs—ugly, tearing sobs. She had never heard such uncontrollable crying from her husband. She wanted never to hear anything so awful again. She straightened her back and forced herself to speak calmly. He had locked the door.

"Jack, what is it? Let me in."

"I'll be all right. Just let me alone, please!"

"I most certainly will not. If you don't come out immediately and talk to me, I'm calling the doctor—I don't care if it's the middle of the night—I mean it!"

He took this as a threat, as if he were a child, and she heard the door unlock. He emerged slowly, wiping his face with a cold washcloth.

"I'm a trained medic, you know. I don't need a doctor."

"Tell me what's wrong."

She led him into the living room as if he were a child and sat with him on the sofa. She handed him the glass.

"Sip this slowly."

"Better if it were whisky."

"That's the last thing you need now," she said quietly. "Now talk."

"I never wanted you to know—not you, Bess, my parents—nobody." He halted, struggling against silence.

'Know what?" she asked, again as if talking to a child and suddenly afraid that he was just that. She stroked his shoulder, but he removed her hand gently.

"Please. Just let me talk. Say it."

Frima moved away a few inches, and Jack slowly began to talk into the silence.

"You can't imagine it. The photos can't convey the stench. We were moving through pretty country, near Weimar, which had been bombed, but you didn't see that. But the stench! We thought we were near pig farms. You know, like in New Jersey—Secaucus—but so much more putrid. Word came down the line that we'd come to Buchenwald. A prison camp? We didn't know what to expect. And that's all I remembered until tonight. I ran away, they told me. They found me in the woods. I didn't recall anything before that. Temporary amnesia from the shock, they said. They couldn't say if and when I would remember. They didn't call me a deserter or anything like that . . . I think there were others who ran into the woods. They just gave me an early discharge, and sent me back to the States."

"But, Jack, there's nothing shameful about what you did. Anyone decent human could react the same way."

"No, shh, please. Let me finish. It's what I remember now, what I'd shut out until tonight. When we got to the camp—we weren't the first Americans to get there—there was this confusing number of people: GIs, officers shouting orders, inmates wandering around the enclosure. The SS guards weren't around. Probably they had run away or had been arrested. Some of the inmates were thin, in prison stripes, looking like prisoners of war who had lived through tough conditions, sort of like what you'd expect. But the others . . . Oh, God . . . the ones emerging out of the barracks! The real dead, the naked gray-green skeletons that the Nazis had tried to hide were stacked up like logs, but these coming to us now were the living skeletons. They were in rags and patches and they spoke a babble of languages. Some couldn't walk without help, but some were smiling. They knew we were Americans and they were happy to see us. There was this little old man who looked like my own grandfather. Maybe he wasn't that old . . . even the kids looked old. Anyway, I said something to him, like, Zayde? His eyes lit up and he reached out to me with his arms, and I ran away! I thought he could give me a disease or something. I ran to hide, like a coward! Like the damn SS! I think that old man will reproach me forever—if he doesn't curse me."

Frima put her arms around him. "He will do neither. And it will be better now. You know, it's like an infection draining, this remembering, like a boil lanced. It will be better now."

They sat holding hands silently. When she could see that he was calmer, she got up to make them some tea.

So, you thought you both came out of the war unwounded!

CHAPTER 23

By the time a bleary-eyed Frima entered the kitchen the next morning, Jack was on the phone with Leon, talking hotel business, and Lena was playing with her blocks in the living room. Dishes in the sink, unwashed, naturally, revealed that he had already scrambled some eggs for Lena and himself.

"Coffee is on the stove," he called out.

She poured herself a cup and made some toast. So this was to be a nice normal morning?

"Listen, honey, I called my mother earlier and canceled their coming over tonight. Told her I had a cold coming on. I figured it would be a little too much for you after last night."

And for you. "I have all that food."

"I told her she could come over and pick it up. That's okay with you, isn't it?"

"That's fine," she answered, "We're both too tired for company. But, remember, you have to make your peace with your sister."

"I know. I'll write to her, like you said." He was silent for a few moments, shuffling papers around his desk and seemingly absorbed in business from Ellenville. "If you talk to her today, Frima, I don't want her to know anything about last night.

"She'll have to know something, Jack. No details. Just that the trials,

213

the talk yesterday, brought back some upsetting war experiences. Beth won't pry."

"We're still talking about my sister, right?"

"Very funny. But in some ways I know your sister better than you do." This was the understatement of the year, Frima thought, but added only, "Beth will not pry. She'll keep the peace, and you must too."

"I'll do my best." He came back about a half hour later, looking ready to take on the world, but instead of a quick kiss and a rushed exit, he pulled up a kitchen chair and seated himself on it backward, facing her with a serious expression. Frima waited warily for more speech.

"You know, honey," he began, "there's going to be more and more about the camps and the Nazi war crimes as these trials go on. Without going into detail—there was enough of that last night—I'm only saying there were places worse than Buchenwald. And I don't think you should see them. There's been quite enough upset around here, and in your condition. . . . "

"You think I'm not going to read the papers, that I'll retire to the ladies' room when the movie newsreels come on?" She gentled her tone as she realized with some tenderness that he was gathering about him the shreds of his male authority and protectiveness toward her. "Well, we'll see," she said, as she kissed him goodbye.

With housework finished and Lena napping, she sat down at the piano to warm up with some scales before turning to Mozart for a little uplift, but her hands remained motionless in her lap. No escape here; she was too deep in thought about good and evil.

Frima had been gently reared, as she put it to herself. Not in the class sense—she had no pretensions to that. But her parents in their different ways were both humanists. There was no terrifying concept of evil and damnation in her home; no vengeful, eternal punishment. Neither were there blissful everlasting rewards in heaven waiting for the good. No living creature deserved either such punishment or such reward. You did the best you could and were good to each other, looked out for each other. If you lived together, you loved each other. You also tried to widen your vision—the people and things you looked out for, cared about. You tried to appreciate. This was the good life—and it was its own reward. It astonished her now, as she sat at the piano unable to play, just how much that good life had been envisioned not only in German music, but in the German language.

They had never spoken German in her childhood home; she came from an Eastern European Jewish background and was well aware of the half-humorous cultural antagonism between German Jews and Eastern European ones—a distinction that Hitler had unwittingly blurred forever. Her home language had been English as long as she could remember. Frima understood the Yiddish her parents used together but could now only speak it haltingly, and she knew nothing of the Polish they occasionally exchanged. In high school Frima had ignored the more popular French and Spanish for her required foreign language classes and had enthusiastically chosen German instead, the language of her favorite composers. To her it had seemed soft and a little guttural, like Yiddish, and it was full of pleasing cadences in the art songs of Schubert or Brahms. But now all that was overwhelmed by the hysterical shrieking of Hitler and his henchmen. The Nazis adored Wagner, that arrogant little anti-Semite, with his huge helmeted screaming sopranos. The ultimate anti-humanist. Frima had never liked him, but she had grudgingly recognized his power. Now she'd never listen to him again. She couldn't stand the sound of any German now. Would it always be so? She would hate the Nazis until the day she died, perhaps never forgive Germany or its people for fostering them. Could she ever forgive this enemy?

She didn't feel that way about the Japanese—the other enemy. She was ashamed to say that she barely thought of them, now that peace was restored. But, then, they were still mostly hidden from her. Since childhood, of course, comic strips and animated cartoons had depicted fearsome images of the Yellow Peril—first the Chinese, then the Japanese—but she'd been essentially unimpressed by such nonsense, and living on the East Coast in a provincial Bronx neighborhood, she knew no Japanese Americans. Why, she knew little more about a real living Japanese person than the Mikado audiences did—or Lena. But the Nazis were something else. They were an explicit, graphic horror. Realistic detailed photos and live reports had shown her the depths of depravity, of cold-blooded evil, humans were capable of. And Beth was right; the most frightening part of it all was that they were and are human. The same people who had produced Bach and Beethoven had given birth to Hitler and Goering. Artistic geniuses and monsters and sometimes, like Wagner, a mixture of both. If the Germans could do this, so can we, or the Chinese, or the French. They are not change-lings. They are us.

This was a concept so chilling she was relieved to be distracted by Lena's calling her. She was happy to leave off dwelling on the German character and the heights and depths of the entire human race. Lena wanted a snack. Her child was not one of the poor children in Europe or anywhere else, and she, her mother, could tend to her wants quite easily by opening a box of graham crackers and pouring a glass of milk.

A bit later she called Beth at work, calculating that she would be finishing for the day.

"Bethie, I won't keep you long, but I'm so sorry about last night!"

"You have nothing to be sorry for," Beth responded evenly.

"Then I'm apologizing for Jack. He was very hurtful, very unfair. But there are things he can't talk about yet, upsetting things he saw overseas, and somehow, you—we—brought it all back to him."

"You're being diplomatic again, my dear. It was me. He wasn't angry at you—he never is."

"Be that as it may, he's very thin-skinned right now, so please, Beth, walk softly. He says he's going to write to you and apologize, but I doubt that he'll go into much detail."

"And neither will you, right? As usual with you, still waters run deep."

Frima sighed. "I guess that's lucky for me, married into your family."

Beth gave a short but not ill-humored laugh. "You got that right. Okay, I'll walk softly, but I'll still carry a big stick."

"So, what else is new? Let's talk next week, okay?"

"You bet."

With purposeful lack of subtlety, Frima left some stationery, a pen, a stamp, and Beth's address on the living room desk in full view. Then she gave Lena her bath and supper. When Jack came home he calmly sat down and wrote a short, well-meaning apology, not much different from Frima's spoken one, only adding that he hoped Beth would come to visit again soon.

At sundown, Frima lit the Friday night candles, which Lena loved to see. Then while Jack took the child off to settle her for the night, she warmed up the appetizing leftovers from last night and put out wine glasses. They had learned to like dry red wine from Vinny, and Beth had brought a bottle with her yesterday. Ironic, that. But mostly she felt a renewed peace and good humor after the stormy last days. A pretty, pregnant mommy, a handsome contented daddy who was reading a story to his bright, beautiful daughter; glowing candles, good food, good wine. And, certainly, love later that night.

She would not hide, though. She would not bring up anything more tonight, but she would read the news and listen to the radio and follow the war crime trials. Not every moment or everyday, but she would see what she had to see. Jack could not and should not protect her or himself, for that matter. How could you do anything about such evil if you refused to look at it for what it was? They weren't kids in the playground.

CHAPTER 24

Hair up or down? Beth peered at the mirror. Up, definitely, to expose neck and ears. A better line and silhouette with the open-necked dress, which was sufficiently low cut but not too obvious. Don't pull your hair too tight—you don't want to look like a Flamenco dancer—just a few tendrils allowed to come loose. Beth was lucky her hair was easy. Very dark, thick and wavy, it was a tad coarse but basically easy to control. She left it long because she couldn't afford beauty parlors to keep it in line. Style conscious as she was, she had nevertheless scorned the intricate hairdos of the war years. They were dying out now, those rolls of hair needing lots of hairpins and requiring a personal lady's maid or a flock of beauticians on a Hollywood set to get them right. It made you wonder that in the time of Rosie the Riveter and women piling into the workforce, fashionable hair styles were so elaborate. Probably another class issue. Women factory workers would wear kerchiefs to cover their hair; besides they had no time or money to wrestle with styles so quickly ruined. And you need another class issue like a hole in the head, so just forget it! Lucky she didn't worry about hats. Although she had the height and presence to carry them off, she seldom wore them—too uncomfortable.

It wasn't her habit to spend so much time gazing at herself—mirror, mirror on the wall—but she wanted to get it right. The party at which she would be introduced to Eduardo Ibarra was not until tomorrow night; but from what she had heard, he was worth the time. She wanted to be, to feel, very attractive in her own true style. So here I come, Señor Eduardo Ibarra—ready or not. And if you're not ready, or won't quite do, maybe Mr. Somebody Else!

Beth was more than ready for a new man. There had been nobody since Vinny's death who could remotely be called a partner, which was what she was lonely for. She soon found out that good men were scarce, and not just because of the war. After she ended a period of isolation and mourning, friends went out of their way to introduce her to the few men they thought suitable. She'd had a couple of brief romantic experiments, but none had really panned out. There were certainly men more than happy to share her bed, and in fact that was part of the problem. She was beginning to feel that attached women didn't really want her around their husbands and boyfriends. She was too good-looking and too available, they thought. A young woman who had been around was a magnet for straying men or those who liked to fancy themselves as straying. It was amazing how puritanical and fearful these open-minded, progressive, free-thinking women (and men) could be when there was a dangerous woman about. Beth Erlichman, femme fatale. What a laugh! She knew she was attractive to men, and she still savored her transformation from ugly duckling to swan, but as a dangerous woman she was a washout. She had none of the requisite wiles, subtlety, or heartlessness for that role.

There was another uncomfortable, less flattering aspect to her life these days. She had come to realize that her easy acceptance among Vinny's highly political friends had come from being his girl. On her own, she wasn't much to these same people. Oh, she had made a little stir when her "Pearls" painting had been hung in a small group show, but otherwise they seemed dismissive of her as an artist; and she was sure they considered her a lightweight as a thinker. There were fewer phone calls, fewer invitations. Social-political activities were mentioned casually after the fact: "Oh, I'm sorry, Beth. I thought you knew about that party," or "We didn't really think you'd be interested in that discussion." She felt undervalued and didn't like it. She was not truly chagrined, however, for the bare-bones honesty that surfaced in her at times told her she really wasn't interested in most of this activity. She gladly donated whatever funds she could manage to fighting racism, supporting labor—and she still worked for the NMU, didn't she? But that high wave of camaraderie in its biggest expression, the United Front, was dying now, she felt, with the end of the war.

What seemed to be left was all this talk. Factions and theoretical positions on everyone and everything: Stalin, Jimmy Hoffa, Ben-Gurion; every *ism* possible and, of course, the *masses*. The very word irritated her—so theoretical and abstract. Beth didn't want to talk and she didn't want theories. She wanted to paint and not be *mutchered*. That Yiddish-English word expressed it best, she thought: *mutch'urhd*, pronounced in two syllables, soft almost silent R. How to translate that? To be questioned, heckled, nagged at—all for your own good. Or something like that. Could she ever express this openly? There was, of course, that secret cabinet in her mind she could lock this waywardness in, but she didn't want to. How wonderful to find a man as a companion and partner that she didn't have to hide it from. Not bloody likely, she thought. She was also pretty sure another artist would not be the solution. Artists—serious ones—could make for pretty unsatisfying company as a steady thing. Not only were they in competition with each other for scarce resources and even scarcer recognition, most of them were too busy working at their day jobs and at their personal creative work, like she was. It made for a lonely life, unless you were attached to some really unusual person.

Still, lonely as she was sometimes, she felt offended rather than wounded by the slights of Vinny's social–political crowd, and she really didn't want to be in any other environment than where she was. She was going to hold on to that expanded hopeful vision, the humane, progressive attitudes that she had discovered from living with Vinny, as well as the quirky, still shaky independence he had helped her forge. So, some of the lefties were doctrinaire, rigid, disappointingly conventional. Well, what else was new? At least they strove for something decent. Where else could she find a reasonably compatible partner? Certainly, she couldn't go up to a Catskills resort this summer to hunt for a man. She had neither the money, the time, nor the inclination. Besides, who would she meet there? Another Alphie Pie, another Arthur Midland? Another Vinny? She didn't want another anyone. Someone new was what she longed for. Tomorrow night was an opportunity that sounded quite promising, and she intended to take full advantage of it. Margo, a painter she knew, was married to a veteran of the Abraham Lincoln Brigade, and he had a friend who had also fought in Spain. He was a Spaniard, actually, who had been living in Mexico and had moved to New York a few years ago. He was a journalist, unattached, very interesting. This was not a blind date, Margo had assured Beth. And, she informed her, more than a few women were interested in Eduardo. Still, Margo was ready to give her a leg up. Why didn't Beth come to this Brigade reunion? Eduardo would be sitting at their table, and so would Beth. Margo or Phil would introduce them and she could take it from there.

Knowing that Eduardo Ibarra was a Spaniard and had fought for the Republic, Beth, ever the movie fan, had amused herself envisioning several romantic screen types. Would he be a tall, dark, impassioned Henry Fonda in *Blockade* or a tall, dark, quietly courageous Gary Cooper in *For Whom the Bell Tolls*? Perhaps an earthier peasant type with a beard and beret. The man who materialized was nothing like any of these. He was attractive, all right, smooth-shaven, kind of bony-faced with wire-rimmed glasses; sexy–intellectual, Beth decided. He appeared to be a quiet, well-mannered, thoughtful man who spoke excellent if rather formal English. He was dressed casually but in understated good taste. Expensive clothes, she noted with some surprise (Beth had an eye for these), but no beret, not even a neck scarf, to be seen; just a blameless tie that he soon loosened as it got warmer inside. She was pleased with what she saw. *Just be yourself; don't try to impress him too much.* He was obviously pleased with what he saw also. *Easy does it. A little vino, now, that would help.*

They were hitting it off. Eduardo declared that he was no dancer, but if she wasn't embarrassed to stand up with him, he would venture a foxtrot. Beth meltingly assented. He was not bad, actually. He was a lean, kind of loose-jointed man (not the compact, stalwart teddy bear Vinny had been). She had this fleeting vision of a marionette; if he were strung together more tightly, he might have been shorter than she was. *Short-shmort!* She didn't care; she liked the way they fitted together. A couple of dances later, they were still together when Beth, silently cursing her bladder, had to excuse herself. She had a long, irritating wait for the bathroom, during which she worried that Eduardo would be swept away. When she emerged she found him sitting at a table chatting with a couple of men and quietly smoking a cigarette. He stood up and excused himself as soon as he saw her.

"All this inspiring talk about fighting fascists and bourgeois reactionaries," she commented sotto voce. "The Left needs nothing but their bathrooms to defeat them. Never have I been to a meeting, rally, or even a dance where there were adequate restroom facilities." She felt she'd either charm him or lose him with her irreverence.

Eduardo laughed. "Try Mexico, *gringa*," he retorted, taking her hand. "But if you're willing to get out of here and have a drink with me, I promise to find you a place with the finest facilities available."

Success!

Of course, there were hurdles to overcome. Like the fact that Eduardo had a wife and son. He was quite candid about this, telling her that first night.

Beth stifled a howl. "And just where are your wife and child this evening?" she asked evenly.

"In Mexico. We are legally separated, and we would be divorced if her priests allowed this. She has received a good settlement, and she now lives with my son and another man, whom I understand is very good to both of them. I am grateful for that, and I continue to support them. I write to Manuel often, but I can see him only infrequently. It's not a pretty story, and it stems from an episode in my life that I regret deeply. My only excuse is that I was rash and idiotic at the time. We were both still in our teens." Eduardo took a sip of his drink. "Strange, isn't it? I regret that whole episode in my history, but I can't regret my boy. I'm happy he exists and is thriving. The marriage, well, that's another thing. I only tell you this because I hope that we will be seeing more of each other, and I find it is wise to be honest about one's entanglements."

She was relieved, of course, that he seemed to have no current romantic or domestic involvements she needed to worry about. Fearful of marriage and motherhood as she was, it was probably a very good thing that it was out of the question for the time being. She was a little wary, however. His words bespoke considerable experience, and he was so convincing, so articulate about this history, she was suspicious that it might be a well-rehearsed explanation—a set piece for the new woman, whoever she was.

She would discover soon enough that she had misjudged him. Eduardo turned out to be rather quiet and private by nature. When he did talk, he was articulate, persuasive. He was a journalist, after all, so he was adroit with words, but he had little patience for fakery, and in their personal life, he demanded a core honesty.

One thing surely was easy and open between them—their physical comfort and pleasure in each other. She would have been quite ready to bring him home that first night but for strategy and caution, and it was clear he felt the same. She couldn't say why she felt so bone-of-my-bone, flesh-of-my-flesh about him, but there it was, and she loved it.

Eduardo had heard tell of Vinny but had never met him. He was interested in her relationship with him, though careful not to be overcurious. Beth wanted him to see the "Pearls" painting. She didn't know why, exactly, but it was very important that he see it. He was genuinely interested and spent some time studying it.

"You know, I'm sorry I never met him. I would have liked this guy," he said.

Beth was delighted. "He was extremely likable, and quite charming, really." She was quiet for some moments; then she took the plunge. "Of, course, it wasn't all peaches and cream. It's very possible we would have gone our separate ways after the war, if he hadn't died."

"And why is that, do you think?"

"How can I put it? He was someone who painted within the lines. He had a broad vision, but still. . . ." She was amazed at how easily she had said this and at how accurate her words were.

Eduardo gave a quiet laugh. "He was a Communist—with a capital C?"

"You know, I believe it was only a small C, but that was only because he was a labor organizer and a political coalition builder and it was probably a tactical thing. His hero and mentor was Harry Bridges, who would always mean more to him than Marx or Lenin."

"Ah, the Nose!"

"You know him?"

"Only indirectly. Your Vinny was fortunate. He was tutored by the genuine article, I think."

"Meaning?"

"He had his eye on the ball, as you people say; I think Bridges is a great organizer and negotiator for labor."

"And so was Vinny. But I have to say I had some trouble with some of the people around him. So doctrinaire, some of them—small minded—for all that they think of themselves as the vanguard who sees the bigger picture. Not Vinny—he was too generous and good-hearted—but there were some I could really do without. And they could clearly do without me. None of them ever tried to recruit me to do or be anything."

"You sound indignant. Do you want to be recruited into the Communist Party?"

"Well, no."

"I'm glad to hear it, because you wouldn't be here with me if you did."

"But you're a Brigade veteran."

"I certainly am, but that doesn't mean I'm a party member. I'm afraid I cannot be a dependably loyal member of any political party. You see, I was brought up as a Roman Catholic, Spanish variety, and that has been tough enough to recover from. I don't need another orthodoxy—or hierarchy."

"Vinny was brought up as a Roman Catholic, Italian variety, but to be honest I don't believe he was entirely free of it, though he claimed he was. He wasn't a believer or churchgoer, but the mentality of staying within the lines, well, that was still with him. I mean, I hate to say he was dogmatic or doctrinaire—he was so genuinely nice and easy to be with."

"Perhaps he was just principled."

Beth grinned at him. "You are so right. You do him justice. And you? Are you principled?"

Eduardo, sighed and put his arm around her. "I hope so, *preciosa*, I hope so. A good part of the time, at least."

This was love, the genuine article. Beth was sure of it. Nevertheless, both she and Eduardo were determined to act rationally. She had learned something of the dangers of her own impetuousness and her emotional need for male guidance. She knew now she'd had more luck than brains when she'd flung herself into Vinny's life. It could have been a disaster, if he hadn't been such an essentially good person. Whatever independence she'd made for herself in the three years since his death had been hard won and shaky. But it was precious to her.

As for Eduardo, he too was careful about commitment. He had a wife and child who were the offspring of his adolescent rebellious youth. It was a union that had made both husband and wife unhappy, to say nothing of their son and extended family. He shouldered the blame for this, for he realized that his insistence on solitude, privacy, and intellectual freedom was difficult for any family to live with but was necessary to him, possibly more necessary than the comforts of domesticity and of one particular woman's love. To Beth, Eduardo was quite complex, not easy to know. He was honest but, nevertheless, reserved. Confession, of any kind, he said, was an activity to treat with suspicion.

This much he readily revealed about himself. He was the youngest and only son among four children of a wealthy Madrid family. Conservative Catholics, his parents had nothing good to say about the formation of the Spanish Republic and even less about their teenage son's enthusiasm for it. They had left Spain and settled comfortably, fortune intact, in Mexico City, where they had both business and family connections. There they meant to sit out the Republic—they were confident it would not last—and support Franco and his insurgents from a safe distance. The angry, rebellious Eduardo had soon attached himself to this girl, sufficiently poor, uneducated, and *mestiza* to be a slap in the face to his prosperous rightwing family. They were apoplectic. It was one thing for a young man to experiment; another thing for this young idiot to marry his experiment. Divorce was impossible. The girl, obviously pregnant, was also a devout Catholic. His family arranged for the couple's legal separation and a settlement for the mother and child, and they shipped Eduardo off to England for an expensive education. There he studied history and economics and repaid their prudence and generosity by joining the British division of the International Brigades as soon as it was formed. He was welcomed because of his knowledge of Spain and its languages and regional cultures, and he promptly landed back in Madrid to fight for the Republic.

Eduardo returned to Mexico after the defeat and resumed university studies in Mexico City, but his proximity to his parental family made them all miserable. He remained basically socialistic and passionately anti-fascist; his family celebrated Franco's triumph. Within a year, he had migrated to New York City and made his home in Greenwich Village. He had discovered during his recent time in Spain that he had a facility with language and could become conversant in Western European tongues fairly easily. He was, needless to say, completely at home in Spanish and English, and he was also fluent in Catalan and French. He saw a path for himself as an independent journalist who could write for both the English-speaking and foreign press, and he concentrated on refining his skills and making a respected name for himself in left-leaning circles.

"My God, you've done so much—been to so many places. I've done practically nothing." Beth mused.

"So how come I find you fascinating?"

"I don't know—you tell me."

"You are fishing for compliments, Beth. Seriously, except for my time fighting for the Republic, I've been a child of privilege, and that's the only reason I have been able to travel and explore the world. I have independent means, an inheritance from my mother's side of the family. My father would disown me if he didn't fear being murdered in his bed by all the doting women who brought me up."

"Funny, my father would disown me also, if he had anything worth withholding. As it is, he won't be in the same room with me."

Eduardo smiled and took her arm. "So, *querida*, we have some things in common after all."

So here I am, again, Beth thought. How ironic. My stock in these parts has gone way up, because I'm on the arm of a man with a lot of status. All veterans of the International Brigades were honored and respected for fighting the good fight. She could bask in his reflection. But Eduardo didn't see himself as a hero, and he didn't enjoy the role. It was not just Beth's charms that had made him rush her out of that Brigade reunion to be alone with her. He didn't want to stay for the speeches and singing, he confessed. He had no regrets about fighting for the Republic, but war was a dirty stinking thing that made either side capable of atrocities. You didn't emerge with your hands clean. No one did. He seldom spoke of Spain or of his war experiences, though he dreamt of them, restlessly tossing and mumbling in a rapid slangy Spanish Beth could make nothing of. She began to see how painful the experience was for him when she discovered an album of dusty black records in his music collection, covered in jackets with no labels on them. They evidently had not been moved for years. When she asked him about these he explained what they were, but he was reluctant to speak at length.

"These are songs sung by young teenage girls at a public school just outside of Madrid that was established by the Republic. I've carried them with me since I left as a teenager. The school was later completely razed—bombed by the Fascists. I don't know if there were students in it—probably so. I can't listen to these recordings, but please play them sometime when I'm not here. The songs are lovely. He picked up a paper insert that had lyrics. I'll translate these for you, if you like, but I can't listen to the music."

When she was alone she did listen to them once, and they were lovely. She wondered briefly if an adolescent Eduardo had been in love with one of the singers. She liked that romantic notion, somehow. The songs were not love songs, however, but playful children's songs: sweet ballads and folk songs about flowers, shepherds, animals. They were totally innocent, without any political content; and the singers were devoid of any of the slick polish and sentimentality of Hollywood child stars, singing and parading as short adults. That Eduardo cherished this music taught her a lot about this man she loved.

In Eduardo, Beth felt she had found a rare combination of support and freedom, intimacy and space. Secure for a lifetime? Oh, come on, that could only come with time, if ever. They had both felt like they belonged together almost immediately, but they waited almost a year before she moved into his home on Bedford Street. He owned a whole townhouse, but used only a small part of it for an office and living space, which had been furnished sparely. To Beth it was the height of luxury. She had never experienced living in such lavish light, air, and space. She kept her job until Eduardo tempted her with a studio in the wonderful light-filled attic apartment of the house. And she worried not at all if her family approved of her new life.

CHAPTER 25

Frima hung up the phone gently but with a drawn out sigh. So, Beth was busy building a painter's studio for herself, happy as a pig in you-know-what, and she, in contrast, was thinking about having her beloved piano shipped up to the hotel, where it would sit unused and faithful, waiting for the spare half hour that Frima had to make a little music during the summer and maybe a few weekends out of season. To Jack, the piano was in the way in their city apartment. That had been increasingly clear, since the birth of baby Rosalie, and the interesting little conversation they'd had yesterday pretty much settled its fate. She slammed her way about the kitchen, and expelled her breath rudely in a Bronx cheer. Well! At least her husband's sudden yearning to fight for Zion was over, and with any luck permanently.

What an improbable Zionist he would make. The ones Frima knew of were socialists of sorts; not Jack's type at all. Of course every Jew she knew personally wanted to see a homeland established for Jews, especially for all the refugees and displaced persons in Central and Eastern Europe. Everyone knew someone who had immigrated to Palestine before the war or knew of people desperate to get there. Even Frima, whose entire extended family had come to the United States well before the rise of the Nazis, felt a kinship with these poor displaced souls. They looked like her grandmother or great uncle in those faded family pictures. Except for the ultra-Orthodox Jews, none of whom lived around here, everyone admired David Ben-Gurion and dropped spare change into those little blue donation cans for the Jewish National Fund. No one she knew had any intention of emigrating themselves. They were Americans and felt their luck. But her husband, she discovered, had an itch.

He had begun quite casually, perched on a kitchen chair. "You know my old high school buddy Lou Kurlansky?"

"Uh-huh."

"I met him on the subway on the way home last week and then again yesterday. I asked him what he was doing in this neck of the woods because he lives further east, near the zoo, and would ordinarily take the Pelham line. He was carefully dressed, if you know what I mean, and I thought maybe he had a girlfriend around here. He was pretty good with the girls when we were in high school. I start to kid him about this, so he sets me straight. He tells me he's having supper with Mrs. Sussman; you know, who lives on the other side of the building from us? Her granddaughter goes to kindergarten with Lena? He visits with her when he has time these days. He likes to talk with her, and she's a good cook."

"A bit long in the tooth for him, isn't she?" Frima said this affably enough, but silently she was wondering what issue Jack was circling about and just when he would home in on it.

"She is a very interesting, intelligent person, as it happens," he said testily.

"We have no argument there. So?"

"I would really appreciate it if you would just listen without comment. It interrupts my train of thought."

Frima just rolled her eyes.

"It happens they are connected by marriage. Mrs. Sussman's youngest son married Lou's sister. Anyway, she has some important relatives over there in Palestine—archaeologists of international reputation, actually—who are Zionists, of course, and also very high up in the Haganah. You know, the paramilitary organization fighting for establishment of an Israeli state?"

"I do."

"Well, one of these men, a famous archaeologist, is visiting here, and Mrs. Sussman invited Lou to meet him. What a lucky guy, don't you think?"

"I didn't know Lou was interested in archaeology. Nor you, for that matter."

"It's the Haganah that interests him. Especially their determination to smuggle displaced Jews from the European camps to Palestine. I'm sure he wants to be a crew man on one of those boats. He didn't say this directly, of course. The operations are secret and illegal."

"Then it seems to me you shouldn't be talking about them, either."

"It's only to you, for God's sake, Frima!"

"Well, why are you so sure that's what he wants?"

"He cares a lot about all those poor people. He joined the Navy when he was seventeen, trained as a frogman, but the war was over before he could be in combat. He wants to do something for the Jews. He calls them 'my people.' I admire him, and I envy him for being able to do this. It would make up for a lot!"

"Are you trying to tell me that you want to do the same?" She was instantly enraged, could hardly get the words out. "Lou has no wife and children, to say nothing of parents, and he is a trained seaman."

"And I, if you remember, am a trained medic!" He stopped himself right there. "Of course I know I have obligations that he doesn't. I know I can't do what he can do, and I would never do anything to hurt the family I love. Where are you going?"

"Be back in a jiffy," Frima said. "I think the baby's up from her nap."

The baby wasn't, but she needed those few minutes by herself. It took a mighty effort in that brief time to stifle the scorching words she felt like saying, including, of course, that his own first encounter with "our people" was not exactly heroic and that he wouldn't be a prime candidate for that kind of perilous activity. Returning to the kitchen table, she kept her voice even.

"It seems to me that if you need to support Zionist causes, you can do it from here in New York. If you want to help the Jews, you can do it right here. At least half the kids you'll be teaching are Jews—probably more. You have a real talent for teaching and a way with kids. Teach them chemistry and good values. Teach them how to learn and think for themselves. Believe me. You'll be doing your part."

Jack was silent for a minute or two, collecting himself while Frima pretended to busy herself at the sink.

"You're absolutely right, honey. And that being the case, I'd better hit the books."

"Where are you going?" she asked, seeing him put on a muffler and a jacket.

"Just to the library at Fordham." He glanced at the piano. "There's barely any room to spread out my books here, to say nothing of the noise."

He said this smoothly, easily, and Frima, suddenly enlightened, made no reply. So this was the bargain he offered. She decoded it quite calmly. He was indirect, of course, but the terms were clear. The thing that crowded him so much was her piano. It wasn't the first time he had made that known. The thing that was noisy (damn him) was her piano. He couldn't make it clearer: If I'm to put away my chance to be heroic and redeem myself of my feelings of cowardice, you can put away your dreams of being a musician. If I sacrifice for my wife and children, you sacrifice for me.

She thought again of Beth's news. How ironic that Beth, in a perilous relationship by conventional standards, feels loved and secure because she can be honest with Eduardo and is free to express herself—encouraged to express all she is. And she, Frima, married to the good catch and possessed of a picture-perfect loving family, can only be safe and secure by suppressing a big part of herself. She stood silently for a few minutes. Did she accept the terms of Jack's bargain? Well, yes, sort of. What choice did she have?

So, here she was, getting ready to hang her wet laundry on the roof again, escaping the steaminess and heat of an apartment full of infant demands and adult rancor. She stood quietly for a moment gazing out at the city view with its water towers to mourn her lost dreams. Looking anew at the closest water tower, the one on the roof of her own building, it no longer appeared to have the inviting contours of her youthful daydreams. Now it was a big awkward structure, looming and forbidding, seeming perhaps too heavy for its flimsy supports. So much for adolescent fantasies. The only ones that had come close to realization happened in bed; not in a lofty studio, not even on a rug before a fire or in a rose garden.

You really have only a couple of alternatives, she told herself with grim humor. You can strangle yourself in this clothesline, jump off the roof—that would certainly make a splash—or you can go downstairs and take care of your two priceless little girls who love and need you and for whom there really is no substitute, and also your handsome, desirable husband who loves you and works his head off for you. And he is mostly a decent guy, as husbands go, she thought, even if she was tempted to go after him with the first handy blunt object from time to time. She would have to—what were Jane Austen's words?—learn to be a philosopher.

The phone rang as she entered her apartment again. It was Mama in Ellenville. By the time she got off the phone, Frima had forgotten all about Jack's latest. Grandpa had died. He went peacefully in his sleep, evidently. When he hadn't been seen by midmorning, they went to check on him. It was his heart, the doctor said. It seemed to have just stopped; there was no sign of struggle. "As if he were ready," Mama said. "His affairs were all in order, his burial wishes clear."

"He seemed so hale and hearty last time I saw him," Frima said.

"Joking and cooking up schemes for a Western trip with Moe Ginsberg. Maybe he was depressed or sick and didn't want us to worry."

"I don't think so. He wasn't exactly thrilled with the way things were developing up here—not at our place, but in general. Still, he wasn't a man who got personally depressed. It wasn't his nature. So I wouldn't worry that he was hiding anything from us. He and Moe were still plotting their trip, up to the last. All in all, it wasn't a bad way to go, I suppose. Looking forward to some excitement, and then the lights just gently go out. No suffering."

CHAPTER 26

June 1950

"Go West, old man! Arthritic knees, Yiddish accent, and all. Now I've heard everything!" Jack's laugh was good-humored.

Oh, no, you haven't, Frima thought, but she remained silent. A lot of her spontaneous responses to Jack were silent these days, she was finding. Still, his amazement was understandable at this latest bulletin from Ellenville: Moe Ginsberg had announced that he would soon move out to California for good. This was no pipe dream. Moe's two sons had settled their families north of San Francisco, and he had spent some of the cold months with them. He loved the country out there. He had no intention of retiring in the sun, however, under the care and supervision of his sons, "like some geriatric kindergartener," he announced, but it was time for a change. There were stirrings on the coast that intrigued him. He was excited about a community of pensioners, as yet small, but with the potential to expand in a progressive direction. According to Mama and Leon, the old light was in Moe's eyes again; the one that had been missing since the violent death of his wife, Judith. Her unknown assassin—for that's what they all called him—had never been found, and that no one in authority had looked very hard was a bitter truth to Moe, augmenting his abiding sorrow. But now he seemed once more to be the genial, shrewd mover and shaker of the old days.

"And why shouldn't he move on?" Mama commented. "He sees the handwriting on the wall." Frima knew what she meant. The community he loved of small farms, boardinghouses, and modest country hotels was vanishing. Soon kosher style food and a few old jokesters would be the only remnant of the older rural Jewish settlement.

"Still, I hate to see him go," Mama said.

"Me, too," Frima said. "And what if he gets sick on the train or dies out in the middle of nowhere with no one to take care of him—like Grandpa Joad in *The Grapes of Wrath*?"

"What a comparison! He will not be buried on the side of the road. He's off to see a new part of the world, with money in his pocket and renewed enthusiasm and curiosity. If he should die in the process, well, that would be very sad, but he knows that is better than to sit still and molder. You are too young to think this way, but Moe isn't. Believe me, I worried also, but he convinced me that this is what he wants. It's a great gift at his time of life to be able to seek something new with that kind of enthusiasm and energy."

Moe had decided to take a long train route through the Canadian Rockies and down the West Coast. He wanted to see something of North America. Frima was seeing him off at Grand Central Station, and she was happily surprised to see Beth there also. Moe stood tall, eager, full of excitement.

"Ah, my two beautiful young ladies, how can a man leave you? Yet I have always longed for the romance of trains, especially fancy-schmancy train travel, and I hear the food is terrific. Bacon and eggs for breakfast tomorrow, hmm? And cocktails in the bar before dinner, and perhaps after," Moe added, "if I find I have trouble sleeping in a Pullman car."

"No scandals, please. And write, you hear?" Frima was suddenly very happy for him.

"For you, my dear girl, I will keep a journal better than Mark Twain," Moe assured her.

Beth wrapped her arms around him. "If you don't write to me, I'll haunt you," she said. She had tears in her eyes. Beth, who was not a weeper.

"I didn't know Moe meant that much to you, Bethie." Frima said after the train departed.

"I love that man. I can't really explain it. But I hate crying, and the only remedy is lunch. Do you have time? My treat."

"Absolutely."

"We're here at Grand Central, so do you want to go to the Oyster Bar?"

"Oysters! You? I don't believe it. After your early experience? When did you get so adventurous?"

"I've learned a thing or two," Beth said.

—

Now, far from feeling adventurous herself, Frima sat in the hotel station wagon, which was almost splitting its seams with clothes and supplies and their family of four. The kids were singing and horsing around in the back seats, but she and Jack were quiet. He whistled absent-mindedly between his teeth as he drove, his ear tuned to the radio, waiting for the Yankees game to begin. She was silent, fanning off the heat from the road and the crowded car. Again she was fleetingly reminded of the Joad family, but, shamefaced, she dismissed any comparison. The Joads had packed their family and possessions into that old wreck of a truck to face a desperate unknown. She and her family were just going up to Ellenville to their hotel for the summer. More accurately, she and Lena and Rosalie were spending the entire season at Eisner's. Jack was teaching summer school and would only be there weekends. Frima was fine with that. No use kidding herself, they needed some time apart from each other. Still, she noted dryly, both the fictional Joads and the real Eisners were bidding a permanent farewell to a farm they loved.

As long as Grandpa was alive, Mama would have continued managing and living at the hotel, but since he was gone, she really wanted time to relax and do some traveling with Leon. Running a family vacation farm was exhausting work, especially when your own family spent so little time working there with you. Frima was abashed when she looked honestly at how little time she and Jack had spent in Ellenville in the last few years since Rosalie's birth. It was easy to tell herself that the weekends and holidays they had spent in the city rather than the country were just breaks in their routine. She loved being up in the country, and she'd thought they could at least spend summers there, which would have been a help to Mama and would have given her a chance to be with her grand-children. In truth, Frima felt she could be quite happy there all year round, but evidently she was the only one in her household who felt that way. The kids had no real attachment to the place; they were too young. Lena was just as happy to go to a city day camp with her school friends, while Rosalie was too little to care where they spent their time. And Jack, she had discovered to her pain, didn't miss much about the hotel at all. His affection for their "little haven," as he had called it during their courtship, had worn away. He had more than once offered a whole lot of reasons why they shouldn't commit any time to the hotel or property.

"I have to say, Frima, that I vastly prefer beach vacations. We could spend a couple of weeks at the Jersey shore or out on Long Island or Far Rockaway. It would be fun for the kids and easier for us. I know you're not crazy about sand and salt water, but I bet you'd come to like the beach more, and you could read and relax to your heart's content. I'm sure we can find a place with enough trees and grass to suit you. Also, that way I could continue working the rest of the summer. They need people to teach summer school or tutor. And we could use the money, right?"

"I don't actually see why you have to work in the hot city most of the summer, but I can't force you go to the farm, if you truly don't like it. Funny, I thought it really had a place in your heart."

"It did, but we all have to grow up, you know. Both you and your mother are entirely sentimental about those acres of ground. It isn't really a farm anymore, and it can't compete with the more luxurious hotels."

"The whole point is that it doesn't want to compete with the bigger resort hotels, and it does quite nicely being what it is."

"Well, you can't start a family dynasty up there. It's completely impractical—you can see that, can't you, honey?"

Honey, my eye! I can see, she had thought resentfully, that you are being patient and reasonable because you know you've already got your way.

The ball game began, and Jack listened intently to it on the car radio. Frima had given up wondering how he could possibly be so engrossed in the game and drive at the same time, but evidently this was a feat easily mastered by baseball fans, which she and her daughters were not. Invariably the female members of the household wandered off or nodded off to the unending roar of the crowd. Today, she was glad not to have to make conversation while the game was on. She was still sore about Jack's disloyalty to Eisner's, and she wanted time to muster a powerful argument to counter his. She wasn't quite sure why, since the farm was being sold, anyway.

She waited until they had arrived in Ellenville and were preparing for bed to continue her argument. "You say Mama and I are romantic about Eisner's. Well, it's because we have loved it. I'm not in the least ashamed of feeling sentimental and nostalgic about this place. But I can't see either of those feelings as driving my mother. She loves it and is proud of it, eyes wide open. And she certainly created a thriving business here."

"So I've noticed, and so she's told me often—and in more detail than I care to know."

"And just what is that supposed to mean?"

"Well, we've had some discussion about whether you and I would want to take over the place. I told her that realistically it wasn't a possibility." Jack stifled a yawn.

"We? Where was I during this discussion? I wasn't to have some say in this?" She wanted to shout at him, but kept her voice down. The walls were thin.

"Now, Frima, be reasonable."

"I'm sick and tired of being reasonable. All that means is letting you have your way."

Clearly prepared for this, Jack launched into a speech. A highly aggrieved one, though he kept his voice down. "I'm trying to do what's best for my family! I want you and the kids to be able to walk the streets, having the whole neighborhood and community around you. I don't want them or you to have to wait for a school bus or a ride to go to a store or movie. The girls shouldn't have to think buying a hot dog or an ice cream cone is a big event. And even more, I want them to grow up in safety with their own kind—knowing that they are Jews and proud of it. Yeah, there are Jews in the Catskills, but they're mostly summer people. What kind of kids would they grow up with and what kind of schools would they go to? And, yes, I want them to feel superior. Every other people feel that about themselves. They should honor their religion, their traditions. And I want my wife to have the luxury of being a full-time wife and mother. I don't want to see her slaving away in a store like my own mother. Or in a hotel, for that matter. You know how hard your mother works. She's barely has time to sleep."

"Okay, I get the point." She removed herself to the bathroom. Oh, he was good at this! He had a positive talent for self-righteousness, and she wasn't skilled at countering this with noble sentiments of her own. And manipulative—my God! Did she have to be hit over the head with a hammer before she got it? Prime example: that famous episode just after the war. Jack never had the slightest real desire to risk his life aiding the Haganah to rescue Jewish refugees. He just wanted Frima to think he did and adamantly object to his doing any such thing. That way he was off the hook. He could get credit for courage and the right sentiments and win her gratitude for the sacrifice of his ideals. After all, he was only doing what was best for his family. And he could get rid of the piano, as well! Two seconds later, the reflexive reaction: was she being too harsh? And then her new answer: so what?

Odd, but she felt quite tranquil after she had deciphered all of this. She was armed with insight, at least, and it gave her some power. So no more arguments tonight. Talking to Mama, now, that was something else altogether. She'd have plenty to say to her about leaving Frima out of the decisions about so vital a part of her life. She'd wait until Jack left for the city on Sunday, and then she'd demand an explanation.

As soon as she saw the exhaust of Jack's car Sunday, she went in search of her mother. There was a rare lull in activity this pre-season afternoon hour. She spied Leon grabbing a nap in a hammock with a newspaper shading his balding pate from the sun, which meant Mama would most likely be alone in her office.

"We need to talk, Mama. Let's go for a walk. Whatever you're doing can wait an hour or so. I'll help you later."

Seeing her sober face, Mama rose instantly and joined her. They walked some way down the wooded lane, until Frima finally broke the silence.

"There's something that I can't understand, and it really bothers me," Frima began. "I hear you had some talk with Jack about our taking over the hotel, and you didn't consult me. I had no say in the fate of this place that's meant so much to me. I can't believe you would do that—do you think I'm a child, an idiot?" Frima had rehearsed this opening in private, for she wanted to appear calm and adult about this, yet she found herself fighting tears.

Mama looked pained and was silent for some moments. She

guided Frima to a log where they could sit down and took her hands into her own. She began to speak haltingly with many pauses, not at all her decisive, managerial style.

"I'm so very sorry that I've hurt you by doing this. And in no way was it because I don't value your opinion. Of course, you aren't a child or an idiot—quite the opposite. In many ways I feel that you are the one with the adult strength and intelligence—expansiveness of mind—in your household. Forgive me for saying this, but it's the way I feel."

"Then why wasn't I consulted?"

"Perhaps that was a mistake. It was difficult to know what to do, but I thought I should test the waters with Jack first. If he were absolutely against the idea of taking over the enterprise there was no way it was going to happen, regardless of how you felt about it, and it would only cause bad feelings. I would be putting myself between you and your husband, and I didn't want to do that. I know how attached you are to this piece of earth of ours—or I should say that was ours—which was why I approached him in the first place, though I was pretty sure he would refuse the offer. Jack was adamant, so I thought it better not to pursue it."

Frima was silent. There was truth here.

Seeing her daughter's face, Mama sighed, then continued, choosing her words carefully. "Your husband is not a man who likes to take risks. I believe you know this, my dear, and maybe better than I. He is . . . how shall I say this? Very aware of his personal safety zone, and he defends it carefully and well. He wants safety and comfort for himself and his family, a conservative at heart and quite conventional in his vision of what a family should be."

"Maybe because he never really had a family before now."

Mama nodded her head in agreement.

"You don't like Jack very much, do you, Mama. I never realized."

"You shouldn't think that. Jack is a good man. He works hard for you and the girls and he is affectionate and devoted to his family. He's hard not to like, he's so attractive and intelligent and engaging."

"But?"

"I don't always approve of him—a mother-in-law's prerogative, you know. And, well, we all have our ways, Frima."

"And his are?"

"He is sometimes selfish. Now don't look at me like that. I don't mean with his money or his time. It's just that he is very fond of his own way, and adept at persuading us that his way is best."

"You don't mean us; you mean me, don't you? And just what is it that you think he has persuaded me to do?"

"Well, your piano, for instance. Why is it here where you can hardly touch it?"

"Oh, that. You know there was no room for it in the city."

Mama went no further. She saw very well that her daughter had just shut the door again. "It's really cooling off. Look at those clouds. Maybe we should get back before we are drenched," she said.

They walked back arm in arm, not hurrying but moving apace. Reaching the lobby, they were surprised that the staff was already setting up for dinner. Frima glanced at her watch. They had been gone for well over an hour. Yet they had said so few words, really. Their meaning and connection were in the silences between the words, permeating and swelling in stillness, like the rain filling the air.

CHAPTER 27

"I've got a surprise for you," Mama announced the next morning. She sat on the porch swing, motioning Frima to sit besides her. "Beth just called me. She wanted to know if there would be room for her and Eduardo to come up for a week. I told her there would always be room for them, so they are coming up next Sunday, actually."

Frima's face brightened. "They are both coming? Why, that's super! But aren't we full up?"

"Leon and I have a home, you know, a stone's throw from here, and we can manage quite nicely. Most of our personal stuff is already there. All I need to do is empty a couple of drawers, and they can have our room and bath right here in the main house."

"Now that's service," Frima said with a grin.

"Well, Beth says that Eduardo has been working like a man possessed, and she has insisted that he take a week off. And she, herself, wanted to be here one more time before Eisner's is no more. Eduardo has never been to the Catskills, and he's quite curious about the region. And I'm very curious to meet him. I hope this place isn't too lowbrow for him."

"I doubt it. Eduardo is very intelligent and educated, but from what I know of him, he's an easy guy to be with. Quite genuinely courteous and unassuming. I think you'll like him very much, indeed."

"If he loves Beth, that's good enough for me. However, Jack, we all know, does not approve of him or of Beth's attachment to him."

"Oh, I wouldn't worry about Jack," Frima said, with surprising ease. "My husband may like things the way he likes them, but he's not stupid. He knows when he's outnumbered, and he'll behave himself. Besides they'll only have a little time in each other's company. After all, they arrive on Sunday morning and Jack leaves for the city on Sunday afternoon."

They lapsed into a comfortable silence, and Frima kicked off her sandals. "I'm only sorry Eduardo won't get a chance to meet Grandpa, Moe, and Judith, poor woman. They're all gone. All of them the genuine article, if you know what I mean."

"Excuse me?" Mama retorted. "But Leon and I are also the genuine article—even you!" She smiled good-naturedly as she said this, and Frima grinned back.

"Yup, that's me—Jewish pioneer in the New World—the genuine article. Now I guess I'd better collect my offspring, who certainly are no such articles, and tell them that breakfast is served." She slid her feet into her sandals, then turned again suddenly to face her mother. "You know, maybe Beth will take Eduardo to meet Max. Now he's the real goods!"

Mama watched her move buoyantly down the path. My daughter, she can tiptoe through the tulips, but there's steel in her, I know it. I hope she never needs it, but I'm very glad it's there.

Frima had judged shrewdly. The meeting of the adversaries was entirely civil, if not overflowing with warmth. Beth and Eduardo arrived at about ten in the morning, having gotten up in the middle of the night, according to Beth. Frima and Mama greeted the couple like long-lost, beloved relatives. Jack ambled over in his bathing trunks with a towel around his shoulders. He kissed Beth lightly on the cheek and shook hands with Eduardo. Then he casually excused himself.

"Sorry, folks, gotta take my little bathing beauties swimming. And, oh, Hannah, I'll bring the kids back for lunch, but none for me. I have to get back to the city early today."

"Do you want the kitchen to pack a lunch for you?"

"Maybe just a sandwich. I ate a ton of breakfast." Then, turning to Frima, he added, "See you in a couple of hours, honey."

She was impressed. His busy schedule was clearly by his own design, but he was handling things well. He wasn't falling all over himself with friendliness, but what could you expect? Still, she wasn't sorry to see him leave. Ordinarily she would have missed him, especially during what she still sometimes thought of as romantic summer nights. But now a five-day interval without him was like a vacation from school.

She and Beth together were like school girls. As soon as Jack was gone, they sat down with the others for lunch and begin cracking themselves up with Borscht Belt jokes.

"You heard this one?" Beth started. "A garment worker boards the train in Hoboken on route to the mountains. A hoity-toity conductor is punching tickets, when he comes to the man sitting in an aisle seat with a large suitcase obstructing his way. The man is happily singing to himself:

"'Yoo, hoo, hoo! Going to the Catskills, Ah, hah-hah, lying in the sun.'

"'Sir, your suitcase is in my way. Kindly remove it.'

"'Yoo, hoo, hoo! Going to the Catskills.'

"'Remove that bag at once, sir. If it's here when I come back down the aisle, I'm gonna throw it off the train. Do you understand me?'

"'Hoo, hah! I'm going to the Catskills! Yoo, hoo, hoo, I'm gonna sleep so late!'

"'I don't care where you're going, move that suitcase—you should have stowed it before we left the station! It's still here? Okay, I warned you!'

"'Hoo boy, I'm gonna eat like a schoolboy. Ah, hah, five pounds I'll gain.'

"The conductor grabs the suitcase and throws it off the train. 'There, how do you like that?'

"'Ah hah, hah, going to the Catskills. Hoo boy, dhat is not my valise!'"

"How about the Moskovitz Diamond?" Frima suggested.

"Enough! You'll give us all indigestion," warned Mama.

After lunch Frima and Beth decided on a stroll. Eduardo opted for a book and a lawn chair.

"This man is without doubt the most physically lazy creature alive," said Beth, turning to Hannah. "He exercises only his eyes and his fingers at the typewriter, eats like a horse, yet remains thin and fit. It's disgusting!" she said lovingly.

"A most irritating trait," Hannah agreed. Then she turned to Eduardo. "Do you mind if I sit here for a few minutes? I don't want to interrupt your reading."

"Please do," he said, gesturing to the seat next to him with a smile. "It's my pleasure to get to know one of Beth's most formative influences. She calls you a light in the darkness."

"Does she?" Hannah was pleased. "But she doesn't seem to be in the dark now. She looks beautiful and happy walking in the sunshine." Her eyes followed the two friends as they walked down the path from the house.

"To me she's beautiful even on the dark days. But I think she is talking about her childhood and adolescence, when you were one of the rare adults who encouraged her. She sees her young girlhood as Dickensian."

Hannah chuckled. "Not exactly a workhouse child, but she felt she was an ugly duckling and unappreciated. And then there was that big handsome brother, who could do no wrong. I knew she would be a beauty in her own time, and I always thought she was gifted, like my own daughter, only different."

Eduardo nodded. "They are quite different, but complementary—lovely to see them together."

"You do understand!"

"I understand from Beth that Frima is a gifted pianist."

"Yes, I believe she truly is. But she plays very little now."

"Is that her piano in the house? It looks like a fine instrument."

"As fine as her father and I could afford at the time. That piano used to be the most important object in her city home, but she shipped it up here, where it soon will be unavailable to her. I've begged her to take it back, but I don't think that will happen. Jack . . . her family . . . doesn't think there is room for it."

"Do you think she might play something for us some evening? Forgive me if I'm talking out of turn."

"She might, if you asked her and it was before the weekend."

They exchanged glances but said nothing more. Edward offered her a cigarette, which she declined. "Don't mind me," Hannah said, embarrassed, "I'm the one who's speaking out of turn. I'd better get back to the office and let you get on with your book."

"Oh, don't go yet—not without telling me." Eduardo, said, rising politely.

"Telling you what?"

"About the Moskovitz Diamond."

Mama shook her head gently. "Now, now, no more Borscht Belt jokes."

"Does it come with a curse—Moskovitz?

"You've heard it already, you sly man!"

"No, but I've heard about the Ibarra Tiara."

"Well, that's certainly not Borscht Belt."

"More like garbanzo soup country."

"Frima and Beth should both know better. I don't know who coined that name for this area, but it always has something demeaning in it—a synonym for lowbrow—you, know, like Borscht-Belt Chopin or Borscht-Belt theater."

"I didn't know. But maybe they were joking as if we were all what

Beth calls MOT. She sometimes compliments me by allowing me to be a Member of Our Tribe, though with my background she's taking a pretty big risk, I'd say. My family like to think they are descended from Torquemada."

"I'll risk it also. As far as I'm concerned, you are MOT."

It was clear by the time that Frima and Beth returned that Hannah and Eduardo were pals.

"And another woman hits the dust," Beth murmured to Frima.

Beth had described Eduardo as a very private man, and Frima could believe it. There was a quality—not exactly reserve—but something hidden and unknowable. Yet here, relaxing on vacation, he was quite friendly and engaging, though he was seldom the instigator of social contact. He wears well, this man, she said to herself.

What really surprised and delighted her was his way with her children. The couple of times that Beth and Frima could drag him away from his books for a swim, he good-naturedly played with them in the water and left the two women to loll on the grassy beach. And even better, he read to them and told them stories, mugging and clowning and making silly noises. By the third day of their visit, Rosalie wanted no one but him to read her storybooks, except at bedtime, when she still wanted Frima. Even Lena, who was quite a good reader herself and proud of it, hung around when Eduardo told stories. She was getting a crush on him.

"Lena wants to ask you something," Frima said in a low voice to Eduardo, "but she's kind of shy about it."

"Ask me what?" He smiled at the little girl.

"Do you have a nickname? I really want a nickname. But Mommy says my name is too short, like hers. Rosalie has a nickname—Daddy calls her Rosie. Aunt Bethie has a nickname—her real name is Bethesda, but it's silly, so nobody calls here that." The adults hid their smiles. "And Eduardo—that's a long name too." Lena spoke a little breathlessly. "Do your friends call you Eddie? Could we call you that?"

Eduardo considered this seriously. "Well, I'll tell you the truth, Lena. If you called me Eddie, I probably wouldn't answer, because I wouldn't remember you were talking to me. I'm not used to it. But if you called me Lalo, I'd answer, because that's what my family calls me."

"Lalo—that's a funny name."

"Yes, it is, but it's a very common nickname for Eduardo in Spanish.

"Can we call you Lalo?"

"Yes, But it's a secret. It's a silly name, and I don't want anyone else to know about it."

"Does Aunt Bethie call you Lalo?"

"Sometimes, but only in our house, when no one is around."

"But I still don't have a nickname."

"Well, where I come from, people sometimes add *ito* to a name for a boy or *ita* to the name of a girl. It's like a nickname for some one they like. So we would call you Lenita."

"Lenita, I like that!" Lena said after thinking about it for half a second.

"I want to be an ita too!" Rosalie chimed in.

"How about Rosalita for you?"

"Yes!"

Lena was excited, catching on immediately. "So Mommy would be Frimita, and Daddy, Jackito?"

"Well," answered Eduardo seriously. "You have to be careful. It's usually for kids, not for grownups, unless you're really sure they like it. Some grownups might think it was disrespectful. As if you called your father, Jacky, instead of Daddy. If I were you, I'd just keep these nicknames a secret for now. Just like my nickname. So people don't think we're silly."

Rosalie looked puzzled, but Lena was satisfied. "Okay, but when we're alone with you, it will be Aunt Bethie and Uncle Lalo." Both of them skipped away, excited. "Don't tell!" they heard Lena warning her sister.

Eduardo lit a cigarette, his expression blank.

"My God, Lalito, what have you wrought?" asked Beth, grinning. "Can you see my brother when he hears about Uncle Lalo?"

"That's why it's a secret," he said soberly and turned to his book, ignoring the simultaneous grins from the ladies.

Frima had a lot of work that week, as much as she'd ever had at the hotel, but with Beth and Eduardo there, it was truly like a vacation—a family vacation. Beth quickly pitched in with the office work, and with Eduardo entertaining the kids for an hour or so, Frima managed to take a little time each day at the piano. She needed encouragement, even pushing from the others to do this, and it didn't take her long to realize there was a gentle conspiracy to get her playing and performing again. This conspiracy most obviously did not include her husband, whose name was never mentioned by any of them in connection with her music. She was grateful for that. She wanted no further confrontation with him this summer. As for herself, she was a bit uneasy. What if she was opening a Pandora's box, stirring up a longing she couldn't fulfill? Still, after several hours of practice and considerable coaxing, she consented to play for the others. Mozart, the "A Major Sonata," she thought, though she was a little worried about the scherzo; Chopin, the "Raindrop Prelude." Also maybe a little Schubert. Beethoven? Not yet. She decided on an informal, unannounced mini-recital for anyone who wanted to listen in the late afternoon on Thursday. She figured it would be a time when there weren't too many people around.

Frima assumed that only Mama, Leon, Beth, and Eduardo would be there, but more people gathered, as they stopped to listen for a moment and stayed for more. Mama, Leon, and Eduardo, she noted, were smiling steadily, very pleased. At a pause after the Mozart, Beth slipped away, and Frima wondered about that, until she saw that she quickly returned to a seat behind the others, pad and pencil in hand, and began to sketch her at the instrument. It was all very gratifying.

Jack returned Friday evening, relieved to be out of the city and finished with the long, hot drive. By the time he'd had a quick swim and a cold beer, he was in good spirits, happy to be back with Frima and the kids. In their excitement at seeing him, the girls forgot momentarily about Uncle Lalo. Dinner was later on Friday nights, so the girls had eaten earlier with the other children. With luck Frima could forestall their saying anything about Eduardo until tomorrow morning. No longer than that, though, because the kids loved to get up very early with Daddy. Meanwhile, her mood remained light, and she would not allow anything to deflate it. The weather had begun to cool deliciously, and she looked forward to a stroll with her husband after dinner and to their nighttime intimacies with the renewed enthusiasm that followed their weekday separation.

At dinner, Jack was borderline cool to Beth and Eduardo, but inoffensive. Mostly he didn't talk to them directly if he didn't have to. He passed the salt if he was asked to, and did so courteously, but with no real interest, as if they were casual acquaintances who happened to be seated at the same table. When Eduardo complimented him on the brightness and charm of his daughters, he graciously thanked him, giving Frima all the credit. He would not be engaged any further. There was naturally a little tension in the atmosphere. Still, Frima was optimistic that no storm would break out.

"My sister is looking pretty good, I have to admit," Jack said to Frima as they strolled together down the road after dinner. "She looks downright prosperous, not exactly one of the laboring masses. Those clothes she's wearing—a bit too look-at-me for a modest hotel, don't you think? I'll bet she can't afford them on her own earnings."

"She looks terrific—she has a real flair," Frima agreed, careful to keep any envy out of her voice. It was true that Bethie was doing the most with her striking looks by wearing the bright colors and exotic fabrics she loved. And it was equally true that Eduardo very likely paid for them, but that did not make her a fallen woman. Anyone who knew Beth and was sympathetic to her recognized that her clothes were an expression of her liberation from the repressive, sometimes self-inflicted, admonitions of her youth: you're too tall, too thin, too awkward, all the don't-call-attention-to-yourself warnings. However, Frima was not about to encourage Jack's resentment by talking about this any further. She was still high from her recital, and wanted to maintain the feeling.

"The kids are looking good, aren't they?" she commented.

Jack smiled dryly at her obvious change of subject. "They sure are," he said.

Considering how deeply he resented Beth and Eduardo's arrangement, Frima figured he was doing the best he could.

By breakfast time the next morning, things were different. "So now there's an Uncle Lalo in the picture. How sweet! And we have a Lenita and a Rosalita—even Frimita. And my sister, Chiquita Banana? It's not enough to have charmed the pants off my sister, he has to start on my family."

"Oh, come on! You're making a big deal over nothing. The kids like him—why shouldn't they? They asked him if they could call him Uncle Lalo. What's he supposed to say? Now we've been having a lovely time here, and you can too, if you'd make an effort. This is the perfect opportunity to bury the hatchet—or at least begin to." As they walked to the dining room, Frima could almost see Jack silently weighing his options. It reminded her unpleasantly of her father-in-law, whom Beth referred to as the adding machine. Of course, Jack wasn't crass, and the situation had little to do with money. Still it was a resemblance she didn't want to contemplate.

Jack gave a sacrificial sigh. "Okay," he said. "Let's have breakfast—one happy family."

To their surprise no effort was needed. When they came to the family table, Beth was having a last gulp of coffee, and Eduardo was already out the door. Beth greeted them gaily.

"We decided at the spur of a moment to drive Leon to Monticello. His car is at the mechanic's, so we're dropping him off there and then we're going on to the Alpine. I'm dying to see the place again. We'll be back before lunch. Enjoy your privacy a little," she said, giving Frima a peck on the cheek.

This was odd. Beth never got up before she had to. For them to be leaving so early, they would have had to arrange it beforehand. Well, everyone looked happy enough, and she had to admit breakfast was more relaxed and cheerful with the others gone.

CHAPTER 28

Beth wanted to weep out loud. Her buggy little cabin in the woods was gone. The most beloved place at the Alpine for her, be it ever so humble. Here, she'd enjoyed her first tastes of adult intimacy and freedom and accepted self. Oh, she had wanted Eduardo to see it before anything else. Of course she should have expected this. Everything was changing so fast. She had almost missed the side road leading to the cabin, so transformed was it from a half-hidden dirt path to a macadam road with a discreet painted wooden arrow pointing to the Lodge. This turned out to be a handsome two-story structure with log siding and screened picture windows. Landscaped trees and greenery surrounded it. It would have intimidated any stray mosquito. It certainly intimidated Beth.

"We'd better drive round to the front of the main entrance. 'Parking for Lodge guests only,' it says here. Very fancy-schmancy!"

"It's called progress."

"I bet Rhubarb wouldn't even be allowed in here."

"Rhubarb?"

"I never told you about Rhubarb? Well, it was a while ago. He was a dog who adopted me when I worked here. Very comforting and adoring. I could do no wrong according to Rhubarb, who was an old hand around here—a meeter and greeter—one of Max's mutts, actually." She peered out at the porch as they drove up to the main entrance. "Speaking of the devil, I believe that's the man himself. I don't know if he's been renovated but he certainly looks prosperous and spruced up."

Beth usually found that places revisited always seemed smaller than in memory, but not Max and not the Alpine Song. Everything seemed larger, grander. She wasn't surprised at the new tennis courts, the renovated pool area, the added cottages, for she'd heard that Max had done well and was expanding the place. But even the unchanged main house and the older cottages gave an impression of development. Everything was newly painted and landscaped, presenting an image of a solid, well-maintained estate. Nothing cheap and postwar looking here; more like old-money suburbia, the kind of community that wouldn't allow Jews, she thought ironically. She didn't like it as well as the old place, but she had to hand it to Max; it worked, if you liked that sort of thing. The man who came down from the porch was no longer the lean man in work boots and pants, but a smiling, well-fed proprietor, who would seem quite at home on a golf course in his light tan slacks and striped cotton T-shirt. He had added a few pounds and shed the worry lines on his forehead.

"Well, well," he said, coming to greet them. "So this here is Bess! Beth, I understand, according to Hannah Eisner. This is the same young thing that used to have Vincent Migliori, may he rest in peace, hanging around her and also my old dog Rhubarb sniffing at her heels. He's gone too."

"Poor Rhubarb! He wasn't hit by a car or anything?"

"Just age, my dear. It happens to the best of us. But look at you! Hannah told me you were, as she says, drop dead gorgeous, and now I see she wasn't kidding."

"You're looking pretty spiffy yourself," Beth countered. "Positively prosperous and sleek."

"That's what comes of living and eating at your own hotel," Max said. "Besides, times are better than before the war. So, are you going to introduce me to your gentleman friend?"

"Of course. Max Kalish, meet Eduardo Ibarra."

"My pleasure," said Max.

"And mine."

Beth jumped right in, hoping to avoid any of Max's uncensored questions about their relationship. "You see that interested, curious expression on Eduardo's face? I call it his interview look. He's a journalist, you see. And he's very interested in the Catskill resort country. I'm sure he'd like to hear some of your history here."

"I certainly would, if you would do me the honor and can spare the time," Eduardo added.

"An hour I can spare. Unless you want to stay for lunch. Can't? Well, come into my office where it's quieter. Coffee okay? Hey, Mikey, bring us some fresh coffee from the kitchen and some of that breakfast coffee cake—that's a good fellow."

Max was happy to talk about his history. Eduardo could bring that out in people. Also, Beth realized, her old boss probably didn't have much audience for this kind of reminiscence.

"Like the others, I was an immigrant Jew on the Lower East Side, originally from Minsk. But I didn't want to be a farmer, like Jake Eisner and the others. When did a small farmer ever have a chance in Hell? Only in fairy tales. Me, I started as a cook when I still lived on Rivington Street in Manhattan. Better than being a pants presser in a tenement, like my father, or a peddler with a pushcart. When I got the opportunity for a little land up here, I took it, but I wasn't going to raise chickens. From the very beginning I liked to think of myself as an innkeeper, even if I was really only a cook in a boardinghouse.

"My sister was the bookkeeper and the housekeeper when I started to live here. Without her, I never could have survived. In my family she was the educated one, which is unusual. It's mostly the sons who study, you understand. But she went to classes at the settlement house on the Lower East Side, where she learned about American deportment and culture. The rich ladies taught the girls. For these women, it was like donating to charity. Then she went to night school to learn typing and bookkeeping. She read everything she could get her hands on. Also a couple of summers she was a waitress in Asbury Park, so she learned about nice manners, how to set a table and fold a fancy napkin. I was a bum until I started working in a delicatessen. There I learned to cook, and I loved it; and I was very interested in food management, I suppose you'd call it.

"You, know, this was an interesting community in the old days. Everyone worked their heads off. It wasn't no workers' paradise, but everyone worked. This place as it grew became my life and my family. I had ambitions. I wanted my Jewish guests to enjoy the luxury of being waited on and catered to like any other Americans at a hotel. They should enjoy a vacation. It's a fantasy for them, a romance—nothing wrong with that. That's what I still want to give them." Max halted and expelled a sigh.

"Still, some things I don't want no part of, you know? Like this racetrack they're gonna build right here in Monticello. Some of the big owners with influence, other hoo-ha businessmen—they try to tell me it's good for business, brings in more guests, adds revenues to the area, jobs." Max was getting excited, they could see, and didn't pause for any response. "Revenues, my foot! Gangsters is what it will bring in! Now, Beth can tell you, people that come here to the hotel, some of them play a lot of cards. But we're talking about a friendly game. I don't spy on them, but I don't take any cut, either. This is not a casino. It's not like Las Vegas. With a racetrack you get the pros, big casinos coming in. Big-stakes con men—I don't care, Jews or gentiles—they are out to make their profits off the ordinary guys who come up here for a little break from work, a little relaxation. The little guys always lose—that's the way it's supposed to work." Max stopped talking then, shaking his head, his face somber. Neither of the other two made any immediate comment, but Eduardo who had been scribbling rapidly, looked up from his notepad and smiled at Max pleasantly and steered him in a new direction.

"You know, I'm intrigued by the name of this place. So many hotels we passed on the road were named for the proprietors, like Grossinger's or Eisner's, or for obvious landscape features: The Pines, Green Acres. The Alpine Song—now that's a lyrical name. How did you decide on this?"

Max looked pleased at the question. "I guess it was a hidden romantic streak in me. Believe me, I didn't know from the Alps— French, Swiss, or German. But when I was a young man, there was a kind of music in the wind through these trees. You can't hear it now. Not enough trees left."

"Why Max, you old softie, you really are a romantic at heart!" Beth teased him.

"Was, my dear girl. For about ten minutes, maybe. Mostly hotel keeping is a lot of drudgery and hard work."

"Still, a handsome resort of this scale and comfort is a proud accomplishment," Eduardo prompted him gently.

"Well, yes, it is. But from me you won't hear no Horatio Alger story or any such fairytale. I worked hard, way longer than factory hours, believe me. But without the others—I mean Moe Ginsberg and his kind—I couldn't have made it. Personally, I think some of them are a little softheaded about the working class, even though I am and have always been a worker, I won't deny it. But without the insurance cooperative, the credit union these fellows organized, the sharing of the risks they pushed for, I wouldn't have this. That Moe, and Jake Eisner, too—I was sorry to see them gone—smart men. Jake, he should rest in peace, was just a farmer, you could say, but clever. A real head on his shoulders, and he knew how to get along with everyone. He was persuasive, could convince people to act together. And Moe, you think he's just easygoing with his joking, but he's an educated man who studies things: mathematics, economics. He is sharp as a tack and practical and principled both. They both hated this racetrack thing also. I'm sure that's part of why they decided to leave. Then there was Judith, Moe's wife, God bless her." Max was still again for a few moments, his expression suddenly looking worried rather than indignant. Eduardo silently signaled Beth not to say a word, and Max soon spoke again.

"I don't know, maybe it's a good thing Moe is not here. It's hard to figure—is he better off not knowing? Maybe I shouldn't be telling you this, but they found the miserable animal who shot Judith. Moe's wife—you know about her?"

"Who? What did they find out? Who found her? How did you find out?" Beth bombarded him with questions.

"Well, I live so close to town—I hear things from my suppliers, shopkeepers. You know, word gets around. I don't know the details, and I don't really want to know, but it was a local rube, a shit-kicker, the *goyem* would call him (you should excuse me, Beth), even though he was one of them. He made some kind of cockamamie deathbed confession, they say. A confession or a boast, who can be sure? He should live forever in *drerd.*"

"Did any of us know him?" Beth asked.

"I don't think so. Though from the police you'd get nothing. They weren't exactly dropping dead in their hurry to find the bastard, you should excuse me."

"That's what Vinny said. He didn't think there would be any investigation at all. I was shocked he was so cynical. What did I know?"

"The worry is, should someone tell Moe? Would it help him or hurt?"

"I have no idea," said Beth. She turned to Eduardo, her face questioning.

"I think I would want to know," he said. "But that's me. I wouldn't spread this around, but I'd guess you could ask Hannah or Leon. They know him so well."

"So, maybe, you could tell her," Max said, feeling relieved of his burden.

"Let's leave it for now," Eduardo said pleasantly. "Beth and Leon are cooking up a happy surprise for Hannah, and we wouldn't want to ruin it."

"I do want to tell Frima about Judith," Beth remarked, when they were on the road back to Ellenville. "Just not today."

"Right. Now tell me about this dog. Rhubarb? Did you name it?"

"No, Max did, I guess. I once asked him why. 'Who remembers?' was all he said. I thought it was maybe because his skin and tongue had a pink, rhubarb-like cast."

"Have you been pining for a dog?" Eduardo looked at her quizzically.

"Not anymore, really," Beth answered. "It's just that I always wanted one when I was a kid, but my father wouldn't allow it. One of the rare things he was probably right about—a dog in a cramped apartment. Still, dogs have great personalities," she said a little wistfully.

"All of them?"

"You know what I mean. They are right upfront, honest in their feelings. They can't lie or be sly about anything. Give a dog a little attention and it is loving and grateful. Totally unselfish; not a mean bone in its body."

"You've heard about a dog with a bone, of course."

"You know very well what I mean."

'How about a cat? Do you like cats?"

"I never thought about them, actually. Do you?"

"I like both cats and dogs. I'd always had them around the house before I moved to this country. But they were companion and working animals who ate and slept in the kitchen or some outside shelter."

"Like the other servants and peons?"

Eduardo grinned, appreciatively. "What I mean is they weren't useless overbred creatures who sit on your sofa or your lap and share your bed, shedding hair, as they go."

"Where is this all going?" Beth asked.

"I'm just trying to find out if you've been longing for a pet to keep you company and if I've been depriving you of it."

"Well, it might be something to think about, if you want one too, but for the moment, I already have one overbred hairy creature in my bed."

"Woof," he responded. They reached the hotel and walked shoulder to shoulder to the front porch.

CHAPTER 29

To anyone looking at the two couples relaxing in the shade with cool drinks, they made the perfect picture for a vacation brochure. Except that not everyone was really that relaxed. Beth couldn't contain her excitement. She turned to Frima.

"You know that drawing I began of you—'Frima at the Piano?'"

"What drawing?" Jack asked.

"Something I did while you were in the city. Frima will explain. Anyway, Leon looked at it and he really liked it, and he wants me to do a painting from it. He's commissioned me to do it. I said I would do it for free, but he insisted. He wants to give it to your mother as a surprise belated wedding gift. It has to be a secret. But I need you to pose for me, Frima. Maybe at some time in the afternoons here, while they're away, and then some more in the city."

"A painting of me? Why, I don't know what to say. What a sweet man he is—how generous of both of you! So that's why the three of you scurried off this morning. So you could plot." Frima turned to Jack. "What a surprise!"

"Sure is," he answered lightly, with a little smile.

Although she saw at once that he was making an effort to show enthusiasm, his face was clouded. Her spirits drooped a notch, but she refused to let him spoil the moment for her. Of course, Bethie, in her excitement, had managed to make him feel left out of the process, the decision-making. All she would have had to do was tell Jack first—or direct the conversation to him. Okay, so she wasn't the most tactful person on earth, but couldn't Jack be generous about it? Apparently not.

"I didn't know you did portraits. A commission? Well, well! I know you'll do your best to do her justice." Jack took a swig of his drink. "Frima has a rare beauty that I imagine you would find hard to capture. I mean, she's not very proletarian looking."

He simply couldn't stop himself, Frima saw. She felt like smacking him.

Beth looked at him warily. "Well it's not meant to be a completely lifelike portrait, you understand."

"Oh, I do understand," he continued smoothly. "Being realistic is not your style."

Before Frima could respond, Eduardo was already up. He stood for a moment behind Beth's chair and put his hands on her shoulders protectively.

"Now might be an opportune time for Frima to sit for you," he said gently. Then, not changing his tone, he looked pointedly at Jack. "And I'm sure that Frima and Leon and Hannah, of course, will know this painting to be a work of art and of love, and they will appreciate what an honor you are bestowing in creating it."

"I'm sure they will," Jack responded tonelessly. "Frima, if you're going to sit for your portrait, I'd better find the kids. Maybe they'd like me to take them for a swim before dinner, since Uncle Lalo is busy."

Left to themselves, the two women were silent for a few moments. "Well," Beth began, "for a Beth–Jack confrontation, that was actually pretty mild. But why couldn't Jack be happy about this, I ask you?" She seemed genuinely puzzled.

Frima expelled an exaggerated breath. "Because he felt left out. Because he's a little jealous. Because he wants to be paterfamilias. Because the kids are temporarily full of Uncle Lalo and Aunt Bethie, and he wants to be first in their hearts. Don't you know your brother, you knucklehead?"

"And because he is a horse's ass," Beth retorted.

Frima allowed herself a little snicker. "He has these moments, but I'm sure that Jack will be thoroughly ashamed of himself by now. And since all of this is about a wonderful surprise, we'll all be hunky-dory at dinner, right?"

"Right." Beth's face brightened. "But admit it—wasn't Eduardo splendid?"

"He certainly was."

At dinner, Mama was curious about Beth and Eduardo's visit to the Alpine Song and their reaction to it. Even Jack was interested; he remembered old Max. Since nobody would mention Leon's surprise or the news about Judith Ginsberg's murderer, the conversation was unexceptional.

"What's all this about a race course in Monticello?" Beth asked. "Max didn't seem at all happy about it."

"That will change things, won't it?" Jack commented. "Will it be trotters or flat?"

"Trotters, I believe," Frima answered.

"Trotting, running, or flying, I don't like the idea of racing," Mama said.

"You don't enjoy the sport of kings?" Eduardo asked her.

"I do not." Mama replied. "Neither do I enjoy kings."

"I love horses of every kind," Frima said, "but I like to see them happily grazing in a meadow or racing each other for fun, not running to exhaustion for someone's fun or profit."

"That's a nice romantic notion, honey, but horses are expensive as the devil to maintain, and they have to work to support themselves somehow. And, by the way, so do I," he added. "Hannah, I'll have an early breakfast with the kids tomorrow and head home just before lunch," Jack announced.

"So soon?" Mama asked.

"I have Teachers' Guild business. We can get a lot of work done during the summer, those of us remaining in the city, and I'm the new representative for my school.

"Is that the Teachers Union?" Beth asked, interested.

"Not yet. The so-called Teachers Union is completely commie, and the Guild broke away years ago—specifically to get away from the reds and the battling of their Marxist factions. And now the AFL and even the CIO are wising up and expelling the red unions."

"I'm not sure that's wise, to say nothing of just." Eduardo commented. "This country already has powerful blacklists operating in this Cold War atmosphere. And then, of course, there's McCarthy and HUAC, and now the arrest of the Rosenbergs—not exactly strengthening to a democracy."

"Somehow I'm not surprised you would think that. After all, you do live with my sister, and she's enamored of the comrades."

"You have no idea, Jack!" Beth was making a great effort not to call him a pungent name.

"I'd like to clarify, if I may," said Eduardo, turning to Jack, but putting his hand over Beth's. He spoke coolly, as if he wouldn't dream of disturbing the peace, but it was evident that he too was keeping his anger in check. "What I meant is that red-baiting is a perilous tactic for a labor movement, and in doing so, it is losing some of its best organizers and thinkers—even though I sometimes disagree with them, personally. And, yes, Beth and I might be called comrades, but not in the way you sneer at. We prefer to think we are intimate companions in the best way we can manage in our circumstances. And, by the way, it would be nice if you actually called Beth by her name. I have yet to hear you refer to her as anything but 'my sister,' with obvious irony."

"She doesn't like the name I call her, 'Bess'—the name she was born with."

"Well, then, you could call her the name she likes."

Mama looked worried. "That's enough! No more politics or arguments at the table. Other people will hear what is none of their business."

"My apologies, Hannah," Eduardo said.

Jack modulated his tone, as he put down his napkin. "It's certainly enough for me. We're finished aren't we?" he asked Mama pleasantly. "If you'll excuse me, I've got things to do."

Nothing but a coma was likely to relieve Frima's discomfort. Evidently Jack couldn't bear to lose; not to Frima, or Beth, or Eduardo. Not to anyone. You thought everything was settled, but he just bided his time. After a few moments. Frima rose from her chair, saying simply, "I'd better follow him." It was a necessary gesture, but she knew there would be no more talk between her husband and herself this evening about what had commenced at dinner, and she assumed the others would remain mute also. She left them to their dessert and coffee, if anyone wanted them.

Frima "had a headache" that night, and stayed in bed as late as possible in order not to join the others for breakfast. She refused to witness any sequel to the previous day. She didn't leave their bedroom until she heard Jack's car pull out of the driveway. She needed a respite from his anger and her own. Going directly to the kitchen for coffee and toast, she found her daughters impatiently waiting for her. Lena plunged right in, obviously troubled.

"I don't understand what Daddy said. And why was he mad at us?"

"I'm sure he wasn't mad at you, sweetheart. Tell me what happened?" (No respite, evidently.)

"Well, you know how I want a cousin? So I said to Daddy, I wish Aunt Bethie and Uncle Lalo would have a baby so I could have a cousin. And he said they couldn't have a baby because they weren't married and we didn't have any uncle and probably never would. I didn't know they weren't married. I thought people who lived in a house together were married or, you know, related, like me and Rosalie."

"Not always."

"Why don't they get married?"

"Because sometimes people can't or they have to wait for a while. It's hard to explain, but you'll understand when you are a little older."

"Boy, do I hate it when people say that!"

"I know, and I'm sorry. But it's true."

Lena hesitated, scuffing the ground with her sandaled foot before she continued. "Is Uncle Lalo a bad man?"

"You know Daddy said we shouldn't call him Uncle Lalo," Rosalie said uneasily.

"Is Aunt Bethie bad?"

"Did Daddy say that?"

"No, but he sounded like it, you know?"

"I do know." Frima took a daughter under each arm. "Now listen to me, girls. Eduardo is a good man and Aunt Beth is a good woman and they love each other, and you. And Daddy is a good man, but you know when grownups are tired or a little upset, they say things that they don't really mean. And remember Daddy and Aunt Bethie are brother and sister, and they sometimes quarrel. But then they make up, just like you and Rosalie, right?"

The kids were silent.

"And remember that Eduardo said Lalo was a silly name and also a secret name."

"So when Daddy is there, he is never Uncle Lalo. Just Eduardo."

"That's right, Lena. You know that all the grownups call him Eduardo anyway."

Rosalie piped up crossly. "Well, I want to call him Uncle Lalo—at least sometimes—when Daddy isn't here, and I like it when he calls me Rosita or sometimes Rosalita. I'm the only one with two *itas*," Rosalie said, asserting herself. "And you, Lena, don't you be bossy. I'm not a baby!"

Frima smiled in spite of herself. She always got a kick out of Rosalie defending her territory. She kissed them both and stood quietly with an arm around each for a few moments until she could feel them relax.

"Are you feeling better now? Do you want to join the other kids? Good. It looks like they're going to pick blueberries, so run back to your room and put on long sleeves and pants. Lena, help Rosie, and don't let her get scratched."

She continued on into the kitchen to get some coffee, though what she felt she really needed was a stiff drink. Damn him! What Jack had said to the kids was cruel. She didn't know he had it in him. No matter how rough their marital waters, she had always had faith in him as a loving, supportive father. That he had left her with the burden of soothing and explaining his behavior was a minor irritant compared to the stony fear inside her that she would have to protect her daughters from their father's ruthlessness. She found that the hand that held her coffee cup was shaking, and she hastily put the cup down as her mother came into the kitchen.

"I heard Jack leave about a half hour ago, and Leon has taken Eduardo off with him somewhere. Says he wants to talk business with him—I've no idea what. Why don't you join Beth in the dining room? She's still at the table. The kitchen is still open, so eat something please. You look like you need it. Poached eggs on toast okay? I'll have them bring it to you right now."

Frima nodded, and Mama patted her shoulder, her face rather abstracted. She wondered if Mama had heard something of Jack's little interchange with the kids.

Beth obviously had not, judging by the placid way she was pouring another cup of coffee. "I'm glad to see someone as lazy as me," Beth greeted Frima with a languid smile and a huge yawn, immediately interpreted by Frima as meltingly postcoital. "Peaceful isn't it?" Beth commented.

"I'll say." Frima was amazed at her own ability to restore outward calm to herself. She was getting good at it. "Beth, would it be all right if we waited until the afternoon for me to pose? I need to get a little exercise."

"No problem. I would actually prefer to work when the living room light is better. I'll need to work on your hands at the piano, and hands are always a challenge for me. Besides we should wait until your mother isn't around."

"Join me for a walk?"

"Sure."

They walked in silence for a while, and Frima assumed that neither of them wanted to bring up the tensions of the weekend. When Beth did begin to talk, she surprised Frima.

"You know it's so sweet to see Eduardo with the kids. I think he misses Manuel, his son, more than he is willing to say. I also wonder if I'm not depriving him of a great happiness in not having a child with him. But I still don't feel easy about having a baby, and I don't know if I ever will be. It makes me feel so guilty."

"It must be a shared happiness, Bethie," Frima said with feeling. "You should never have a child if you don't want one. Especially to please someone else! Every child should be planned and wanted by both parents—but especially the mother."

Beth looked at her quizzically, surprised that Frima was so emphatic. It was on the tip of her tongue to say she sounded just like Judith Ginsburg, but considering what she'd learned yesterday, she thought better of it.

"Yet you had Lena without planning—forgive my frankness—and she seems a happy, thriving child."

"True, but she was not unwanted. That's the most important thing. I wanted both my children, and so did Jack. I'm not saying that either of us thought things out very clearly, and I'm just as capable of doing something against my inclination or judgment because my man wanted it—that should be quite apparent—but that doesn't mean I don't know what's right. A child is too important. If you don't want it, don't get pregnant."

"Would you have another child, Frima?" Beth didn't look at her as she asked this.

"I think not."

"Not even if Jack really wanted one?"

"Frankly, I don't think he gets to decide. I'd never have a child against my will."

"Would you have an abortion?"

"You're not asking me all these questions because you're pregnant, are you?"

"I'm not."

"Well, then, all I can say is I plan on not having to confront that situation, and I do what I need to prevent it. Still, if I had an accidental pregnancy and my only decent or reasonable choice was to end it, I would do so—and early—probably before the man in question knew anything about it." Frima stopped right there, suddenly conscious of what she was saying. The man in question? This was her husband she was talking about. The two women walked on in silence for a few minutes.

"You're not very happy with Jack, are you?" Beth asked this softly, understanding with certainty that this was true. "Don't be angry with me for asking, and don't answer if you don't want to—if you feel it's none of my business."

"It is your business. He's your brother. And no, I'm not very happy with him at the moment, but that has nothing to do with my advice to you. Have a baby when and if you want one and are happy to care for it and cherish it. And not a moment sooner."

"You know, Frima," Beth resumed haltingly, "if you feel that you had to leave Jack, it would be okay with me—not that I'm encouraging you to do any such thing. I just wanted you to know that it wouldn't change the way I feel about you, and I would try to help, if you would let me; and I think Eduardo would feel the same."

Frima was touched. "Thank you for that, Bethie. Really. But please don't think I have any intention of leaving Jack. Or he, me. Things are a little rocky just now. It happens in every marriage, according to the agony columns. Nothing serious."

"Because of me and Eduardo?"

"Well, no, not entirely. That's just the usual fireworks. We disagree over some things. What couple doesn't?"

"And if we were at some future time to have a baby out of wedlock, Eduardo and I, you would be happy for us? Consider it family?"

"Gladly. What a silly question!"

"Not so silly. Jack and my parents would probably shun it as a bastard."

"If they did it would be their loss." This was not something Frima needed to take seriously at this time. There were enough real problems to grapple with.

Although they were due to return to the city that afternoon, Eduardo arranged for Beth to spend a few more days in the country. Beth said she would be happy to take the bus back to the city Thursday morning. It would be like old times. In the meantime, Beth and Frima told Mama very firmly that they would help in the office mornings so that she could go off with her husband afternoons to shop and plan their belated wedding trip to Europe. They would work on the portrait while she was out. By the time the four days were over, Beth was confident that she could finish the work in her city studio and that they could present it to Hannah at the end of the summer.

With the departure of the visitors, Frima could almost see the aura of vividness and excitement that surrounded them vanish into thin air, leaving her once again heavy with unspoken fear and anger about her husband. But as the days passed and the visit faded somewhat, she found she was reasonably calm again. If the novelty of their presence was gone, so was the edginess and conflict created in her household. Jack returned somewhat chastened and more thoughtful of everyone. He regained something of his old engaging self now that his chief antagonists were out of the picture. Frima was loathe to disturb the peace of her last remaining days at the old farm acres she loved, and the family at Eisner's drifted into what could pass as tranquility for the remainder of the season.

CHAPTER 30

"Frima at the Piano." What to make of Beth's portrait of her? Frima couldn't say. She had no language for it. She saw herself suddenly as a teenager, when she and Bess would go to the museums downtown. Bess would always head straight for a painting, ignoring (and despising) the printed descriptions and analyses, the docents' lectures. Frima found those aids interesting, and she would be a bit ashamed of herself for this weakness, since Bess declared that "the language of real art has no words." That was the adolescent Bess, of course. The adult Beth would not be so severe and uncompromising. Still, there was something to this. Frima had known from a very young age that music was like that for her. She recalled that when she wasn't yet in kindergarten, she had by chance listened to a simple Irish ballad sung in Gaelic and how her eyes had filled at the harmony, not understanding a word of the lyrics; how, later, the most subtle adjustment in phrasing or tempo could make something change from ordinary to splendid. Oh shut up! She wished she could turn away from herself in disgust. All this silent babbling. Words failed her? How about feeling failed her? She felt nothing about this painting. No more than for a blank canvas.

Everyone else had opinions. "It doesn't do you justice," Jack commented to her privately. "I doubt that my sister has the technical skill or the patience for portraits. It looks kind of raw to me, though it's probably very artistic and all that. But as I've said often enough, I don't have the eye for that sort of thing."

Leon seemed very pleased with the final product, if for no other reason than Mama's evident happiness with it. And Eduardo, whom Frima credited with real penetration, contemplated it often with interest and evident pride and pleasure. Beth had not allowed him to see it as a work in progress. The artist, herself, was reticent, even shy about talking of the work, as she always was—with her painting, that is. Only when she saw Mama's response did her eyes brighten with tears.

For Mama's reaction was extraordinary. Of course, she was delighted with the sweetness, the thoughtfulness of Leon and Beth, the cleverness of the conspirators in keeping it a complete surprise. After she hugged and kissed, made all the appreciative noises, she spent a long time in front of the painting with clasped hands and a quiet smile. Then she burst into tears, and Beth burst into tears and they hugged each other.

And Frima? She was left out. They understood something, saw something she didn't, and she resented this. A lot. The painting became something else not to mention.

—

The weeks had moved so fast, heading to the end of an era; a personal one for Frima. For the Catskill counties, it was still early in what would become the heyday of the mountain resorts: palaces and pleasure spas that would employ—and so finance the college educations of—countless waiters, busboys, counselors, and maids. The places that hired and introduced to the world so many comics, musicians, actors, singers, and dancers; whose golf courses and card rooms encouraged numberless business deals. They offered the dream vacation: ease, comfort, continuous entertainment. They would specialize in enticing packages for families with children, for honeymooners, for singles looking for the perfect someone to share your life with. All bathed in respectability: the American Dream, kosher style.

Eisner's was something else: it arose from the dreams of tenement and *shtetl* dwellers for a little place in the country; fresh air, a fresh pond or damned up creek to cool off in, abundant fresh food, some time to relax with a good book and good talk. Papa and Mama and Grandpa had taken that vision about as far as it could go. It was wonderful, but it was over. The new owners would undoubtedly change everything. If all this had to end, Frima was relieved the end had come. It was better than dreading it.

They had spent the final week divesting the place of the family's personal belongings. The piano was to be sold, even though Mama made a last ditch attempt to return it to Frima. "Is there no way to make room for it? I don't see why Jack couldn't have a desk and things in the bedroom. Other people do that."

"There's no way, Mama, it's way too big. The kids want a television. All their friends have one or are getting one. I'm sick of battling with them about this."

"And Jack? What is his opinion?"

"At first he backed me, but now he's starting to change his mind. As long as it doesn't interfere with homework time, he thinks it's okay. He says not having one would only make them envious. Besides he thinks television is the wave of the future—you can't stop progress, et cetera."

"This he calls progress?"

"I don't continue battles I can't possibly win. I realize you feel bad about the piano, but I can find an instrument to practice on outside the house if I need one. I really don't have enough time to practice anyway."

"It's not my feelings I'm concerned with."

"You know, this is really my business. Jack's and mine." She said this gently, not eager to inflict injury.

"Meaning, of course, that it's none of mine. Well, I suppose it isn't. But, my dear daughter, if it is your business, mind that you take heed of this one thing I say. You need to take care of yourself as well as your husband and children. And now I'll keep quiet. I have no wish to argue." Mama rose and walked out of the room.

A couple of days later, she asked Frima to come with her to the office. They needed to talk privately, and, no, it couldn't wait. Frima sat down trying to control her apprehension. She reminded herself that she was a big girl now.

"You haven't been sent to the principal's office, so relax." Mama began. "It's just that for me, this is a time in life when financial planning becomes more important. You understand that both Leon and I have done well for ourselves in these hills, and though neither of us are millionaires, there will be enough money for us to help our children. We've talked about this seriously and have taken certain actions. Leon's assets will rightfully go to his children, at his death. Mine will be dispersed somewhat differently. What I have will go to you, naturally. It won't be a fortune, but it will certainly make things easier. And I've arranged things so that you won't have to wait until I die, which with luck will not be anytime soon."

Frima smiled, relieved that Mama's subject was not anything that she, Frima, need be uncomfortable about. "From your lips to God's ear," she said. "This is so generous of you, but you're sure you don't want to keep it for yourself? You never know."

"I'm entirely sure. Do I look like I need it?"

"Of course not." Frima expelled a breath. "Well, this is a happy surprise. We'd really love to have enough money to send both girls to college—they're both so bright, you know—but we wondered if we could ever make that happen. This will help so much. Jack will be as happy as I am. Or does he already know about this?" she asked, suddenly wary.

"Please! Give me some credit. I don't make the same mistake twice. Jack knows nothing of this; nor should he, in my opinion. Don't look at me like that. And let me finish. I have already arranged for some funds that are in trust for Lena and Rosalie's education. The funds will be managed by a professional in a conservative way. I'm hoping there will be enough to finance their schooling as far as they want to go, but if not, they are bright girls and can get scholarships or part-time work, if need be."

"I hardly know what to say. This is so generous of you. But why shouldn't Jack know?"

"Oh, it makes no difference if he knows about this, as long as he knows he will not have any control over it. Now, Frima be reasonable. Jack doesn't really know anything about investments and neither do you or I for that matter; we were none of us born Rockefellers. And you, my dear, you need a professional to manage your money."

"My money?"

"Yes, that's what I really want to talk to you about. If you'll let me finish."

Frima was silent.

"I've put some money in trust for you. The proceeds from your piano will go into the trust, you understand, but mostly it will consist of savings bonds that will mature at intervals and other safe investments that will yield dividends and interest. A law firm that handles our affairs, Leon's and mine, will manage the trust and control disbursements."

A lot of fancy words to say that I have money but I can't manage it, Frima thought, but she remained silent.

"You may have money whenever you wish, though the trust managers will surely advise you not to be impulsive about it."

"As if I'm likely to be!"

"The only stipulation is that this money is for you—not for your children or for Jack. It is to be used for your benefit alone. If possible, a married woman—any woman—should have some money that is hers, independent of anyone else, whether through work or through fortune. You may not see that yet, but you will."

"What I see is that you don't trust Jack to take care of me and mine, and I'm not that sure that you trust me."

"Oh, I believe Jack will take care of your physical well-being quite willingly and conscientiously. But not your spirit, your soul. That, you'll need to honor and cherish yourself." Mama ignored the last part of Frima's accusation.

"You really hate him," Frima said softly, things beginning to roil inside her. "You and Beth, even Eduardo." Beth's words flashed into her mind again. She felt panic rising.

"Nonsense. Eduardo doesn't hate Jack. He's only interested in protecting Beth, and Beth doesn't hate him, though she thinks she does sometimes. And me? I've always liked and enjoyed him—a lot actually. But, I'm sorry, I can't always trust him."

"What has he ever done to you?"

"It's what he's done, or may do, to you."

Mama was chipping away at her as if to reveal something awful.

"You don't know what happened to him. None of you do. You can't understand!"

"Nor can I, if you don't tell me."

"It was at the camp, the concentration camp. What he saw—what happened to him."

Mama looked confused. "I don't know what you mean. What camp? He was never an inmate—I mean, he couldn't have been."

"Buchenwald. He was with the troops that came in when the camp was liberated. Things he saw—it was like shellshock. He ran away, and he didn't remember anything for a long time. He came out of it, but he was so ashamed. He didn't want anyone to know, and now I've told you and betrayed his confidence."

"No you haven't. Not really." Mama said this as if she were thinking out loud. And Frima saw at once that she would not receive a great outburst of sympathy and remorse from her mother, who went on, almost talking to herself.

"A terrible experience, it must have been, and I'm truly sorry that he—that anyone—had to go through it. Still, he was a witness, not a victim, thank God, and without our soldier witnesses, how could that unspeakable suffering ever have ended? But, who knows . . . what do I know? I didn't have to go through it." She paused for a few moments. "It does make some of Jack's behavior, his opinions more understandable. But that's not enough. Understanding doesn't mean condoning. And does it occur to you that in swearing you to secrecy, he puts a burden on you—you who are so loyal—for he doesn't allow you the aid and comfort, at least, of talking about this to someone else?"

"He didn't want to burden me! I forced it out of him. He kept it to himself as long as was possible."

"I'm sure he did, darling, but be that as it may—" She interrupted herself with a sigh. "My God, you were both so young when you married."

Frima turned her eyes to the painting of herself that still stood in state in the office, where Mama would personally supervise the movers' handling of it. She continued to look at it as she spoke.

"You think I made an awful mistake in marrying him, don't you? You and Beth. What is it with you two? She tells me it would be okay with her if I left him, that she would help me. You leave money to me—to me, not to us. It tells me you have no confidence in us as a couple, and neither does Beth. And that painting!"

"Frima, look at me. Regardless of what Beth said or offered, there is nothing between us but our care and love for you. She is your sister in a way that most real sisters can only long for, even if she isn't the most subtle of people. No one is saying you should leave Jack. We are only saying, look out for yourself, also. I've said it to you before, and I'll say it again. Now, why are you so angry about the painting?"

"You and Beth—you cried and hugged each other, as if you have this private comprehension, and I don't. And, after all, it's supposed to be a portrait of me!"

"And you don't like it?" Mama's tone had become calm and almost conversational, and Frima suspected this was deliberate, like a doctor or a schoolteacher dealing with an agitated pupil.

"I don't know."

"And Jack? What does he say?"

"Now, come on! You know Jack wouldn't like it. He would want a conventional portrait of his little peaches-and-cream blond—the closest he can come to Abie's Irish Rose and still stay an MOT." She surprised herself, saying this.

"And the kids?"

"They think the colors are pretty—oh, what does it matter?"

"You're right. It doesn't really. Reactions to a work of art are very individual. And, much as I'd like it to be otherwise, people are entitled to their opinions. But, naturally, I'm very interested in yours."

"I told you. I don't understand it. I don't have an opinion."

"I don't believe that for a minute, Frima. If you have no opinion it's because you will not take the blinders off and really see. And for that, I do blame your husband."

"How can you say that? You make him out to be a monster!"

"Not at all. What ails him is too common to be monstrous. And it isn't all he is, by any means. But this I will say. His problem has little if anything to do with his war experiences, terrible as they were for him. He suffers from a selfishness that makes him the center of his world and those around him satellites. In this way, I'm afraid, the apple doesn't fall far from the tree."

"Meaning he's like Sam? Well, what about Beth? She's Sam's daughter, don't forget."

"Very true, but Beth wasn't any kind of apple in her family. More like a changeling, bound to disappoint them."

"And me? What about me? What kind of apple am I—if any!"

"You are, and always will be, the apple of my eye. Now, why are you so angry? Have I said anything you haven't seen yourself? And, again, that's not all your husband is. You know his fine qualities as well as I do."

Frima was shaking with rage at her mother. "When I feel I need a psychiatrist, I'll go to a real one. After all, now I have that money to pay for it. I don't need you to analyze me or my marriage!" She almost knocked over her chair in her haste to get out of there.

"Frima, please—don't leave like this!" Mama sighed, her eyes filling with tears as her daughter ran out of the office.

They cried and hugged and made up by the next day, but it wasn't over and they both knew it. Never before had Frima been eager to leave Ellenville to go home to the city, even as she knew she would never be at the farm again. At home, away from the open conflicts of this place, away from Mama, she and Jack could be happy. She was relieved to see Mama and Leon off at the dock where they set sail for a long European tour. As she wished them bon voyage, she wondered if she would ever again experience the ease and intimacy she and Mama had shared.

She would not. And she was to know this soon enough. Not two months later, she received the telegram. Mama and Leon had been driving the steep hills of Tuscany late at night. Perhaps they had been sleepy. They had both been killed instantly, it was thought, as the car crashed and tumbled them out of their world.

Everyone was kind, of course. Neighbors visited and made meals while Frima and Jack sat shiva. Jack was at his best. He took charge of the funeral and burial arrangements, complicated by there being "two departed loved ones," as the funeral directors put it. He was careful of her; physically tender, and protective of her comfort, good with their girls. He and Beth even declared a kind of truce for Frima's sake.

And Frima? Most of the time during those weeks, she went on with the routines of her life: filling lunch boxes, doing laundry, reading, listening to the radio, as if nothing had happened. Then, perchance, she might think to herself, I have to tell Mama what Rosalie said this morning; and then she'd remember that she couldn't because there was no Mama. Those times when disbelief and denial suddenly lifted were terrible, and mercifully short. For then with certainty she knew she was an orphan. Papa, Grandpa, and now Mama, all three gone without warning. The only ones in the world who could give her a sturdy unconditional love were gone, and she had never had the chance with any of them to say goodbye, or I'm sorry, or I love you. Those times, she knew that she had only her husband and children. Would they go suddenly as well? She could not let that happen. She had to shelter them, take care of them—in a sense make do with them.

There was Beth, of course, always more sister than sister-in-law. Dear Bethie! She was deeply grateful for her support and love, but it was difficult to have her around sometimes. It was not lost on either of them that Beth, who could well do without both of her parents, was still burdened with the two of them, while Frima's, much beloved, were gone.

"Think how lucky you were to have the family you did. They will always be with you. The only way I could envision anything remotely resembling that kind of love was having a dog." Beth said this without irony.

This was true, but not very helpful. And then there was all her urging for Frima to "get involved." Beth loved to throw herself into progressive causes, even as she chafed at doctrines and restraints. She loved chanting her head off and picketing for the social good. It was an antidote to the intensity and privacy of her painting. Whether it was ban the bomb, do away with blacklists, or defeat McCarthy, Beth was for it, heart and soul, and she could come home to the safety of the tolerant Eduardo and be secure and economically protected—no livelihood to lose. Frima wanted nothing of politics or causes, and Beth was like a gnat buzzing around her head about this. For Frima, gently brushing her away, her answer was always "later." At some time, but not now.

"Hannah Eisner was a light in the darkness." Beth had said this at the funeral, and she had never spoken truer words. For Frima, as the months after her death passed, it was as if a window to that light gradually closed in herself. She was living in a muffled, not unpleasant grayness. Perhaps beige was the better description. She remembered ironic social advice from somewhere: "Smile and wear beige." Mama would never follow that advice, but Frima was comfortable doing just that. With two children, she had enough things to do to fill the days. She had the comfort of her husband in the dark. Maybe she'd crave something more some day, but for now, a nice safe beige was all she wanted.

In just this frame of mind she opened her mailbox at the usual time and found a surprise: a letter from Moe Ginsberg.

January 1951

My dear Frima,

I hope you are well and happily engaged in your life back in New York. Maybe you think this is a stodgy way for old Moe, the joker, to begin a letter to a young lady who is also an old friend, but I don't know how to do otherwise at this time, understanding, as I do, the loss you suffer.

The loss of Hannah, your mama, the loss of Judith, my wife; different but the same. They were beacons of courage, energy, love—both of them. And both snatched away from us without warning. I can only say to you, Frimaleh, your mama was worthy of your grief and your enduring and loving memory, as was Judith to me. But as your mama, herself, would say: not every hour and not all the time. In that way those gone can be a comfort and a courage in your heart. This is exactly what Hannah did write to me last summer, when Judith's assassin had been discovered, after those many years.

It was good advice, and so I'm taking it. I'm actually getting married again. This is maybe more an issue of Social Security than romance, but that's also as it should be at my age. Rachel, my intended, is an intelligent lively companion, and we prop each other up, you could say. She is a handsome Jewish widow, a good cook, also good politics, and a sense of humor. But, between you and me, these California Jews are different from us. Rachel was actually born near Los Angeles, and she doesn't even know from Ellis Island. Also up here in Santa Rosa, which is in a county north of San Francisco, they wouldn't recognize a good bagel or a bialy if they tripped over one. Their chopped liver isn't anything to write home about, either, if you ask me, but I admit to prejudice. But guess what? They know all about egg farming. Rachel is actually the widow of an egg farmer.

Just south of where I live, a bunch of Jews moved here a few decades ago to become farmers, like your Grandpa Jake and I did in the Catskills. They came to this country from the same shtetls and Eastern Europeans cities, escaping pogroms and persecution and soul-killing poverty in crowded tenements, with the same dreams we in the Catskills had, but also different. They tried to build a utopian collective of Jewish egg farmers—Stalinist yet—in sunny California. I can well understand how California beckons, especially this coastal area. It's so beautiful. But chickens? Why do so many Americans, Jew or gentile, think that chickens will make their fortune? That these birds will allow them to live a pastoral dream of a modest, yet prosperous family farm? They could have asked me or Jake—or your Mama, for that matter. A small family farm is a struggle, always. Did you ever read The Egg and I? Believe me, if you happen to have a prosperous, picture book, family farm, it started out that way, probably with settled money. "Farming, that's the fashion, farming," like Danny Kaye sings about. No mortgages, and other people to do the shoveling. And a socialist collective based on chickens? There is absolutely nothing cooperative or utopian about a chicken, Stalinist or Trotskyist.

Okay, so I'm joking again, but that's just my way. I'm not making fun of them. I think it was an admirable attempt, even if it could not be sustained for long. Also it is very nice for me to have some of these left-wing Jews around, when I feel the need for a good argument or discussion, or a chess game. In my mind, I'm always contrasting the fate of the Catskill Jewish communities to this one in Petaluma, but I don't talk about it much, because when I do, I can be very boring. But you, I hope, I can bore a little. You'll understand.

We were socialists, many of us, back in New York, and we all saw the need for cooperatives and collective action, but we also had entrepreneurs, like Leon or Max, or Jenny Grossinger. And such a different future we made compared to our landtsmen out here. The Catskill Jews, they started boardinghouse farms and hotels to eke out a living on plots not particularly good for farming, but very attractive to a whole lot of sweatshop Jews and crowded apartment dwellers in New York City and Newark, who were not welcome elsewhere. To these summer guests, it was farm-schmarm: more like a week or two in heaven to have such fresh cool air, abundant kosher food cooked by someone else and served to you. Word gets around, and before you know it, the boardinghouse is a hotel, and, bingo! Here comes the Borscht Belt. Maybe not that easy. You still work your head off, and there are plenty of failures, but like it or not, call it whatever, it's something of a miracle.

I believe that could never have occurred out here, but not because in the Catskills we were better or smarter. It's more a question of geography or topography. These wide open spaces here, even with fences, they call them ranches, not farms. You see sheep, dairy and beef cattle grazing, pleasure horses, and more and more vineyards only a few miles from San Francisco. Why would ranchers and growers with large properties break up these fertile stretches for chickens, which can survive and produce in far more crowded conditions? Poultry and egg farming is fast becoming industrialized, like it or not, but not on expanses of quality acres. So these Jewish chicken farmers, just like their gentile counterparts, are absorbed into the work force and become shopkeepers and clerks and insurance agents and schoolteachers, like normal people. And they didn't risk their futures opening summer boardinghouses and vacation inns because there weren't many sweltering city dwellers who needed them.

I'm not saying there aren't poor people in San Francisco and Oakland, living in squalid conditions, but there is this immediate escape. All they have to do is walk a couple of blocks and there is fresh air and beautiful vistas around them. Anyone can walk down to the beach or to the park or to the wharfs and be in another world. These cities are on one of the most beautiful bays in the world, and if you take a ferry across the bay and dock at either end, you feel as if you have just gently bumped into a city fancifully laid out on a hillside. With the Golden Gate Bridge, you can be in the country or the city in no time at all, compared to the East Coast.

Even though I am a country boy (hah, hah) at heart, I love to go to San Francisco. Vinny Migliori always used to talk about it with such affection, so I was eager to see it. He was born there, you know. It is perched on the hills, just like in the picture postcards, and it is a quite small city built to a much more "human" scale than New York. It is rarely very hot or cold, and even with its famous ocean fog—San Francisco air conditioning—it is still very light compared to Manhattan, because there aren't many skyscrapers keeping it in shadow. In sunlight, it's gorgeous. From every hill there are beautiful vistas. Yet there is something about this city that reminds me of New York in the thirties and forties; the distinct neighborhoods and street life, the look of the buses and the cable cars—much like the old trolleys. Also it is still a union town. Vinny would be happy to know that.

Speaking of Vinny, I do correspond with Beth Erlichman from time to time. Vinny was a lasting connection between us, as was Judith. Beth has told me that Judith and I were kind of parent figures for her, as was your mother. This I find touching and sad. But she seems happy and busy now with her Eduardo and with her painting, politics, and so on, and that is very good to hear. She also tells me that she fears you are despondent and that you avoid engagement with the world. Now don't be angry with her, Frima, or with me, for mentioning it. We both love you. But as an old man, I see in a way Beth can't yet see, that people are so various and complex in their reactions and their promise, and lots of paths are good. Beth enjoys carrying banners. Her way isn't your way, nor should it be. Your mother used to say that underneath your delicacy and beauty, the still waters of your nature, there lies keen intellect, talent, and ribs of steel. You come by it honestly, my dear. You will continue to find your own way and your own truth, and it will be very good, I know. I think of you with love and hope. Think of me, this way too, Frimaleh. Not exactly Mark Twain, as I once promised you, but your loving and devoted friend,

Moe

Frima sat at the kitchen table reading and rereading the letter. Then she reached for the phone to call Beth.

CODA

You are walking to the bakery on Jerome Avenue to pick up the seeded rye, sliced, that your wife forgot when she was out shopping. She doesn't bake bread anymore, except for the challah for Friday night. You've just come home from work, but there are no longer any children at home to hustle off on this errand. Out of the nest and married; making their own nests now. And alive and well, thank God. No casualties of the Depression, war, polio, or any other blight. It's late spring, and with Daylight Savings Time, it is bright out still, and as always you enjoy taking a little walk in the neighborhood. You feel like a benign watchman: Thursday night and all is well.

You walk along the edge of the park lined with the large indestructible benches put in by Franklin Roosevelt during the heyday of his public works programs. Functional they are but not elegant, certainly. Neither are the lumbering cars of the Lexington Avenue subway line that climb up to elevated tracks in the Bronx as they reach Jerome Avenue and Yankee Stadium. The tracks are almost directly above your head right now, between the boundary of the park and the row of apartment houses across the avenue. The trains run round the clock, roaring, clacking, and shrieking at stops—the noisy arteries of the city. They can wake the dead, but if you dwell in these parts, you barely notice the sound. The people in the apartments don't even acknowledge a train's passing. Neither does the man stretched out asleep on one of those long park benches.

You are not distressed to see him there. He is not bothering anyone. Maybe his navy blue pea coat is a little seedy. Is he a vet down on his luck, or a stray hobo? Everyone, child or adult, seems to own one of those coats. Postwar military surplus; cheap, warm, and durable. You recognize the cop on the beat as he stops to look at the sleeping man. He is just checking that he is okay; he won't issue a summons or wake him and force him to move on.

Walk up to the nice policeman, the very first one you meet,
And simply say "I've lost my way and cannot find my street.
But I know my name and address and telephone number too."
And he'll be kind and help you find the dear ones who wait for you.

How many public school kids, city kids like his own, had learned that little ditty in first grade. The kind policeman—what a concept. Only in America!

So, okay, you aren't naïve. You know how fragile that human connection can be. If the man on the bench had dark skin, it would be a whole other story. You are aware of different unpleasant conflicts brewing as well, but they are still shadowy; they can be ignored in your gratitude that you and yours have come through the hard times and can feel safe and optimistic again. It's a moment in time, and you savor it.

Those two young women, standing on the stoop of that apartment building—you are startled by the sight of them. Another moment in time, but this one from the past. Why, it must be ten years since you've seen them together at the same spot. Two lovely looking girls they were then, but most definitely they are young women now. Character, that almost indefinable quality, is etched into their faces. A gentle etching, to be sure, and they are still a pleasure to look at. Bess—no,

Beth—has changed much more than her name, if her dramatic looks and dress are any indication. She could be an Ava Gardner, except for the defiantly long nose. No, she's not Hollywood. She's more bohemian and quite arresting. She has a look-at-me attitude. Here I am, take me or leave me. Frima has changed her name also; she's Erlichman now, creating with her husband, Jack, a picture-book family, with her blond beauty, his dark good looks, their two engaging little girls. But there's more there; still hidden. She looks—how to say this—chastened, or maybe subdued. Still, her smile is lovely, if a little ironic; her visage revealing a strong intelligence. Both stand tall, graceful. No hot dogs this time, you notice. They are reading a letter together, smiling.

You are a little sobered, looking at them. What will their future be? You allow yourself a pin prick of envy. In this quiet moment in time your own future looks short and uneventful. Still, you've had your time, much of it good, and if you have a few regrets, well, who doesn't? You are at peace with yourself. But these two—that sense of promise—what of them? Neither will long be able to hide her light under a bushel. Whether she wants to or not.

The story continues in
Take the D Train: A Novel of New York in the 1950s

ACKNOWLEDGMENTS

My appreciation to all the people who did critical readings, supplied valuable insights, and encouraged me in this endeavor with very special thanks to Anne Ackerman, Erin Almond, Richard Almond, Steve Almond, Grace Chappell, Elaine Elinson, Julie Gantcher, David Greenberg, Dan Lettieri, Carol Rothman, Laura Rosenthal, and Robert Wernick. My gratitude also to the members of the San Francisco Village Writers' Workshop who with their golden memories and fresh insights still write and encourage me to do so as well. I'm greatful also to all the editorial and production staff at She Writes Press for their professional dilgence and their guidance throughout this publishing process. Finally, many thanks to Jordan Kushins for generously sharing her technical expertise and outreach savvy and to my publicists Linda Quigley and Louise Crawford. All three have patiently and skillfully kept me on track during days and enabled me to sleep nights.

ABOUT THE AUTHOR

Alice Rosenthal was born and raised in the same Bronx neighborhood as her protagonists, though a generation later. With a master's in English from NYU, she settled in the Village-Chelsea area of Manhattan, where she maintained her life style by copy editing for academic and educational presses. In 1976, she moved to San Francisco and began a new worklife teaching ESL at City College of San Francisco, which rekindled her interest in the varied experiences of immigrants to this country. She enjoys reading, gardening, baking, and shmoozing with her friends and family. She takes pleasure in good music of any kind, most especially when she engages in choral and ensemble singing. She still loves to dance—when she can. She is the author of *Take the D Train: A Novel of New York in the 1950s* as well as articles published in the *San Francisco Chronicle* and *Jewish Currents* magazine.

SELECTED TITLES FROM SHE WRITES PRESS

She Writes Press is an independent publishing company
founded to serve women writers everywhere.
Visit us at www.shewritespress.com.

The Sweetness by Sande Boritz Berger. $16.95, 978-1-63152-907-8
A compelling and powerful story of two girls—cousins living on separate
continents—whose strikingly different lives are forever changed when
the Nazis invade Vilna, Lithuania.

All the Light There Was by Nancy Kricorian. $16.95, 978-1-63152-905-4
A lyrical, finely wrought tale of loyalty, love, and the many faces of resis-
tance, told from the perspective of an Armenian girl living in Paris during
the Nazi occupation of the 1940s.

The Belief in Angels by J. Dylan Yates. $16.95, 978-1-938314-64-3
From the Majdonek death camp to a volatile hippie household on the
East Coast, this narrative of tragedy, survival, and hope spans more than
fifty years, from the 1920s to the 1970s.

An Address in Amsterdam by Mary Dingee Fillmore. $16.95, 978-1-63152-133-1
After facing relentless danger and escalating raids for 18 months, Rachel
Klein—a well-behaved young Jewish woman who transformed herself
into a courier for the underground when the Nazis invaded her country—persuades her parents to hide with her in a dank basement, where
much is revealed.

Tasa's Song by Linda Kass. $16.95, 978-1-63152-064-8
From a peaceful village in eastern Poland to a partitioned post-war
Vienna, from a promising childhood to a year living underground, *Tasa's
Song* celebrates the bonds of love, the power of memory, the solace of
music, and the enduring strength of the human spirit.

Arboria Park by Kate Tyler Wall. $16.95, 978-1631521676
Stacy Halloran's life has always been centered around her beloved neighborhood, a 1950s-era housing development called Arboria Park—so
when a massive highway project threaten the Park in the 2000s, she steps
up to the task of trying to save it.